WHAT LOYALTY DEMANDS

WHAT LOYALTY DEMANDS

CAROL ASHBY

For I know the plans I have for you," declares the LORD,
"plans to prosper you and not to harm you,
plans to give you hope and a future."
Jeremiah 29:11 (NIV)

"Blessed are the peacemakers,
for they will be called
children of God."
Matthew 5:9 (NIV).

And we know that for those who love God
all things work together for good,
for those who are called according to his purpose.
Romans 8:28 (ESV)

*To my children, Paul and Lydia,
for their love, support, and encouragement
and my granddaughters, Payton and Kaila,
for the joy they bring to our lives.
And especially to my husband, Jim,
who brings out the best in me.*

And most of all, to Jesus.

Soli Deo gloria.

Loyalty. It's faithfulness to something or someone that doesn't waver despite any temptation to reject, abandon, or betray. We expect it of a man or woman of honor. We want our friends and family to see us as loyal people who can be counted on in challenging times.

But loyalty can be a dangerous thing. Each of us must decide who and what is deserving of our loyalty. Unwavering faithfulness to what we have chosen as worthy of our support can be a good thing...or a bad one. It depends on what we choose as the object of our loyalty.

The problem comes when we choose something that doesn't deserve the deepest commitment of a loyal person. Perhaps it never did, but we were fooled into thinking so at one time. Perhaps it once did, but it changed into something that no longer deserves the dedication that loyalty demands. Perhaps we learn there's a higher goal, a deeper purpose, or a special calling from God, and old loyalties keep us from responding. But how can honorable people know when their loyalties should change?

And how should we live as Christians when loyalties conflict and animosity flourishes because of it?

In his early life, Rogatus knew rejection, abandonment, and betrayal too well. No one in his family deserved his loyalty. But in the Roman military, he found belonging and appreciation. Every year, he swore an oath of loyalty to Rome and her emperor. He finally had something he thought deserved his dedication, and he gave it wholeheartedly.

Sulio was born the son of a chieftain of the Brigantes tribe. His sense of loyalty to his father, to his clan, and to Brigantian ways was great enough that he hated Roman rule. He even disliked his male cousins who were raised as Romans and chose Roman ways.

Narina considered herself both Brigantian and Roman, but her true loyalty was to God and His son Iesu. She was kind to everyone, and as God had commanded, she tried her best to be a peacemaker between the Brigantian and Roman sides. When the Roman officer wants her friendship and her Brigantian cousin wants to protect her from him, she leads both to examine whether their extreme loyalty to human groups like clan and empire might need to change.

Today we're faced with sharp divisions in our society. If people can disagree about something, many choose to do so with a passion that builds impenetrable walls between people. Our loyalty should always be to God, and we're called to be His agents in this troubled world. As Jesus said, "Blessed are the peacemakers, for they will be called children of God." - Matthew 5:9 (NIV).

Paul's instructions to Timothy speak powerfully to us today. "Have nothing to do with foolish, ignorant controversies; you know that they breed quarrels. And the Lord's servant must not be quarrelsome but kind to everyone, able to teach, patiently enduring evil, correcting his opponents with gentleness. God may perhaps grant them repentance leading to a knowledge of the truth, and they may come to their senses and escape from the snare of the devil, after being captured by him to do his will." - 2 Timothy 2:23-26 (ESV).

I want to be a peacemaker who leads others to consider what God wants of us and then choose to follow His ways as loyal children of God.

I hope you enjoy the story of Rogatus and Narina and how her kindness and loyalty to God first opened his heart to love and then opened his mind to find the one person worthy of his loyalty...God. May we always choose to live in loyalty to Him so others will see it and choose to love and serve Him as well.

Characters

The Romans:

Proculus Trebonius Rogatus (29): tribune serving as prefect of the auxiliary cavalry unit (*ala*) at Isurium

Julius Valentinus: legionary tribune in Deva

Prefect Atilianus: commander of the Tungrorum cavalry before Rogatus

Sextus Cornelius Dexter: legionary tribune in Eboracum

Gallus, Martialis, Rufus, Bassus, and Plantus: other tribunes stationed in Eboracum

Germanus: lead decurion in Rogatus's Tungrorum cavalry ala

Adolphus: decurion in Tungrorum cavalry ala

Marcus Trebonius Rogatus: Proculus Rogatus's father

Publius Visulanius Crescens: Rogatus's maternal great-uncle

The Lucanus family: Roman citizens and Brigantian tribal members

Narina Lucana (23): raises horses and produce, oversees Isurium taberna; a Christian

Marcus Ulpius Lucanus (deceased): Narina's father, a Roman citizen after 25 years of military service

Minconus Ulpius Lucanus (31): Narina's oldest brother and guardian since her father's death.

Lucania (11): Narina's younger sister; a Christian

Veldicca (36): family servant and friend of Narina; a Christian

Atto (15): farmhand who works at the Isurium taberna

Bikka and Vinda: women from Narina's farm

Trenus: Narina's farm foreman, Bikka's husband

The Brigantes

Bellicus (62): son of Catus, Narina's uncle, tribal chieftain within the Brigantes tribal federation

Sulio (26) and Albiso (30): Narina's cousins who are unhappy with Roman rule

Iesu: the Celtic name for Jesus (Iesus in Latin)

British Tribes: Brigantes, Coritani, Otadini, Parisi, Selgovae

The Horses

Bena: Narina's brown mare

Boreas: Rogatus's tan dun stallion, means "North Wind" in Latin
Zephyrus: Rogatus's silver dun stallion , means"West Wind" in Latin

HISTORICAL PEOPLE

Hadrian: Emperor from 117 to 138. Received notice Aug 11 of Trajan's death.

Trajan: Emperor from AD 98 to 117. Died August 9, 117

Agricola, Cerialis, Frontinus: Legates and governors of Britannia

Vespasian and Domitian: two of the three Flavian emperors

For more about these people in Britannia, see historical note after the story.

MILITARY UNITS

Cohors III Brittonum Equitata: mixed infantry/cavalry auxiliary cohort. Narina's father was cavalry centurion AD 75-100. Rogatus commanded as prefect from AD 112 to 115.

XX Valeria Victrix: Legion headquartered in Deva (Chester). Rogatus served here as equestrian tribune from AD 115-117.

IX Hispana: Legion headquartered in Eboracum (York). As ala prefect, Rogatus reports to its legate.

Ala I Tungrorum: Auxiliary cavalry unit assigned to IX Hispana. Rogatus became prefect August, AD 117.

FAMILY RELATIONSHIPS AND SOCIAL STANDING:
WHAT ROMAN NAMES TELL US

The rules for naming a Roman citizen were well defined, leaving little room for creativity but revealing a lot about the person and their relations.

The Roman *familia* was the Roman family unit consisting of the *paterfamilias*, his married and unmarried children regardless of age, his son's children, and his slaves. Wives and freed slaves (freedmen) were sometimes considered part of the familia. When a paterfamilias died, his oldest son became the new paterfamilias of his father's familia. His daughters and other sons became *sui iuris,* a person who is not under the power of another person. Each of the sons became a paterfamilias over their own children and any slaves they acquired.

Romans took names and what they said about family connections very seriously. The three-part name (like Proculus Trebonius Rogatus) meant you were a Roman citizen of the clan Trebonius and family Rogatus. Using a three-part name if you weren't a citizen was actually a crime. Which name of the three you called someone depended on the closeness of your relationship. There were only twenty male first names in common use, and one-in-five Romans was named Gaius. Only close friends and immediate family called you by your first name. Others used your last name, both your second and third names when being formal, and sometimes your first and third names.

Women were named the feminine form of their father's clan and family names. Married women kept their maiden names because they officially stayed part of their father's familia, not their husband's.

When a noncitizen auxiliary soldier retired and became a citizen, he took the first and second names of the emperor at that time. His personal name became his third name.

When a male slave was freed by a citizen so he became a citizen, too, he took the first and second names of his former owner with his slave name added as his third name.

For the definition of special terms used for Roman-era things and people and for the meanings of Latin words, see the Glossary after the story.

Locations

TOWNS

Clusium: town near the Rogatus villa, about 100 miles from Rome, present-day Chiusi della Verna

Coria: also known as Corstopitum, present-day Corbridge

Deva: home of the fortress of the XX Valeria Victrix Legion, present-day Chester

Eboracum: home of the fortress of the IX Hispana Legion, present-day York

Hispania: Roman province, includes present-day Spain and Portugal

Isca Silurum: home of the fortress of the II Augusta Legion, present day Caerleon

Isurium: present-day Aldborough, Yorkshire

Isurium fort: auxiliary fort on main road 17 miles north from Eboracum

Londinium: present-day London

Luguvalium: present-day Carlisle

Mamucium: present-day Manchester

Moesia: Roman provinces in the Balkans south of the Danube,

Petuaria: port town nearest York, present-day Brough-on-Humber

RIVERS

Abus: present-day Ouse, flows into the Humber Estuary

Fossa: present-day Foss, flows into the Ouse in York

Isura: present-day Ure that flows into the Ouse near Lintor on Ouse

ROAD NAMES

The original Roman names for many major roads have been lost, so I have applied typical naming practices used for Roman roads to create names for the major roads in this book. Major roads were often named (Via + the name of the one responsible for their construction). So, for roads built during the empire, I use the name of the emperor under whom a road was built.

Via Claudia: Ermine Street from London to Lincoln (Londinium to Lindum Colonia)

Via Flavia: Ermine Street from Lincoln to York (Lindum to Eboracum) and Dere Street north of York (built by Agricola in AD 79)

Via Vespasiana: road from Deva to Eboracum

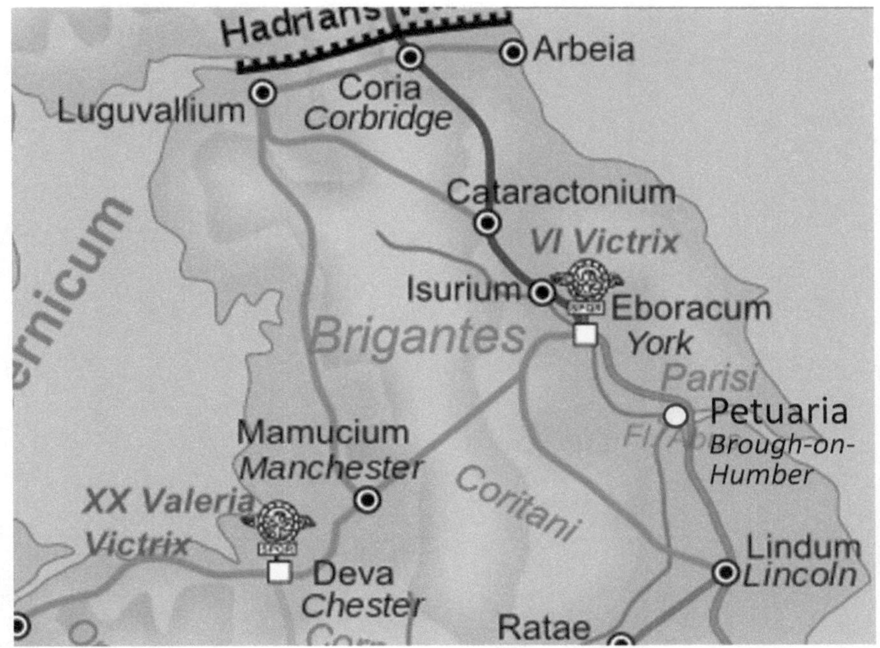

Public domain edited by Carol Ashby

The map shows Roman Britain around AD 150. So, it shows the VI Victrix Legion in Eboracum instead of the IX Hispana. The Victrix moved into Britain around AD 122 to replace the IX Hispana after it lost so many men in the uprising between AD 117 and 119.

Eboracum is sometimes spelled Eburacum. Both spellings are found in Roman-era writings, and maps might use either. The Latin version comes from the Britonnic word Eburākon.

For the definition of special terms used for Roman-era things and people and for the meanings of Latin words, see the Glossary after the story.

Chapter 1

A New Assignment

Near the legion fortress in Deva, Britannia, AD 117, Day 1

The raised cups and raucous laughter of his fellow tribunes drew glances and a few frowns from the Britons at the adjacent tables. Tribune Proculus Trebonius Rogatus forced a smile because it was expected, but he drank the farewell toast with pleasure.

Julius Valentinus, another of the five equestrian tribunes of the XX Valeria Victrix, had finished his three years as military tribune with the legion and was heading east to take command of a cavalry cohort in a different province. Another half year and Rogatus would leave the Twentieth to become a cavalry prefect as well.

Since the day Rogatus arrived in Deva to start his legion tribunate, Valentinus had said and done whatever he could to undermine him. Why the sustained hostility? Maybe the gods knew, but he would bet on jealousy.

Rogatus had barely dismounted to hand off his horse and pack mule to the stablemaster when Valentinus appeared. He'd greeted him with a smile and words of welcome, offering to show him to quarters. As Rogatus unpacked, Valentinus had seen his *armillae*, and those silver bracelets inspired the envy.

In Rogatus's first prefect posting, he commanded a cohort *equitata*, with 120 cavalry added to the usual 480 infantry of an auxiliary cohort. He'd led dozens of sorties against mounted raiders who sneaked across the Danube to pillage Moesia. Those hinged cuffs honored his skill at planning counterattacks and leading his men in battle.

Valentinus's first cohort had only been infantry in the peaceful province of Hispania, and not a single skirmish had broken the monotony of his three years as prefect.

Rogatus traced the rim of his cup with his middle finger. If only Valentinus had never seen those cuffs. The fleeting frown followed by calculating eyes and a fake friendly smile—Rogatus had seen those too many times before he left home to take his first post in the *tres militiae*. Even though his father, as *paterfamilias*, owned everything else, his military pay remained his. Nine years and three officer postings would earn him the 100,000 denarii required to stay equestrian, no matter what Father did to him later.

Rogatus's grandfather had named him Proculus because he was born while his father was away. He'd been a big baby, and Grandfather thought he must have been conceived before his father came home on leave. To avoid any scandal, Grandfather kept him and named him. When Father returned, he shared Grandfather's doubts and divorced his mother. Then his father and two older brothers never let Rogatus forget his questionable pedigree.

How that arrogant firstborn son of a newly elevated senator learned his family history—Rogatus had no idea. Over the past two and a half years, Valentinus made sure every tribune questioned Rogatus's lineage. Only family and good friends should call a Roman by his first name. Valentinus was neither, but he used Proculus whenever he could to promote the slur Grandfather had bestowed.

But even after his nemesis was gone, one of the others would tell the man who replaced him.

"Proculus. Where was it you came from again?" A sneer curled Valentinus's lip before he flicked a raisin at Rogatus's face.

Rogatus caught it and popped it into his mouth. "Protecting Rome from her enemies. Maybe you'll get to do that yourself someday."

A few chuckles and an amused snort from the other tribunes earned a glare from Valentinus.

Six more months, and Rogatus would get his own cavalry cohort somewhere else in the empire. What Valentinus and any of the others thought wouldn't matter anymore. It barely mattered now.

The serving girl returned to fill the empty cups, and Rogatus waved her away. He'd never been one to get drunk, and a wise man only let down his guard among friends.

The shadow of a man standing in the *taberna* doorway fell across their table. Then the optio who served as the legion commander's personal assistant strode toward them.

His fist hit his chest. "Tribune Rogatus. You are to report to the legate immediately."

"What's he done wrong this time?" Valentinus slurred his words.

The optio's head drew back, and he stared at Valentinus.

Rogatus rose. "Ignore him. Drunken questions deserve no answer." He tipped his head toward the door. "Take me to him."

The murmurs around their table faded as he followed the optio into the street. As far as he knew, he'd done nothing wrong in the past two and a half years. But his jaw still clenched as he strode behind the fast-walking soldier.

Life had taught him that a man could be punished for something that wasn't his fault, and too many took pleasure in another person's misfortune.

He was off duty and wore only his tunic and dagger, but the guards at the fortress gate saluted anyway. The optio marched past Rogatus's quarters, allowing no time to don the armor that protected him in battle and commanded respect as an officer of Rome.

Two more guards saluted as he passed through the double doors of the legion headquarters.

"Wait here, Tribune." The optio opened the legate's door and slipped inside, closing it behind him.

Rogatus spread his legs and stood with his hands clasped behind his back. But without his helmet, armor, and sword, parade rest felt less safe than hunting raiders.

When the door opened, Rogatus strode into the room and stopped four feet from the desk. He struck his chest. Fist on flesh sounded weak compared to fist on bronze.

"Legate."

His commander closed a wax tablet and slid it to the side. "Rogatus. I understand you commanded an equitata with distinction in your last posting. That you earned armillae for leading actions against tribal raiders."

"Yes, Legate." Rogatus never spoke of that honor himself or wore the cuffs on duty. How did the legate know?

His commander placed clasped hands on the desktop. "A courier just delivered an urgent request from the legate of the IX Hispana. One of his cavalry prefects is dead. With the unrest among the Brigantes, he can't afford to wait more than a few days to replace him, and he doesn't want someone who's never commanded cavalry. It would take too long for an experienced ala prefect to transfer from another province. He asked whether I could provide an immediate replacement."

Rogatus's heart rate ramped up. Was this headed where he hoped?

"You've shown you know what to do and did it well." The legate rubbed his lower lip. "I'm going to transfer you."

Rogatus tightened his lips to stop the grin. "Thank you, Legate. I look forward to this opportunity to serve."

A nod and fleeting smile spoke his commander's satisfaction. "Plan to leave for Eboracum tomorrow. You'll be in command of the Ala Primae Tungrorum." The legate reached for a tablet. "You're dismissed."

Rogatus saluted, executed a parade turn, and strode from the room.

He kept his lips straight until he walked past the headquarters guards. Then a satisfied smile broke free.

There was time to return to the farewell party just long enough to share his news. They'd drink the customary toast, whether they meant it or not.

And the look on Valentinus's face would be priceless.

Day 2

With his two midsized trunks strapped to a pack mule, Rogatus led his troop of four legionary cavalrymen toward the fortress gate. Today he wore the solid bronze cuirass of a legion tribune. As an ala prefect, he still would… most of the time. But one trunk held his chain-mail body armor. When a man went into battle, it gave him the freedom to twist and bend as he swung his sword that a solid bronze cuirass couldn't.

Valentinus had laughed at him having the chain-mail shirt before picking it up and holding it to his chest. Rogatus had folded it around the cuffs, and the cloth he'd wrapped them in caught on the armor rings. The engraved silver bands tumbled out and lay in plain sight. Then Valentinus held the chain mail over the trunk and dropped it atop Rogatus's proof of excellence. His half-mocking smile turned into a fake-friendly one, revealing an antagonist who would never become a friend. Soon after, the rumors about Rogatus's past began.

As they approached the gray stone gatehouse, Valentinus stood to the side of the right archway, arms crossed.

"Proculus." He curled his fingers and took a step forward.

Rogatus raised his hand, and his escort halted. "Wait for me outside the gate."

The men rode past, and when the pack mule disappeared through the stone arches, Rogatus rode toward Valentinus. His escorts would be returning to Deva when he reached Eboracum. Whatever Valentinus wanted to say, they didn't need to hear and repeat it later.

He reined in facing Valentinus. "What?"

"You couldn't resist flaunting your early promotion, trying to take over my celebration. But it didn't work. After you left, no one said another word about you." Valentinus scrunched his nose as if smelling something foul. "But at least you spared them pretending to celebrate your next command in six months."

Rogatus fixed a chilling stare on Valentinus. "You're assuming I care what you and the others think of me. I only care about the opinions of men I respect." He pointed at Valentinus's face. "You are not among those men."

He turned his horse toward the gate. "But I wish you well in your next posting. You're likely to see action, and that could mean you or your men dying for Rome. For the sake of your troops and for Rome, may Fortuna smile upon you in battle, and may the gods guard the safety of you all."

Rogatus's condescending smile as he nudged his horse into a trot turned his enemy's frown into a scowl.

He rode through the gate and past his escort without slowing. Eboracum was a three-day ride to the northeast. The cavalrymen of the Ala Primae Tungrorum would become his as soon as he arrived. The best time of his life had been leading his men in Moesia. If Fortuna smiled, the coming years in Britannia would be even better.

And in Eboracum, where no one knew his family history, maybe he'd even find a friend.

Chapter 2

A New Opportunity

The Lucanus farm north of Eboracum, Day 2

Narina Lucana leaned on the top rail of the corral, watching the mare and her new foal. With legs looking half again as long as they should be for his body, the wee beast wobbled as he walked around his mother. When he began bumping her belly and trying to suck, the mare shifted to help him find the milk he was seeking.

Many small head and neck jerks announced his success, and Narina straightened. With his rich chestnut coat and star-shaped blaze, he'd bring good money someday from a noble of the Brigantes or Parisi tribes. Or maybe some Roman in Eboracum.

Her gaze drifted across the field where several other mares grazed with foals beside them. Father would be proud of the family herd. Twenty-five years in an auxiliary equitata cohort had earned him and his children Roman citizenship. Fifteen years as centurion over its cavalrymen let him marry and earned enough for this farm and the taberna with upstairs lodging in Eboracum. Ten years of shrewd trading added the matching inn at Petuaria where the sea-going ships loaded their cargos.

Before he died five years ago, he put her in charge of the farm and herd so her two older brothers could run the businesses in the fortress town and the seaport. She was only eighteen, but he made the right choice.

She'd only been six when Father brought his wife and three children back to Brigantes country. Getting along with Brigantian neighbors had been easy for her, but her older brothers were more Roman than Briton and not eager to change. Even now, after seventeen years back in Britannia, her uncle's sons didn't welcome the rest of her family at clan gatherings, and both brothers chose Roman wives.

The hoofbeats of a trotting horse drew closer, and she spun toward the sound. Mounted on a fine Lucanus stallion, her oldest brother, Minconus, slowed to a walk and stopped beside the corral. He slid off and wrapped his reins around the top rail.

When he turned to face her, he was beaming.

"It's good to see you, Minconus. What has you so happy today?"

His broad smile became a grin. "I've just come from Isurium, and I made the greatest purchase of my life."

She stared at him. He'd never liked Isurium. Too tribal for him, just like their uncle and cousins were. Brigantian men took offense so easily, and the slightest offense could turn into a fight. He much preferred the legion town where his "own kind" lived. Words, not fists, settled disagreements there.

So, after she turned fifteen, Father had her help him sell the family horses. Whether Brigantes in Isurium or Romans in Eboracum, she could convince almost anyone that a Lucanus horse was what they wanted. He said her smile charmed them, but it was the horses.

Father had built a herd of quality mares and impressive stallions. She still raised fine animals, so they really sold themselves. She only pointed out their strong points that a man who didn't know horses well could miss. God didn't approve of lies or cheating, so unlike many horse traders, she never did either.

"What did you get?"

"I bought a house with a shop attached that's perfect for a taberna. There's plenty of space for serving food at inside tables, and there's already a counter along one wall that only needs a few stools. It's on the street connecting the fort's gate with the Via Flavia. I got it cheap because it's been empty for a while, but the owner had no idea that it was about to become valuable."

She barely stopped her nose from wrinkling. She'd been down that road recently. If it was the one she suspected, it should have sold cheap.

"Why do you think that? The fort is down by the river, and Isurium is much higher on the hillside. Hardly anyone who's not a legionary uses that street, and only the centurion has much money."

"That's about to change." He tugged first one, then the other sleeve of his tunic until they covered his wrists. "The tribunes of the Ninth ate lunch in the taberna today. The senatorial tribune said a decision was made just before they came to eat. They're moving the Tungrorum cavalry cohort to Isurium. There's only one century in the fort right now, so you're right that it's too few to earn much profit. But that ala will be almost five hundred men with sixteen decurions and a tribune. They're the ones with money in their purses and a taste for something better than garrison food."

He twisted their father's signet ring that he now wore. "And I've never met a soldier who didn't like to drink."

She rubbed her cheek. Isurium was a Brigantian tribal center. One century in the riverside fort could mostly be ignored, but a full cohort wouldn't be welcomed. At least his "greatest purchase" was some distance from the town. Mix young Brigantes with Roman soldiers and let some get drunk—how could fights not break out?

"I suppose that could bring enough customers. When are they moving?"

"As soon as their new prefect arrives. A courier went to Deva to get someone who's commanded cavalry."

"What happened to Prefect Atilianus?"

"I heard he died."

Both hands covered her mouth. "I sold him a horse only eight months ago. What happened?"

"I haven't heard, but it doesn't matter." He nudged her. "Maybe the new prefect will need a good horse. Bring some to town in four, maybe five days. He should be here by then. He'll recognize their quality and be willing to pay for it."

She tightened her lips. It did matter. Atilianus was a nice man, and he'd sent others who bought her horses.

"I sold one of the four-year-old warhorses to Atilianus. The other one I want to stand at stud. There's a three-year-old who's fully trained and strong for his age. He's already as good as what I sold Atilianus, and when he's older, he should be better. I can bring that one."

"Good." Minconus slapped her arm as his smile grew. "We need the money for setting up the taberna."

She sighed. Minconus was paterfamilias now, and Father had made him her guardian when he died. She needed his approval in financial matters, but he didn't always make the wisest choices where money was concerned.

God, don't let this be a foolish move that hurts the family.

"Some, but not all."

"Of course not. Father put you in charge of the horses." His smile turned sheepish. "I can always count on your help. Like when Martina broke her arm."

Her brow furrowed. That comment seemed out of place unless…

"Who's going to take care of the Eboracum *caupona* while you get the new taberna started?"

Father's first inn had both food and lodging, and some who rented rooms were not nice men.

"I will. I'm not leaving Eboracum."

"Then who's going to get your new business ready and run it?"

"You are." He bounced his eyebrows at her.

She narrowed her eyes. "I run the farm and raise the horses. That's more than enough."

"But you can do all three. Father always said you could do whatever was needed, even more than most men. You'll need to hire locals to do some things, and you work better with Brigantians than I do."

He was right, but often men, tribal or Roman, didn't like a woman telling them what to do.

"Maybe I do." Palm up, her hand swept the corrals and farm buildings. "But this doesn't run itself."

"It's only a three-mile ride if you take the trail by the river. You can visit here every day if you want. But our people know what to do. They should keep doing it as long as you drop by every few days to make sure they are."

It was all she could do not to roll her eyes. He had no idea what he was asking.

"But I've never run a taberna."

"Of course you have. When Martina broke her arm, Father sent you to take over everything she helped me with in Eboracum until she healed."

"He did, and I was glad to help. But helping and running something are very different things. I couldn't possibly do everything both you and I did."

He rubbed his jaw. "But you can take Veldicca and Lucania with you to share the work. Veldicca's a great cook, so she can oversee the kitchen. Her stews"—he kissed his fingers—"I serve some of her specialties, and the tribunes often order seconds."

She crossed her arms. "She could, but Lucania is only eleven."

"Eleven is mostly grown. She can help cook or serve."

Her lips tightened. "I am not putting my almost-grown sister into a room full of men who've been drinking. I hated dealing with the ones who wanted more than food when they paid for a meal."

"That shouldn't be a problem. She still looks like a child. You were fifteen, friendly, and pretty enough, so what did you expect? I thought you handled it well enough. And if you're serving yourself…well, you are twenty-three, and that's not as tempting." He shrugged. "Besides, if they see the dagger you wear selling horses, they'll back off. They won't know you wouldn't use it."

She slapped his arm. Twenty-three wasn't that old, even if most Brigantian women were married by twenty and the Romans even younger. Pretty enough? Lucania was pretty, but she'd call herself plain.

"After a few drinks, some men don't care about age or beauty. Isn't there someone you can hire to run it?"

"Maybe, but not quickly enough." He wrinkled his nose. "I don't want the officers to get used to going somewhere else before we start serving. I expect to make a lot of money there, and I need to know a man well before I give him that kind of temptation. There's no one I can trust like I trust you."

He reached for her hand, then held it in both of his own. "But I'll find someone trustworthy. Then I'll train him in Eboracum so he'll know what to do. It shouldn't be for too long."

She pulled her fingers free. Minconus could always persuade her to help him when she was a girl. Too often, that led to trouble. But she was many years past being a girl this time.

She leaned against the railing, and her gaze locked on the big oak at the edge of the woods. When she'd climbed so high she was too afraid to climb down, Minconus had come up to get her. She couldn't ask for a kinder, more loving brother toward both her and Lucania. What he was asking wasn't unreasonable as long as it wasn't for more than a few weeks.

She closed her eyes. *God, should I help him?*

Was that small nudge toward yes from God or from years of being a good sister when he needed her?

It was only three miles, but he shouldn't think she agreed too easily.

"Are you sure it won't be for too long?"

His grin returned. "I'll start looking for the right person to take over tomorrow."

He turned his back to the corral and focused his own eyes far up the tree. "You used to climb to see beyond our farmyard. I think you'll like spending more time in town and meeting more people." He joined her at the rail and prodded her with his elbow. "Who knows…maybe another Christian like you might start eating there. You could finally find someone you'd be willing to marry. Isurium is where the tribal chieftains meet, and one of their sons could be the right husband for you. They won't care what Rome thinks about Christians." A wry smile curved his lips. "Or about anything else, for that matter. Just like our cousins."

She forced a deep sigh to make sure he heard it. "I'll do it. Come get me tomorrow, and we'll ride in to look at what you've bought. Then we can make plans for getting it ready to open."

He wrapped his arm around her shoulders and drew her against his side for a hug. "You're the best, Narina. Together, we'll make it a great success. You'll see."

She blew out a slow breath. Would she see? Only God knew.

Chapter 3

Better Than She Expected

Isurium, Day 3

When Narina and Minconus left the Via and started down the road to the fort, her brother nudged his horse into a trot. She followed two horse-lengths back. She might need time to hide her first reaction if his "greatest deal" wasn't so great.

They slowed to a walk when they reached the short row of buildings between them and the gatehouse. He twisted and rested his hand on his horse's rump.

"It's the last one on the right near the fort."

She faked a smile. The one she'd feared. It had been months, maybe over a year, since she'd ridden down that street, and that house had been empty then.

The wattle-and-daub outside walls seemed in decent shape, and the thatched roof appeared thick enough it shouldn't leak.

"The door on the right is the shop, and those three shuttered windows open into it." Minconus pointed to each in turn. "And that left-side door leads into a courtyard house with the rooms opening under a portico around a small garden. So, you won't get wet when it's raining. Plenty of herbs there for Veldicca. The shop has a door into the courtyard, too."

He dismounted and opened the gate of a small corral that ran the length of the building. A shed at the rear had two doors, each split across the middle. "Since you'll be riding back and forth, you can get some hay put in one stall. Whatever you ride over can use the other one."

She followed him into the corral and dismounted. "Will we be here long?"

"Maybe. We want to look at everything and make a list of what needs to be done. I'll get what we need in Eboracum and bring it up by wagon. Or by boat if that's cheaper."

Maybe almost always meant yes with Minconus, so she took off the bridle and hung it on a corral post. "We want to get some of it here. It's a good way to meet the vendors you'll be trading with later."

"Fine, as long as you'll do it." A wry smile accompanied his shrug as he did the same. "You don't seem as Roman as I do. You'll get a better price."

"I probably will." Narina blew out a slow breath. "While you're looking for that trustworthy man, make sure he's comfortable dealing with Brigantians. If he can speak Brittonic without a Roman accent, that would be best."

"Even I can't do that, and I've lived here half my life." His smile faded. "You just made it harder, but I'll try."

She closed the gate behind them, and they returned to the street. He pulled a chain from under his tunic and gripped the larger of two keys. One quarter turn, and with a satisfying click, the door unlocked. He pushed it open and slid a stone over to hold it there. With spread arms, he turned in a circle. "Behold, the future Taberna Lucani."

With one foot, he tapped the gray-green floor. "Slate, so it will be easy to clean up when there are spills."

She scanned the room. No gouges in the walls to patch, no stains on the floor where the roof had leaked. It was much better than she expected.

He patted a counter that ran the length of the front wall. "Add a few stools, and our customers can eat and drink here. They can even see out when the shutters are open."

With fingers spread, he raised his hands and, palms out, spread his arms to sweep half the room. "There's room for ten or so tables with chairs. The house is furnished. There's one table that can seat six there and another that could hold four. But they both have benches. I'll get some chairs made. The tribunes prefer them."

She pointed to the corner opposite the door. "For the man who wants to eat alone or with one friend, there could be a small table over there."

He nodded. "I'll get three more tables that seat four made so they can be put together for a banquet. That should be enough to start. We can add more as we get more customers."

"Where's the kitchen?"

His smile turned sheepish. "There isn't one now, but the storeroom behind that wall is big enough to turn one end into one. It just needs a window added and a brick floor oven with a metal top to heat pots."

She narrowed her eyes. "Veldicca can't cook without a kitchen."

"But there's one in the house, and there's a door into the courtyard from the storeroom. She can cook there and use a pushcart to bring the pots over. We can keep the large jars of mead and amphorae of wine in the first room on the right. That way they won't get too hot when she heats the oven."

Hand over her mouth, she turned slowly as her gaze swept the room. It was much nicer than she'd feared. Maybe he had made a great purchase.

"Veldicca knows how to get what she needs to make the food, and I'll send up mead, beer, and wine from my Eboracum supply as you need it."

She drew her finger along the counter. Dusty, but not dirty. It shouldn't take long to get ready. "I could get the beer and mead here."

"Don't do that. Roman officers demand quality, and a single bad drink could keep them from dining here again, even with food as good as Veldicca cooks. The legion tribunes mostly drink mead. Good mead is close enough to white wine, but for the ones who want red, there's no substitute."

He handed her the key chain. "You'll need these. I should stay in Eboracum tomorrow. I expect the tribunes to bring the new prefect to dine with them. It's only three days to Deva, and the legate wanted a prefect immediately. I'll be able to tell him that he'll have a good place to eat in Isurium by the time he leads his ala here."

The shutters opened easily, and he leaned through the window to look up and down the street. "It's a great location. The prefect might eat here every night if the ala cooks aren't good and we feed him well."

He closed the shutters and slid their three bolts into their catch plates to secure them. "Don't forget to bring those two stallions to the stock fair. I'll let him know about that, too."

"I won't forget."

She stared at the two keys. She should have expected he'd leave her to do all the hard work of getting ready to open. But Veldicca would know what to do, and she'd ask one of the young men to stay in Isurium and help until Minconus got her replacement.

"I'd like to see the house now."

"It might take some cleaning, but nothing you and some women from the farm can't finish in a day or two."

She drew a breath through her teeth. When a man said "might" about cleaning, that meant it would. "Some" usually meant a lot. But the building wasn't that large. Surely, she and Veldicca with Lucania and a couple of the women could get it livable in a day. She wasn't some hard-to-please Roman noblewoman. Besides, she wouldn't be there more than a few weeks, and she could put up with anything for that long to help the brother she loved.

Chapter 4

A Better Horse

A village east of Mamucium, Day 3

From Deva to Mamucium, Rogatus and his troop made excellent time. He rode the horse he'd bought in Londinium when he first came to the province. He'd weighed the pleasure of riding a spirited stallion against the lower cost of a serviceable gelding, and he'd chosen to save the money. He'd only be selling it when he left the province in three years anyway. It had no trouble on the six-day ride up to Deva. But that road was almost flat the entire way, and he hadn't been in a hurry.

This time speed mattered, so he alternated trotting with walking to let the horses rest. His horse seemed no more tired than the mounts of his escorts when he turned it over to the stableman at the inn where they spent the first night.

But today the road grew steeper as they climbed into the mountainous country that separated the western and eastern coastal plains. By the time they'd traveled twenty miles, the distance his horse could trot between walking breaks grew shorter.

It was late afternoon when the village ahead drew his sigh of relief. Stopping for an early dinner would give all the horses the rest that his truly needed. Dusk came late in the summer, and they could ride farther after they ate.

He lingered over the caupona's tasty stew and fresh bread, listening to the companionable conversation among his escorts. Would he find such friendship among the tribunes in Eboracum? Or perhaps among the decurions under his command, like the two centurions who taught him what it took to be a worthy commander of his cohort. They'd been more like fathers to him than the man who questioned whether Rogatus was his own.

Too soon, it was time to mount and ride ten more miles or whatever it took to reach another inn to spend the night. He paid for all the meals before stepping outside, leaving his men to finish their drinks.

A commotion where their horses were tied drew his gaze and then his frown.

His horse was closest, and a trio of small boys were throwing large pebbles at it. Each time one hit, the horse shied, tugging on the halter rope that tied it to the hitching rail and bumping the horse beside it.

His jaw clamped when the boys laughed at the frightened animal.

Like a scout sneaking toward an enemy camp, he crept up behind them and grabbed the closest boy by the shoulders. The other two shrieked as they ran.

He spun the boy to face him and gripped his upper arms. The boy squirmed and tugged, trying to break free, but Rogatus tightened his grip.

"Stop fighting me and listen." Wearing his fiercest scowl, he leaned over so the boy could hear his soft-spoken Brittonic. "Every good man knows to treat a horse better than that. Would you do that to your chieftain's horse?"

The boy stopped struggling. His eyes widened, and he shook his head.

"I'm chieftain over five hundred warriors. What you wouldn't do to your chieftain's horse, you shouldn't do to mine. Should you throw rocks at the horse of any man in your tribe?

Another shake of the head accompanied the boy's swallow.

Rogatus relaxed his scowl into a slight smile. "That's right. You should never throw rocks at any horse, not even an old cart horse. This time, I won't punish you. But never do that to a horse again, or I will. Understand?"

The boy's rapid blinks accompanied several quick nods.

When Rogatus released him, the boy stepped out of reach, but didn't run.

His men walked past, eyeing the pair of them.

"Mount up." Rogatus untied his horse, tossed his leg over its back, and settled into the saddle. The boy remained in place, staring up at him.

Rogatus's fleeting smile raised the boy's eyebrows before getting a smile in return.

With a forward flick of his hand, he led his escorts from the town at a trot.

Coritani or Brigantes—in this hill country, the boy could be either. But when he grew up, he could tell his clansmen at least one Roman chieftain was not an enemy because he chose not to punish a small boy's foolishness.

Eboracum, evening of Day 4

It was early afternoon when Rogatus led his men past the cluster of buildings lining the road from Deva and onto the bridge across the Abus River. It arched over the water, leaving room for the masts of the larger riverboats to pass underneath.

He scanned the riverbanks as they crossed. Large boats and small lined the quays on both sides, close to the warehouses that made Eboracum the trading center of the region.

But the view straight ahead triggered his smile. The towering stone walls of the legion fortress stretched before him, and its double-arched gate whispered welcome home.

The fists of the legionary guards struck their chests as he rode past. Straight ahead lay the *principia*, where he would report his arrival to the legate. But first, he led his troop to the stables that lay to the right of legion headquarters.

When the soldier in charge approached, he signaled the man with the pack mule to hand off the lead.

He turned his horse to face his escorts. "You'll return to Deva tomorrow. Report to one of the decurions to find where you'll bunk tonight. You're dismissed."

They saluted, dismounted, and led their horses away. As legionary cavalry, they knew what to do.

But he wasn't sure himself. He'd be quartered with his ala, but until he reported to the legate, he wouldn't know where that was.

"Tribune." The stablemaster struck his chest. He looked askance at the weary gelding, but said nothing.

Rogatus dismounted. "This one wasn't up to a quick trip from Deva. As soon as possible, I'll need to get two more horses fit for cavalry service. I'm Trebonius Rogatus, the new prefect of the Ala Tungrorum."

The stablemaster's face relaxed. "Welcome, Prefect. You'll be operating in hill country here, and I might have part of what you need already. Prefect Atilianus had a fine stallion, well trained for maneuvers and battle. He's a beauty as well. He hasn't been reassigned to anyone since Atilianus's death."

Rogatus smiled at the prospect. "The stallion I rode when I commanded an equitata in Moesia was my partner in battle. I want to find others like him."

A smile warmed the stablemaster's eyes. "Since you've commanded cavalry before, you'll appreciate what you're getting." He shrugged. "Atilianus hadn't, so he bought the horse for its appearance. Fortuna smiled on him even without him knowing what he needed."

The stablemaster summoned a soldier with a curl of his fingers. "Tend to the gelding. Leave the trunks on the mule to take them to the prefect's lodging."

With a broad smile, he turned to Rogatus. "Follow me."

They walked along a stone building with many half doors opening onto the walkway. Through each of the open top halves, Rogatus saw three horses tied to rings on one wall. After passing fifteen doors, the stablemaster opened the one at the building's end.

A single untied stallion turned to face them. With a dark tan body, a nearly black stripe down its back and across its withers, and mottled black extending from black hooves to above its hocks and knees, it was a classic dun.

Rogatus's fingers gripped the bolt, and he raised his eyebrows at the stablemaster. The man's nod gave permission, and Rogatus entered the stall.

The stablemaster closed the half door and leaned on it. "Broad chest, short back—he's as fast as he looks. Those hindquarters—strength and stability for lunging or spinning to face the enemy. You won't find better in these stables."

With cautious calm, the stallion watched Rogatus approach.

"Any temperament problems?"

"None I've seen. He's not afraid of anything, and he doesn't start fights. Never needs a muzzle."

Rogatus reached the horse and stroked its neck, patted its shoulder, and placed a hand on its back.

"Can I mount him here?"

"You can."

With some mane in his left hand, Rogatus made a stepping jump and swung his leg over the stallion's back.

"High withers, thick muscles on both sides of his spine—he's a comfortable ride when you're not in drill or battle."

Rogatus settled on the stallion's back, and the horse turned its head to contemplate him.

"I'll have to ride him first to be certain, but he's much like the horse I left in Moesia. I never saw a better one in action. He was ten when I left there, and I sold him to serve as stud for a man I trusted to care for him."

"It's good this one is going to a man who'll appreciate him."

"What did Atilianus call him?"

"Boreas."

Rogatus slipped from the horse's back and stood in front of him. When he gripped both sides of the halter, a single toss of the head was the response. He stroked the forelock, and confident eyes stared into his. North Wind. A fitting name for a fine animal.

"I'd like to find another like him. Where did he come from?"

"He's a Lucanus horse. They bring horses to the stock fair sometimes. The next is the day after tomorrow."

"Have him ready for me first thing tomorrow. I'll take him for a ride, and if he satisfies, I'll shop for one from the same stud."

The stablemaster responded with broad smile. "If Fortuna smiles, you'll find one, Tribune."

Rogatus left the stall. As soon as he spoke to the legate, he should know where he'd be living.

With a horse fit for an officer, he was now more than ready to lead his ala wherever Rome needed them to go.

He headed across the street to the principia. The guards saluted as he entered, and he strode across the courtyard to the desk by the legate's office.

The legate's orderly stood. "Tribune, may I help you?"

"Trebonius Rogatus, reporting to the legate. I've just arrived from Deva."

The optio closed the tablet that lay open on his desk. "He's not here at the moment. You weren't expected to arrive so quickly."

"My former commander said there was urgency to your commander's request, so I came promptly. Can you tell me where my quarters are?"

"No, Tribune. But for tonight, you can have a guest room in the *praetorium*. The guard there can tell you which one." The optio's brow furrowed. "Do you have baggage?"

"Two trunks on a pack mule. The stablemaster knows where those are."

"Very good, Tribune. I will send someone to transfer them to your room." He clapped once, and one of the guards came to him. "Get Gallus's optio to fetch Tribune Rogatus's trunks from the stablemaster and take them to the praetorium's guest rooms."

Someone cleared his throat, and Rogatus turned.

A tribune stood behind him.

"We've been expecting you." He placed his hand on his chest. "I'm Sextus Cornelius Dexter. Welcome to Eboracum."

"Trebonius Rogatus. I've come from the XX Valeria Victrix to assume command of the Ala Primae Tungrorum." He donned his friendliest smile. Perhaps Dexter wouldn't notice he'd shortened his own introduction to the last two names. Or if he did, would think nothing of it.

"Our garrison cooks aren't the worst, but they aren't the best, either. I'm joining the other tribunes for dinner. There's a taberna that belonged to a retired cohort centurion where the food is always good and men of the legion are always welcome. His oldest son runs it now. Join us."

Rogatus returned Dexter's smile. "With pleasure. But first I need to leave my sword in my quarters."

"I'll take you to the visitor quarters, and then we'll go meet the others."

Palm up, Dexter motioned toward the exit, and Rogatus walked beside him to his room in the praetorium.

Dexter leaned against the doorpost while Rogatus wrapped the strap around his scabbard and placed it in the cabinet. When two soldiers appeared carrying his first trunk, Dexter stepped aside for them to pass.

"Put them there." Rogatus pointed at the wall beside the cabinet. This time, he'd wait to open them until he was alone. Only a fool would risk anyone he didn't know well seeing his chain mail or armillae. Valentinus had seemed as welcoming as Dexter…until he saw them.

When Rogatus entered the taberna with Dexter, the other tribunes were already seated at a table with six chairs. Rogatus made seven. But as they walked by a table with an empty chair, Dexter grabbed it and brought it with them.

"This is Trebonius Rogatus. He's come to replace Atilianus. These are Gallus, Martialis, Rufus, Bassus, and Plantus."

Rogatus exchanged nods with each one in turn.

"Welcome to Eboracum." Gallus lifted his cup. "Where were you posted before Deva?"

"I commanded the Cohort Brittonum Equitata in Moesia Superior."

A man too well dressed to be a servant took a pitcher from the serving girl and came toward them.

"I'm Minconus Lucanus, and I welcome you to my taberna. Wine or mead?"

Rogatus glanced at what the others were drinking. "Mead."

Lucanus filled an empty cup and set it before Rogatus. "My father served in that cohort for twenty-five years. He was a cavalry centurion and fought the Dacians under Domitian."

"I saw the *phalerae* from that war on the cohort standard. Two bronze and a silver disc for valor…I was honored to lead such a cohort. My cavalrymen continued its proud tradition against the Jazyges raiders."

Lucanus stood a little straighter. "I have the ones my father earned. Our family lived in Viminacium until I was twelve. Father brought us all to Britannia when he retired. He bought a farm and this inn when we settled here."

Dexter tapped Lucanus's arm. "And we officers of the legion are glad he did. There's no better place to eat and relax than this taberna."

He turned a smile on Rogatus. "So, I thought the best introduction to Eboracum for Rogatus would be a good dinner here. He just rode over from Deva to assume command of the Ala Tungrorum."

Lucanus's smile dimmed. "We were sorry to hear of Atilianus's untimely death. It was always a pleasure to see him when he could join all of you."

Rogatus drew the cup closer and traced the rim with his finger. "I'll be riding one of his horses. Boreas. The stablemaster said he was a Lucanus horse. Any relation?"

"A dark tan dun?" Lucanus drew a thumb along his jaw.

Rogatus nodded.

Gallus tapped his cup, and Lucanus added more mead. "He's one of ours."

"He reminds me of the stallion I left in Moesia when I came to the Twentieth. I'll be looking for another like him."

Lucanus set the pitcher on the table. "I might be able to help you with that. We'll have some horses at the stock fair this week."

A diner across the room raised his hand, and Lucanus waved back. "I hope you enjoy our stew tonight." He tipped his head toward the diner. "If you'll excuse me…"

Several nods sent him to his other customer.

Dexter leaned back in his chair. "You'll enjoy the stew. Everything Minconus serves is excellent. When you're in Eboracum, join us anytime."

The others put on social smiles and spoke conventional words of welcome. But that was how most first meetings went, and it was enough.

Rogatus took his first sip. As good a mead as he'd had in Britannia. No wonder the tribunes ate there.

As the conversation of the others swirled around him, any worries about fitting in faded away. He'd always been a man who listened more than he talked. It wouldn't be long before joining in the conversation would feel natural, and watching each word he spoke could become a thing of the past.

Chapter 5

New Responsibilities

Eboracum, morning of Day 5

After an early breakfast of still-warm bread, cheese, and hard-boiled eggs, Rogatus swung his legs off the couch in the praetorium's guest dining room. He was the only man in armor. The other three diners dressed in Celtic-style tunics with trousers. Given the choice between sitting at a table made for four with three Britons he didn't know and reclining alone, he opted for solo dining. After a few glances, they ignored him, so his choice suited them as well.

He stopped by his room to collect his helmet before going to the principia to report. It was past the time when the legate of the Twentieth was in his office. The commander of the Ninth probably kept the same hours.

When he entered the headquarters courtyard, the same optio sat by the legate's door. He strode toward the desk, but he hadn't reached it when the orderly rose.

"Tribune." The man's fist thumped his chest. "The legate isn't here."

Rogatus blew out a slow breath. "When do you expect him?"

"I don't know. He didn't say when he left."

"When was that?"

"Yesterday morning."

Rogatus fingered his lower lip. Should he assume the legate would be there soon and wait, or ride Boreas now to see if the stablemaster was right about Lucanus horses?

"If the legate returns this morning, tell him I was here, but I've gone to see about getting suitable mounts. I expect that to take no more than the morning. Tell him I'll return by this afternoon."

"I will, Tribune."

Rogatus stopped the sigh before the orderly heard it. At least he had something to do while he waited. The stablemaster should have Boreas ready for him. On the training field, he could try the maneuvers all cavalry horses must know. With a gallop up the road for a mile, then trotting back, he'd test whether the stallion had the stamina that cavalry on campaign required.

He strode past the saluting door guards and crossed the street to the stableyard.

His smile grew slowly and ended up broad. It had been two and a half years since he sat on a horse that was pure delight to ride. It would be good to do it again.

Isurium, afternoon of Day 5

Narina carried the bucket of dirty water from the kitchen to the ditch by the long-abandoned garden. Next to its old gate, a dozen yellow wildflowers raised their heads above the grasses that had reclaimed the land.

After dumping the water, she straightened and arched her back. She'd spent yesterday and today cleaning the taberna and the rooms of the house, and she'd lost count of how many times she'd emptied and filled that bucket. But at least she had a well of her own only a few steps from the kitchen door.

Atto had taken Bikka, Vinda, and the two-mule cart back to the farm. He would return with the smaller cart and a single mule that would let her shop for supplies in Isurium. With only Veldicca, Lucania, and herself to finish cleaning, she was long past tired. But nothing satisfied like a job well done, and the taberna could open tomorrow.

If Minconus's venture with this place survived, she would plant vegetables there in the spring. The low fence that once kept hares out would need fixing before then. Some Britons revered the hares, but most Romans loved the taste. Eboracum was a legion town, so no one was upset that Minconus raised hares for his kitchen. But Isurium was a tribal center, and many were offended by Roman ways.

It might be wiser to bring a few from the farm as she needed them. She'd be riding home at least twice a week until her brother found her replacement.

Yesterday she'd left home at first light with Veldicca, Lucania, and her work crew in a cart. Stuffed with bedding, cleaning supplies, and much of what she'd need to live there for a while—there was barely room for it all. Bikka and Vinda came to help with the cleaning, and they sat atop the load.

With both Narina's best friend and her little sister on the seat beside him, Atto drove the two-mule team. At fifteen, he already had the building skills for keeping the place in good shape. As tall as a man and now filling out, he was eager to do more than farmwork. With his quick smile and friendly ways, he would do well serving their customers, whether Briton or Roman.

Narina had ridden the older mare she would keep in Isurium. No longer one of the breeders, it was no loss to the herd to have Bena there. She was one of Father's first mares and one of Narina's favorites. How often she'd have to ride the river trail to the farm, only time would tell. But Bena would take her the three miles in no time at all, and Narina would enjoy the ride.

Lucania stuck her head out the kitchen door. "It's here, and you won't believe how much Minconus sent."

Narina followed her sister through the kitchen, courtyard, and taberna to the street.

A mule-drawn wagon stood before her. A half dozen stools for the counter and a pair of chairs that tribunes would like were stacked behind the driver. Past those were amphorae of wine, urns of mead, and crates holding cups, plates, and whatever else Minconus thought she'd need to open before the ala arrived.

Veldicca opened the small chest at the back. "He sent the herbs and spices I'll need for the best of my stews." She directed a hopeful smile at Narina. "Now all we need are the men who will eat them."

"It's too soon to know"—Narina lowered her voice as a group of legionaries walked by—"but I've been praying for Minconus's success with this. I don't know if he spent money he can't afford to lose."

"I've been praying, too." Veldicca picked up the chest. "Lucania is as well."

The driver joined them at the back of the wagon. "Lucanus sent this for you."

She took the wax tablet and stepped away so he could climb onto the wagon bed. As he began pulling crates to the open tailgate for her work crew to carry inside, she read her brother's message.

> Narina,
>
> I think I sent everything you'd find hard to get in Isurium. If not, send your requests back with the driver.
>
> Or tell me yourself when you bring the stallions to the stock fair tomorrow. I've met the new prefect. Rogatus has already taken over the horse you sold Atilianus, and he's looking for another like him. No one around here has that except you. I told him we'd have some horses at the stock fair. I expect he'll look for them.
>
> He needs to buy one for me to have the money to cover enough of the start-up costs. I'm finding those much higher than I first thought. In case he doesn't like the three-year-

old, be sure to bring that silver dun. I don't think I've ever seen a prettier horse, and tribunes like showy mounts. As Father used to say, you can charm anyone into buying a horse with your smile. Whichever he buys, get him to pay top money for it.

Thanks for all your help with getting the taberna opened so quickly. I couldn't do it without you. You're the best.

Minconus

Bring the silver dun? Zephyrus was the best she'd ever raised. The stallion Father had used to start the herd had died, and she'd planned for Zephyrus to replace him. Father had made Minconus her guardian, so she had to bring him. But she'd do nothing to draw attention to him. If she stressed the excellence of the three-year-old and showed the tribune what he could do, the bay should prove irresistible to a cavalry officer.

Charm a Roman tribune with her smile? Narina rolled her eyes, even though no one was watching. Nothing was less likely. Rich Romans might be eager for her horses, but not for someone like her.

Mother had been a Roman beauty with the stately manners and dark brown hair of Narina's grandmother. She had Grandmother's brown eyes as well, not the blue eyes of her Germanic grandfather.

Tall and imposing in his centurion uniform, Father had won Mother's heart in Moesia. She used to say his blue eyes and almost-blond hair looked more like a Brigantian chieftain than a Roman, and she liked it that way. Father and Uncle Bellicus could have passed for twins, and Uncle was a chieftain now.

Her brothers and Lucania got the dark hair and brown eyes of their Roman mother, but she looked different. While Lucania had inherited Mother's beauty, Narina had no illusions about her own appearance. Except for her medium brown hair with golden strands spread through it, she looked like her father. Mostly. His eyes were a rich, deep blue, and hers were the color of a rainy-day sky.

When she rode a Lucanus stallion, men looked at the horse, not her. It really was the quality of a Lucanus horse, not the charm of her smiles, that made every sale.

She stepped inside to place the tablet on the window counter. Then she joined the others carrying the crates into the storerooms. Veldicca would know what else they might need, and Narina would leave all the money she had with her for her faithful servant and best friend to buy it.

At first light, she would ride to the farm to get the stallions and a couple more horses that ordinary buyers might want. Then she and one of the men would take the river trail to Eboracum.

God, please let that tribune pay enough for the bay stallion to cover what Minconus needs. I wish I knew how much that is. I don't want to sell him for less than he's worth, but if my brother's desperate for the money…"

A deep sigh escaped. She'd stop by the inn to find out before taking the horses to the fair. He'd probably tell her, but he might not. A paterfamilias didn't have to explain himself to anyone, not even a sister who only wanted to help him succeed. But if Minconus wasn't there…

She set her crate down and headed back to the wagon. No point in worrying about things she couldn't change. It was time to leave it in God's hands.

Besides, even a legate should be proud to ride any of her stallions, and she was good at getting a horse's true worth from a man who had the money. This time should be no different.

Eboracum, afternoon of Day 5

When Rogatus returned to the stable, the stablemaster met him. "Did Boreas satisfy you?"

Rogatus swung his leg over the stallion's head and slid off. "More than satisfied. It was like riding my horse in Moesia again. He did every maneuver as well as I've seen, and his speed and stamina are what I'd hoped for."

"I thought he would." The stablemaster took his reins. "I saw the legate. He should be in the principia now."

Rogatus acknowledged that with a nod. "As soon as I know where the ala is camped, I'll want Boreas again."

"I'll have him ready, Prefect."

After a final slap to his stallion's shoulder, Rogatus strode across the street to receive his command.

When he approached the reception desk, the optio saluted and opened the legate's door.

Rogatus stopped four feet from the legate's desk, and his fist struck his chest. "Tribune Trebonius Rogatus reporting. I've come from the Twentieth at your request."

The legate closed a wax tablet and set it aside. "To command the Ala Primae Tungrorum. Right now, it's encamped on the other side of the Fossa River. But you'll be taking it to its new fort in Isurium."

Isurium? Rogatus blanked his face, but had the legate seen his surprise before he did? Where that was…he had no idea.

A wry smile curved the legate's lips. "Coming from Deva, I wouldn't expect you to know where that is. Isurium is a Brigantes tribal center seventeen miles north on the Via Flavia. There's been an undercurrent of discontent lately, and a strong presence there should quiet things down."

"Is that fort garrisoned now?"

"A century has been stationed there since before I took command of the Ninth."

Rogatus drew a deep breath and held it. Only a century? Fewer than a hundred men. In Moesia, that size of garrison needed no more than a fortlet and lacked anything for horses. His equitata's fort had barracks built especially for cavalry with the riders bunking above their mounts.

He exhaled slowly lest the legate question his reaction. "Has it housed an ala before so it has enough nearby grazing for the herd of two hundred extra mounts?"

The legate rubbed his chin. "I don't know."

Rogatus blinked fast, then hoped the legate hadn't noticed. He'd be taking almost five hundred men and seven hundred horses to…what? And what would happen if he got there and the fort was grossly unsuitable?

"Then I request permission to inspect it before moving the ala there."

A reasonable request, but would it seem insubordinate?

"Permission granted for up to a week. You may stay in my guest quarters until then. Anything else?"

Rogatus stayed at attention, but he relaxed inside. At least this legate saw the wisdom of looking before leaping with five hundred horsemen along.

"No, Legate. I'll ride out now to meet my decurions and partly inspect the ala. Tomorrow I'll inspect the fort."

"Good. If you've no further questions, you're dismissed."

Rogatus struck his chest again, made a parade turn, and strode from the office. Probably the stablemaster could give him directions. A cavalry camp of five hundred men was impossible to hide.

His mouth twitched, then relaxed into a smile. He'd enjoyed commanding a unit well away from the legion fortress in Moesia. The political maneuvering and petty jealousies like he found among the tribunes of the Twentieth had no effect on him there. Seventeen miles wasn't that far, but it was far enough.

Today he'd meet his decurions and arrange for at least one to accompany him to inspect the fort tomorrow. He'd go early to the horse fair so they could ride to Isurium by noon.

If Fortuna smiled, he'd have his second mount and could begin its training to be a warhorse like Boreas. He'd do some himself and have the decurions identify someone to work on the rest.

A good day's work made a man hungry and let him sleep well. Minconus's taberna would satisfy the first. He hadn't slept well last night, but after meeting the legate, tonight should be different. In a new town with new duties where he'd surely excel, sleep should come easier than it had in years.

Evening of Day 5

The tribunes were already seated when Rogatus entered the taberna. But Dexter raised a hand to summon him and got an extra chair from the adjacent table. Rogatus settled into it between Dexter and Plantus.

"So, what did you do today?" Dexter took a sip of mead.

"The legate is back. I learned I'll be taking the ala to Isurium. I rode out to meet my decurions across the Fossa, and the most senior will be joining me tomorrow to inspect the fort there."

Minconus brought a clean cup and set it before him. "I already have a taberna in Petuaria near the wharves for the sea-going ships. I will be opening another like this one near the fort in Isurium.

"Will be? How soon is that?"

Not that Rogatus cared, but it felt polite to ask.

"Within a few days. Probably by the time you take your ala there. No need for bad food if you don't want it." Minconus chuckled as he poured Rogatus a cup of mead.

Rogatus traced the rim with his middle finger. "I plan to eat with my men most of the time, like I did in Moesia. I knew my men well, their strengths and weaknesses, because of it."

Minconus's smile dimmed, but only for a moment. "At least try the taberna. It will be as good as here. Your decurions will also love it. Knowing them well…that's important, too. My father truly appreciated when a prefect rewarded his centurions with a dinner far better than what their cooks made."

Dexter looked up at Minconus. "I'll be sure to try it if I'm in Isurium." He slapped Rogatus's arm. "On my day off, maybe I'll ride up, and we can try it together. Plantus likes a good day's ride, so maybe we'll both come."

Plantus sipped his mead and wiped his mouth with the back of his hand. "I do. I'll join you."

Rogatus answered both with a nod and a smile. It was seventeen miles one way. Why would two men he'd just met want to spend a day in the saddle to join him for lunch?

"We can do that."

What else could he say? It probably wouldn't happen, anyway.

Across the room, a diner raised a hand. "Minconus."

"If you'll excuse me…" With a smile genuine enough to show in his eyes, Minconus moved away. When he reached the other table, a wave of the man's hand invited their host to sit, and the innkeeper settle into the offered chair.

The servant girl came with a tray of bowls balanced on her hip. As she set one before him, Rogatus acknowledged it with a smile.

Maybe his time with the tribunes of the Twentieth had made him too suspicious. Maybe these men were how tribunes usually were, a group of comrades who enjoyed each other's company. Men who were willing to let him be one of them, even with no questions asked.

Chapter 6

WORTH WHAT SHE'S ASKING

Eboracum, early morning of Day 6

A heavy rope stretched between several trees with a few wraps around each of them. Different traders displayed their horses between each pair of trees.

Narina leaned against the third tree in the row. Senorix had beaten her to the fairgrounds, and he'd snagged the first spot today. But his horses weren't even competition with the two ordinary horses she'd brought. Compared to her stallions, they looked like cart horses.

She'd tied the bay so the prefect would see that one first. Zephyrus was farthest away from where the prefect would approach if he came straight from the fortress. If he liked the bay, she'd never tell him Zephyrus was for sale.

She stepped away from the tree when the glint of bronze caught her eye. The prefect was coming, and she was ready.

But before he reached her first horse, Senorix stepped into his path. "Can I help you, Tribune? I have fine horses here for anyone looking for the best."

The tribune cast an appraising glance at the mix of mares, geldings, and a couple of stallions that Senorix had tethered to the rope.

The corners of his mouth turned down. "Are there any Lucanus horses here today?"

"No. It's not often they bring any. But I have some fine ones that might be exactly what a tribune like yourself would want."

The tribune's frown deepened. "I was told some Lucanus stallions would be here. The two you have are…" His mouth twitched. "They might satisfy some, but I'm not looking for something that merely looks good to ride. I need something fast, strong, and intelligent, one I could train to be a good warhorse."

Senorix offered an oily smile. "Then I'm certain you'll want to try the chestnut. He's the best you'll find in Eboracum."

With crossed, muscular arms resting on his bronze-encased chest, the tribune tilted his head to look down at the liar. "The best in Eboracum? I don't think so. I have a better one back in the legion stables, and my next horse must be just as good."

His arms fell to his sides. "But your horses look decent, and I'm sure someone else will find them suited to their needs."

Narina eyed the tribune as he stepped back from Senorix. It might be the prefect, but even if it wasn't, he would have the money Minconus needed for the taberna. She and the others got it clean enough to open as is, but it wasn't as inviting as the Eboracum one. Some better tables and comfortable chairs instead of rough-made stools would encourage officers to linger over their food and make them want to come back.

She stepped away from the tree and headed toward her intended customer.

The farmhand who'd come with her whispered as she passed. "Good luck, Narina."

She flashed him a smile. He meant well, but luck wasn't what she believed in.

God, please let him buy my bay so Minconus won't be in trouble.

He'd turned his back toward the line of horses. Was he planning to leave already?

She lengthened her stride as much as her long plaid tunic allowed.

◆

A tall woman, probably mid-twenties, with a strong, square jaw and gray eyes approached Rogatus.

"Are you looking for a showy horse just to ride or one with the stamina and strength that a military man can count on in battle?" Palm up, she swept her hand toward a bay stallion tethered just past the next tree. "If the second, come see what I have."

A woman horse trader? Not what he'd seen before.

"One like I left in Moesia. Fearless and understanding what he needs to do without reins telling him."

She rubbed her jaw. "Why did you leave him? Those are hard to find."

Not a question he expected, and not anything she needed to know. But something about those gray eyes made the question seem genuine.

"I bought him from the officer I replaced, and he'd served long enough. The next prefect might not know horses well enough to appreciate him. So, I sold him to a man I knew would take good care of him, as he'd taken care of me. He's standing at stud now."

"Faithful service deserves a reward." A prettier smile than he expected softened her face. "Come see what I have here today. Everything I train does what I tell them with only my legs, and they seem brave to me. If one interests you, we can take it into the country to test. I'll ride another one out with you. After you see what makes it special, I'll answer any questions you have."

His eyebrow rose. A young woman should be more careful, even a plain one. She was dressed like a Briton, but she spoke like an educated Roman. The horses she had were as good as he'd seen, so her family had more wealth than most. But who chose her to sell them where the scoundrels often outnumbered honorable men?

"You'll go away from the town alone with me?" He tipped his head toward her helper. "You could send him."

Her laugh was musical. "How else will you know whether a horse suits you? He can't show you what I can. My father was an auxiliary centurion. He would trust a tribune not to do what he shouldn't when he's only looking to buy a horse. So will I."

She shifted the fringed purse that hung from a strap across her body. A sheathed dagger rested against her hip. "But he taught me and my brothers to take care of ourselves, too." A wry smile curved her mouth. "And my stallions like me, not you. So, I'm not unprotected."

"Humph." His mouth twitched. She was right that he wouldn't hurt her, but men like Valentinus? A bronze cuirass sometime covered an evil heart, not an honorable one.

Palm up, she swung her hand toward her tethered horses. "Shall we?"

With a single nod, he fell in at her side as she started toward them.

"I heard you ask Senorix about Lucanus horses."

"You were listening?"

So, she knew the answer to her first question before she asked. Why did she ask it?

"When I hear my name, it catches my attention. I'm Narina Lucana."

They'd reached the rope where her horses were tethered, and she stroked the nose of a bay stallion that stood first in line.

"This bay is three and a half, but he's already showing the speed and strength of many four-year-olds. He's ready for service."

She looked over her shoulder at him, and the smile appeared again. "Feel free to look him over closely. I think you'll like what you see."

He stroked his jaw. Three and a half might mean closer to three. A horse wasn't at full strength and stamina for at least another year. His gaze shifted from horse to horse along the rope until it settled on a silver dun at the far end. Tall, solidly muscled, calm as it looked back at him. A mature animal that should be at its best.

"I need something older. Tell me about that one." He pointed, and her smile wavered before steadying.

She led him down the rope to what he might be looking for. The stallion bumped her with his head before she wove her fingers into his forelock and pulled them through.

"This one is four and a half, also ready for service."

He ducked under the rope and began his inspection of the silver dun. The horse turned its head to watch him. With an almost black chin, slate-gray muzzle, and black tips on its ears, the face was stunning. The mane was gray, but a black stripe started at its withers and ran down its back to the tail. While most of the tail was gray, the black strip continued into it, like a black ribbon atop steel. The black at the hooves turned into horizontal black stripes near the knees and hocks. The stripes stopped half way between knees and body, fading into a silvery gray.

He'd spent his whole life around the expensive horses of Rome's elite, and he'd never seen such a striking animal before.

But he'd told her he didn't want pretty. He wanted a warhorse, and it didn't matter what those looked like as long as they could do the job.

"How much?"

Valentinus gave him no end of grief over the gelding he'd bought for less than two hundred denarii. His nemesis claimed he never spent less than six hundred on a horse for himself, and sometimes a thousand. The stallion Valentinus rode was a pretty animal, but only a fool would pay that much.

She flashed him a smile that took away some of her plainness. "We can only discuss that after you've ridden him."

She took off her belt and draped it across her shoulder. Then she grabbed her long tunic by her knees and pulled it up to her waist. With one arm holding it in place, she flipped the belt around her waist before cinching it, turning it into a thigh-length tunic. She'd worn a pair of trousers beneath.

His eyebrows shot up, and she laughed at him.

"Don't look so surprised. I came dressed for riding, and how a proper woman dresses wouldn't let me do what you need."

He shrugged. "I've known Sarmatian women who fight as cavalry. They dress like men as well. It was how you changed, not how you ended up that surprised me."

"That's not the only surprise you'll have today." The winsome smile he'd seen several times appeared. "I'll ride the three-year-old out. He's fast and strong for his age. You might want to try him, too. Either would serve a military man well."

She gripped the younger stallion's mane and jumped to swing her leg over his rump.

He mounted the silver dun, and the animal felt solid beneath him.

Her calves tensed, and the bay started walking. Then she turned in the saddle and placed her hand on his rump. "But I won't show you the real surprise until you've ridden one of them for a while."

He moved up beside her. Before he could speak, she nudged her mount into a trot, then a canter.

He did the same, and a smile leaked out as he felt the power between his legs. With effortless, fluid motion, the stallion caught up with her. When she moved into a full gallop, he followed suit.

He'd thought Atilianus's horse was exceptional, but this one…it could leave Boreas eating its dust.

They'd gone more than a mile when she reined in by an open field. "How do you like him so far?"

"He's a good horse."

Good wasn't the accurate word. Amazing fit better. But if she knew he thought so, she'd set a high price.

"How much are you asking?"

"Seven hundred denarii, and a bargain at that."

His head drew back. Half a month's wages. He'd never paid that much for a horse, and he wasn't about to now.

"That might sound like a lot, but I'd like to show you something before you decide. Let's trade horses."

She slid off her horse and dropped the bay's reins. It stood as if tethered, and she stroked its nose while she waited for him to make the trade.

He dismounted and handed her the reins. As soon as she was seated, she turned the silver dun into the field.

Then, without using the reins, she started the moves he'd done to test Atilianus's horse.

Tight right-angle turns, then tight circles with quick reversals of direction. Cantering straight before a sharp left without breaking stride. A sharp right turn into a gallop. Back and forth between gallop and canter before a sudden stop, only to gallop again. The horse reared and stayed there, striking out with his hooves. She shifted, and he turned while rearing, then planted his feet and stood still. She dismounted, and the horse backed up to wait behind her.

He covered his mouth and patted his cheek. A true warhorse stood before him, and he wanted it.

◆

Narina reveled in the power of a stallion beneath her, but nothing compared with the exhilaration of riding like the cavalryman her father had been. He'd taught her before he took her horse trading the first time. First with reins, then with legs alone, her own body moving in harmony with the horse. Every stallion they raised had a chance to learn this, and the best ones loved the routine as much as she did herself.

When Father's health failed, she'd taken over the training. Since he died, she still trained every stallion willing to learn.

As she rode back to the prefect, the look on his face was priceless. Amazement, then desire. Any tribune should have the money, and he was ready to make the deal, whether he knew it or not.

It pained her to do it, but she gave him what Father had called her horse-trading smile, guaranteed to make a sale.

"For a horse that can already do battle maneuvers and catch anything you're chasing…seven hundred is not too much. How much is the life of a man worth? Father was a cavalry centurion. He always said in the heat of battle, the right horse can be the difference between winning and dying. How do you put a price on that?"

◆

Rogatus stared at her in silence. She watched him back. She showed none of the signs of a person trying to take advantage of him. Nothing in her eyes or the curve of her lips suggested she was lying. She really thought the horse was worth what she was asking, and maybe he was.

His monthly pay had risen from 1000 denarii a month as an equitata prefect to 1500 as a legionary tribune. Except for buying the horse in Londinium, he'd spent no more than a hundred a month, even though Valentinus and the others mocked him for the gelding he rode and for eating garrison food most of the time. So, he'd saved 75,000 denarii already. As ala prefect, he'd still earn 1500 a month. In less than nineteen months, he'd reach the 100,000 denarii that made him equestrian in his own right, and nothing his father did could ever change that.

So maybe this once, he would spend more of the money he usually saved. A true warhorse and the most magnificent mount he'd ever seen wasn't something he should pass up.

"I'll take him."

Her smile dimmed as she nodded. "Zephyrus should belong to someone who appreciates all he is, not just his beauty." She moved a loose strand of hair behind her ear. "And he already knows Fortis. They got along fine as long as there was no mare to fight over."

"Atilianus called him Boreas, so I do, too. Zephyrus fits this one, so I'll keep that name as well. I won't confuse him with a name change."

She turned cool gray eyes on him. "So, no matter which one you ride, you'll be riding the wind."

He crossed his arms. She'd made her sale at the price she asked, but she didn't seem as pleased as he expected. "As I like to do. Who trained Boreas?"

She gave him a warmer smile and a shrug. "I did. I train our stallions like my father taught me. Any good horse can do well for just riding. As a soldier, you need a partner who knows his job. That's what Father always said. I train partners, not just rides."

He answered with a nod. "I'd like to ride him back."

They made the switch and rode back to town in silence.

But he found himself glancing at her without intending to. Narina Lucana wasn't a woman that men's eyes would follow, but anyone who had seen her ride would never forget her.

Chapter 7

PREPARATIONS

Isurium, late morning of Day 6

With his lead decurion at his side, Rogatus reined in on the low rise before the road descended to cross the Isura River. Alternating trotting and walking to keep the horses fresh, he and Germanus had traveled the seventeen miles from Eboracum in three hours.

He'd chosen Atilianus's horse for this first trip, and the stallion seemed as fresh as when he mounted him. Yesterday, Boreas was the finest horse he'd ever ridden. Today, he was only second best.

The corners of his mouth turned down. While he was paying Narina Lucana, she told him she'd left home when the first blush of pink lit the clouds and had ridden Zephyrus over ten miles that morning. She should have known a cavalry officer didn't need her to tell him to use another horse if he planned a long ride today.

But the way she rested her forehead against Zephyrus's nose and whispered goodbye kept him from letting his irritation show. It was how he felt himself in Moesia when he said goodbye to his horse-partner after three years.

Atop a high hill to the east sat the large town of Isurium. A tribal center of the Brigantes, where chieftains might meet to plot against Rome and hot-headed young men could be stirred up to turn their plans into actions.

The fort that would be his lay ahead near the river. The sight of it triggered his satisfied smile.

Not a fortlet for a century, but an auxiliary fort built of stone like the one that served his equitata. Not far from the main gate, a village had grown up on the road connecting the fort to the Via Flavia. Perhaps a mile separated the fort from Isurium. Close enough for a commander to see what was done in public. But who could he trust to be his eyes and ears among the men who chafed under Roman rule?

An undercurrent of discontent. That's what the legate said. Rogatus blew out a slow breath. Discontent could fester like a splinter you couldn't remove until pus pushed it free or you cut it out. He and his cavalrymen might be the scalpel Rome would use.

Rogatus pointed toward the hilltop. "The legate said the Brigantian leaders sometimes gather there. Do you or any of the other decurions know someone they trust who lives here?"

"I don't." Germanus's nose twitched. "Many of the ones who know some Latin pretend they don't. But I know they do from the way they listen to us. Pretending they aren't but reacting to what we say."

Rogatus rubbed his forehead. Headaches were his frequent companions, and he could sense one starting. But after years of practice, he could mostly ignore them.

"Do any of the others speak Brittonic?"

"What the others know…" He shrugged. "I only hear Latin and sometimes Germanic in camp. That's all I need."

Rogatus stopped the frown before Germanus would think he'd caused it. More times than he could count, he'd known where to find the raiders he hunted because some of his men could talk with the locals. They'd find someone willing to reveal what he needed. He'd learned a little Brittonic when he commanded the Brittorum because his men spoke it among themselves.

Valentinus had poisoned the other tribunes against him, so he'd spent most of his off-duty time alone. He spent it wisely, learning more Brittonic. Sometimes he could figure out what Britons said when they thought he couldn't understand their words. But he needed more. If his decurions found which of their men knew at least as much as he did, they could become his spies.

"When we get back to the ala, find out who among the men can understand Brittonic. If they can speak it, that's even better."

The guards saluted as he and Germanus rode through the arched stone gate. Even before he dismounted at the headquarters building, the number and design of the barracks declared it a fort for an infantry cohort but not an equitata. The small stable was sized for fewer than two dozen horses, and his ala would have at least seven hundred. Five hundred lived close to their riders, ready to saddle and mount at a moment's notice.

Past the barracks, then between the headquarters building and the commander's house, along another row of barracks, between the hospital and granary, and circling back to the headquarters—Rogatus and Germanus rode in silence.

As he dismounted by his future quarters, the centurion in charge of the garrison strode toward them.

"Tribune." His fist hit his chest. "Welcome to Fort Isura. Let me show you around and answer any questions you might have."

With the fort centurion on his right and Germanus on his left, Rogatus took the official tour.

"Are there any special problems in the area?"

The centurion snorted. "Nothing out of the ordinary for Britannia. Most of the people around here consider us an enemy army. Some of the Brigantes welcome the money my men and I spend, but that's all. Some of the younger ones would welcome an uprising. Or the chance to hurt a Roman soldier. I tell my men not to go to Isurium alone, and even in a group, don't get too drunk."

Rogatus rubbed his jaw, "It wasn't that bad in Deva where I served the Twentieth, but it's been seventy years since the Cornovii were conquered."

One corner of the centurion's mouth lifted. "Cerialis thought he conquered the Brigantes almost fifty years ago, but that's not the way the Brigantes see it."

With nods and occasional questions, Rogatus let the centurion show him everything again. It wasn't as bad as he'd feared, but it wasn't all that he needed.

As the tour ended, a low rumble came from Rogatus's gut. Germanus's mouth twitched as he cast a quick glance as his commander. But his decurion probably ate breakfast.

He'd only grabbed a roll and a handful of raisins for breakfast to get to the horse fair before the best animals sold. But the solution to his hunger should await outside the gate.

"An innkeeper in Eboracum said he was opening a taberna near the fort. Where is it?"

The centurion's eyebrows rose. "There hasn't been one since I've been here, but I've seen people working around an abandoned house that had a shop on the front and a corral beside it. It's on the road to the Via."

Narina Lucana's words about treating his junior officers to a good meal echoed in Rogatus's mind.

"Join us there for lunch?"

The centurion's smile confirmed the wisdom of her advice. "Not today. I doubt it's open yet, but if the food is any good, maybe next time."

Rogatus and Germanus strolled through the gate. The first building was two hundred feet from the fort walls. Farther than normal in a peaceful province, but this was Britannia.

He'd be eating with the tribunes this evening. If Minconus asked, he could at least say he tried to eat there. If it wasn't as good as Minconus claimed, he would save Dexter and Plantus a full-day ride, assuming they had meant what they said. He'd never ride a day to eat with anyone but a close friend, and he hadn't had one of those since childhood.

The door was open, and on the outer wall next to it hung a wooden plaque divided into two columns. On the left was Latin in the block letters used for inscriptions. Someone had written, "Welcome to the Taberna Lucani. Please enter, then eat, drink, and relax for a while." On the right were words he couldn't read. But he'd bet it was the same message in Brittonic for the few who could read it.

Whether the owner realized it or not, that wasn't just an invitation to enter. It was an invitation to trouble. Roman soldiers, young Brigantes, and too many cups filled with mead was not a recipe for relaxation.

Rogatus stepped through the doorway and scanned the room. No one sat at the counter by the front windows. Two tables, one with stools, the other with two chairs, stood in the middle of the large room.

"It's past lunchtime, but maybe there's food left over in the fort." Regret tinged Germanus's voice.

"Is anyone here?" Rogatus raised his voice as if addressing his troops.

A pretty, dark-haired girl of about eleven scurried out of the back room. Her head drew back as she stared at Rogatus's red horsehair crest.

"Prefect?" Her question was Latin, and her slight accent reminded Rogatus of Moesia.

Rogatus nodded. He wore the crested bronze helmet and cuirass of a tribune. But the girl knowing his exact title—that was odd.

"We weren't expecting you today, but"—the girl waved toward the table with chairs—"please take a seat. Veldicca just made us something I'm sure you'll enjoy."

Rogatus lifted his helmet off and set it on the table before sitting. His decurion did the same.

"What is it, and what do you have to drink?"

The girl's eyes widened. "I'll get Veldicca." She spun and disappeared into the back room.

Germanus raised one eyebrow. "Expecting you today? Why would she expect you at all?"

Rogatus stretched out his legs and crossed his ankles. "The owner of a taberna in Eboracum said he was opening a new one. He knew the ala would be stationed here before I met him, and he was eager for me to try it. Maybe he told her."

"What the girl said sounded like we'll be getting what the servants eat." Germanus leaned back in the chair. "Not what I'd want a customer to judge my cook by. But at least these chairs are comfortable."

A smiling red-headed woman who looked well past thirty came through the doorway. "Welcome. Lucania said you wanted something to drink while I prepare your lunch. Minconus sent up some red wine and mead that the legion tribunes like."

"Mead." Rogatus glanced at Germanus and got a nod. "For both of us. She said there might not be food except what you prepared for the household."

"There's plenty of soup for two more, and fresh bread I baked this morning. Shall I bring some for you both?"

"What does it cost?"

Valentinus's scornful words about only a poor man asking the cost of a meal played again in Rogatus's mind. But only a fool didn't know what he was spending before he spent it.

Veldicca's mouth opened, but no words came out. Then her smile returned. "It's not a regular dish on the menu, so I don't know. But maybe a quarter of what you paid Minconus for dinner?"

"Bring two servings and the mead."

"Yes, Prefect." She dipped her head and disappeared into the back room.

The girl replaced her in the doorway. Two cups filled with mead sat on a tray, and she placed one in front of each of them. After a bow, she left.

One sip, and Rogatus knew he'd be drinking here with his officers.

Veldicca had returned with two bowls of soup and the bread. He inhaled the rich aroma and ate the first spoonful. Garlic and rosemary and something he couldn't identify made him lick his lips to get every last drop.

At least as good, maybe even better than Minconus's stews in the legion town. It would have been worth at least twice what she asked for it. If dinners only cost what Minconus charged in Eboracum, an occasional treat for some of his decurions wouldn't cost too much.

He filled the spoon again and slipped it between his lips. Definitely better than camp food. He would still mostly eat with the garrison, but he might indulge himself once a week with something that made his mouth water instead of his nose twitch.

Isurium, late morning of Day 6

Narina handed Atto the basket of onions to place in the one-mule cart with a bag of ground wheat and more bags of lentils, chickpeas, broad beans, dried peas, barley kernels, and dried carrots. She'd had him bring it back from the farm when he took the women home in the wagon. A mile was too far to carry the supplies Veldicca would need when the prefect and his decurions started eating with her.

"Narina." The familiar voice made her turn.

"Albiso. Sulio. It's good to see you."

Her cousins crossed the street, and Sulio leaned on the wall of the cart.

"Buying what you usually grow? Did something go wrong at your farm?"

Narina bit her lip. What should she say? Maybe the simple truth was best, even though they wouldn't like it when they heard it.

"It's for Minconus's new taberna."

Albiso's eyes narrowed. "New taberna? In Isurium? I thought he wanted nothing to do with this town."

Narina smiled at him as she shook her head. "I wouldn't say that. He's just too busy to leave Eboracum much."

He crossed his arms. "Where is it going to be?"

"Off the old road. He found a good building for a low price, like Father did in Petuaria. It's the seaport, but it's also the Parisi tribal capital. Minconus thinks Isurium is going to be the new capital for us Brigantes."

Albiso snorted. "Us Brigantes. I'd wager he didn't say 'us Brigantes.' You're the only one in your family who's not mostly Roman."

He scrunched his nose. "If it's in the village just outside the fort, he made a bad deal, no matter how little he paid. It's so close to the fort there will be too many Romans for any Brigantian man to want to eat there."

Sulio tapped his brother's arm with the back of his fingers. "But the Romans know they're not wanted where we drink in Isurium. Minconus isn't Brigantian enough to care who drinks there as long as he makes enough money."

Albiso returned the tap, but harder. "He won't make much then. There's only ninety Romans there, and the only one with much money is the centurion. The others...they'll only buy his drinks if they're cheap enough."

"That's ninety Romans too many." Sulio elbowed his brother. "But at least they stay down by the river where we can ignore them."

Narina dropped her gaze to her cousins' feet. Maybe a century could be ignored. But the five hundred Rogatus was bringing?

She fixed a friendly gaze on one, then the other.

"Not everyone hates the Romans like you do. Dubnus says the Romans, Greeks, Gauls, and Parisi all get along at the Petuaria taberna. Minconus will serve Veldicca's stews here. You've had those before, and you have to admit those are worth coming a mile for. I agree with Minconus that it will be a great place for both Brigantes and Romans. If we spend more time together over some good food, we'll all get along better."

Albiso's eye roll accompanied Sulio's snort.

Sulio rested his hand on her upper arm. "You're the only one in your family who's Brigantian enough to be worth talking to. But you're right that

Veldicca's stews might be worth putting up with a couple of Romans, as long as we don't have to share a table."

She placed her hand atop his and patted it. "I hope so. It's always nice to see you." She flashed a smile at Albiso. "Both of you. After I get the taberna open, do come and eat with me."

"Will there be Romans?" Albiso's nose twitched.

"In the taberna, probably. But if it's that important to you, we could eat in the house instead."

Sulio nudged his brother. "We'll come. If you need some help while you're here, let us know."

She gave them her warmest smile. "I will. Thank you."

With a wave, her cousins strolled away.

Narina sighed. Her tribal cousins had never liked her brothers because they were too Roman. They made Minconus feel like he didn't belong in the clan. She'd do almost anything for Minconus, and she liked these cousins who'd always made her feel welcome. Nothing could be better than getting her cousins and her brother to care about each other like family should.

But would Minconus opening a taberna here to serve so many Romans be more help or hindrance?

Eboracum, late afternoon of Day 6

Rogatus's stomach clenched as he approached the legate's office. How does a man who's only seen his superior officer once report an urgent problem?

The optio announced him and held the door open. Rogatus stopped four feet short of his commander and saluted.

"Legate, I have a report on the state of the Isurium fort."

The legate set aside a stylus and clasped his hands. "Proceed."

Rogatus cleared his throat. What was the right way to deliver both good and bad news to the man he knew nothing about?

"The fort was built in stone for a full auxiliary cohort, and it is in good repair." He drew a deep breath. "But it was built for an infantry cohort, not for a cohort equitata. It has stables for no more than twenty-four horses. The ala needs five hundred quartered with their riders and another two hundred in a reserve herd."

His heart rate ramped up. "So, I must request the building of stables against one of the walls of the fort with a palisade around them. In the event of a Brigantian attack, it will need more than one deep trench and the dirt piled to make a high embankment with stakes atop it."

The legate's eyebrows plunged, but Rogatus forged ahead. "Basically, we need to add part of a legion marching camp that can be entered through the fort gates on that side. There's ample room by the south wall for the addition. I believe three centuries can complete construction in two or three days."

Through pursed lips, the legate blew out a long, slow breath. "One of my tribunes should have mentioned that when we discussed stationing the Tungrorum ala out there."

The optio had followed Rogatus into the room and was on one knee gathering some wax tablets from the floor by the desk. The legate turned to him. "Which tribune is over the century that's already out there?"

"Tribune Dexter." The optio stood, and his chin held the tablet stack steady.

"Hmph." The legate's eyes narrowed. "Tell Dexter to get two more centuries out there to get that fort ready to receive the ala as soon as possible."

"Yes, Legate." With only the tablets he'd already picked up, he strode from the room.

"Since Dexter has no idea of what cavalry requires, I'm putting you in charge of directing the construction."

Rogatus barely stopped his head from drawing back. Placed in charge of another tribune's men? Would this turn Dexter into an enemy instead of a friend? He was the obvious choice for the task, but what would it mean for Dexter…and him?

"I can do that, Legate. An ala is four times what I had with the equitata, so for me, it's only a matter of scale, not something different from what I've overseen before." He cleared his throat before speaking maybe dangerous words. "I know what's needed, but a man who hasn't commanded cavalry has no reason to know that a fort that is well suited for an infantry cohort would need so much added to make it suitable for cavalry."

The legate's frown relaxed into a wry smile. "It looks like my colleague over the Twentieth was doing what's best for Rome, not for his own command, when he sent you. I like my tribunes to work with, not against each other. You would have fit in well here.

"I have met your tribunes, and I believe I will work well with them." Even though Rogatus stayed at attention, the uneasiness drained away.

"I'm sure you will. If there's nothing else, you're dismissed."

Rogatus struck his chest, spun, and strode from the room.

He tightened his lips to keep from grinning. If this legate had seen what was tolerated in Deva, he'd be appalled.

The urge to grin faded. It was one thing to want your officers to work together for the good of Rome, and quite another for an ambitious man with a ruthless streak to do it when his commander wasn't watching.

Chapter 8

A Woman Worth Talking To

The clear sky of dawn had been replaced by light cloud cover, but the day was still pleasant as Narina worked at her loom under the portico.

"Narina!" Lucania burst through the back-room door. "The soldiers are here."

"Was Zephyrus leading them all?"

"I didn't see any horses. There are two groups of them with men at the front holding poles with round metal plates on them and a hand on top."

"No horses? There should be at least five hundred if the whole ala is there." Narina placed the shuttle on the small shelf at the top of the loom. "And it should be a dragon head with a tube of cloth, not a hand on the top. That's what Father's cavalrymen followed."

She accompanied her sister back through the taberna and into the street.

The men marched in rows of four and wore layered bands of metal as armor.

Narina sucked a breath between her teeth. Where were the auxiliary cavalrymen?

As she stared at the marching men, her hand covered her mouth. These were legionaries like she'd seen every day when she helped Minconus at his taberna. With only two standards, only two centuries were joining the one already there.

Was the ala not coming? Had Minconus wasted his money and her profits from the finest horse she'd ever raised on a taberna that almost no one would visit? It would fail with only three junior officers and the rest ordinary soldiers who would buy the cheapest drinks on the rare occasions when they came.

She bit her lip. Had she parted with Zephyrus for that?

When the last of the legionaries entered the fort, she noticed at least fifty men digging about a hundred and fifty feet out from the fort. A wall of dirt rose between them and the stone wall. But what were they doing that for?

Lucania's hand shot out. "Look. Just past the fort. That looks like Zephyrus."

She drew a deep breath and blew it out slowly. Rogatus with his bronze cuirass and red horsehair crest sat atop her horse. Zephyrus walked past the men digging in line with the back of the fort and stopped by a centurion. He dismounted and stood, arms crossed. As the centurion pointed at different things, the tribune would nod once.

A small group of soldiers began raising a long tent fifteen feet out from the wall.

Trenches, a growing dirt wall, tents, the prefect overseeing it—the legionaries were expanding the fort, not moving in.

She placed her hands on Lucania's shoulders and drew her sister back against her before kissing the top of her head.

"It's him, and that's the commander of the cavalrymen who are moving here."

She'd worried for nothing. The ala was coming, and all should work out well.

Noontime of Day 7

Rogatus had ridden up shortly after dawn, well before the legionaries arrived. With the help of the centurion and a few of his men, he'd marked out where the several buildings to house the horses should be.

He'd eaten more breakfast than yesterday, but his stomach declared it lunchtime anyway. The centurion he'd invited to dine with him before was busy directing his men. But eating alone was fine with him. Solitary dining was much better than eating with bad company.

It was a short stroll to the taberna and a mile to Isurium. He'd left the *spatha* he used in cavalry actions in his quarters. It was too long for a short man on foot, but his shorter *gladius* hung comfortably at his side. He could safely ignore the centurion's policy of his soldiers not going into a Brigantian town alone.

When he entered the taberna, an iron triangle now hung from a ceiling beam just inside the door. A sign in Latin and the other language on the outdoor sign said to ring it and someone would come.

As he moved the metal rod around the triangle, the ringing was almost musical. It should make the girl or maybe the cook appear.

He was gazing out the open door when he heard someone behind him.

When he turned, his head drew back. The last person he expected to step through the doorway was Narina Lucana. Dressed in a plaid tunic with a cord wrapped around her torso to shape it, the Brigantian horse trader had transformed into a Roman woman.

She greeted him with the smile he saw in the horse market. "Welcome, Prefect. Veldicca said you were here yesterday. I'm glad you liked her soup well enough to come again."

"It beats field rations and most garrison food." An understatement if he ever made one.

She laughed, and it sounded as natural as the first time he heard it.

"From what Father told us, that isn't saying much. After twenty-five years of garrison cooks, it's no wonder he appreciated what Veldicca prepared so much. After she joined us, it was her recipes he used in the Eboracum taberna. Minconus still does."

Palm up, she invited him to sit at the table with the comfortable chairs.

He shifted his sword as he lowered himself into one and placed his helmet on the table.

A youth walked through the back-room door and froze.

Her friendly eyes stayed focused on him. "We're not ready to serve many people, but you're welcome to enjoy our lunchtime soup and whatever you'd like to drink."

"Same price as before?"

It was worth twice as much, but he liked a bargain.

"That seems fair."

"Then mead and the soup will do." He pointed at the other chair. "And some conversation while I eat."

Her eyebrows rose, and she paused before replying. "I can do that today." She turned toward the youth. "Atto, would you please let Veldicca know the prefect would like a bowl of her soup and some bread?"

Atto nodded and took a step toward the doorway.

"And a cup of the best mead." She pulled out the second chair and seated herself as gracefully as any elite Roman.

"How is Zephyrus doing for you?"

One corner of his mouth rose. "As well as you expected. The stablemaster at the fortress thinks he's even better than Boreas. My decurions were all impressed."

A wistful look flitted across her face. "As they should be. He's the best I've raised. I'm glad you appreciate him." Her smile dimmed for a moment. "He would be a great stud, given the chance."

Rogatus leaned back in his chair and crossed his arms. If he raised horses, he would have kept Zephyrus to stand at stud. Why hadn't she?

Atto appeared with a cup and filled it with mead before returning to the back room.

"You told me you train all the Lucanus horses." He traced the cup rim with his middle finger. "I didn't expect to find you here."

"It's only temporary. Minconus asked me to help him get this started while he trains someone to take over running it for him. I'm usually at the farm three miles south along the river. I raise the horses there and fruit to sell."

He took a sip. Had she sold Zephyrus to help Minconus start this place? But who was Minconus to her? She looked nothing like him, so maybe his wife? But she wasn't wearing the stola over her tunic that would declare her a married Roman.

"Minconus's food is a favorite with the legion tribunes." He swirled the mead before the next sip. "Roman officers aren't welcome everywhere, but since he's Roman himself..." He shrugged.

"Father was Brigantian. He enlisted when Frontinus was raising auxiliaries for Vespasian. His twenty-five years gave us all citizenship."

Sister, not wife. For no particular reason, that pleased him.

"Minconus was twelve when we came home from Moesia." She flashed a smile. "He'll always be more Roman than Brigantian."

"And you? Are you Brigantian or Roman?"

The laugh he liked accompanied another smile. "Both. I was only six. I remember Moesia a little, but Britannia is home."

"You speak excellent Latin. I don't hear that much here."

"I look nothing like Mother, but she was the youngest daughter of a Roman equestrian. He was prefect of Father's cohort during Domitian's war with Dacia. A Sarmatian arrow almost killed him, but my father saved him. Mother met Father when he came to check on how my grandfather was recovering. When she fell for the dashing centurion who saved Grandfather's life, he permitted their marriage. She taught me to be a lady like her. Father taught me to be a horsewoman."

Her soft chuckle brought warmth to her eyes. "I liked his lessons better. Mother was so beautiful. My little sister looks like her, but I ended up plain and looking like Father."

He stopped the frown before it escaped. The girl he saw yesterday was pretty, but Narina wasn't so plain when she smiled. "But you also have his skill with horses. That's better than being pretty."

Her laughter filled the room. "That's what Minconus used to say. He meant it as a compliment, but it's not what a young woman wants to hear."

His ears heated. He'd never been skilled at making a woman feel admired. But insulting her was the last thing he meant to do.

She made no move to leave, but silence stretched out between them.

"How did your mother like living in Britannia?" Not that he cared, but getting Narina talking again was worth his asking.

"She always said that wherever Father was, that place was home." Her smile faded. "It broke Father's heart when she died."

Her eyes had softened as she spoke about her parents. She had loved them, and they probably loved her.

He rubbed his jaw. What would that have been like? Grandfather had banished his mother after his birth and refused to let him see her. As a child, he'd dreamed of meeting her when he was a grown man. But she died before he could. Father loved his brothers and sister, but he'd treated his favorite slaves better than him.

Veldicca entered with a bowl of soup and some bread on a tray. As she set it before him, Narina pushed back her chair.

"Don't leave."

Her eyes widened. He wanted her to stay and talk, but why had he said that aloud?

"I'd like to know more." He picked up the spoon. "About the area."

Veldicca leaned over and whispered in Narina's ear.

Narina's single nod sent her servant from the room.

She fingered her lip. "I'm not sure what to tell you. About the fort or the town or what?"

"Either or both. No one in Eboracum told me much about this area. I'm adding stables to the fort because it wasn't built for cavalry. The legate didn't know that when they decided to move the ala here."

"About the fort then. It's on the old road. It was built after Agricola thought he'd conquered the Brigantes. The first bridge across the Isura is just past it. But as Isurium has grown, they built a new road through it and put in another bridge. Most travelers pass through Isurium now." She swept her hand across the room "That's why this place was empty for so long."

Rogatus furrowed his brow. "Thought he conquered?"

The fort centurion had used the same words.

Her eyes sobered. "Yes. A tribe is conquered only if it admits it is. Many Brigantes…they tolerate the Roman presence, but they would die before admitting Romans have the right to rule here."

Veldicca returned and placed some soup and bread before Narina.

So, he wasn't eating alone after all. That triggered a smile. She was as far from being bad company as he'd ever met.

She picked up her spoon and pointed at his bowl. "You'd better eat it while it's hot. It's better that way."

When she turned her attention to eating, he followed suit. Every time he glanced at Narina, her gaze was on her bowl. But when he kept looking at her, she felt it and gave him a smile before filling her spoon again.

Eating together in silence wasn't the same as eating alone.

When he scooped up his last spoonful, she rose. "I'm sure you have a lot to do, so I won't keep you. It's been a pleasure chatting. I hope you come back soon."

"I will. It's been a pleasure for me as well."

After a quick flash of the smile he liked, she carried her empty bowl into the back room.

He replaced his helmet and strode into the street.

Lunch today had provided him with more than a full stomach. He'd made the first step toward knowing someone he might trust to give him advice about the locals, like he'd had in Moesia.

He'd be back for the good food and for more conversation. She was a woman worth talking to, even if what she said had no military value at all.

◆

After the prefect was gone, Narina and Veldicca reentered the taberna. While Veldicca stacked her bread plate with his on the tray, Narina strolled to the door and leaned against the doorframe. Rogatus was almost back to the fort.

"Minconus will be glad to know the prefect has started eating here. He even said he'd be back." She moved back into the room. "After eating your cooking twice, how could he resist?"

Her grin triggered Veldicca's chuckle. "He asked you many questions. I think he liked your company as much as my soup."

Narina rolled her eyes. "What choice did he have? It was me or no one."

She swept some bread crumbs onto her hand and dropped them on the bread plate. "He's just new to the area and doesn't have anyone better to talk to. When he asked me to stay, I couldn't say no without offending him. That's the last thing Minconus needs. He was comfortable asking because he bought Zephyrus from me. Other than the legion tribunes, I might be the only person he knows here."

Veldicca's smile turned teasing. "You talked about more than horses. I heard him ask about your family."

Narina tapped Veldicca's arm. "He's just a curious man. My Latin sounds more Roman than most around here. That got him asking about my background. Anyone might do that."

"He's coming back for more." Veldicca bounced her eyebrows once.

That earned another eye roll. "He wants more information about the area, that's all. He's being friendly to learn what he needs to command here. I'll try to answer his questions, but he won't get anything from me that might hurt Uncle Bellicus or my cousins. And they won't get something from me to hurt him either. Iesu said, 'Blessed are the peacemakers,' and I want to be one of them."

"Maybe that's only an excuse to get you to talk with him. I don't know anyone who doesn't enjoy your company. Your cousins can barely stand Minconus, but they go out of their way to talk with you. No matter what you say, I think he likes you."

"He'll have no interest in me like you're implying. He's an equestrian prefect, just like Grandfather back in Moesia. He earns ten times what Father did, and just being equestrian means he's from a rich noble family. So, those wages probably don't even matter to him."

She moved the chairs back under the table. "I know the world he comes from. We lived with Grandfather most of the time while Father served as centurion. Rogatus will take a rich Roman wife someday."

"But your mother wanted your father, not some rich Roman."

"Mother was so young, and she fell in love with the noble warrior who saved her father. It doesn't get more romantic than that. But it turned out well for them. They were truly happy together."

She pushed a loose strand of hair behind her ear. "But I'm not young, and I've never been romantic. I don't want just any man. I want someone who loves Iesu as much as we do. One who'll love me for the beauty that God gives me inside, even though I'm plain. That's never going to be an equestrian tribune."

Veldicca's smile faded. "I suppose you're right. But I still think he likes you, even if only for friendly conversations. He'll keep coming for those."

"It better be your food that keeps him coming. I'll be going back to the farm as soon as my brother trains my replacement. I need to go back every few days to do some training even before then. You can keep him eating here until you teach someone your recipes like you did in Eboracum. I don't mind helping out Minconus for a while, but it will be good for us both to be home again."

Narina returned to the front door and scanned the sky. "It looks like it might rain. We should probably get glazing for one of the windows so we can keep the weather out but let the light in during the winter. This place could feel like a cavern otherwise."

Rogatus had disappeared, so she watched the soldiers. They'd marched into the fort in armor, but they were only wearing their red tunics as they wielded picks and shovels.

"I'd hate to be one of those men working on the fort if it rains. They're moving so much dirt. I wonder what it will look like when they're done."

Veldicca joined her by the doorway. "They'll pile the dirt up to make a wall and put a fence of pointed wooden stakes on top. I saw them do this for practice when I was a girl near the legion fortress in Isca Silurum. Put it up, take it down, over and over. When the legion moves in wartime, they make a new fortress by doing that every night and take it apart in the morning before they march."

Narina shook her head. What a waste of men's time and effort. War always was, but Rome didn't see it that way. Father had worshiped Mars, the Roman god of war, and he and Uncle Bellicus had more than one argument over whether the Celtic war god Camulus or Mars was the greater one.

Father had scolded her later for rolling her eyes, but how could she help it when she knew there was only one real God, and He commanded peace, not war?

How many times would Father have built and destroyed an earth-and-wood fortress in twenty-five years of soldiering? One might have kept him alive fighting the wars, so maybe it wasn't all waste.

He was proud of Rome and all she'd conquered. Proud of his service to four emperors, whether they were good men or bad. Proud of his part in making the greatest empire in history.

But that wasn't what Iesu said mattered. His was a kingdom of the heart and mind, and the Prince of Peace was the only ruler she ever wanted to serve.

Chapter 9

A Nice Enough Man

South of Isurium, early morning of Day 8

After a breakfast of bread and cheese, Narina mounted Bena and climbed the hill to Isurium. The community of round thatched houses wasn't laid out in a grid like a Roman town. She wove her way around the houses and public buildings on mostly empty streets. All but a few shops were still closed as she rode through the town center. Then she descended to the docks to catch the tow road along the river.

As she started downriver, she nudged Bena to a trot. To one side, trees arched overhead, and scattered blue and yellow wildflowers brightened the undergrowth. On the other side, the murmuring river proclaimed the beauty of God's creation.

Thank You, God for how well things have gone so far. Please let everything continue to go smoothly. Thank You for bringing Rogatus to eat with us so quickly. Please keep him coming. He seems like a nice enough man, and that makes it easy to encourage him to join us often.

The ala wouldn't be moving in until the construction was done, and even though what the legionaries had already built was astounding, they should take one more day to finish everything.

But the ala might be arriving tomorrow. Would Rogatus bring his decurions with him to eat, like Minconus was counting on? Once they tasted Veldicca's cooking, would his men come regularly to buy meals and drinks with their own money?

She was doing all she could. Rogatus liked the food, and he seemed to enjoy chatting with her. She'd seen the arrogance of equestrian tribunes when she helped Minconus eight years ago. He was remarkably undemanding for an equestrian officer, so she didn't mind hosting him. He wouldn't need her conversations anymore when he had his men for company.

She reached the side path to her farm and turned. After a short ride through the trees along the river's edge, she passed her barley and wheat fields. Beyond them was the pasture with mares and foals. Closest to the farmhouse were the young stallions she was training. The pair of two-year-olds would get her full attention after she checked with her farm workers.

Bikka was cooking while she was getting the taberna started, and she expected some mumbling about missing Veldicca. But they shouldn't have to suffer too long. Atto would stay at the taberna, but her sister would come home with her as soon as Minconus trained her replacement. Veldicca would return as soon as she taught his new cook her recipes.

Each stallion had a small corral, and her heart twinged when she passed the empty one. Would she ever have another horse that equaled Zephyrus?

But at least she got to see him, and the prefect did appreciate him. Rogatus and whoever was assigned to tend his horse would take good care of her all-time favorite. And even though people like her cousins complained about the Romans ruling over them, words weren't likely to turn into swords. Zephyrus should never end up carrying Rogatus in battle.

Maybe she could get him back from the prefect when he left Britannia. Then he could stand at stud for her, like she'd always hoped. Rogatus did that with his warhorse when he left Moesia. Why wouldn't he do it again if she asked him the right way and at the right time?

Isurium, noontime of Day 8

When Rogatus entered Narina's taberna, he expected another good meal made better by enjoyable conversation. He rang the triangle, and Atto's head peered around the corner. The youth raised a hand in greeting and ducked back into the storeroom. When he returned, he brought a cup and a small pitcher of mead.

Rogatus sat in his usual chair and set his helmet on the table. "Bring a second cup. I'd like to talk with Narina."

"She isn't here." The youth shrugged.

Rogatus's felt the frown start and stopped it. "Where is she?"

"She went to the farm."

The frown returned unbidden. "When did she go?"

"First thing."

He'd been watching the construction since dawn, so she should have passed him if she took the main road.

"I didn't see her leave. Which way did she go?"

Atto set the cup before him. "She took the short road."

"Short road?"

Legion-built roads aimed for the shortest distance between two points, and he'd ridden the Via Flavia each time he came from the legion fortress. It went straight except for one bend at a junction with another legion-built road.

Atto pointed toward Isurium. "There's a tow path along the river where mules can pull boats up from Eboracum. She uses that."

"So, would I find that starting where the boats dock in Isurium?"

"Yes." The youth poured mead into the cup until Rogatus signaled a stop when it was half full. He had questions for which he wanted answers before the youth finished pouring and left.

"Is the farm right on the river?"

The youth rested the pitcher on his palm. "It touches the river. We put out a dock when it's time to load the harvest and take it downstream."

"To Eboracum?" Rogatus took a sip, then tapped the cup for the youth to add more.

"And on to Petuaria sometimes. Dubnus runs the taberna in the seaport. He's not as picky about the mead he serves." Atto grinned. "He's not serving tribunes who know really good mead when they drink it and only want the best. So, what we make at the farm is good enough for him."

Rogatus rubbed his jaw. Minconus was Narina's brother, but who was this Dubnus?

"What is Dubnus to her?"

Atto's head drew back at his question. "Mistress Narina's other brother."

Rogatus fingered his lip. Why had he spoken that thought aloud? She'd think it strange if she knew what he asked after only talking with her twice. But maybe her servant wouldn't tell her.

He acknowledged the youth's answer with a nod. "Minconus said he had another taberna. So, if I ride down the short road, will I find the farm? I'd like to see the other horses she has."

Atto's friendly smile returned. "If you know where to turn off the tow path." He squinted one eye. "You might miss it if you don't. There's also a dirt road that we use with the carts that comes off the Roman road. But you could miss that one, too."

"Hmm." Rogatus traced the rim of his cup. "How far is it to Eboracum on the tow path?"

Atto scrunched his nose. "I don't know exactly, but Mistress Narina would. I'd guess thirteen or fourteen miles from Isurium."

"How far to the farm?"

"Three miles."

Veldicca appeared in the doorway, and Atto carried the pitcher past her.

She set a bowl before him, and he inhaled its aroma. Another savory soup that tantalized even though it had no meat in it that he could see.

"Atto said Narina went to her farm. When will she be back?"

She placed the bread plate beside the soup bowl. "Maybe today. Maybe tomorrow. She didn't say."

"What did she ride?"

This time, he'd made the cook's head draw back. She hesitated before answering. "A brown dun mare."

Suspicious eyes asked why he wanted to know, but she said nothing before returning to the kitchen. Both these servants knew better than to question him about why he wanted to know something. But when they got out of earshot, could they resist discussing it?

What they thought didn't matter. And if they told Narina, that wouldn't change whether she talked with him when he wanted her to. She seemed to enjoy their conversation as much as he had.

"What are you serving tonight?"

"A lentil stew. It's one of Narina's favorites."

He offered her the closest thing he had to a disarming smile.

"I expect it will become one of mine."

Suspicion faded into satisfaction. "I do, too." With a slight bow, she stepped back and returned to her kitchen.

He could see the corral from the gate of the fort. As long as she didn't put the horse into the stall, he could know when she was there.

He sipped the first spoonful. Different, but at least as good as what he'd had before. But without Narina for conversation, he ate it quickly. When he finished, he set the money on the table and rose.

At the scrape of the chair legs on the floor, Atto peered into the dining room.

Rogatus pointed at his coins, then strode out the door.

The tow path should prove useful. Three miles shorter than the legion road. Half an hour quicker if he was walking his horse. Only two hours if he switched between trotting and walking.

Getting to know the region around the fort before any trouble started was essential. He'd have seven hundred horses and a small herd of cattle to graze, and it wasn't good to leave them in one spot too long. Maybe she'd go riding with him and show him where he should do that.

If she wanted to ride Zephyrus, he'd be willing to ride her mare for a while. It would be no worse than the gelding Valentinus mocked. From what he'd seen of her horses so far, it should be far better.

If he ever had the chance, he'd gladly ride his old warhorse again. Surely, she felt the same, and he'd see that smile that made him want to smile back.

Chapter 10

Not What She Expected

Evening of Day 8

The expansion of the fort should be complete by noon tomorrow, and the hard day's labor meant hungry soldiers eager for a good meal. If good only meant ample, the garrison cooks would satisfy them. But after eating Veldicca's cooking, ample was no longer enough to satisfy Rogatus.

He strode to the gatehouse and looked up the road toward Isurium. In her corral, a brown dun mare drank from the water trough. He pursed his lips to stop the smile.

For him, dinner would not be the slop served as stew to the legionaries. Whether soup or porridge or stew, what Veldicca prepared should be better. He wasn't a betting man, but if he were, he'd bet something delectable awaited him in the taberna.

Tasty food made even better by good conversation. A lentil stew that was one of Narina's favorites should put her in a good mood, no matter what she had been doing today.

But he'd never seen her in a bad mood, so even garrison food wouldn't dim that smile.

He stepped into the gatehouse. "Should your centurion want me, I'll be eating at the taberna."

"Yes, Prefect." The soldier saluted as Rogatus turned and strode away.

At the taberna, he rang the triangle, and Atto appeared.

"Welcome back, Prefect. I think you'll like what we serve tonight. Veldicca made one of Mistress Narina's favorites."

"So she informed me at lunch." He settled into the chair that faced the door "A cup of mead and a serving of that stew should do." He removed his helmet and set it on the table. "If your mistress is back, I'd like to ask her about the road along the river."

"She's back." Atto stepped into the back room and returned with his cup of mead. "I'll go tell her now."

It was longer than he expected before he heard footsteps in the back room. He leaned back in the chair. Narina should step into view, wearing the smile she usually gave him along with her words of greeting.

Only Atto appeared, balancing a tray holding a bowl of stew and some bread on a plate.

Rogatus crossed his arms as the youth unloaded. "Where's Narina?"

"She said to bring you your food. She'll be with you shortly."

Atto left, and Rogatus pulled the bowl in front of him. He could see lentils, carrots, and peas, but that couldn't be all. The first whiff made his mouth water. The first taste lived up to the aroma.

He'd eaten almost half of it when Narina came.

"Good evening, Prefect." She pointed at the bowl. "From how fast you've eaten that, I think I can tell Veldicca that you like it."

She tilted her head back and rubbed under her chin, keeping her smiling eyes trained upon him. "But eating something fast could mean it tastes terrible, and you're trying to get it down as fast as you can."

He pointed toward the chair, and she sat. "I think you know which of the two is more likely. My compliments to Veldicca on yet another delicious offering. Will you join me for dinner?"

She shook her head. "I've eaten already. Atto said you came at lunchtime, and you had some questions for me about the tow road."

"I do." He set the spoon in the bowl. The longer it took to finish, the longer she'd talk with him. "He said it was much shorter than the Via. He didn't know how much, but you would."

She clasped her hands on the tabletop. "It's three miles shorter between Isurium and Eboracum, but it's not wise to ride it alone."

He narrowed his eyes. "But you do."

She waggled her finger at him, but her smile signaled she meant no offense by it. "I'm not a Roman soldier. You are exactly what a hotheaded young Brigantian would like to kill for the bragging rights among his friends. I'm just a Brigantian horse trader and farmer, and I look like one. Besides, I've lived here most of my life. Anyone lurking in the woods would likely know who I am and would think it too dangerous to bother me."

"Do you wear that dagger where they can see it?" His smile mirrored hers. "You said your father taught you how to use it."

"Yes, but that's not why. Most know my uncle is a chieftain, and he or my cousins would go after anyone who hurt me."

He barely stopped his head drawing back. "Your father a centurion and your uncle a chieftain? I'd wager that disturbed the peace at your clan meetings."

"There have been times…" She shrugged. "I've done what I can to promote peace among us, but not everyone does. Grandfather lost a son to Cerialis, so he wasn't happy about Father joining the auxiliary. He told Father he was out of the family if he joined. But Father was only a younger son so he wasn't going to inherit much anyway. Uncle Bellicus was the heir and became the next chieftain. He didn't hold that choice against Father when we returned. Father was able to buy a farm and the first taberna with what the Romans paid him. That made some cousins jealous, and some don't like how Roman Minconus is. But they like me well enough."

His response was a nod. How could anyone not like her?

"But I wouldn't say there's been so much family friction that it's a problem now." Straight lips and wistful eyes were not what she usually showed him. "I'm just sorry everyone doesn't get along better. I wish more wanted to live in peace with everyone."

Rogatus stirred his stew before fixing his gaze on her eyes again. "I want peace for everyone, too. The legate moved the ala out here hoping that us being here would discourage anyone from starting something. Or at least let us stop anything that starts before it spreads."

"Uncle Bellicus saw what happened last time. He would agree with you."

The prospect of the local chieftain being an ally in keeping the peace triggered his broadest smile. "I'd like to meet him to talk about it."

Narina leaned toward him. "Don't expect that. It's one thing to want peace and to tell young men not to start something. It's quite another to meet with the ones they call enemies. Our chieftains rise up from among the people because they are trusted to be good leaders. That talk might be seen as a betrayal by a chieftain who should be replaced. The transfer of power to a different family…that never happens without a fight."

"A fight of any kind is the last thing I want to cause. Forget I asked."

He tore a roll in two and offered her half.

She hesitated before taking it, then turned solemn eyes on him. "I didn't expect an ala commander to say that. You earn honors and wealth with war, not peace."

"I've had enough blood on my sword to know those honors don't satisfy like I expected. But sometimes it takes battle to bring about peace. It's my job to win quickly so fewer innocent ones have to die."

As she tore a piece from the roll, she raised her eyebrows. "I didn't expect you to be a philosopher, either."

"I'm not. I'm just experienced. I try to do what's right when I can."

Her smile warmed him in a way he wasn't used to. "As far as it depends on me, I do my best to live at peace with everyone. It almost sounds like you agree."

She opened her lips, as if to say more. But what she was thinking remained unspoken, and she popped some bread between them instead.

The girl who had served him when Narina was gone stuck her head through the storeroom doorway. Narina summoned her with a curl of her fingers. When the girl reached her side, Narina slipped an arm around her waist.

"This is my sister, Lucania."

Palm up, she held her hand out toward him. "And this is Prefect Rogatus."

"He came when you were gone." Lucania's smile was as welcoming as her sister's. "It's nice to see you again. You're our only customer so far. Veldicca will have a different soup tomorrow." She licked her lips. "It's one of my favorites. You won't want to miss it."

His lips twitched. It was hard not to laugh at the sales pitch, but she probably meant every word.

"I plan to be here."

With a beaming smile, Lucania left the dining room.

The girl looked fully Roman and spoke good Latin, but with a Brittonic accent. Narina looked fully Briton, but her Latin was polished and had no accent at all. If he hadn't met Minconus, who looked as Roman as he did himself, he'd have doubted the two were sisters. But he knew from painful experience how different people with the same parents could look.

The nanny who raised him swore his mother had been faithful to his father, no matter what his grandfather thought. He was the image of his mother's father, but that proved nothing about his own parentage. If he'd looked like his father's father or even like his brothers, would Father have willingly claimed him as his own?

Not that it mattered now. In a year and a half, he'd have saved all he needed to be equestrian in his own right. His brothers' taunts about their father's plan to pronounce him illegitimate and cast him off used to upset him. But whether Father left him his rightful share, a pittance, or nothing at all made little difference now. He had made his own way, and the men who'd made his childhood miserable had lost the power to hurt him more.

He tipped the bowl to get the last spoonful. "Atto said this is one of your favorites. I can see why."

"It looks like it might become one of yours as well." She put her elbow on the table and rested her chin on her palm. "If we know for certain you'll be coming for dinner, Veldicca can make sure we serve it that evening."

"After the ala comes, I'll be busier during the day. I won't make it as often for lunch, but I expect I'll eat here most evenings."

Her smile faded. "I hope you'll still come for lunch when you can." A teasing gleam lit her eyes. "You're our best customer." She wrinkled her nose. "Actually, our only customer, but I hope your decurions will enjoy dining here as well."

"I expect some will." He fingered his lower lip. The taberna would close if they didn't. She'd move back to her farm full-time, and their relaxed conversations over a delicious meal would be a thing of the past.

"Your brother mentioned how much your father's fellow centurions appreciated a good meal as a thank you for a job especially well done. I think that's a good policy."

Her smile brightened. "I do, too."

He donned his helmet and stood. "Until tomorrow." With a final smile, he turned and entered the street.

◆

Narina got the tray from the storeroom, gathered the dirty dishes, and carried them into the kitchen.

Veldicca scraped the last stew from the pot and plopped it into the bowl Atto held. With a grin and a spoon, he headed for the now-empty dining room.

"So, what did your tribune want to talk about tonight?" She bounced her eyebrows once.

"How far it is to Eboracum on the tow road. I told him, but I warned him not to ride it alone." Narina set the tray down on the counter. "I don't know that he listened. And he's not my tribune."

"Are you sure? He was disappointed when you weren't here to eat with him at lunch."

Narina pushed away her friend's words. "Disappointment is part of life. I'm sure he bore up under it well." She tapped Veldicca's arm with the back of her fingers and got a grin in return.

"But I did learn something surprising about him tonight."

"What?" Veldicca tore the roll she'd set aside for herself in half and handed one piece to Narina.

"He's won military honors like Father did, but he said they don't satisfy like he expected. He looks on battle as a way to bring peace, and winning quickly as a way to spare the innocents who suffer in a long war. He hopes just having the ala stationed here will be enough to persuade any rebels that they can't win before they start something and find out they can't the hard way."

Veldicca inhaled sharply. "Until your father bought me, I'd spent my whole life around Roman military. I never heard any of them talk like that. I can't imagine your father saying that, either."

"Neither would my cousins. It's good that a man who wants peace instead of war is in charge of the ala. If Uncle Bellicus can keep our young men from doing something stupid, maybe both sides can learn to live together."

She closed her eyes and tipped back her head.

Oh, God, please let it be so.

Chapter 11

A Satisfied Customer

Late morning of Day 9

Lunchtime was approaching when Narina pulled the tray of rolls from the oven. She'd added more honey to her usual rosemary wheat bread recipe, and the first taste should tell whether she'd chosen the right amount.

Veldicca turned from stirring the soup. "Well?"

Narina took one from the tray and tore off a bite. "Maybe I made it too sweet. But our customers are all men, and Atto says nothing is ever too sweet."

Lucania bounced through the storeroom door. "Something smells wonderful."

"It does, but is it too sweet?" Narina offered the roll to her little sister.

After inhaling deeply and smiling at the scrumptious aroma, Lucania popped a small piece into her mouth. "I think it's just right, but there's a better way to find out."

She tore off another small piece before disappearing into the storeroom.

After only a moment, she reappeared. "It's fine for the sweetness, and whatever else is in it…he heartily approves."

"He?" Narina nibbled her sample again. Perhaps it was just right if a customer liked it. "Tell me it's someone besides the prefect. We need more than one steady customer to keep this place going."

Veldicca patted her arm. "We're not really open yet, so I don't expect any."

"It's not his fault he can't resist your soups." Lucania nudged Veldicca and got a kiss atop her head "I was just coming to tell you he was here for lunch. He said he wants to ask if Narina could do something for him."

"This is early for him." Narina stroked her throat. "I'll go see what he wants. Please bring him some of the soup, a roll, and the mead he likes." She laid her hand on Lucania's shoulder. "Minconus says to treat every customer as if they were the most important. Since we only have one, I suppose he is."

She took a deep breath before stepping through the storeroom doorway. What could a Roman tribune possibly want her to do beyond feeding him better than his garrison cooks?

As soon as she entered the room, his face brightened, and his straight lips curved into a slight smile.

"It's good to see you again, Prefect." She clasped her hands at her waist. "I'm sure you'll like the soup today. It's one of our favorites."

He crossed his arms and leaned on the table. "After that sample Lucania brought me, I have high expectations for the bread, too."

"I tried something different today, so I'm glad to hear you liked it. Lucania said you wanted to ask me to do something." She tilted her head. "What is it?"

Lucania joined them, carrying a tray with two bowls of soup and two rolls on a plate.

He smiled at the girl. "Tell Veldicca thank you for sending Narina some soup as well." Then he turned the smile on Narina. "I was wanting to talk with you for a while."

Narina sat and picked up a spoon. The mouth-watering aroma rose from the steaming bowl as she stirred. "Soup is always better hot. So, if it might take a while for me to answer, we should eat first."

"It might." He stirred his soup and tipped his head back as he inhaled. "I don't know how Veldicca does it, but each one she's served me is better than the last." He took a bite of his roll. "And your bread is a fitting accompaniment."

He lifted it as if in a toast. "To your excellence as a baker."

She closed her eyes and tipped her head to acknowledge the compliment. His eyes looked like he might be sincere, but it was probably only flattery.

He pointed toward her bowl. "I won't delay the pleasure for either of us. My question can wait until after you finish."

They ate in silence, and he timed his final spoonful to match hers.

She clasped her hands on the tabletop. "So, what did you want to ask me?"

"You trained my horse well." He opened his mouth, then paused. "I need someone to train me, and I think you're the right one."

Narina was glad she had no soup in her mouth. With the laughter his words triggered, she might have spit it on him. "You know how to ride a warhorse already. What could you possibly need me to teach you?"

He rubbed the side of his nose. "I learned some Brittonic with the Cohort Brittonum. I learned more in Deva. But I don't know as much as I'd like." He raised his eyebrows as a subdued smile curved his lips. "I was hoping you could teach me more. I'll be here for another three and a half years, and it's wise to understand what the people around you are saying. It's even better if you can talk with them to avoid misunderstanding what you heard."

"But I don't know how to teach someone a new tongue."

"What I'm asking is easy. I'll tell you the words in Latin, and you can tell me the Brittonic. Just recognizing someone is talking about something, whether I understand it all or not, can be protective." He lowered his gaze to the table, then focused it back on her. "And I want to speak it well. For that, I'll need to practice with someone who's willing to talk with a man who knows only a little at the start."

Lucania set a cup of mead in front of him. "I can teach him if you don't want to." She flashed him a smile. "What would you pay?"

"What do you think is a fair price?" His lips straightened when his gaze turned from Narina to her sister.

She looked at Narina and raised her eyebrows. "What should I say?"

"Consider your time, how hard it is to teach, how badly your customer needs it, how badly you need the money, what your customer can afford." Narina raised a finger for each new point.

"Let me think about it, and we can tell him the next time he comes."

Lucania nodded, and disappeared into the storeroom again.

He fingered his lip. She'd opened a window into the mind of a trader. Seven hundred for Zephyrus…how had she chosen his price? Why didn't she ask for more? He was certainly worth it.

"How long did it take you to train Zephyrus?"

"I start training the horses for riding when they're two. The stallions that show promise for cavalry mounts…before they're three."

"Did he learn fast or slow?"

"One of the easiest I've ever trained." Her eyes softened. "If you give him a chance, he'll be more than a warhorse. He'll be a faithful friend."

A playful smile curved her lips. "Remember how I told you the stallions like me, not you? If you had tried to hurt me, he might have killed you."

He snorted a laugh. "So that's why you weren't afraid to ride out of town with me. You were right to trust me, but don't be so quick with others." His mouth straightened. "There was a tribune in Deva I wouldn't trust near my sister or alone with any young woman. Some of the others…" He shrugged.

She stared at him. The last thing she expected from a virtual stranger was concern for her safety.

He cleared his throat. "I'll try to earn that loyalty from him. The time may come when I'll need it."

"I hope not."

His eyes warmed, and she bit her lip. Surely, he didn't think his safety was that important to her. They barely knew each other. She did care about him, but no more than she cared about everyone, like Iesu said she should.

"That would mean he was in danger, too. I hope you'll never have to put him in that position."

His mouth twitched before relaxing into a wry smile. "I'll do what I can to take good care of your horse. But I can't promise I won't put us both in danger. No soldier can."

"I suppose that's all I can reasonably ask." She picked up a spoon and stirred her soup.

A soldier's promise to avoid danger—it was too easy for someone else to force him to break it. When Mother asked Father for that promise each time he left, he kissed her forehead and said marching toward danger was a soldier's duty. But he would promise to do his best to come home afterwards."

He leaned on the table again. "You never know what another person considers reasonable until you ask. If someone had told me I'd spend seven hundred denarii on a horse and think it the best bargain I'd ever found, it would have proven he didn't know me. If he'd told me I'd do it without haggling because a young woman had trained the finest warhorse I've ever seen, I couldn't have held in the laugh."

"So, I could have charged you more, and you'd still think it a bargain?" She gave him her best horse-trader smile. "If you start feeling guilty about how little you paid, I wouldn't be offended if you paid me more."

He chuckled. "If I'd argued you down to seven hundred instead of that being your first offer, I might. Otherwise…no. I trusted you to start with a first offer well above what you expected to get. I save most of my wages, and that was far beyond what I planned to pay."

A teasing smile played on his lips. "But now that I've heard you tell Lucania how to set a price for something, I can tell you a few of the things you told her to consider. I do want to learn to speak Brittonic well, but I'm not desperate to do it, and I hope you aren't in desperate need of money. I know you'll find me easy to teach. I expect I can afford what you'll ask, but I hope you'll find the time we spend enjoyable enough that you won't charge me as much as you could."

His raised eyebrows and hopeful smile were so like Lucania's when she asked for something. That look on an officer of Rome triggered her heartiest laugh. "I'll keep all that in mind."

"Then I expect I'll be a highly satisfied customer again."

Chapter 12

CAREFUL WATCHING REQUIRED

Midday of Day 9

Sulio guided his horse down the road leading to the fort, scanning the buildings for Minconus's new taberna. It wasn't often his favorite cousin was close enough to drop in for a visit without riding a few miles. She might not be there long, and hunting had been good that morning. She should like what he was bringing her.

He neared the end of the road when he saw it, but it wasn't the taberna that held his gaze. Soldiers digging a trench near the fort, a tall embankment with a wooden stake fence atop it, and large tents just to the south of the stone wall—what were the Romans up to?

A corral with a mare and a mule stood alongside the taberna, but he rode his horse to the back and tied it in the shade of a tree. He untied a sack from the back of his saddle and the hare as well. Veldicca should be in the kitchen, and the path connecting a well to a door told him where that was.

He opened the door slowly. Veldicca stood by the stove, stirring a pot of soup. He crept up behind her, then reached past her to get the spoon. She jumped before slapping his hand. Then, as he expected, she offered the spoon for him to taste.

"I need to drop by more often for some of your cooking. It's been too long."

She patted his cheek. "If it's near lunchtime or dinnertime, I'll have something for you. You always were my favorite of the cousins, but don't tell Albiso that."

"I brought you a present." He pointed toward the hare on the table. "Just what you need for one of your stews. And it's only fair that I get to join you all when you make it."

"You're always welcome. You know that, so come tomorrow."

His grin broadened her smile, like it always had. "Where's Narina?" He held up the sack. "I have a present for her, too."

"Through there." She flicked her fingers toward the door. "She's either weaving or in the taberna."

He entered the courtyard with the surprise. Narina wasn't at the loom under the portico, so he headed toward the door opposite the kitchen.

Her laugh, always musical, reached him as he entered the storeroom. But as he walked toward the doorway to the serving room, a deep male voice speaking Latin struck his ears.

He shifted the sack from his right hand to his left. His freed hand dropped to the handle of his knife, and with narrowed eyes, he stepped into the room.

Narina sat in a chair at a small table to his right, and across from her, looking as if he owned the place, sat a Roman. Not just any Roman, but one wearing bronze body armor with a red-crested helmet on the table beside him.

Sulio's breaths came faster. What was a tribune doing talking with Narina?

The tribune's face turned toward him as he shifted focus from Narina to Sulio. His back straightened, but his hands still cradled a cup of something.

Narina's back was to Sulio when he entered, but she twisted in her chair to face him. A smile lit her face. "Sulio. It's good to see you again. Is Albiso with you?"

"No. I just stopped in to give you something."

She stood and walked toward him. "Something in that sack?" She peered at it. "Did I just see it move?"

He held it out, and she took it from his hand. After setting it on the empty table, she loosened the tie and peeked in.

"Baby hares! They're so cute. Thank you. Where did you get them?"

He raised his chin as his eyes met the Roman's. "I heard them when I was taking the arrow from their mother. I gave that one to Veldicca. She was by her nest. Since these are big enough to forage for themselves, I figured it was better for you to have them than to let the foxes eat them."

Narina retied the cord. "I'll be riding to the farm tomorrow or the next day. I'll take them there when I go." She gave him her biggest smile. "As a thank you, let me feed you."

She waved her hand toward the table where the Roman sat, tracing the rim of his cup with the middle finger of his left hand. His right hand was under the table. With that arm so close to his body, he might be reaching across his stomach so he could draw his dagger swiftly enough to counter an attack.

"I'm sorry I don't have a third chair yet. Minconus is having some more like these made in Eboracum, but"—she picked up a stool from the second table—"these are the right height. Chair or stool for you?"

He took the stool from her hand. "Veldicca gave me a taste. I won't say no to any of her soups."

The Roman's unreadable eyes stayed focused on him. His empty soup bowl said he'd come for something better for lunch than what a garrison served. But what did her empty bowl mean? And why the laughter? How long had she known a high-ranking officer of the occupying army? And how well did she know him?

He'd left his bow and quiver hanging on his saddle. He still had his hunting knife, but the Roman had dagger and sword.

He drew a deep breath. Today was for talking, so none of that mattered. But it was good Albiso wasn't with him. His brother wore his hatred for Rome for all to see. It was better if this tribune didn't suspect what was simmering behind the closed doors of the tribal council.

The Roman had seated himself facing the door. Sulio set the stool in place by the table with Narina to his left and the Roman to his right.

"So, who's your new friend, Narina?"

He spoke Latin and tried to make his words sound as friendly as the fake smile he offered, but they still had an edge.

"This is Trebonius Rogatus." Narina glanced at the Roman before fixing her gaze on Sulio. "He's prefect of the Ala Tungrorum, but he used to command the Cohort Brittonum. That's the one Father served in."

Sulio nodded, as if that was a good reason to have him there. The Roman was about his own age, much too young to have served with her father.

The tribune's gaze shifted to his cousin at her first word and stayed there while she was speaking.

"And this"—she rested her hand against his upper arm—"is my cousin Sulio."

A formal smile curved the Roman's mouth. "It's a pleasure to meet a cousin of Narina."

His eyes didn't match the smile.

Sulio turned his head slightly and tilted it to acknowledge the polite but false words. It wasn't his pleasure to meet the Roman, either.

"It's not often we see an officer of Rome in these parts." He tipped his head in the direction of the fort. "Except for the centurion. But he doesn't often come into Isurium, and never alone. A wise choice on his part."

The Roman crossed his arms and leaned on the table. "He'll be moving back to Eboracum soon."

That news triggered Sulio's genuine smile. "I'm sure he'll like being in a town that welcomes Romans again. Cousin Minconus likes to feed your kind. If he eats there, he won't have to wonder if someone spit in his drink."

The twitch of the tribune's mouth was unexpected. He must think Sulio was joking. He wasn't.

"Are you with the legion there?"

Rogatus tightened his lips as if to stop a smile and shook his head. "No. I'm bringing the ala to the fort here as soon as the expansion to house the horses is completed. So, in three, maybe four days, this will be home for me."

Sulio drew back. A cavalry cohort coming? That was five hundred men, not fewer than a hundred like was there now. And this man was its commander.

Had Narina known when he and Albiso saw her with her cart? Did Minconus know when he bought this place? His gaze locked on Narina. She rested her hand on Sulio's arm and smiled like she had no idea how wrong it was for her to have this man here. To be feeding and talking with the enemy. To be laughing over something he said.

If Albiso had been with him, his brother couldn't have resisted saying something that would get the Roman's hackles up. That could be dangerous. He'd be more than a little angry that Narina was friendly with the enemy. So, it was better not to tell him.

Sulio rubbed the hinge of his jaw. At least not yet.

But she worshiped that Christian god that she'd told him loved everyone. The one who said you had to love your enemies like yourself. And she lived like she believed it. She'd always tried to smooth things over between Sulio's side of the family and her brothers who were mostly Roman with only a trace of Brigantian.

"I'll get your soup." Narina picked up the sack of hares and disappeared into the back room.

She left Sulio alone with a man he had no desire to talk with. Or did he? He'd be telling Father about the ala coming as soon as he got home. But why it was coming…that was worth finding out.

"That one century has been in the fort for as long as I can remember. Nothing that would need more ever happens around here. So, why cavalry instead of infantry?"

Sulio couldn't ask the real question: why five times more than were here now.

The Roman shrugged. "The legate of the Ninth could tell you. It was his decision."

"I thought legates discussed such things with their tribunes. Isn't that what you're for?"

"Sometimes. I was tribune with the Twentieth in Deva. I came a few days ago at the request of the Ninth's legate."

Sulio's head drew back before he could stop it. "What's so special about you?"

He narrowed his eyes. This Roman needed to know Narina wasn't unprotected, even though she had only Atto and Veldicca here to defend her.

"And how do you know my favorite cousin after so short a time?"

A chuckle was the Roman's first response. "Many might ask that. It's not something you need to know. But as Narina's cousin, I respect your desire to protect her, so I'll answer your second question. I bought a horse from her. I also have the one she sold another prefect. He died, and I came to replace him. Both animals are extraordinary."

"Hmm." Sulio traced a grain in the wood without taking his gaze off the Roman's eyes. "She raises some of the finest, and her training makes the best even better."

"Without a doubt. And her cook is exceptional as well. I'll be eating here often for the food and the conversation. You can join me when I'm with her." The Roman traced the cup rim again, but this time with his right hand. "Narina might like that."

The look in the Roman's eyes and the way he said "might"—was that an invitation or a warning?

Narina's footsteps approached, and she came through the door with a bowl and a cup on a tray. Behind her came Lucania.

The girl danced over to Sulio and gave him a quick hug. "Veldicca said you were here. Thank you for bringing the babies. They're darling. Can I keep one as a pet?"

Lucania always brought out his warmest smile. Who wouldn't smile at this miniature version of Narina, even if she did look just like her Roman mother?

"You'll have to ask Narina. I gave them to her."

The girl took Narina's hand. "Can I, please?"

Narina laid her free hand on her sister's cheek. "We'll talk about that later."

Lucania's grin anticipated her sister's answer. "I'll go pick out the one I want."

She gave Sulio another hug. "Thank you. See you soon."

When Lucania disappeared into the storeroom, the Roman drained his cup and stood. "Time for me to go. I'll be back for dinner."

"We're not totally open yet, but you're welcome any time."

Narina's smile was too much like the ones she gave Sulio, and his jaw clenched.

The Roman donned his helmet. He gave a smile to Narina and a slight tip of his head to Sulio. Then he strode through the doorway and headed for the fort.

Sulio crossed his arms and tried to keep the scowl from forming. He managed to stop at a frown. "What's going on with him, Narina?"

Her head drew back. "What do you mean?" Her eyes widened. "Nothing is going on. He comes to eat. That's why Minconus opened this place, and I'm only helping my brother until he trains someone to run it like the one in Eboracum."

"It's one thing to take his money and feed him. It's another thing entirely to sit and talk with him, to laugh at what he says. Any man can get ideas about a woman who does that, and you do not want that to happen." He took her hand. "Romans like him take what they want, and there's nothing and no one to stop them. You have Atto to help here. Let him serve the Romans."

He ran his fingers through his hair. "I'm not going to tell Father or Albiso what I saw today. They'd be furious."

Her lips tightened, and she rammed her fists onto her hips. "You didn't see anything that should upset them. I've done nothing to be ashamed of. You forget I helped Minconus when his wife broke her arm. I can tell a decent man who just wants to eat and talk a little from one who wants what you're afraid of."

She clasped her hands atop the table. "But not telling them is still a good idea. Albiso is filled with hate for anything Roman, and your father would rather not know about something his precious council might get upset over. But I'm going to keep treating everyone with kindness, whether Brigantian or Roman. It's what Iesu told us to do, and I obey him first, not your father or you."

She touched the back of his hand where it lay on the table. "Let's not talk about this anymore. Neither of us will change our mind, so there's no point." She leaned back in the chair. "So, how is Albiso's new baby doing?"

"He's healthy. He's just like any other baby."

She slapped his arm. "You know that's not all I'm asking. Tell me some of what he's doing now. It's such a cute age, and things change so fast."

He rolled his eyes, then started his report. What was it about women and babies? He liked his nieces and nephews well enough when they were born, but they were just…babies.

If she'd only let him, he'd help her find a good man to marry to give her babies of her own. But he knew no Christian men, and she'd sworn she would marry no other kind.

No matter what she thought of that Roman, he'd keep an eye on him. With her father dead and her brothers so far away, it was up to him to do what he could to protect her…even from herself.

As Rogatus strode toward the fort's gate, Narina occupied his thoughts. Those steel-gray eyes that warmed when she first saw him. The friendly smile that sometimes turned teasing. He found himself letting his guard down with her. It felt safe, even though he barely knew her.

But her cousin Sulio was like a fake-friendly dog that was waiting for the right chance to bite. He couldn't fault the cousin for wanting to protect her. He felt protective toward her himself.

Her extended family was so mixed up. She had a centurion father who'd won honors serving Rome as he earned citizenship for them all. Her brother enjoyed treating Rome's soldiers well.

But she also had at least one cousin who disliked Romans, even though he'd mostly kept a polite facade in place. A friendly man's hand didn't rest on his knife when he entered a room. He didn't try to erase a scowl before another man saw it. His words wouldn't have that edge, like he almost said something before he thought better of it, but couldn't resist hinting at his true thoughts.

Sulio was around his own age, old enough to be part of the planners of rebellious acts. Who was the Albiso she asked about? Another young man? Someone with romantic feelings toward her? But she hadn't seemed disappointed that he wasn't with her cousin, so she probably didn't feel any toward him.

Was Sulio the son of her chieftain uncle or some other relative? If the chieftain's son, did he agree with his father's desire to get along with Romans? It seemed more like he wanted to get rid of them.

His mouth twitched. For certain, Sulio wanted to get rid of him. But it was only Narina's opinion that mattered, not that of some cousin. Since he first became a prefect, he'd been the target of women who pretended to like a man to get his money. She was nothing like them. Her smiles and laughter felt genuine, and the words she spoke felt like the truth.

The Brigantian had been bothered by the expansion of the fortress. Why cavalry instead of infantry wasn't the question he'd wanted to ask. It was five hundred cavalry versus a hundred infantry that he didn't like.

Her cousin would need careful watching. A man with no interest in defeating an enemy didn't worry about an increase in that enemy's strength. He didn't bristle at meeting the enemy's commander with a cousin he liked.

Rogatus had years of practice at sorting a man's words into truths, halftruths, and outright lies. If the cousin came often to her taberna and ate with them, he could take the man's measure and decide what his intentions were, even if he tried to conceal them.

The sound of fists hitting chests as he passed through the gatehouse ended his focus on the friendly woman and her hostile cousin. For now, he had a more pressing problem.

Maybe one more day, and they would finish construction. He should spend tomorrow finding good pasturage for the ala herds. His gaze swept the barracks, headquarters, and commanding officer's quarters. Within three days, he'd be leading the ala to its new home.

Home. One corner of his mouth rose. The closest thing he'd ever had to one was with the Cohort Britonnum in Moesia. Perhaps Britannia with the Ala Tungrorum would soon feel the same.

Chapter 13

What Are They Up To?

Bellicus's farm near Isurium, late afternoon of Day 9

Sulio sat on the bench by the corral, sharpening his knife. Father should be home soon, and he had unpleasant news to share.

Trotting hoofbeats raised his eyes from the blade to the man he admired most. As both father and chieftain, Bellicus had shown Sulio what a good man should do and, even more important, what he should be.

He stood and approached his father after he dismounted.

"Son." His father's smile spoke of fatherly pride without any words. "Were you waiting for me?"

"I was, Father. The Romans are up to something, and I wanted to tell you as soon as possible."

Father's eyebrows plunged. "Up to something?"

Sulio pulled a deep breath. Albiso was riding over to join them, and Sulio knew how his brother would react. But this couldn't wait until Father was alone. He let out the sigh.

"Yes. They're moving a cavalry ala into the fort. That's almost five hundred men to replace the single century."

Albiso had reined in beside them, but he was still mounted. A string of curses flowed from his lips. "Narina didn't tell us that was coming when she was buying supplies three days ago for Minconus's new taberna."

Sulio leaned back against the corral's top rail. "Calm down. Her brother might not have told her everything. He's always been that way. She said she was only helping him until he could train someone to run it. Ever since we've known her, he's been able to get her to do whatever he asks. Remember a few years ago when she helped him with the Eboracum taberna when the Roman he married broke her arm? She knows what to do. Of course she'd say yes."

"Albiso." Father sounded like an irritated mother bear as he cleared his throat. "What Narina told you isn't the point. It's what the Romans are up to that matters." He turned grim eyes back on Sulio. "How do you know a full cohort is coming?"

After slipping his knife back into its sheath, Sulio straightened. "I dropped by Narina's taberna to give them a hare I shot this morning, and I found many more Roman troops than I usually saw just south of the stone fort. They were digging trenches and making an embankment with a wall of pointed wooden stakes on top. I planned to ask Narina what was going on, but I found a tribune eating in her shop. He'd come to buy lunch because he knew Minconus from the taberna in Eboracum."

Father's head drew back. "Tribune? There hasn't been one of those around here since before you were born."

A shrug was Sulio's first reply. "He called himself prefect of the Ala Tungrorum. He was overseeing the expansion of the fort."

Father's frown deepened. "So, you talked with him?"

"I did. He said he planned to eat there often after he leads his troops up from Eboracum." One corner of Sulio's mouth rose. "He invited me to join him whenever he's there."

The curse Albiso uttered was a creative one. "The arrogance of a Roman to even suggest you'd want his company."

Sulio chuckled. "I don't think he wants me to, so I intend to do it." His smile faded. "Narina's too nice to everyone, and I want him to understand that doesn't mean she'd welcome his advances. I'll keep an eye on him to make sure he knows she's got men watching out for her."

Albiso punched his palm with his fist. "We can talk to him together and make sure he knows what will happen if he tries anything. Even better, we should stop him—"

Father raised his hand, silencing Albiso. "Eating with him…that's a good thing. If the Roman thinks Sulio likes Roman company, he might get careless and reveal something about what they're up to." His father's eyebrows lowered. "Does he know you're my son?"

Sulio shook his head. "Narina introduced me as her cousin. Beyond that, he only knows I gave her some game I'd killed, like any man looking out for an unmarried cousin might. I said nothing about you being chieftain and me being your son."

"Good. Your uncle told me many stories about being a Roman cavalry officer." The corners of his father's mouth turned down. "They don't move troops around with no goal in mind. And they wouldn't move such a big unit out here without a big enough reason for doing it."

"I remember his stories." Sulio tapped his brother's sword arm. "Albiso would, too, if he hadn't thought Uncle Lucanus too Roman to listen to."

Albiso hit Sulio's arm with the back of his hand. "The only good thing about Lucanus coming back here after his twenty-five years is him bringing Narina. She's the only one from that family who's Brigantian enough to be worth anything."

Sulio tapped him back. "I'd say the money he earned from the Romans was worth something. He got that farm and the taberna with it. I'm glad she got her share when he died. Lucania is worth something as well. It's not her fault that she looks like her Roman mother. Inside, she's a smaller Narina."

"That's enough, Albiso." Father's glower could silence anyone, especially his oldest son. "My brother was a good man. I understand why he left. As the fourth son, there wasn't much for him here. Coming back when he left their army showed that he thought himself more Brigantian than Roman, even after they made him a citizen."

Albiso opened his mouth, but Father's raised finger silenced him.

"I have something for both of you to do." Father rubbed his jaw. "Sulio. Get to know that tribune and see if you can learn what the Romans are up to."

He pointed at Albiso. "I need you to let the nearest chieftains know the Romans are moving troops around. We need to discuss what it means that an ala that has been at Eboracum for more than a year has moved north. I want to know whether other large units of their army are moving. So, invite the chieftains to a council meeting in ten days. It looks like it will be a good harvest this year. Tell them we will claim they are coming for an early celebration of the harvest where we will plan a joint celebration for all the farming goddesses after each clan celebrates alone. They should tell no one why we are really meeting. The Romans must not suspect it might be for our gods of war."

Sulio rubbed his palms together. "I can drop in to see Narina each day. The tribune has been eating lunch and dinner there. Perhaps I can learn what the Romans are planning."

"Good. We'll start tomorrow." A quick nod of Bellicus's head declared the discussion over. As he led his horse toward the stable, Sulio whistled to call his over to the corral fence.

He'd be riding to Narina's taberna for dinner with his target. It might take a few days to soften him up with pretended friendliness and then get information out of him.

But more importantly, he could douse the Roman's interest in Narina. A rich, handsome, powerful Roman could have no honorable intentions toward his kind-hearted but too plain cousin.

She'd always laughed at his own compliments and called them flattery, even when he meant them. But she might be more vulnerable to that Roman's flattering ways.

He'd make certain no evil intention became dangerous action that would hurt his almost-sister. He liked his cousin much more than the sisters with whom he shared his parents' blood. While he'd defend them out of duty, he'd protect her out of love.

The fort, late afternoon of Day 9

Rogatus stood beside the fort centurion, surveying the work the legionaries had performed that day.

"They've done a fine job. Tell your men I'm very pleased with the progress they've made."

A satisfied smile curved the centurion's lips. "I'll pass that on this evening in the dining hall."

"Should you need to speak with me, I'll be dining at the taberna again." Rogatus stroked under his chin. "A local man came there at lunchtime. Do you know anything about a Brigantian named Sulio? He's my age or maybe a little younger."

"Perhaps." The centurion pursed his lips. "I only know of one. It's not a common name. I don't go into Isurium often, and then I go with a group. So, I don't talk much with tribal men. I encourage my men not to let their guard down with the locals, so mostly they don't talk with Brigantes. But there are some who go in a group to a taberna where they're tolerated."

He looked toward the buildings on the hilltop. "I've joined them a few times. The last time I did, there were two who looked like brothers. One was muttering something and glaring at us. The other one took his arm and tipped his head toward the door. I don't know what he said, but as they were leaving, the first one called the second one Sulio. There might have been a fight if he hadn't taken the angry one away."

"Hmm." Rogatus rested his hand on his dagger. "That might be him. The one I met wasn't pleased to see me there, but he acted friendly enough."

The centurion snorted. "Acted. That's the best it gets around here. Given the chance, I wouldn't trust any of them not to kill one of us."

"I expect I'll be seeing him again. I'll keep that in mind."

As Rogatus headed toward the gate and another tasty meal at Narina's taberna, two desires wrestled within him. He wanted Sulio to accept his invitation so he could figure out whether her cousin was part of the threat he'd come to reduce. But reconnaissance required battle-ready alertness, and it had been a long day already. He'd much rather enjoy a relaxed conversation with the woman who was becoming a friend.

Narina's house, late afternoon of Day 9

Narina sniffed the enticing aroma before taking a sip from the spoon Veldicca held out.

"Mmm." She licked her lips.

Veldicca stirred the stew before taking a sip herself. "Good enough for our best customer, if he comes."

"He will. Tonight, he expects me to tell him how much it will cost to learn more Brittonic words and practice speaking it with me." She laid her hand on her chest. "I've never taught a grown man before."

Veldicca's lips twitched before a smile appeared. "You can ask as much as you want. He likes you, and it's a way to get you to talk with him more."

"I don't think so. He's perfectly willing to have Lucania teach him instead of me."

Veldicca tipped her head back to look down her nose. "Was that his suggestion or yours?"

"Neither, actually. Lucania brought his mead just as he was asking, and she told him she'd be glad to do it. When he asked what that would cost, she asked me to set the price."

Veldicca's knowing grin made Narina's ears heat. "So, what did you decide to charge him?"

"I haven't yet. He said that he trusted me to set a reasonable price and that he'd be glad to pay it. But he said he hoped I'd enjoy doing it enough that I wouldn't charge as much as he'd be willing to pay."

Veldicca pointed the spoon at her. "That man likes you."

"I admit it might seem so, but I can't see why he would." Narina arched her eyebrows and shrugged. "Although he did seem more worried about my safety than I expected when we'd done nothing more than exchange names. He couldn't possibly have liked me then."

Veldicca turned back to the stove. After sweeping the edge of the pot with the spoon to prevent the stew burning, she looked over her shoulder. "What did he do?"

"He didn't think I should risk leaving Eboracum alone with him to show him the stallions. He suggested that the man I had with me could do it. First, I told him Father would trust a tribune, but I showed him my dagger. Then I told him Father taught me to defend myself, and the stallions would defend me, too."

Veldicca's head drew back. "That is unusual. I'd never expect it from a young, handsome man who's used to people doing what he tells them. They often think only of themselves."

"I suppose it is." Narina traced a cut in the countertop. "But that doesn't mean he likes me that way, especially since all I've done is sell him a fine horse and talk with him a little while he eats a good meal."

With tightened lips, Veldicca nodded. "Your father would have approved of your prefect."

Narina rolled her eyes. "There you go again. He's not my prefect, and I'm sure he has no intention of being so. He's just a nice man who's loves your cooking and wants someone to talk with while he eats."

"Think that if you want to." The twitch of Veldicca's lips revealed she was laughing on the inside. Then her eyes sobered. "You're probably right. If he were a centurion, he might be here for years and even stay in Britannia when he retires. But the tribunes don't stay long or get attached while they're here."

"So, we're in agreement." Narina set a bowl, a spoon, and a plate on the tray, ready for their best and only customer. "He wouldn't become my tribune even if I was as pretty as Lucania or equestrian order like Mother was. You can be sure he wouldn't want me if he knew I was a Christian, but I wouldn't want him because he isn't."

Chapter 14

What People Might Think

Dinnertime of Day 9

Rogatus had eaten lunch early, so he lengthened his stride as he approached her taberna's door. It was all the fort centurion could do to hold in the chuckle when his stomach started growling during his final meeting of the day with the three centurions.

He almost asked the three men to join him for dinner, but he hadn't warned Narina that he'd be bringing so many. Veldicca might not have prepared enough since he'd been their only customer since Germanus returned to the ala.

Besides, he wanted some private conversation with Narina tonight. She was supposed to tell him whether she'd teach him more Brittonic and how much she'd charge. But what started as a business discussion would probably turn into some playful remarks and personal questions. He didn't want the junior officers hearing any of that.

But he had one more request which she might not want to do. He had the authority to make her, but he didn't want to force her. He wanted their friendship to grow, and nothing could end one faster than making someone act against their will.

The centurions would consider that weakness, so he couldn't let them witness that conversation, either.

He rang the triangle when he entered, then strolled to his usual table and settled in. The first person through the doorway was the woman who made him feel welcome no matter when he came. A woman he could ask questions without worrying whether she'd take offense because he put something awkwardly.

"It's good to see you, Prefect. You're in for a treat tonight." The smile that made her plain face almost pretty curved her lips.

"Everything you've served me has been a treat." He pointed at the other chair, and she took it. He wouldn't tell her yet, but each conversation was a treat as well.

"So, what have you decided about teaching me?"

"Lucania is eager, and I'm willing. So, she and I will take turns answering your questions and chatting with you. I'll put any money aside for her dowry. As to what we'll charge…" Her brow furrowed. "Until I know how much time it will take, I can't set an exact price. Let's do it for a while, then decide."

She flashed him the smile he remembered from the day he bought Zephyrus. "I think you're an honorable man. I trust you to help me figure out what a fair price is."

He was, and she could trust him. But hearing her speak the words still satisfied something deep inside him.

"That suits me, too. When your taberna gets busier, it might be hard to do it here. But we can have privacy in my quarters at the fort. I can be flexible about the time of day to fit it around when you need to be here."

Her eyebrows shot up, then dipped. The closest thing he'd seen to a frown appeared. "I'm not comfortable with my sister going there. I don't want Brigantian men or women to see her entering the fort often. I probably shouldn't do it, either. I can't risk our reputations that way."

He squeezed the back of his neck. He hadn't thought about that risk, but she was right. "So, how would you like to do it here?"

"Well, you can come to buy food and drink. It must look like we're serving you as a frequent customer. If you bring your list of words for that day, you can read them to us, and we'll tell you the Brittonic."

She ran her fingers through her thick hair. It was mostly medium brown, like his old warhorse, but it had strands of gold spread through it. He hadn't noticed that when she wore it braided, but she'd left it loose today. He liked how it framed her face, softening her square jaw.

"It's learning to converse that I want most, so we'll need to talk as well." He leaned his crossed arms on the table. "I can speak some, but I'd like to do it better. I know it has a few different endings on each word that names a thing, depending on its role in what I say. That's like Latin, but the way the words that tell what something's doing change, that's quite different. And you can't rearrange the words and expect someone to know what you said just from the endings."

A quick nod of her head, and the deal was made. "We'll do the words you want, and we'll start by practicing things like you'd use in meeting people or shopping for something or asking someone to do something. As you learn more words, we'll build on it from there."

"Excellent." He offered a wry smile. "You'll be surprised by how fast a learner I can be."

A playful roll of her eyes and her light laugh turned his slight smile into a broad one. Whatever she decided was a fair price, he'd agree to it. She was an honorable woman, and she wouldn't ask more than was right.

"If your cousin Sulio is a chieftain's son, maybe I can practice the art of friendly political discussions with him."

Her snort was less than lady-like. "He is, but he won't be any more eager to discuss such things than his father. You'll have to settle for the people of my household. Veldicca came from Isca Silurum and served in a Roman prefect's household there, so she's the best prepared for those conversations."

A sip of mead hid the deep satisfaction her answer triggered. She might have asked why if she'd seen his smile.

Sulio was the chieftain's son, and his self-assurance when questioning a man in authority fit that. The sons of important men often assumed they shared that importance and expected respect. But the only men he respected earned it by their own actions, and most were not the sons of important men.

His lips twitched as he fought a smile. A warhorse fit to carry him in battle, a friendly advisor that he could ask questions and trust the answers, a young man who resented Romans that he could watch—his acquaintance with Narina was providing far more than he expected.

But would it provide what he needed even more?

He took a deep breath. Her answer to his next question must end with a yes before he could bring the ala to the fort. She might not agree at first. At least, not without some persuasion, but the friendly daughter of a cohort centurion should understand why he needed it. She might even be glad to help him then.

And he'd enjoy her company while she did.

◆

When the tribune drew a deep breath and held it, Narina tensed. That was never a good sign with any man.

He released it. "I'll have seven hundred horses and some cattle after the full ala arrives. They need pasturage. I'd like you to go riding with me to show me where I can find good places to graze my horses. My men will be moving the herd around so we don't overgraze anywhere. I'd like to find places where they won't cause problems with any Britons who use the pastures, too."

"Seven hundred?" She covered her mouth with her hand. "I thought there were five hundred or so in an ala. Why so many?"

"Spares for when a mount gets injured or too tired for action the next day. That's why I have both Boreas and Zephyrus."

She fingered her lip as she stared at the tabletop. Riding around the countryside with an officer of Rome…too many were bound to see them and draw the wrong conclusion.

When she returned her gaze to his face, he looked confident about her answer. She'd have to disappoint him.

"I'm not sure that's a good idea."

His expectant smile vanished. "Is it being seen with a Roman officer that concerns you? Are you afraid people will think you're helping the enemy?"

"Some of my cousins might. And I don't want to start gossip about us. Just like I don't think it wise for Lucania or me to be alone with you in your lodgings in the fort."

He blew his breath out through his nostrils. "I'm never actually alone there. There's always a guard on the door."

She chuckled, but it wasn't because what he said was funny. "Do you think any Briton would expect that to stop a Roman tribune from doing what he wanted? More likely your guard would stop anyone from reaching you to stop you hurting me."

"You're probably right." He scrubbed his face." But I must find grazing before the ala comes, and I think you're the best one to help me find what I need. You can keep me from going beyond what's acceptable to the locals for where to graze and how long to leave the herd there."

She bit her lip. His request wasn't unreasonable to ask a man, but for a single woman to do it…

He crossed his arms and leaned on the table. "If you're only concerned about what people would say, what do you think would let you help me while protecting your reputation?"

She covered her mouth, but only to hide her smile. A tribune was a powerful man in the Roman army. He had the right to order her to help him, and she couldn't refuse. But he'd chosen to ask, and his concern for what others would say about her…even Father would have been surprised if an ala prefect showed such consideration for a woman he barely knew.

"That's hard to say."

"There must be something. Will you at least think about it?"

"I will." She clasped her hands and looked away. She didn't want to take sides in any dispute between Rome and the Brigantes. But if she did this, she'd be seen as favoring the Romans instead of putting her tribe first. That could be dangerous for her and Lucania. But what choice did she have?

When she stole a glance at him, he'd wrapped both hands around his cup and relaxed in the chair. But he was waiting for her to propose a solution, and she had no idea what to tell him.

◆

Sulio entered the taberna through the front door, only to find the Roman with his back to the wall and Narina sitting across from him. She rose and came toward him with arms extended.

"Welcome, cousin." She gave him a quick hug. "It's good to see you again so soon. Come join us."

Sulio grabbed a stool and followed her. He plunked it down and stretched out his legs beneath the table. That should keep the Roman's feet on his own side tonight.

His father had told him to get friendly with the prefect to spy on what the Romans were up to, but protecting Narina took priority over forming a fake friendship, even when Father requested it. Besides, seeming too friendly too quickly after their first meeting might make Rogatus suspicious.

A quick glance at the tribune's face caught the flicker of irritation before Rogatus hid it. But a Roman frown had no power to keep him from interrupting a conversation that shouldn't be happening anyway.

"Veldicca told me to come tonight since she'd be using the hare I gave her for tonight's stew."

Sulio turned a fake smile on Rogatus. "Lunch or dinner…I find you here whenever I come. It looks like you never eat at the fort." He raised his eyebrows. "You know, that's quite an insult to your garrison cooks. Are you sure that's a good thing to do?"

The Roman's hearty laugh was not what Sulio expected.

"My cooks are all soldiers, not oversensitive civilians. Even when a cook is decent, the men tease him with insults, and he gives it back to them." The tribune's eyes chilled. "My men all know how to do their jobs well, and they don't need my presence or my praise to make them excel at it."

The edge on those words revealed more than the words themselves and confirmed that laughter was as fake as his own smile.

Narina rose. "I'll let Veldicca know you're here for dinner. She'll be delighted you came." She tapped Sulio's upper arm. "You two behave until I return."

She'd scarcely disappeared into the storeroom when Sulio crossed his arms. "You seem like a smart man. I'm sure you know what people think can be more important than what the truth is."

With arms still crossed, he leaned on the table. "Why do you even come here? Narina hasn't opened this place to the public yet. Why are you eating what Veldicca makes for the household? They don't need the expense of feeding you."

The Roman's chin rose, and his jaw clenched. Then his mouth relaxed into a polite smile.

"Because Veldicca is a fine cook. Good enough to cook for a senator in Rome." The false smile broadened. "Officially, they are open. I pay for what I eat and drink. Narina makes a good profit off me, like her brother at his taberna in Eboracum."

The tribune rested his crossed arms on the table, mirroring Sulio's position. "It was he who asked me to try the food here. Among the officers, he's known to be a good man, so I said I would."

Rogatus's smile faded, leaving straight lips and emotionless eyes. "I'm a man of my word, and I expected to eat here once so I could tell him I did." He tipped his head toward the back room. "But Veldicca prepares some of the tastiest food I've had the pleasure of eating." His next smile turned wry. "I notice you eat here often as well. Maybe your household cook is feeling insulted that you prefer Veldicca's soups over whatever she makes. I doubt she's as thick-skinned as a soldier."

Sulio glared at him. "This isn't about food. It's not good for Narina for people to see you coming so often."

The tribune locked gazes with him. "She welcomes me each time I come. She enjoys our conversations as much as I do. She's not afraid to speak freely to me. If she wants me to stop, she'll tell me herself."

Then a slow smile curved the tribune's lips. "But since you're concerned about what others think, perhaps you'd like to join us tomorrow. No one could object to a chieftain's son watching over his cousin while I'm shown where I should pasture our horses. I like to move them around so they don't damage the grazing, and I don't want to interfere too much with where the local people graze. Coming with us would be a service to both her and your people."

Sulio swallowed the retort he almost spoke. The Roman wouldn't understand a Brittonic curse, anyway. "So, you want my suggestions on where to graze your horses?" He stroked the underside of his jaw. "I understand there's fine grazing in Germania and Gallia. The other side of the sea is a good place for all Roman horses to stay."

The laughter that burst from Rogatus as his palm slapped the tabletop sounded as genuine as any Sulio had heard.

He stared at Rogatus. Did the Roman think he was joking?

As quickly as it came, the laughter died, and the Roman's eyes chilled.

Narina returned and took her seat. "What's so funny?"

The tribune's eyes warmed when he turned them on her. This soldier had no right to look at her that way.

Sulio flexed his jaw to unclench it.

Rogatus flicked a gaze toward Sulio before turning his eyes back to her. "Your cousin will come with us tomorrow when we look for good pasturage. I expect between the two of you, I'll get excellent recommendations."

Her eyebrows shot up, and a delighted smile appeared. "You'll go with us? What a wonderful idea. I'll have Veldicca pack us a lunch for three. What time shall we plan on leaving?"

Sulio had to unclench his teeth again before he could answer. "Early is better for me."

The last thing he wanted was to help this Roman find pasture for his mounts.

Or maybe he did. He felt the smile start, but he stopped it.

There was no better way to know where the horses might be if the Brigantes decided to launch an attack.

And he'd be making certain Rogatus didn't try anything with Narina. That was worth a few hours in the Roman's company, whether he was spying on the enemy or not.

Veldicca carried a tray with three bowls and a large plate of bread into the room and set it at the center of the table. "I hope you all enjoy this. It wouldn't be possible without Sulio's hunting skill." She squeezed the top of his shoulder. "But he's always been one to share good things with us."

Narina patted the table between her and the Roman. "Would you like to join us?"

A shake of Veldicca's head accompanied her warmest smile. "Thank you, but no. I'll eat with Lucania and Atto. I'll be back later to see if you want anything else."

Narina picked up her spoon. "Shall we?"

When she closed her eyes for too long, Sulio watched the Roman. Did she realize she was putting herself at risk by praying to her god, even silently, when an officer of Rome was watching? No one ever did anything about it in Brigantian lands, but Rome had declared her religion illegal.

Was that one more danger this Roman posed to his favorite cousin?

She spoke openly to him and Albiso and Father about her god. She'd even tried to convince him to become a Christian himself.

Was she as unafraid to speak freely with him as Rogatus claimed? What if she said something that caused the Roman officer to ask what she believed? She'd never lie about it to save herself. And that would put Lucania and Veldicca at risk as well.

Rogatus was right that no one would question Narina riding out with him as long as a cousin escorted her. He could also prevent any deep conversations between them about religion or anything else.

And before he said goodbye tomorrow, he'd remind her to say nothing about the faith that made Rome her mortal enemy.

Chapter 15

Finding Pasture

Early morning of Day 10

Narina tightened the drawstring on her brown riding trousers before slipping the long-sleeved, blue-and-brown plaid tunic over her head. It reached halfway to her knees, making it easy to straddle a horse while training it. A leather belt cinched it in at the waist.

She'd woven her hair into a single thick braid that hung down to her waist. When she wasn't riding, she usually wrapped the braid around itself to make a bun. When she was Lucania's age, Mother had taught her how to make several braids to weave in different patterns, creating elegant hairstyles, but she'd switched to the single braid after Mother died. Nothing she did could make her look anything but plain, so why waste the time?

The hair picks that held the braid in a bun had belonged to her mother. Soon she would divide what she had with Lucania, giving her sister the pretty ones with the butterflies and birds and keeping the plainer ones for herself. After she taught Lucania the fancy braiding that her mother had taught her, she'd pass on Mother's treasures.

But plain or pretty, she didn't want to lose any that Mother had worn. So, she wouldn't risk them loosening and falling out while she rode. The simple braid would keep her thick hair under control today.

She closed her eyes and blew out a slow breath.

God, please help me find what Rogatus needs quickly where it won't be a problem for anyone. Please protect us as we look. Keep Sulio from saying or doing anything that starts a fight. Let our day go smoothly with nothing to upset anyone.

Peace washed over her. *Thank You, God.*

When she entered the kitchen, Sulio was already there. He leaned against the wall, arms crossed, frowning. As she walked toward him, he pushed off the wall, and the frown flipped into a slight smile.

Narina gave him a quick hug. "Thank you for doing this."

"I couldn't let you put yourself at risk riding around the countryside with him." Sulio rolled his eyes. "Why didn't you just tell him no when he asked? Just because he wants something, you don't have to do it."

She wrinkled her nose. "Actually, he has the authority to tell me I'm going to do it, and I can't refuse. Only the governor and the legates of the legions have the right to tell him no and he has to accept it."

Sulio's smile vanished, leaving a scowl behind. "He ordered you to do it? He made it sound like you wanted to."

She rested one hand on his crossed arms. "He didn't, and that surprised me. He asked, just like you would. When I told him I wasn't sure it was a good idea, he wanted me to figure out how we could do it without making our tribe think I was choosing Roman over Brigantian. He was waiting for me to come up with something when you came." She patted his arm before withdrawing her hand. "When you volunteered to go with us, that made it safe for me to do it."

◆

"Volunteered?" Sulio snorted. The Roman hadn't ordered him to do it, but he'd tricked him into it. He could hardly have said no when Rogatus put it the way he did. "He made it sound like you'd already agreed to ride around showing him where to pasture his animals. He suggested I come with you to protect your reputation. Of course I agreed. When he put it that way, I couldn't refuse."

She hugged his arm. "I do want his herds grazing where they won't cause anyone else problems. He wants the same. So, I suppose I did agree that it's a good idea for me to advise him. But it's much better if the two of us help him do that. I'm sure Uncle would like to see that as well."

Sulio's eyes narrowed. "He also said you want him to come here. He thinks you enjoy talking with him."

Narina's gaze flitted to Veldicca stirring the porridge at the stove, then returned to him. "I do want him coming. If he doesn't, this taberna will fail, and Minconus will lose everything he's spent getting it started."

Sulio blew a quick breath out his nose. "He deserves to lose it. He shouldn't be so friendly with Roman soldiers that they think they're welcome in Brigantian lands."

Her smile vanished. "I'd lose what I invested, too." Palm up, her hand swept the room. "What I got for selling Zephyrus to the prefect is paying for part of this."

His head drew back before he could stop it. "You sold Zephyrus? You were going to keep him to stand at stud. He's the best you've ever raised."

"I know." She glanced away, then refocused on him. "But I might get him back in a few years. Rogatus sold his last warhorse to a breeder before he left Moesia because it had served him so well. He wanted to make sure it had a good life after he left. When he's getting ready to leave, I think he'll do that for Zephyrus, too. I'll ask him then. I think he'll give me a low enough price, too."

She shrugged. "Besides, he really is a nice man. He's not like the equestrian tribunes I served in Eboracum. He's as considerate of Veldicca and Atto as he is of me. I don't mind chatting with him a little when he comes, if that's what it takes for him to keep coming every day. He'll bring his decurions, too, and that should be enough to make this place a success."

Sulio rubbed his mouth. A nice man. No Roman officer deserved that description. Not one of them could be trusted. Narina's way of looking for the best in everyone was going to get her hurt if she wasn't more careful.

It was a good thing Father wanted him to get friendly with Rogatus to spy on the ala he commands. If that man went from wanting her food to wanting her…

"Don't go doing anything with him to give the gossips a way to hurt you. If you need me along to stop that, I'll be glad to go with you two."

She gave him her biggest smile. "I won't. Did you eat breakfast before you came?"

"I had some bread and cheese."

Four bowls stood on the counter, and she walked to the cupboard to get another. "Veldicca made plenty. Join us."

Veldicca began dishing out servings of porridge.

Sulio held up his hand. "No more than half a serving for me. I've eaten with you so often lately, and I don't want to cost you too much or have someone go without."

Narina pointed at his bowl and wiggled her finger up and down. "You get a full serving. You're family, and you're always welcome to join us."

Sulio raised an eyebrow. "Does that tribune buy a breakfast from you or expect to be treated like family?"

Narina shook her head. "He's never come for breakfast, and he's never asked to be fed without paying. He's even left extra on the table."

"How often is he here?"

"He's been coming for lunch and dinner. I hope he keeps doing that. Several tribunes eat dinner at the Eboracum taberna most evenings. Minconus is counting on the prefect and some of his decurions doing that here."

Sulio sighed. He'd made no progress in getting her to avoid Rogatus, but maybe she'd listen to reason about the others.

"Don't be as nice to his junior officers as you are to their commander. You think he's a nice man, but you don't know yet. And the others…they're more likely to look on you as a servant who's available. If he's not with them, have Atto serve."

She put her fists on her hips. "I wasn't born yesterday, Sulio. I learned how to read a man's intent when I worked a taberna the first time. If I think one will be a problem, that's soon enough to have Atto serve. We need the decurions to come eat, too."

She picked up her bowl and set it on the tray. Then she added another. "Let's eat in the dining room. I don't know exactly when he'll get here, but we can visit until he does."

As Sulio followed her through the courtyard to the dining room, his deepest sigh escaped. Spy on the Roman and protect Narina. He'd rather have no Roman in Isurium who made him do either, but since there was one, he'd be doing both.

When Rogatus dismounted and tied Zephyrus's reins to the corral railing, anticipation of what lay ahead inspired a smile. By the time he returned to the fort, he would know where to graze his herds. He could finally ride back to Eburacum and lead his ala to a fort well prepared to receive it.

But how he would find those pastures was what he looked forward to most. Exploring the countryside with Narina beside him to answer questions should prove both educational and enjoyable.

His smile dimmed. Sulio would be beside him as well. Her cousin had volunteered to protect her reputation, but he resented how Rogatus had forced him into doing it. His presence would limit what they could talk about, but at least she'd be there. Eating with her in silence was better than eating alone. Riding should be no different.

And any conversation she had with her cousin would tell him more about both of them.

He patted Zephyrus's shoulder. "I've planned a treat for you and Narina today." The stallion turned his head toward Rogatus when he spoke her name. A hopeful look when he stood beside the horse, a turning of its ears when Rogatus was mounted—the horse always responded in some way when he heard "Narina."

Rogatus liked the sound of her name himself. He liked seeing the woman it belonged to even more.

He stepped inside and rang the triangle. While he waited, he stood in the doorway, checking what she would see when she looked out. The fort's arched gate was visible.

Since she'd gone to her farm, he looked to see if her mare was in the corral. When duty delayed his arrival, did she ever look to see if he was coming?

"Welcome to the Taberna Lucani. We're not open for breakfast, but we hope you'll join us for lunch or dinner."

His head drew back before he turned to face her. Why was she greeting him as if he was a stranger?

A soft gasp escaped her. "I'm sorry, Prefect. I didn't recognize you without your armor."

He touched the narrow red stripe on his tunic before resting his hand on his dagger. "I thought this would be enough for today."

She blushed. "You do look different from behind." Then her usual smile of greeting appeared. "You've always had your helmet on when I've looked at the back of your head."

One corner of Sulio's mouth lifted. "I didn't recognize you out of armor either. All you Romans look alike from behind." He stroked his jaw. "Why aren't you wearing it?"

He wanted to frown, but Rogatus forced a polite smile. Her cousin's rudeness was deliberate, and he wouldn't rise to the bait. "Being out of uniform will make us look like three friends going for a ride, not a military scouting party."

Sulio snorted. "Two friends and an acquaintance, not three friends. Friendship is something that has to be earned. You've done nothing to earn it from either of us."

Rogatus's mouth twitched. "Trust is earned, but friendship can grow quickly when another person treats you like a friend." He turned a warmer smile on Narina. "Sometimes a man can recognize a friend after a few conversations."

Her eyes widened, then the smile he liked best appeared.

He turned his gaze back on Sulio. "Others…it can take some time to know whether they will become friends. What starts out cool might warm up over time."

"It can…" Sulio shrugged. "First impressions can prove wrong." Her cousin's wry smile didn't match the coldness of his eyes. "But they can also be right."

◆

Sulio opened the corral gate, and Narina led her already-saddled mare past the men's horses to tie her to the railing.

"We need something to sit on during lunch. I'll be right back."

As she disappeared into the taberna, Rogatus stood by Zephyrus, stroking the stallion's neck. The horse was tall, but without the helmet with its horse-hair crest, its rider wasn't.

Sulio stood on the other side of Zephyrus and rested an elbow on the saddle. "I thought you were tall, but now I realize that's only with that red crest on your helmet. I've seen her beside Zephyrus many times, and you're no taller than she is."

Rogatus's tick as he clenched and unclenched his jaw prompted Sulio's innocent-looking smile.

Then the smile of a politician curved Rogatus's lips. "Being a little shorter never stopped a Roman from defeating a German or Briton in battle. It's knowing what to do and doing it well, no matter the man's size, that decides the outcome."

Sulio snorted. "You talk like you know something about combat. I thought you senior officers stayed back and let your centurions lead the fighting. Narina's father knew how to fight before he joined your army, but he was Brigantian. Her prefect grandfather would have died in Dacia if Uncle Lucanus hadn't saved him."

"If he needed saving, he must have been in the heat of battle, not staying back like you claim." Rogatus's eyes chilled. "You once asked why the legate of the Ninth requested me when the ala's prefect died. I led my cavalrymen in Moesia against mounted raiders many times. The ones we pursued never raided again. I'm prepared to do it again if needed, but I'd prefer that your tribe's young men never make me hunt them the same way." His mouth set to a thin line. "I'd hate to kill someone Narina cares about, but I'll do what duty requires."

"No one needs to be killing anyone." Narina clutched a blanket to her chest as she walked toward them. "There's no good reason we can't live together in peace. It's time to go find the prefect his pastures."

She tied the blanket at the back of her saddle and mounted. "Let's go." She rode her mare into the street, then waited for them to mount and join her.

Sulio wasn't sorry. He'd trained with sword and battle axe until he handled each well, but he'd never had to kill in battle. The man who rode too close to his cousin was a battle-hardened warrior. Had the dagger hanging from the Roman's belt ever ended a man's life? Even if it hadn't, Rogatus's sword had.

He glanced at the sheathed knife on his own belt. He'd used it often while hunting. But would he ever need to use it to kill another man?

Chapter 16

Watching Cousins

The trio started south along the Via, passing the new palisade and a large grassy meadow before entering the woods lining the road.

At two hours past dawn, the sunlight still filtered through the tallest trees that were twenty feet back from the stone surface. Shifting patterns of light and shadow played on the road ahead of them as a light breeze stirred the leaves.

Rogatus rode close beside her on the dirt track paralleling the paving. Paving stones were fine for soldiers in their hobnailed shoes, but the softer surface was easier on a horse's hooves.

"I'd like to keep my herds within an hour's walking distance from the fort. Even closer is better. It's common to split them up into smaller groups. Forty to sixty for the horses. Thirty to forty for the cattle."

She turned to look at him, eyes wide. "That's a lot of cattle."

"Five hundred soldiers eat a lot of meat. Some fresh, some salted or dried. We'll buy pigs here to raise for the bulk of it."

"Veldicca will be glad she'll never have to cook for so many." Her smoke-gray eyes turned teasing. "But she will want to cook for you and your decurions often. She likes to try new recipes, and Father said most soldiers aren't as particular as you might be. They should enjoy the variety, even if some aren't as good as her best. But I've never tasted a bad dish from her, so I think none of you will mind testing what she prepares."

"The roll you tested on me was a worthy companion to her cooking."

She shrugged. "I only added a bit more honey to the dough. Anyone could do that, but she's an artist in the kitchen."

A horse's head appeared between them, and Sulio urged his mount forward, forcing them apart.

But her interfering cousin hadn't considered what a warhorse could do.

With only his knees, Rogatus gave the silent command for Zephyrus to rear, then turn sideways to walk behind the other horses and come up beside her again.

The shock on Sulio's face was almost enough to make Rogatus laugh.

Almost, but not quite.

He glanced at Narina. Her lips had tightened, and she shook her head as she looked straight ahead. Then she turned her gaze on him, and he only saw laughter in her eyes.

Half a mile from the fort, she led them off the road. They rode a hundred feet through the trees to find a lush meadow.

Palm up, she swept her hand across the view. "Will this do for you?"

He dismounted and walked slowly through the grass, gauging the kind and number of plants his horses could eat. It would more than do. It was exactly what he was hoping for.

"It will. I'll need five or six more like this for my horses, another for the cattle."

"I think we can manage that, but some might have to be on the other side of the river."

With the reins draped across his withers, Zephyrus had trailed behind Rogatus like a well-trained dog while she and her cousin rode nearby.

Still on foot, Rogatus took Zephyrus's reins as if to lead him. It was time for the surprise.

"Would you like to trade horses for a while?"

Narina's head drew back. "Really?"

When he nodded, she gave him the broadest smile he'd seen on her yet. "I'd love to ride Zephyrus again." She patted the neck of her mare. "Bena's a good horse, but compared to my stallions…"

"She looks as good as what many of my men ride. She's better than what I rode from Deva." He held out his reins.

She touched his hand as they traded. "Thank you for this."

Even after she withdrew her fingers, the warmth of her touch lingered.

With Sulio listening, Rogatus couldn't say what he wanted, but his nod was enough of an answer. Most women needed words to understand a man. She wasn't one of them.

He mounted her mare right away, but she stood with her forehead pressed against Zephyrus's nose, and it wasn't clear which of the two was happier.

In Brittonic, she whispered, "It's good to see you, dear friend."

Then, with a smile and a happy sigh, she mounted.

As they returned to the road, Sulio took his position on the opposite side of Narina.

"Rogatus." Sulio's voice drew Rogatus's gaze from the happy pair between them.

He raised his eyebrows to give her cousin permission to speak.

"Are your Tungrians Germanic?"

An odd question. Rogatus's eyebrows lowered before he forced them to relax. "Latin and Germanic are what I hear them speak, so they would be."

"So, it would be easy to pick you out if you dressed the same as them. You'd be much shorter. But that red crest does make up the difference. You look like a commander…when you wear it."

Rogatus flexed his jaw to unclench it. He'd grown so used to Valentinus's insults that he totally ignored them. Why were her cousin's words bothering him so much?

"I commanded Britons in Moesia. Many were tall men, like you. When we went hunting raiders, I wore the same chain mail as they did and left the crest in my quarters. They had no doubt who their commander was when I led them in battle."

From what he'd seen in Fossa, his Tungrian troops were tall men. Their Germanic origin made most of them the height of the first cohort in a legion, where the minimum height was five feet ten inches. He was barely five foot seven, but he should have been taller, like his brothers and father.

Most young equestrians had more than enough of the best food and drink. When he was a young child, he'd eaten with his nanny among the servants and slaves. So, portions were small, and meat was a rarity served only when the household celebrated something.

His grandfather hadn't cared about him, but he did send Rogatus to the same teachers as his older brothers. To do otherwise would invite gossip. If it wouldn't have caused a scandal, his father would have shipped him off to one of the estates and left him there with no one to teach him what all young nobles must know.

When Rogatus turned fourteen, his grandfather began to include him in some visits to the forum and in some dinners at the town house. It was expected, so Grandfather did it. Father ordered him not to draw attention to himself and to keep quiet unless spoken to.

But a man learned more by listening than talking. Even now, when only the legates and the governor had the right to command his silence, he chose to listen most of the time.

He glanced at Sulio. Her cousin would be wise to do the same.

But a man who talked too much often revealed what he shouldn't. Since Sulio was the son of a chieftain, Rogatus was counting on that.

He learned even more watching those who were treated as important, even when they'd done nothing worthy of admiration. Too many thought they deserved greater respect because of their ancestors' accomplishments.

They didn't. But he'd learned how to treat them as if they did when it was expected. Real respect…he reserved that for men who truly deserved it.

As for Sulio, Rogatus hadn't yet decided which her cousin would be.

He donned a social smile. "Wise men judge others by what they do, not by how tall they are or where they came from. Your father and uncle…both became important men. Narina's father earned his importance by what he did. Some men only inherit importance from their fathers."

Sulio sucked air through his nostrils. His jaw clenched, and Rogatus would have taken back those words if he could.

An insult to himself Rogatus mostly ignored. An insult to his own father wouldn't have upset him. He'd probably agree with it. But they were fighting words to Sulio.

"But some who inherit it soon earn it in their own right. From what Narina has said, your father is one of those."

Narina moved Zephyrus to place her body between them, blocking Sulio's glare. Rogatus on Bena was shorter than either of them on the stallions. "It isn't the size of a man that matters or what he looks like or how important people think he is. It's what he believes and how he treats people. The same is true for a woman. I've been too tall all my life, but it comes in handy sometimes. I can mount the tallest horse as easily as any man and reach high shelves without a stool. But tall or short, I can still be kind. That's better than being important."

Rogatus lowered his eyebrows and drew his head back for dramatic effect. "I don't think you're too tall. From what I've seen, you aren't 'too' anything. Except maybe too modest."

Her face turned the prettiest shade of red he'd seen on her yet. "You just haven't known me long enough to discover my flaws. I have more than enough of them."

"I look forward to seeing enough of you to know them all."

Her mouth started to open, but her lips closed before she spoke.

"Maybe she doesn't want you to know them." The edge on Sulio's words drew Rogatus's gaze away from Narina. "You shouldn't get to know her well enough to see more than a casual observer would."

Rogatus tipped his head back to look down his nose at Sulio. "That's for her to decide, not you."

"Enough about flaws and who should know what. There's a clear stream just past those trees. Perfect for our lunch." She flashed a smile at both of them. "Race you."

Zephyrus shot from a walk into a run within four strides.

Sulio's horse took off after her.

Rogatus nudged Bena into a canter. There was no point in running the mare. She'd never catch Zephyrus, even if they'd started at the same time. She probably couldn't catch Sulio's stallion.

But he had to admire how Narina stopped a conversation that could have ended the possibility of gaining Sulio's trust. He might thank her for that later when they were alone.

Sulio wouldn't always be with them. Then they could talk about whatever they wanted. Even if they disagreed, her words would be kind, and he'd enjoy the exchange.

That thought triggered a satisfied smile.

As Narina and her companions approached the old Isura bridge from the north, a rider hailed them from a distance.

She stopped the sigh before Rogatus heard it. The last person she wanted to meet on this trip was her cousin Albiso. If he hadn't already spotted them, she might have steered them into the trees so he wouldn't. But since he had, she raised a hand in greeting.

Rogatus leaned toward her. "Who is that?"

"My cousin Albiso. He's Sulio's brother."

Should she say something to warn him that her cousin didn't like Romans? Would Albiso have the good sense to not say anything he shouldn't to a Roman officer?

Before she could decide, Sulio nudged his horse and rode forward to greet his brother.

She reined in Zephyrus. At least she wouldn't have to explain why a Roman was riding her favorite stallion.

It had been tense enough each time Sulio made some comment meant to get a rise out of Rogatus. How the prefect mostly ignored what Sulio said was surprising. But letting a snide remark pass was a far cry from ignoring the outright insults that Albiso was likely to speak.

Iesu had told his followers to forgive those who insulted them, but that wasn't the Roman way. Her years living with Grandfather had taught her how easily Roman pride could be offended, and a serious insult was never allowed to pass.

Sulio was twenty feet from them when he stopped. Albiso reined in beside him.

At least they weren't within striking distance, so words should be the worst things exchanged.

Albiso's gaze raked Rogatus, and Narina gave thanks that the prefect had left his armor and sword in his quarters.

But Rogatus's short, dark brown hair and darker complexion said "Roman" before he spoke a single Latin word, and her cousin knew what those red stripes on his tunic meant.

With his hand resting on his knife, Albiso turned toward Sulio. "Who's the Roman?"

Sulio glanced at Rogatus before answering in Brittonic. "The new fort commander."

Albiso's eyebrows plunged as his head drew back. "Why are you and Narina with him?"

"His cavalrymen are bringing many horses tomorrow. They have to graze somewhere. Father knows I'm helping him find pastures that cause the least problems for the clan."

Albiso's frown deepened. "You could do that without Narina. He's riding too close to her. She shouldn't have to put up with that."

A shrug was Sulio's first response. "I'm watching him. Nothing will happen."

"It better not, or I'll—"

"I said I'm watching him. He won't touch her while I am. Besides, his kind prefer pretty women who know how to please them. She isn't either of those."

When Rogatus looked at her, her cheeks and ears heated. Had he heard? Did he understand? She'd said the same to Veldicca, but somehow it hurt for her cousin to say it.

When he turned his gaze back on her cousins, he remained impassive. No sign that he understood what was being said crossed his face.

But he listened too attentively for him not to be getting some of it. The question was how much.

"Do you want me to join you?" Albiso's horse fidgeted, as if sensing his rider's anger.

"No. We're on our way back to her taberna, so he'll be leaving us shortly. I'll see you later."

With a final glare at Rogatus, Albiso turned his horse and trotted away.

When Sulio rejoined them, he tipped his head toward the bridge. "Shall we?"

He'd slipped back into speaking Latin.

"I've learned all I need." Rogatus turned Bena toward the bridge.

She scratched at the base of Zephyrus's mane, just above his withers, and a soft snort declared his pleasure. "I suppose we should trade horses now."

"You can ride him back to your corral." His eyes were warm as he answered. "I get to ride him whenever I want. I've enjoyed watching the two of you together."

His lips curved into a smile like he gave her when she greeted him for dinner. "Perhaps you can show me the shorter road to Eboracum sometime. You can ride Zephyrus while I ride Boreas. You could visit Minconus while I take care of business."

Sulio cleared his throat. "I can show you that road. It starts by the docks, and it's used enough you can't lose your way. A man like you shouldn't need a guide."

She frowned at her cousin. "Sulio, you know he shouldn't ride it alone."

He shrugged. "Soldiers are used to danger in a land that doesn't want them. He has five hundred men. He can take some as escorts."

Rogatus drew a deep breath, then released it without speaking. "Let's go home." He nudged Bena into a trot and headed toward the bridge.

Narina hit Sulio's arm with the back of her hand. "Don't go telling him to do something that could get him killed. He's a nice man, and he wants to keep things peaceful around here. If he gets killed, the next commander could be so much worse."

"He's smart enough not to take my advice. But it lets him know he's not welcome here."

As he trotted after Rogatus, Narina patted Zephyrus's neck. "What am I going to do with them?"

The stallion looked back at her and nickered.

"So, you don't know either. Please take care of Rogatus…for me and for you."

She closed her eyes.

God, please protect Rogatus and help him do what will keep the peace, even when some don't want it.

With a flex of her calves, she hurried her favorite to join the cousin who loved her and the Roman who maybe liked her more than he should.

Chapter 17

Too Interested

Narina's taberna, late afternoon of Day 10

When Sulio reached the taberna, the Roman had already put the mare in the corral. He finished releasing the straps of the saddle, lifted it off, and draped it on the top rail near the stable.

Sulio rode past to tie his horse in the shade of her tree. Then he sauntered over to the corral and leaned on it. "I didn't expect a tribune to do stableman's work."

Rogatus's lips tightened. "A horse deserves good treatment after a day of work. They don't care who gives it to them." He slipped off the bridle and hung it on a post.

"It was good you let her ride Zephyrus today. He's special to her."

"He's a special horse. He'll serve me well."

"I was surprised she sold him. She'd planned to use him as stud since her main stallion just died."

Rogatus paused as he opened the corral gate. "What changed?"

He stepped through and latched it.

"Minconus bought this place and needed the money. She planned to sell the bay." Sulio's nose twitched. "But he told her to sell Zephyrus if she couldn't. He's her guardian, so she had to do what he said."

The Roman looked past Sulio and straightened. "The bay was too young for what I might need from him."

Sulio looked over his shoulder. Narina was almost there. The glowing smile she'd worn during their ride had faded as she came to give her favorite back to the man who didn't deserve him.

Rogatus's eyebrows lowered for a fleeting moment, then his face relaxed to the alert but emotionless expression he showed Sulio when Narina wasn't with them.

After she dismounted, she rested her forehead against Zephyrus's nose. Her whisper, even though meant for the stallion alone, still reached Sulio and the man beside him.

"Today was good. I'll see you soon. Take good care of Rogatus."

She led her favorite to the Roman and offered the reins. "Thank you for letting me ride him."

The Roman's eyes warmed, and a smile that matched them curved his lips. "Thank you for helping me find all the pastures I'll need for a while. I can go back to Eboracum to get the ala now."

As she returned smile for smile, Sulio tensed. Every time she did that, she encouraged Rogatus to think she welcomed his attentions.

Rogatus mounted but made no move to leave.

She tipped her head back to look up at him. "Will you be eating dinner with us?"

"I can't say until I talk with the centurions, but probably not. If there's time, I might ride back to Eboracum this evening. Otherwise, I'll leave early tomorrow."

Her smile vanished. "If you're going alone, don't take the tow road."

His eyes lit with unspoken pleasure. "I'll take the safer road this time." He leaned forward to pat Zephyrus's neck. "And I'll take good care of Zephyrus for us."

She stroked her favorite's nose. "When will you be back?"

"I won't know until I get there, but I would expect at least two days, maybe three."

She stepped back. "We'll watch for your return, and Veldicca will have something special for you then."

He turned Zephyrus toward the fort, then paused. "Sulio, thank you for serving as escort for Narina. Together, I believe we've found pasturage that can serve my ala while causing the fewest problems for your people. Please convey my regards to your father and tell him I look forward to meeting him soon."

Sulio gave a single nod in response. Spending the day helping the Roman army and watching one of its officers show too much interest in his cousin was the last thing he'd wanted to do. He'd be a liar if he said he'd been pleased to do it.

But Rogatus had earned some grudging respect from him. The Roman's self-control each time he'd said something to bait him was beyond what he'd ever seen among the Brigantes. Father claimed that a cool-headed man was more dangerous than a hotheaded one. Because he thought before he acted, his strike came when your guard was down, and he was less likely to miss when he finally struck.

If Father was right, Rogatus was a very dangerous man.

Sulio leaned against the corral railing and watched Narina. At first, her gaze seemed fixed on Zephyrus as he trotted down the road toward the fort.

Or was she watching the Roman? The trace of sadness she'd shown before she returned the stallion to his new owner had vanished, and a slight smile curved her lips.

But rather than vanishing through the arched stone gate, Rogatus turned south and headed for one of the centurions, who stood with crossed arms as he watched his men. When Rogatus dismounted, she turned her gaze back on Sulio. "Thank you for being my escort today. It was much better having you both for company."

"You're welcome. I couldn't let you go riding around alone with him."

He rubbed his lower lip. She wasn't going to like what he was going to say. But he would be speaking it out of love for her, so even if it made her angry now, she would forgive him. She always did.

"It's a good thing I didn't. There are some things I saw that I want to talk to you about."

She tipped her head toward the taberna. "We can talk inside. Then I can give you something to eat or drink before you ride home."

"I could use some mead."

He settled into the chair Rogatus always chose, and she slipped into the storeroom. She came back with a cup of the mead the Roman liked.

"Minconus sent this up because the tribunes like it. But you deserve the best I have, too." She set the cup before him and took the other chair. "What did you want to tell me?"

He took a long drink before replying. Minconus was way too Roman for Sulio's taste, but he did know how to pick a great mead.

He wiped his mouth with the back of his hand. "You're letting that Roman get too close. The problem isn't just that people might think you're being too friendly with the enemy. He's dangerous. No one has the power to stop him from doing whatever he wants with you."

She crossed her arms. "He's not that kind of man."

A snort was Sulio's first reply. "You don't know him well enough to tell if he is or not. So far, you've been welcoming to him, and he likes it. A lot, from what I saw today. He has no reason to expect you won't continue that. But what is he going to do when you stop? Will he think you've led him on and get angry? Will he act on that?"

He cradled the cup in both hands atop the table, and she rested her hand on his forearm.

"I've prayed about how I should treat him, and God hasn't told me what I'm doing is wrong."

A dramatic eye roll ended in his deepest sigh. Asking her god was often her answer. But even if she believed he answered, that didn't mean he had.

"And that's another thing. I saw you praying before we ate. No one else closes their eyes and freezes for that long before they eat. If he sees that often enough, he's going to ask about it." He leaned closer. "What if he finds out you're a Christian?"

She withdrew her hand. "It wasn't that long, and I don't think he'll question it. But even if he does, I know how to deflect his questions without answering. Veldicca does, too. And when he came for lunch the first time when I wasn't here, she warned Lucania to be careful about what she says about our faith around strangers. We'll both be reminding her when he starts talking with her more."

Sulio drew back. "Why would Lucania be talking more with a man like him?"

"He expects to be here for three and a half years, so he wants to learn to speak Brittonic well enough to talk with people." She shrugged. "So, he asked me to teach him. Lucania heard him ask when she brought him his mead, and she told him she'd teach him if I didn't want to. Then she asked what he would pay. He said whatever I think reasonable. We'll set that money aside for Lucania's dowry."

"You're not going to let her, are you? Does she know he's not a safe person to get close to? She's spent her whole life on the farm. She's never had to deal with people who don't look on her as family. She doesn't know she shouldn't trust everyone, and the more she talks with him, the less careful she'll become."

He'd bent forward and leaned on his crossed arms. She patted one.

"Don't worry. I plan to do most of the talking with him, but she can help with giving him the Brittonic word that matches a Latin one."

"How much does he know already?"

"Some from when he led Father's old cohort, and some from when he was in Deva."

"So, he might have been trying to learn it for six years?" Sulio placed his hand atop his head. "You should have warned me. I would have told Albiso before he met him so he wouldn't say something to make the Roman suspicious."

"They didn't really meet, and what I heard Albiso say…it was only about me being near him, and that's no more than you've told him."

Sulio rubbed his forehead. Albiso's glare had thrown daggers at the Roman "But did he know that was all my brother said?"

"I don't know whether he understood or not. He said he knows some, but

I don't yet know how much that is. He wants to get better at speaking it. So, he'll bring lists of words, and we'll chat about things to give him practice."

He covered his mouth with his hand and sighed into it. "You should never have agreed to teach him. Everything you do that lets him spend time with you increases your risk. He'll come to expect it, and then he might expect more than your time."

"I already told you he's not that kind of man. He won't force me to do anything he shouldn't. Veldicca thinks Father would have approved of him, and I agree. I know you think God doesn't answer prayers and guide us, but He does. And if Rogatus is going to become a problem, God will show me how to deal with it."

He ran his fingers through his hair. When it came to her god, she would never listen to reason. "Maybe you and Veldicca won't say the wrong thing around him, but don't let Lucania talk with him much. She's only a girl and too young to always think before she speaks. If she forgets and says anything that leads him to think she's a Christian, he could assume you and Veldicca are as well. You heard what he said about doing his duty. If the next governor says to hunt Christians, he will."

He reached across the table and took her hand. "I don't want to lose the three of you."

She squeezed his fingers as she smiled at him. "I don't want you to, either. I'll be sure to talk with her again before she spends time alone with him. We're not like Albiso, saying what we're thinking before thinking about what we say."

He squeezed her fingers back and withdrew his hand. "I'll talk with Albiso tonight and let him know not to be cursing your prefect in Brittonic and saying things about hating Rome. Maybe he'll listen to me."

It was Narina's turn to roll her eyes. "I don't know why you and Veldicca call him my prefect. He's not mine, and neither he nor I have any intention of him becoming so. I know it won't stop you worrying, but I will promise to be as careful as I think I need to be."

Sulio closed his eyes and breathed out a heavy sigh. He knew the signs of a man's deepening interest in a woman. Rogatus was already liking her too much, but she was determined not to see the danger.

"I suppose that will have to do." He tipped back his head and drained the cup before he stood.

"Father is expecting me to report on where we told him to graze his animals. Since he's not coming for dinner, I won't stay, either."

She rose and gave him a hug. "Thank you for caring so much. Just because he's not going to be here for the next two or three days, that doesn't mean you shouldn't join us."

"I might."

He strode toward the exit. Before he passed through the doorway, he looked back over his shoulder. When she raised a hand in farewell, so did he.

But as he walked past the corral toward his tethered horse, he turned to scan the fort. No sign of Rogatus.

Whether the prefect rode to Eboracum later today or early tomorrow morning, he'd be going alone down the Roman road. If something happened to him, would the next prefect want to avoid provoking the locals to rebellion as much as Rogatus did? Narina would be safer with Rogatus gone, but would the clan?

Chapter 18

END OF A GOOD DAY

Narina's taberna, late afternoon of Day 10

Narina was in the kitchen when the triangle rang. "I wonder who that could be. Sulio wouldn't ring, and I don't know who else might come."

"Maybe our first Brigantian customer?" Veldicca scraped the edges of the pot with the spoon and continued stirring. "Your uncle knows you have this place open now. He always liked what I prepared when he ate with your father."

"Or maybe Albiso, but I hope he won't start scolding me about being with Rogatus." Narina sighed. "Normally he'd be the next chieftain, but Sulio would be a much better choice. I do love both cousins, but if it is him, I hope Sulio is with him to calm him down."

She'd unbraided her hair when she got back from riding, so she tucked some loose strands behind her ears as she headed through the courtyard.

As she walked through the storeroom, she could see the triangle. No one stood beside it, but whoever rang it had left the door open. It was already late enough that she should have run the bolt across when Rogatus left.

As she scanned the street past the doorway to make sure no one lurked outside, she pushed the door closed and bolted it.

"Trying to keep me in?"

She jumped and spun at the deep voice behind her. Then her whole body relaxed.

"You scared me half to death."

"I'm sorry. That wasn't my intent." Rogatus, still in armor, sat in his usual chair. "But things took long enough that I decided to leave early tomorrow. I was hoping you still had something left for me to eat."

"We'll always have something for you, even if it's only bread and cheese.

But tonight you're in luck. Veldicca has just finished a lentil stew, and you're welcome to a bowl of it."

"Does it come with a companion to enjoy it with me?" He raised his eyebrows and offered the pleading smile like Lucania's that made her laugh.

"It does."

He stood and pulled out the chair for her.

She raised one finger. "I need to let Veldicca know you're here. I'll be right back."

As she walked through the courtyard, she shook her head. What would Sulio say if he knew Rogatus had come for dinner after all? What Veldicca would—she could already hear her friend saying, "That man likes you." Then she'd chuckle, and Narina would feel the heat to the tips of her ears.

She stepped into the kitchen. "It's Rogatus, and you don't need to say it. He only came because he didn't finish in time to leave this afternoon, and he loves your cooking."

Veldicca's chuckle was exactly what she predicted. "Of course he does. And he likes your company, too."

Narina got the tray and put some rolls on a plate as Veldicca ladled stew into two bowls.

"Tell your prefect I hope he likes this one. He hasn't had it before."

"I will, and he's not my prefect."

Another chuckle made her ears heat again. "If you say so."

She stopped in the storeroom to get him a cup of mead. By the time she carried the tray to their table, her ears had cooled. But it was good the late afternoon light wasn't so bright in the back of the room that he'd see what was left of her blush.

She placed the cup and his bowl in front of him and handed him a spoon before serving herself. He waited to eat until she sat and picked up her own spoon.

It had become their custom to eat in silence while the serving was hot, then chat. Most men ate fast, so it was odd how he always seemed to eat his last spoonful while she ate hers.

"We didn't expect you." She picked up a roll and nibbled it.

"I wanted one more good meal before I'm away for a few days."

"A few days?"

"I'll meet with my decurions as soon as I get there, and they'll get everything ready to leave the next day or maybe the day after. I already told them we would be stationed here, so I expect they've prepared some things for the move already."

He leaned back in his chair. "I'll have both your horses when I return.

I'm not sure how late that will be, so I'll probably eat with my men the first night here."

"We'll watch for the ala's arrival. If you change your mind about eating garrison food, just let us know."

"I will."

He ran his finger around the top of the cup. "I want to thank you again for going with me to find the pastures."

"It was my pleasure. Thank you for letting me ride Zephyrus."

"I thought he'd enjoy that as much as you would." His gaze met hers, then he looked at the cup. "Watching you ride…any man would enjoy that."

She focused her gaze on the roll. Any man who loved horses would love watching Zephyrus. Watching her…except when she put a stallion through the warhorse demonstration, no man would choose to do that.

"I've been thinking." He cleared his throat. "Zephyrus should make a fine stud. If you wanted to bring your mares up to the corral here when they're ready to breed. I could let you borrow him. I'll use Boreas that day if I need a horse."

She stared at him. The only stallion she had to stand at stud was the bay. He was a good horse, but Zephyrus was truly fine, even better than his sire had been.

"Would you like that?" His smile faded as she sat in stunned silence.

He must think her an ungrateful fool when she hadn't said yes.

"Would I like that? I can think of nothing better." She reached across the table and touched the back of his hand. "That's the most generous offer anyone has ever made to me. With his sire dead and him gone, I wasn't sure how I was going to find a worthy stud for the herd."

His grin declared him almost as happy as she was.

"It's worth doing for me as well as for you. In three years, I might want to buy one of Zephyrus's foals, and I'll expect a low price."

She flashed him a teasing smile. "Or maybe we can split the profits from his offspring, and you can pay me full price. After all, I train partners, and that's worth something."

"You do. So, we can discuss it when the time comes. Whatever we decide, I trust you'll make it fair to both of us."

"I'll try not to disappoint you."

"I don't think you can."

She opened her mouth, then closed it. Why did he say that?

An uncomfortable silence stretched between them, but she wasn't sure how to break it. Finally, he did.

"I'll be leaving early, so I won't be seeing Sulio for a while. Please give him my thanks for helping us find pastures next time you see him."

"I can do that." She could, but Sulio was likely to respond with a snort and some comment about not wanting a Roman's thanks for what he hadn't wanted to do.

"Did you have a message you'd like me to deliver to Minconus?" He took the cup in both hands and kept his gaze focused on it. "Or is there something you'd like me to bring you from Eboracum?"

Bring her something? The last thing she needed was something that made Sulio think he was buying her presents now. He'd be suspicious enough about what Rogatus wanted from her when he learned of the loan of Zephyrus.

"Please tell Minconus that you've been eating at the taberna, and that you enjoy the food. He'll be glad to know you plan to eat here often in the future. He was having more chairs made, so we'll soon have comfortable seating for more than two. I'm sure your decurions will appreciate that. Other than the chairs, I can get anything I need in Isurium."

Rogatus drained his cup, set the usual coins on the table, and rose. "I'll look forward to seeing you in three days. We can figure out when you'll start teaching me then."

She traced the grain around a knot in the tabletop. There was still time to tell him she'd changed her mind. Sulio would rejoice at that. He'd tell her she'd done the only smart thing by discouraging him now before he got too interested. But she couldn't think of a single good reason to give him, and he'd just done her a huge favor by offering Zephyrus.

"I'll look forward to that. Lucania will need a good dowry, and this way she'll feel like she helped earn it."

She rose and walked him to the doorway. She pulled back the bolt, then she leaned against the edge of the half open door. "It should be safe enough since you're not taking the tow road, but please be careful."

He stood close, gazing into her eyes. When his eyes warmed too much, she stepped back. "I'd hate to see Zephyrus or you get hurt on your trip."

His lips twitched. "I'll be in armor, and he can outrun anything that tries to catch us. We'll be fine."

"Good. We'll have something special to serve you when you return. Just let me know when you'll be with us again."

His smile returned. "I will."

As he strode toward the fort, she closed the door. Then a sigh much deeper than she expected escaped.

She would miss him coming for lunch and dinner. There was something about him…a man trained for war but preferring peace. A man with real power who didn't flaunt that he had it.

Her smile broadened before she even realized she was smiling. A man whose pleasure at seeing her warmed his eyes and brought a smile to those normally straight lips. Sulio was probably right that he liked her.

As a friend at least. He wasn't a Christian, so she'd never want to be more than friends.

Besides, a rich, handsome man like him would someday marry a wealthy elite woman back where he came from. He couldn't possibly want more than friendship with a plain, common woman in a frontier province, and that was fine with her. He wouldn't be demanding anything Sulio feared. But it was gratifying that he respected her and enjoyed her company.

If only Sulio would be nicer to him. His patience with Sulio's barbs and baiting was so unusual for an elite Roman. Unusual for any man, actually. How had he come to have so much self-control when most men she knew would be responding with fiery words or flying fists instead of ignoring the insults or answering the taunts as if they weren't meant to offend?

Her smile faded. But Sulio might be right about the danger of letting him get close to her family. Was Veldicca right about him liking her as a woman, not a friendly acquaintance?

Rogatus was a nice man, and he'd been so considerate of her, asking when he could command. But he was also an officer of Rome, and he had a duty to fulfill, whether he was happy about what he had to do or not.

He'd told Sulio he hoped he never had to kill someone she cared about, but he'd do what duty required.

Father had done what duty required. He'd been among those who took Dacians prisoner, not just warriors but women and children and men who weren't part of the Dacian army. He'd watched as they were sold as slaves and taken away from their homes and families, never to return.

When she'd asked him one time what was the hardest thing about his time in the cohort, that was his answer. He didn't regret killing in battle. He didn't regret ending the rule of a king who'd sent his raiders across the Danube to plunder innocent people in peaceful provinces.

But tearing apart families like his own, sending women and children to work and die as slaves because their king cared more for his power than for his people—that he regretted. He remembered too many of their faces. Too many of their wails echoed in his head. He hoped his tribe would never be foolish enough to challenge the power of Rome and suffer the same fate.

Uncle Bellicus had listened to Father's stories. He knew what rebellion could bring. He'd do what he could to stop it, but he was only one man. If a war council met, would they listen to him or to those eager for battle with no thought of what that could bring.

God, please don't let resentment turn to anger and anger to bloodshed. Protect Rogatus as he tries to keep anything from starting. Guide Uncle as he speaks with the chieftains so they'll see that war carries too high a price and peace is the better way. Don't let Sulio or Albiso get caught up in anything that could get them killed. If anything starts, please protect Lucania, Veldicca, and all our people. Keep Minconus and his family safe, and Dubnus, too.

She drew a deep breath and exhaled slowly. Worrying about what she couldn't change did no good. But it was so hard not to, even though she prayed.

Inside the fort, night of Day 10

Rogatus lay on his bed, listening to the quiet sounds of a fort where most were asleep while a few stood watch.

He'd missed that in Deva. Being part of a legion fortress wasn't the same as having a fort of his own. His time in Moesia with the Cohort Britonnum had satisfied more than anything he'd ever known. With the two centurions who taught him what it took to command well, it was the first time there were men he admired who cared about him and his success. He became good at what he did, and he knew he belonged. It might not be long before leading the Ala Tungrorum felt the same.

But he had something here that he'd lacked in Moesia. Not far up the road was a woman who trusted him as a man of honor, who spoke truth to him when he needed it, who told him to be careful because she didn't want him hurt. He had a friend who knew almost nothing about his past but cared about him anyway.

He'd pulled off a clever maneuver when he delayed his departure until early tomorrow. Sulio hadn't expected him to dine with her, and it was the first time since her cousin showed up that he'd had time alone with her.

Her delight when he told her she could use Zephyrus with her mares… Sulio had made that possible. Her cousin had meant to make him feel guilty over taking her favorite from her. But by telling him that she'd planned to breed him before her brother forced her to sell him, he'd shown Rogatus the best way to reward her for all she'd done to help him.

He laced his fingers and placed them behind his head.

She'd had her hair down. Thick and wavy with golden highlights, it cascaded down her back and across her shoulders. She should wear it that way more often. It hid the squareness of her jaw. The way her eyes lit, the beautiful smile that turned her from plain to pretty…seeing her alone before he left had been a satisfying end to an already good day.

Chapter 19

A Wise Choice

As Rogatus strode across the courtyard toward the legate's office, the optio stood and saluted.

"Welcome back, Tribune."

Then he stepped inside the office and closed the door. By the time Rogatus reached the aide's desk, he'd reappeared and held the door open for Rogatus to enter.

The legate sat at his desk with a tablet open before him. As Rogatus came to a halt and saluted, his commander closed the tablet and set it aside.

"So, is the fort ready for the ala now?"

Rogatus spread his legs and gripped his wrist behind his back. "It is, Legate."

"That was quick."

"With good men under me, preparations have gone smoothly. The centurions and their men who added the stables and fortifications deserve commendation for that. They have made it as good an ala fort as I had hoped."

"What next?" The legate tapped the desktop with his stylus.

"I spoke with my decurions before going to Isurium, and they will have prepared the ala for the move during my absence. I'll review the troops tomorrow, and final preparations can be made for the move to the fort the next morning. We should arrive before noon, allowing time for your legionaries to return to Eboracum before nightfall. I discussed the schedule with the centurions before I left, and they will be ready for the exchange of ownership of the fort when I return."

A satisfied smile curved the legate's lips. "Good work. You just confirmed that the legate of the Twentieth chose wisely in selecting you to fill the vacant command here."

Rogatus responded with a single quick nod. He managed to turn the grin into a fleeting smile before the legate saw it. He always did his best, but it felt good to have a commander who appreciated that.

"Have I your permission to take the unit there as soon as it's ready?"

"You do." The legate leaned back in his chair and clasped his hands atop the desk. "Anything else?"

"No, Legate."

"Then you're dismissed." The legate pulled another tablet in front of him and opened it.

Rogatus's fist struck his chest before he executed a parade turn and left the office.

As he headed for the principia's main exit—

"Rogatus."

He turned at his name to find Dexter approaching. A welcoming smile accompanied the hand raised in greeting.

"Where are you off to in such a hurry?"

Rogatus returned the smile. "I'm going to the ala camp across the Fossa. We'll be moving up to Isurium in two days."

"While you're here, drop by Minconus's taberna for dinner with us. Usual time."

"I might be able to join you tonight, but I'll be eating with my new command the night before we leave."

Dexter widened his eyes and drew his head back, but it looked more for show than genuine surprise. "I'd never choose garrison food over a delicious stew from Minconus's cook. Especially when it could be a long time before you can eat something as good."

"That won't happen." Rogatus fingered the hilt of his dagger. "The cook at Minconus's new taberna is at least as good as the one here. Maybe even better, since the one here uses her recipes. So, it's no hardship to eat what my men do as they prepare to leave. I'll be dining well most evenings after I move the ala."

Dexter raised his eyebrows. "At least as good?" His smile broadened. "Since that's the case, Plantus and I will plan on riding up in a few days to join you for lunch. We'll judge for ourselves whether his Isurium cook can top the one here."

Rogatus stopped his eyebrows from dipping. When he'd eaten with the tribunes before, Dexter and Plantus had said they wanted to do that. He'd thought it something spoken without meaning it, like so many exchanges he'd heard at his grandfather's dinner parties. But they were actually planning to come see him.

"Wait at least three days after I leave. Then the ala will be settled in, and I'll have some free time."

"That's what we'll do." Dexter slapped his upper arm. "Your troops await, so I won't keep you now. See you at dinner."

Rogatus nodded once, and after another quick smile, Dexter turned and walked toward his office.

As Rogatus continued toward the exit, a smile slowly formed. The last two and a half years would have been so different if he'd been with the Ninth instead of the Twentieth. Maybe the Twentieth would even have been fine if Valentinus hadn't poisoned it for him. But the past didn't limit the future, and he could look forward to his time here while men like Dexter served with him.

Isurium, evening of Day 11

Narina pulled her stool from beneath the kitchen table. With room for one on each side of the square top, she settled in between Lucania and Atto. After Veldicca handed each their bowl of stew, she sat across from Narina.

Heads bowed, and Narina closed her eyes. "Thank you, Lord, for this day, this food, and the joy of sharing it together. In the name of Iesu we pray."

All said amen and took their first bite.

"Delicious, as always." She raised her loaded spoon in a toast, and Veldicca mirrored her moves before each slipped their spoon between their lips. "It seems strange to be dining with family instead of entertaining our best and only customer."

Veldicca blew on the next steaming spoonful. "He's probably missing you at least as much as you're missing him."

Narina stirred her bowl and sniffed the delectable aroma. "I'm not missing him like you're implying, but it is nice that he wants to come eat here every chance he gets. It's the only way the taberna will succeed for Minconus." She took a bite. "I do hope he makes it a practice to bring some of his decurions when he comes."

"He brought one the first time when you and Atto were gone shopping." Veldicca loaded her spoon again. "They both ate every drop of the soup that day. I expect that one will want to come again, even if the prefect isn't paying."

"I hope so. He won't need me to sit with him when he starts bringing some of his men."

She tore off a piece of roll and dipped it in the stew.

But was that a good thing? Sulio would say so, but she would miss eating together, even if he never spoke a word from the first bite to the last. His gaze was on her almost every time she glanced at him. And strange as it might seem, it felt like admiration with the way his eyes warmed and that slight smile appeared when she caught him watching.

But it probably wasn't. She had Mother's polished brass mirror, and the plain face with the square jaw and big nose that looked back at her from it wasn't likely to excite admiration in any man who could choose among women who vied for his attention. A handsome, rich man like Rogatus would have been among such men since he grew into manhood.

"I hope he doesn't always bring the decurions so he won't have time to learn Brittonic. I wonder when he'll bring the first words for me to help him with. I think 'friend' should be one of them, since that's what he is now." Lucania selected another small honey roll from the large bowl. Her gaze settled on Narina as she nibbled it. "How much do you think he'll pay to help build my dowry?"

Friend. If Sulio heard Lucania call Rogatus that, he'd be clenching his jaw before scolding her for thinking that. She'd promised to talk with Lucania about being careful around a man whose duty was to Rome, no matter what it asked of him. Maybe now was the right time.

"I haven't decided yet, but there are some things you need to understand about Rogatus before you start talking with him beyond serving him food and drink."

Lucania tilted her head. "What?"

"He's an officer of Rome, and Rome has made following Iesu illegal. So, we must be careful what we say around him."

Lucania drew a sharp breath through her nose. "Is that why Sulio doesn't like him being here? He seems like such a nice man."

Narina patted her sister's hand where it rested on the table. "He is a nice man, and he probably wouldn't want to do anything to hurt us. But he also has to enforce the laws of Rome, even if he might not want to. Father had to help make the Dacian people who weren't part of any battles into slaves because that's what the emperor decided would happen. If the legate or governor said to kill them or enslave them, that's what he and the men he commanded did."

Lucania drew back. "Father made people slaves? Why would he do that? He freed Veldicca and said we should never have any."

"It was many years before you were born, when he was still a centurion." Narina took her sister's hand and leaned closer. "He had no choice. He'd sworn his loyalty to Rome and the emperor, and that meant he had to do what the emperor and the governor and the legate told him. He told me one time that was the worst thing he ever had to do, but it was his duty to do it."

She took a deep breath. "Rogatus is a tribune in charge of 500 men, like Grandfather was before Mother married Father. He can't do whatever he pleases if it goes against what a legate or governor wants. So, we want to be very careful about not letting him know we follow Iesu. That's part of why Sulio doesn't want him around us. He just wants to protect us."

Lucania blanched. "Do I have to be afraid of him? Is Rogatus really that dangerous?"

Narina blew what was left of the breath out. She'd scared her sister, and that was the last thing she wanted to do. If she couldn't fix it, Lucania would act differently toward the prefect than she had. Would that offend him? Would it make him feel unwelcome so he stopped coming?

"There's a difference between being afraid and being careful. You aren't afraid of the stallions, but they can be unpredictable at times. So, you're careful around them before I get them trained. And even then, you don't do things that might make them strike out. And the guard dogs that keep the wolves away. You're not afraid, because they don't plan to hurt you like a wolf might, but a strange dog might attack. Even one you think you know might if its owner ordered it to."

She stood, placed her hands atop Lucania's shoulders, and squeezed. "You can treat him like a friend because he is one, but just be careful not to mention anything about our faith. If he asks about it, tell him you don't understand and change what you're talking about. Or excuse yourself and let me know right away. I'll go talk with him so he won't worry about you not answering."

Lucania's shoulders relaxed, and her usual smile returned. "I'm glad you think he's still a friend, even if he's a tribune. Veldicca says that he likes us and that's why he comes to eat so often."

She wrinkled her nose. "Then she gets a funny smile, and I've seen her and Atto exchange winks when you go out to meet him. I asked why, and she said I'd understand in a few years."

It was all Narina could do not to roll her eyes. "When you're a little older, if you still don't understand, I'll explain it to you. For now, it's enough for you to know he's a friend, but not someone who can know about our faith."

"I'll be careful."

Narina wrapped her arm around her sister's shoulders and pulled her in for a quick hug before sitting back down. "We all will, and everything will be fine."

Chapter 20

An Undercurrent of Discontent?

The Ala Tungrorum camp near Eboracum, morning of Day 12

In the privacy of his quarters, Rogatus opened the trunk that held what had turned Valentinus against him. He lifted out the chain-mail shirt he'd worn so many times in Moesia and placed it on the bed. Then he unfolded it to expose the cloth-wrapped silver cuffs he'd received from the provincial governor for valor and exceptional strategy in recovering what raiders had stolen.

He'd led dozens of successful sorties, but one stood out. When the governor's nieces were kidnapped and a horde of gold taken from an imperial estate, he'd tracked the raiders deep into Jazyges country. With only two of his men who spoke their language, he'd infiltrated the raiders' stronghold, found the girls and the treasure, and brought them out unharmed after making certain those responsible would never repeat their crime.

He placed the first cuff around his left wrist and closed the clasp. It latched with a satisfying click. After donning its mate around his right wrist, he placed the bronze helmet atop his head and headed out to review his troops for the first time.

Without a word, those cuffs would declare to his men that he was an officer who was more than some equestrian making his way through the three postings to become an imperial procurator. He was a man of action they could respect and follow.

Zephyrus awaited him at the entrance to his quarters. The silver stallion tossed his head when Rogatus mounted, then turned it to look at his master.

Rogatus slapped the stallion's neck. "Let's go see what we're leading."

A dip of the stallion's head looked like he was agreeing, and Rogatus reined him toward the gate that led to the exercise ground. Each turma would perform the same set of maneuvers, each one designed to show cavalry in action. With sixteen turmas, it would take most of the morning to complete the review; then the final preparations for heading to Isurium would begin.

A satisfied smile curved Rogatus's lips. He'd be going home to the fort that was his for the next three and a half years. But the fort wasn't uppermost in his mind. Part of what made it feel like home was the taberna where he would eat most days and the woman who'd join him while he ate.

Germanus sat his horse on the low hill beside the field. When Rogatus rode up beside him, his top decurion saluted before riding down to join the Turma Prima that he personally led. They would complete their maneuvers, and Germanus would join him again to review the remaining fifteen.

The Prima rode past him the first time, its dragon-headed standard in the lead with a bright red tube of fabric fluttering behind the bronze head. As the men turned their heads to face him while they passed, he raised his right arm in a salute that allowed each man to see the polished silver cuff on his forearm. He would only wear the armillae on formal occasions, but it was enough for his men to see them once for the message he wanted to be sent and received.

As the column of men fanned out to perform battle maneuvers, he relaxed in the saddle. It was like a dance, choreographed to perfection as the two columns of horses wove between each other and moved on to more complicated maneuvers. Germanus had trained his men well.

As the Prima left the field, Germanus rode up beside him and raised his hand. The Turma Secunda entered the field to take its turn.

Germanus glanced at his wrists, then turned his gaze back on the fast-moving horses. "The armillae. What did you get them for?"

Rogatus replied without taking his eyes off the field. "For leading cavalry sorties against Jazyges who crossed the Danube to raid in Moesia. My first command was the Cohort Tertiae Brittorum Equitata.

Germanus nodded. "So, you commanded cavalry before. Atilianus hadn't."

Before Rogatus replied, the horses began a different pattern, forming a column of twos that split and reformed as the horses moved in circles and rectangles.

"I did. That's why the legate of the Ninth requested me from the Twentieth. He said he wanted someone with experience but couldn't wait for an ala prefect to transfer in from another province."

A quick smile flashed, then vanished from the decurion's lips. "It's good the legate wanted someone who knew what he was doing for a change."

Rogatus glanced at Germanus before watching the horses again. "For a change?"

Embarrassment colored Germanus's next words. "Never mind."

"When I ask a question, you don't have to be careful what you answer. I want what you really think."

Those words triggered another quick smile. "When a tribune comes for their last tres militiae posting, many can't ride like cavalry. And many have no battle sense."

A single nod was Rogatus's first reply. "I understand. I left my legion tribunate early to help your legate, but another tribune whose first command had no horses and never saw action was heading east to lead an ala after his three years in Deva. I hope he listens to his decurions on what to do. Two centurions of the Brittorum taught me what I needed to know when I first arrived. One led a cavalry unit, and I owe my success there to what he taught me."

Germanus turned his head to face Rogatus. "Maybe after this ala you should lead one of the auxiliaries farther north where the Selgoviae and Otadini sometimes raid. We're far enough south I don't expect that problem. The fort up at Coria was built for the Ala Petriana, but it burned ten or so years ago. I heard they were rebuilding, but a regular cohort will be there. The town is a tribal center for the Brigantes, but they're not all peaceful like the ones near here. We mostly don't have a problem."

"Only mostly? So sometimes there is?" Rogatus rubbed under his jaw. "I have Atilianus's horse, but no one ever said how he died. Can you tell me?"

When Germanus turned his gaze back on the maneuvers, silence hung between them. Then he cleared his throat. "No one knows. He went for a ride, and his horse came back alone with a lot of blood on the saddle. The searchers didn't find his body. My guess is some Brigantes ambushed him, and his head's a trophy now. He was only here a few months. He'd served in Gallia and Italia before where riding for pleasure was safe."

He shrugged. "I don't know if the horse came back on its own or if they sent it back as a warning to leave the Brigantian lands. I was surprised the killers didn't keep him. He's a better horse than most chieftains have. But maybe he was too easy to identify, so riding him would be risky for the murderer."

Rogatus stopped the frown before Germanus could see it. The legate said there was an undercurrent of discontent, not that some tribesmen might have murdered the man he was replacing.

"Well, I'm glad they didn't keep him since he's mine now. He's a beautiful animal and well trained as a warhorse. But this silver dun that I just bought from the Lucanus farm is even better."

Germanus glanced at Zephyrus's proud head that kept shifting to follow the moving standard. "Your horse looks like he's judging the maneuvers himself. Whoever trains there, he knows what he is doing."

"It's not a he. It's Narina Lucana. She's been the trainer since her father died a few years ago. When Domitian was emperor, he was a cavalry centurion for the equitata that I commanded in Moesia. He taught her how to train warhorses."

Germanus's head drew back. "A woman trainer? That I'd like to see."

"You'll get to meet her. Right now, she's running the Lucanus taberna that we ate at in Isurium. She's helping her brother get it started. The Lucanus farm where the horses are raised is three miles south of the fort."

The decurion raised one eyebrow. "Is she the redhead that the girl fetched to serve us? That one would have turned men's heads when she was younger. She's not bad now."

"No. She's close to twenty, not forty. Maybe sometime I'll get her to put Zephyrus through his paces while we watch. You've never seen a better rider, like she's one with the horse."

The Secunda was just finishing its maneuvers, so Germanus turned his gaze back on the field as the dragon-head standard of the next turma led thirty men onto the field.

Rogatus rubbed his jaw. If Germanus had met Narina, he wouldn't say anything about her beauty. With that square jaw and large nose, no man would. But there was something about those steel-gray eyes that sparkled when she teased him, her musical laugh that came so easily, and the smile that turned her plain face pretty. They made a man feel good when he was with her. In less than two days, he would see her again.

Even if he did eat with the garrison the night the ala moved in, maybe he'd still drop by the taberna to see how she was doing before dusk turned to darkness and it wasn't wise to be out alone.

Narina's taberna, Isurium, evening of Day 12

Narina had just put the rolls in a large bowl when Sulio came through the back door.

"Join us for dinner? Veldicca's trying something new."

"That's why I came." He picked up a roll and tore off a piece. "It's much nicer to see you when that Roman isn't here."

She put on a smile. Rogatus probably felt the same about him being there since he showed up to eat with her alone before he left. He might have been planning that all along. But she wouldn't share her suspicion with her already suspicious cousin. It was better not to tell him Rogatus came back after saying he probably wouldn't.

"I think you find it too entertaining to bait the man. But it is amusing to see how he never responds like you want. I've never seen anyone seem so unconcerned when someone tries to insult him."

Sulio's mouth tightened. "I don't care how he responds as long as he gets the message that you"—he pointed at her—"are off limits to him."

"I don't know how many times I have to tell you that he isn't interested in me that way."

His rapid head shake spoke his thoughts without words, but he didn't leave it at that. "It takes a man to know a man. You haven't been paying attention to how he looks at you. To the hidden meanings in things he says."

"He's Roman elite, just like Grandfather. He has no serious interest in me as a woman. He'll marry a wealthy elite woman back where he came from. I could be as pretty as Lucania, and I still wouldn't tempt him."

"Not for marriage, maybe, but any man can want a woman he has no plans to wed. And rich men are good at getting what they want with money and flattering ways."

Her teeth clenched. "But this woman has no intention of being 'gotten' by any man I don't plan to marry. A Christian only does that with her husband. And even then, he has to wait until after we make our marriage vows. I tell you, Rogatus is only a friend who likes Veldicca's food and wants me to help him learn to speak Brittonic well."

"You're actually going to do that? Even after all the warnings I've given you about how men with power think? You really think he just wants to learn Brittonic?"

She placed her fists on her hips. "Yes. When we were first talking about it, he even asked if you'd be willing to chat with him in a friendly way about things men are interested in."

Sulio's eyes narrowed. "Such as?"

"Like friendly discussions about politics. Father and Uncle used to have those often. I told him I didn't think you'd be interested, but if you are, he might be willing to pay you as well."

Sulio's dramatic eye roll triggered Narina's best laugh. "He wouldn't be surprised by that answer. He also wanted me to thank you for escorting us yesterday."

He huffed a breath out through his nose. "I don't want that Roman's thanks for something he tricked me into doing to help a Roman army. Besides, I only did it for you, not him."

Her laughter relaxed his frown into a reluctant smile, as she hoped it would. "I told him I *could* do that, not that I would do that. I already knew what you just said would be your response."

She got an extra bowl from the shelf to make five. "But he did find a wonderful way to thank me for helping him find pastures. He's going to let me use

Zephyrus as stud if I bring the mares up here to my corral for him to service. It was so generous of Rogatus to suggest it."

"Hmph." Sulio crossed his arms. "You should be thanking me for that. I told him you hadn't wanted to sell him Zephyrus, that Minconus made you do it. He probably felt guilty about making you lose your best stallion when you didn't have a good replacement."

She patted his arm. "Thank you for whatever part you played in it. It's a wonderful solution to my problem. And there's one more lovely thing that's come of him being here."

"What?"

"We're seeing a lot more of you."

Her teasing grin drew a shrug and a smile from him. "It's not him being here. It's you being in Isurium whether he's here or not. And maybe I'm really coming for Veldicca's cooking, not just your company."

"Maybe so." She pointed toward the courtyard. "Would you please go close and bolt the front door? Since Rogatus can't be with us tonight to entertain you, you can have one of the chairs. They truly are comfortable. Veldicca gets the other one. Her stew tonight—after you taste it, you'll agree she deserves the best place to sit."

Sulio disappeared through the courtyard doorway, and Narina sighed. He would be shocked and scolding her yet again if he knew how much she missed the prefect coming today.

Those thoughts made her uncomfortable, too. It was easy to tell herself Rogatus couldn't possibly be interested in her. But each time she saw him now, he would say or do something that made her wonder if she might be wrong.

Chapter 21

Isurium, early evening of Day 13

Rogatus sat at the head of a long table in the dining hall, Germanus to his right and Adolphus, the decurion of the Turma Secunda, on his left. The rest had arranged themselves according to whomever they wanted close for conversation. The same had been done in Moesia, and the familiarity of it triggered Rogatus's smile.

The food was no worse than he expected after so many meals in the legionary dining hall in Deva, but it wasn't what a man who'd tasted much better would look forward to.

A few hundred feet away, Narina and her family were undoubtedly dining on a stew tasty enough for a senator's banquet. But he'd chosen to eat with his officers the night they moved into the fort, and their obvious approvals of his modifications to an infantry fort to make it cavalry-ready were gratifying.

He'd made the right choice as commander of the ala. Now that he'd fulfilled that duty, he could do something for himself. Being with Narina Lucana was satisfying in a way that he hadn't known before, even when they only ate together in silence. He could relax in her presence. He didn't have to prove anything about who he was or try to earn respect by what he could do.

He rose, and the conversations around the table stopped. "I have something to attend to. First thing tomorrow, I'll show you where our livestock will be grazing and you can decide how to distribute our animals among the pastures." He waved his hand toward their cups and bowls. "Carry on."

Germanus fixed his gaze upon Rogatus, then wiped his mouth with the back of his hand, erasing the start of a knowing smile. But Germanus's knowledge of his friendship with the owner of the taberna wasn't likely to be shared. When he started treating them to meals at her taberna as rewards for good work, they'd all know anyway.

When he started up the street to the taberna, the sun had dropped behind the low hills to the west. How far below, he couldn't tell, but it wasn't getting dark yet. So, he could count on at least a half hour of twilight before he must return to avoid any dangers hiding in the dark.

With five hundred cavalry newly arrived, no one was likely to be lurking between the gate and her doorway. He'd left his armor in his quarters when he went to the dining hall. But he always wore his dagger, and nothing more should be needed.

Knowing how Boreas came to need a new owner had made him more wary.

She'd been wise to tell him not to ride the tow road alone. He wouldn't ask her to ride it with him again. She could be hurt in an ambush meant for him.

When he reached her door, it was closed. He pushed on it. Bolted already. But she'd bolted it when she shut it the last time he visited, before she saw he was already there. She'd said she'd always have something for him when he came, if only some bread and cheese. So, the taberna might be officially closed for the evening, but a bolted door didn't mean she wouldn't welcome him tonight.

With his knuckles, he rapped on the wood three times.

And waited. No answer. So, no one was in the dining room.

With a tight fist, he knocked again.

More silence. If they were all in the back past the storeroom, had anyone heard?

Three times he pounded on the door and began to count. At thirty, he turned away. He'd be showing his decurions the pastures tomorrow, so he couldn't see her any sooner than tomorrow evening. That was what he'd told her to expect, but disappointment still inspired his sigh.

He'd taken the first step when a youthful male voice came from behind the door. "Who's there?"

"It's Prefect Rogatus. Let me in."

The sound of a bolt being drawn back was followed by Atto opening the door a crack to peek out before swinging it partway open.

Rogatus stepped through, and the youth opened the door wider behind him, as if expecting him to go back into the street.

"We're closed now. We didn't think you were coming and ate all the stew."

"I ate already, but I want to speak with Narina." Rogatus settled into his usual chair.

Atto stared at him, then closed and bolted the door. "I'll let her know."

It was too long until the soft sound of approaching footsteps announced her arrival.

She stepped into the room, and the smile he'd missed for three days greeted him.

"Welcome back, Prefect. Atto said you wanted to talk with me."

He pointed to the other chair. "I do."

She was dressed for riding, but she lowered herself into the chair with the graceful assurance of the elite. "We saw the ala arrive. When you didn't send word, I just assumed we wouldn't see you today."

He leaned back in his chair and crossed his arms. "Before I left, I said I'd see you in three days. I'm a man of my word. I'm glad I've been able to keep that promise."

"Father was a soldier. I would have understood if you couldn't. Did you get to see Minconus?"

She ran a hand through her loose hair. With so much wave in it, she'd probably just released it from the braid.

"I did. He was glad I've been enjoying Veldicca's cooking. He said to tell you it would be another week or two before he had the chairs, but he has the carpenter working on them. He also said to tell you that you were the best. Since that's an opinion I share, I assured him I would."

With a flick of her fingers, she brushed away his compliment. "He and Sulio only see the best in me, so they exaggerate sometimes. Don't feel you need to flatter me like they do. I expect you to be a man of truth as well as honor."

He opened his mouth, then closed it. He wasn't a man who flattered, but she'd figure that out in time.

"I'll try not to disappoint."

She clasped her hands and rested them on the tabletop. "So, you wanted to talk with me. What about?"

Nothing in particular, but he couldn't tell her that. "I wanted to deliver Minconus's message, as promised."

"I appreciate that. He's as good a brother as they come."

"It's good of you to be working so hard to get this place started for him. Perhaps he's not exaggerating when he says you're the best."

A flush of pink colored her cheeks. "Veldicca might be the best, but I suppose I'm good enough."

She cleared her throat. "Should we plan on you coming tomorrow? She has an idea for something new."

"I'll be showing my decurions the pasturage we found, so I won't be coming midday. But I should be free in the evening."

"Good. Lucania is eager to start teaching you. So perhaps you can bring a few words when you come."

"I can." He leaned toward her, and she drew back.

Had he done something that offended? He shifted to where he had been, and she relaxed.

"I'm eager to understand more of what I hear around me. And to talk with your tribesmen to build a better understanding between us."

He traced an R that was carved in the tabletop. "When I'm alone and out of uniform, you can call me Rogatus. It will make our conversations feel more natural."

Her eyes widened, but only for a moment. "If that's what you wish, I suppose I can. But when anyone might overhear, I'll still call you Prefect."

"That's fine. I want to learn how I should talk with someone formally, like with your uncle."

He traced the R again. "Or with a close friend like…"

He stopped midsentence. He'd almost said like her. It wasn't true yet, but he hoped she'd soon want it to be. After her comments about flattery, she wouldn't believe he meant it tonight.

She chuckled. "You almost said like Sulio. He wouldn't say he's your friend now, but I have great hopes that will change before long."

"So do I."

He rubbed his lower lip. Would Sulio be more open to friendship if he didn't think Narina might like him too much? Would her cousin be so protective of her if he was a Brigantian man?

He wasn't looking for what her cousin feared. He would never treat a woman that way.

Right now, he wasn't in a position to make lasting plans with a woman. But in three and a half years, he would have made his 100,000 denarii and have fulfilled the tres militiae requirements. Someday, whether Father died or disinherited him, he could go wherever he wanted. Do whatever he wanted. No matter how much Father might want to hurt him now, what that man wanted would never matter again.

How Narina would fit into that—that remained to be decided. But for now, he could enjoy her advice and teasing along with her smiles and laughter as their friendship grew.

"Was there anything more you needed tonight?" Her quiet words drew him back to the taberna and the woman sitting across from him.

"No."

Simply coming had satisfied him that all was well with her.

She stood. "Then I'll bid you goodnight. We'll look forward to seeing you tomorrow." She flashed him a smile. "Veldicca is eager to see whether you like her newest dish."

He rose as well. "If I were a betting man, I'd wager I will without even smelling the odor."

"Aroma." Her chuckle was almost a giggle. "Odor makes it sound like something that smells bad. We'll teach you the Brittonic words for both so you don't insult a good cook." She flashed him a smile. "Or even a bad one. Maybe especially a bad one if she's going to cook for you again."

She moved toward the door, and he followed. When she slid back the bolt and opened it, he stepped through. But before he walked away…

"Good night, Narina. Sleep well."

"May you do the same, Prefect."

His mouth twitched. She'd forgotten.

"It's Rogatus when no one else is listening."

"Of course. Rogatus. It might take me some time, but I'll try to remember."

She slowly closed the door, and he headed back to the fort.

His name sounded good coming from her lips.

As he approached the guards at the gate, he didn't care whether they wondered about his grin.

◆

Narina bolted the door, then leaned her back against it.

Why had he really come so late in the evening when he'd already eaten?

Not to fulfil a promise to Minconus, no matter what the prefect said. Her brother would never have asked him to call on her only to tell her the chairs would be there in a couple of weeks.

Casually telling someone you'd see them again in three days, like he had with her—that wasn't a promise that had to be kept by dropping in so late with nothing important to say.

A niggling voice in her head whispered what she didn't want to hear. He likes you, like Veldicca's been claiming. Like Sulio's been fearing since they first met.

But there was no good reason for a man like him to find her attractive. If she looked like Lucania, maybe he could be infatuated. But with a nose and jaw fit for a cohort centurion, that wasn't likely.

She heaved a sigh. Veldicca was sitting in the courtyard, wondering why the prefect came. She'd never believe the reason he gave any more than she had.

Veldicca had been part of the family for eleven years. Father first bought her to take care of Lucania when Mother died giving birth. She'd belonged to an ala prefect who was heading home to Rome, and he was selling the slaves he no longer needed. Father used to say no one ever did him a greater favor than the man who'd brought her to Eboracum and made that sale.

Father had freed her and kept her on as a paid servant as soon as he knew she'd be a good second mother to his girls. His sons were already young men. But she'd loved on them, too, and she'd made their family whole again.

He couldn't have chosen better. She'd done far more than care for a tiny baby and console a heart-broken girl of twelve. She'd introduced Narina to Iesu and shown her how much God loved her. She'd done the same for Lucania, and the three of them were sisters in Christ, bound together forever in His love.

Narina strolled through the storeroom and settled onto the portico bench where she and Veldicca were chatting when he came.

"What did the prefect want?" Veldicca shifted to face her.

"He said he was keeping a promise to deliver a message for Minconus."

Veldicca straightened. "Is everything all right with your brother?"

"Yes."

"What was the message?"

"That the chairs should be finished by next week, and he'd send them to us when they are." Narina shrugged.

Her friend scrunched her nose as her head drew back. "That doesn't sound like something so urgent that you'd need to be told the same day the prefect returned." Her slow smile turned into a big grin. "That man likes you, and he didn't want to wait another day to see you."

Narina fixed her gaze on the entrance to the storeroom. "I'm afraid you might be right. I can't think of any other reason he'd come so late with no intention of eating."

As she turned her eyes back on her dearest friend, she sucked air between her teeth "What am I going to do about that? And what is Sulio going to do if he learns Rogatus came by so late just to check on me?"

"I wouldn't tell him unless he asks." Veldicca traced a half-circle on the floor with her sandal. "Which I don't think he'll do. But if he says anything to me, I'll remind him that your father would have no objections to such a nice young officer. Besides, I'm watching over you, too, and I see no harm in him wanting to talk with you."

"But that's not all." She bit her lip. "He wants me to call him Rogatus, not Prefect, whenever he's out of uniform and no one else will hear us. He wants 'natural' conversations between us as I'm teaching him Brittonic. How could that not encourage him to like me even more?"

A shiver passed through her. "I hate to admit it, but Sulio might be right about the danger. I've already committed to spending time with him, and there's no way to take that back without hurting his feelings. Maybe even making him angry, like Sulio keeps saying. He claims it takes a man to know a man, and I'm walking a dangerous path."

Veldicca took her hand. "Maybe not. Sulio doesn't know God like we do. We'll ask Him to guide and protect you. I'm sure He will."

Narina drew a deep breath and let it out slowly. "Yes. Should we say anything to Lucania?"

"She's too young to understand." Veldicca released Narina's hand and patted it before withdrawing her own. "But we'll be asking God to make Rogatus content to be a friend instead of something more. He knows what's best, and He delights in giving it to His children."

A sigh drained Narina's lungs. "At least he won't be coming for lunch tomorrow. Maybe by dinner God will have shown me what I should do."

It was growing dark in the courtyard, and Narina stood. "Let's go to bed."

As they headed toward their bedrooms, she turned her face to the sky.

God, please help me with this. Help us all become friends and nothing more.

Chapter 22

KEEPING A PROMISE?

A pasture near Isurium, morning of Day 14

Sulio was the first to enter the meadow from the path through the woods, but Albiso was right behind him.

Not twenty feet to the left, Rogatus, in his bronze cuirass and tall red crest, sat on Zephyrus. Next to him, a man who was at least ten years older sat astride a stocky bay. His helmet sported a plume of long red horsehair that hung down the back of his neck.

A senior decurion, the leader of thirty cavalrymen just like Uncle Lucanus had when he retired as a cohort centurion. A calm but alert man with a well-muscled body, expert in the ways of war, afraid of nothing when facing danger...that was how Father described his brother and all the junior officers like him. The man looked like he fit that mold.

Rogatus was pointing at different places around the meadow, and each time, the decurion nodded once, and a fleeting smile revealed his appreciation and respect.

Albiso moved up beside Sulio and uttered a choice curse in Brittonic. "I count sixteen and Rogatus. What are they doing out here?"

"This is one of the pastures we found the day you saw us."

Sulio would have slipped back among the trees, but Rogatus spotted them and raised a hand in greeting. There was no avoiding the meeting now.

He clenched his teeth. The last thing Father would want was Albiso provoking the prefect and his officers. That was also the last thing Albiso could resist doing.

"The prefect knows some Brittonic. He might understand what we say, so we need to be careful. If you can't make what you say sound friendly, don't say anything at all. Let me do the talking."

"Hmph." Albiso nudged his horse and started toward the Romans.

The two decurions closest to Rogatus turned their horses toward the pair and urged them to a trot. When they reined in behind the prefect and the man he'd been talking to, their hands rested on the hilts of their swords.

Rogatus turned Zephyrus to face Sulio. "It's good to see you again, Sulio." His hand swept the meadow. "My men are deciding how to divide our herds among the pastures. All commented on how well they should serve us."

He tipped his head toward the officer beside him. "This is Decurion Germanus. He commands the Turma Prima and is my second-in-command." Palm up, he held out his hand toward Sulio. "And this is Sulio, son of Bellicus, the Brigantes chieftain over the area around Isurium. When we eat at the taberna, you're likely to see him again."

Sulio exchanged silent nods with Germanus, but the man's fleeting smile barely counted as one. Suspicion lurked in Germanus's eyes as Rogatus's second-in-command took Sulio's measure.

The prefect continued speaking. "Sulio helped identify all the pastures we will be using. Without his help, it would not have been possible to choose good grazing where conflicts with the needs of his tribe should not be a problem."

Suspicion was replaced by acceptance on the decurion's face. "The pastures we've looked at should serve us well. We appreciate you helping our commander find them."

Sulio forced a smile. "It's my cousin Narina you should thank. She first agreed to help."

Germanus's sideways glance at Rogatus accompanied a twitch of his mouth. Rogatus's second knew about Narina already, but what had his commander told him?

Without even looking, Sulio knew Albiso was stewing beside him, barely holding in some comment about Romans needing to stay away from Brigantian women. It was time to get away from the Romans before that happened.

He fixed his attention back on the prefect. "I'll be at Narina's tonight. If I see you there, we can talk more about where Roman horses should graze."

A snort was what he expected from Rogatus, but he got a smile that could almost pass for friendly.

"I look forward to seeing you there."

Sulio reined away and headed across the meadow to enter another path. He nudged his stallion into a trot, and the hoofbeats of Albiso's horse sounded behind him. When they passed into the trees lining the path, he slowed to a walk.

Albiso came up beside him. "That arrogant Roman dog introduced you as a chieftain's son and said nothing about me."

"What did you expect?" Sulio furrowed his brow. "I've been talking with the Roman since before Father told me to. I've even been somewhat friendly except where Narina is concerned. He's seen you once at a distance, and you two didn't speak."

With arms crossed, Albiso huffed. "You didn't introduce me, either. I'm Father's oldest son, not you."

A shrug was the answer that deserved. "Rogatus didn't introduce the two who rode over like bodyguards to either of us, and you didn't see them getting angry. They all lead cavalry units like Uncle Lucanus did, so they are men of rank among the Romans. They don't have to put up with anything from anyone except their commanders. Then it's"—his fist struck his chest—"'yes, Prefect,' and they do what he says right away."

Sulio tapped his brother's upper arm. "Besides, would you have shown them the respect you would show the son of another chieftain?"

After a snort, Albiso returned the tap. "Of course not."

"Then it's good he didn't invite you to insult his men by introducing you. He's one who watches without speaking, and I can't tell what he's thinking more than half the time. Maybe he remembered what you said when you saw Narina and me with him the other day and figured you wouldn't control your tongue."

Albiso rolled his eyes. "I watched him, too, and he showed no sign he understood. That's why I only spoke Brittonic."

With a flex of his calves, Sulio started his horse walking again. "At some level, so does he. And he doesn't show his anger even when what I say would earn a curse, if not a fist, from a normal man. Be careful what you say around that one. Maybe a man can get away with kicking the leader of a wolf pack when the animal is alone, but only a fool would do it when the pack is with him."

He turned in the saddle to face his impulsive brother. "Father is wise when he tells us not to start something. If you'd ever listened to Uncle Lucanus's stories, you'd know Rome doesn't care who they hurt as long as it ends in their victory, and once they start, they don't stop until they win."

Albiso waved his words away. "They still have no right to be using the pastures that belong to our clan. Someone should do something about that."

Sulio glared at him. "That someone better not be you. Father is trying to protect us all by keeping the peace. If his own son was the one to start something, no Roman would believe he hadn't told you to do it. Roman men don't even own anything until their father dies, and a son has to obey his father, even if the son is a provincial governor. You'd be drawing the wrath of their armies down on the clan. Keeping them from using a few pastures isn't worth what it would cost all of us."

"It wouldn't come to that, and you have no right to be telling me what I should and shouldn't do. I think for myself."

Sulio bit his tongue before the words that would start a fight came out. If his brother actually thought before doing something, no one would need to tell him what to do. But since he didn't...

Albiso trotted away, and Sulio let him get some distance down the path before following.

Was Albiso just talking this time, or was he so big a fool that he'd light the fire that would consume them all?

Narina's taberna, late evening of Day 14

Rogatus had returned to the fort too late for any stew to be left at Narina's, so he'd dined with his decurions. But yesterday she'd said she looked forward to seeing him today, and he'd told her he'd come to try Veldicca's new recipe. Keeping his word to her wasn't only a matter of honor. It was a source of pleasure.

When he reached the taberna, the door was closed and bolted. He knocked, and no one answered. But before he could knock again, the scraping of the bolt being drawn back stayed his hand. The door swung inward.

Was it Atto or Narina herself? Her surprise at his unexpected arrival might end in her best smile. That always triggered his own, but even if the youth seated him, she'd come talk with him for a while.

His hand dropped to his dagger when a tall man's hand gripped the edge of the opening door.

He let it fall away when the door opened halfway and Sulio stepped out.

"The taberna isn't open." Her cousin closed the door behind him. "And it's late enough you should know that without me telling you."

The near-sneer that curved Sulio's lip provoked a sharper response than Rogatus usually allowed himself, especially with a man he was studying to see if he might be a rebel.

"It's only Narina who can tell me that, not you."

Sulio towered over him, so Rogatus moved back three steps as he shifted his hand closer to his dagger again. Close enough for a quick draw, but not resting on it to imply a threat. He still wore his armor, but her cousin didn't seem foolish enough to attack him even if he didn't.

"She won't. She promised Minconus she'd help him start this place. She needs the money you spend, and she's hoping you'll bring your decurions so the taberna earns enough to stay open. She'll encourage you all to come, like her brother does you tribunes in Eboracum. But that doesn't mean she wants you here when you're not buying food or drink."

Sulio crossed his arms, and his glower relaxed into a milder glare.

There wouldn't be a fight with her cousin this night, but did he have accomplices lurking nearby? It was already early twilight, and soon it would be dark enough to be risky outside the fort alone.

Her cousin jabbed a finger at him. "So, since she won't tell you, I will. I know you'll keep coming here to eat, and that's fine. But otherwise she's off limits to the likes of you."

He took a step closer.

Rogatus crossed his arms and didn't move. "For years, I've dealt with women who tried to get close to me as if they liked me when they only wanted my money. They say and do whatever they think will get it. She isn't one of them. You insult her by suggesting she is."

He drew a deep breath and blew it out. Letting her cousin anger him wasn't the best way to handle Sulio. But would he listen to reason?

"But I can tell mere acting from truth, and your cousin is a truthful woman. As I told you before, she knows she can speak freely with me, as I can with her. I know you want to protect her, but no threat from a cousin is going to change what I do. But I will assure you that I have no intention of hurting her...ever."

"Maybe you don't, but what of the others?" Sulio tipped his head toward the fort. "That decurion, Germanus—I could tell you've talked with him about her. It's bad enough that you won't leave her alone. The decurions better not start thinking they can do what Roman officers are famous for with innocent women."

Rogatus replied with a wry laugh. "Your best assurance that won't happen with any soldier is for them to know she's important to me. I'll be bringing my decurions here as rewards for work done well. They'll soon see she's a woman deserving full respect."

◆

When Narina entered the dining room, silence greeted her. Where was Sulio?

The bar across the door had been lifted from its brackets and the bolt drawn back. He'd gone outside, but why?

As she approached the door, the deep voice that she'd know anywhere was proclaiming her worthy of full respect.

She heaved a sigh. Sulio and Rogatus were out there arguing again, and this time it was about her.

She swung the door open. The two men, arms crossed, stood less than a long arm's length apart. Close enough for a shove or a punch if anger overrode self-control.

Three steps put her beside them. With Sulio frowning and Rogatus straight-lipped, they both turned to face her.

"What are you two doing out here?"

Rogatus's mouth relaxed into a smile. "Discussing when the taberna isn't open. I took my decurions to see all the pastures today. I knew it was too late for any of Veldicca's stew to be left when we returned, so I ate with my officers. But I'd told you I'd come and eat her new stew. Please apologize to her since I was unable to taste it, as promised, but I kept the part of my word that I could."

Sulio clenched his teeth, and she could easily imagine what he wanted to say just then. At least he had the good sense not to say it.

"Since you didn't make it in time, Atto ate your share as well as his tonight. A youth of fifteen is never truly full, so we never have to throw any food away."

Rogatus's smile broadened as he chuckled. "That's true at the garrison as well. The youngest cavalrymen are always eager for seconds."

"I suppose young men from everywhere are the same." Narina let her smile mirror his. "I'll give Veldicca your regrets. It was excellent, so I'm sure she'll make it again."

She walked back into the dining room and gripped the edge of the door. "We're closed now, and Sulio was just leaving. But I hope we'll see you both tomorrow."

Rogatus took a step back. "I expect you will. Goodnight, Narina." His eyes warmed as he smiled at her, then cooled as he turned them on Sulio. "Sulio."

After a quick tip of his head directed at her, the prefect started toward the fort.

When he'd gone far enough to be out of earshot, Sulio turned on her. "Why is he coming so late? He knew you wouldn't be serving any food."

Narina drew a deep breath and released the sigh. "He did tell Veldicca he'd be here to try her latest creation. I suppose he didn't want her to think he failed to come without a good reason."

What would Sulio say if he knew about Rogatus coming last night? About him wanting her to call him by his name instead of prefect when they were alone?

"Humph." Sulio pointed at the distant figure. "That man is too interested in you. You need to stop encouraging him before he decides to do something about it."

She stopped herself just before she bit her lip. "I will admit he does seem to like to talk with me even when he doesn't get a meal here. But he's not going to 'do something' that he shouldn't. I've talked with Veldicca about your concerns, and she agrees with me."

She joined him at the edge of the road again and rested her hand on his forearm. "But thank you for caring enough to watch over me. Even when I don't think it's needed."

Sulio placed his hand atop hers. "Your brothers aren't here to do it. I'm not sure they would even if they were. Minconus got you to run this place where you'd have to be nice to Roman officers. He should have known better."

She pulled her hand from beneath his. "He taught me how to do this safely. I know what I'm doing, and I am the obvious person to get this taberna started so it will succeed. Rogatus is ready to start bringing his decurions, and that's what this place needs."

After moving away from him, she paused in the doorway. What would convince him to stop trying to drive the prefect away and ruin it all?

"Besides, this is only temporary. As soon as Minconus trains someone to run it, I'll be back at the farm. Veldicca's going to train someone to cook her recipes, then she'll come home, too. The prefect and his men will keep coming for the food, and he'll soon decide it's the food, not my conversations, that make him want to come here."

A frown that was almost a scowl curved Sulio's mouth. "You don't understand him like you think you do."

"Perhaps I don't, but let's stop talking about it tonight. Neither of us will change our minds." She stepped back inside. "Are you going to stay for a while longer?"

"No, but I'll come tomorrow." Something about her cousin's smile didn't look right. "I need to get to know your prefect better before I can stop worrying about what he might do. Good night, Narina.

She gave him her warmest smile. "Sleep well."

Her dearest cousin strode down the street, along her corral, and headed toward the tree in back where he always left his horse.

She closed, bolted, and barred the door. Then she leaned her forehead against it.

God, please help Sulio and Rogatus get along better. I think Rogatus is harmless. Please open my eyes to see clearly whether he's as nice as he seems...or not. And if he is, please let Sulio stop seeing him as an enemy instead of a friend.

Chapter 23

THE PEACEMAKERS

The taberna, early morning of Day 15

In the room beside the kitchen, Narina sat on the bed by Lucania with Veldicca and Atto on a bench opposite them.

"For all these blessings, and especially for Your Son Iesu, we thank You, Father. In His name we pray, amen."

Three quiet voices had just joined her in the amen when the muffled sound of a fist pounding on the taberna door drifted across the courtyard.

Atto slipped off the bench. "I'll go tell whoever that is that we aren't open yet."

Narina stood and brushed the creases from the front of her tunic. "I wouldn't expect anyone to come this early. Not even Sulio does. I wonder who it is."

Lucania nudged her. "I can think of someone."

To hide any blush, Narina covered her mouth. "He's never come this early before. There's no reason he should now."

The blush deepened when Veldicca softly cleared her throat and grinned at her. "Perhaps."

Atto stuck his head in the doorway. "It's the prefect. I told him we weren't open until lunch. But he said you'd want to speak with him now, so I seated him

After a roll of her eyes, Narina pointed at Veldicca. "Don't say it."

She covered her mouth with both hands as her gaze shifted between the storeroom door and her friend. "What am I supposed to do? He just dropped in two nights in a row after he already knew we couldn't feed him dinner, and now he's showing up at breakfast time."

She rested crossed hands on her chest. "And what is Sulio going to do if he learns Rogatus is doing this?"

Veldicca raised her hands, palms out. "Don't panic. There might be a perfectly good reason other than him wanting to see you. Don't assume until you know. But I can pray for you as you find out."

Narina drew a deep breath as she rose. Veldicca reached out her hand, and Narina gripped it. After a loving squeeze, Veldicca released her.

Through pursed lips, Narina blew out the breath. "Of course, you're right. He usually has something reasonable to ask me when he comes. I've just been listening to Sulio too much."

When she stepped into the dining room, she found him seated at the usual table, in full armor except for the helmet. She offered him her usual smile of greeting.

"It's quite a surprise to see you so early, Prefect. We're never open to serve breakfast, but is there something else I can help you with?"

"There is." He swept the room with his hand. "Even though I'm in armor, there's no one here. So, feel free to call me Rogatus."

Even if she'd rather not, she had no reason to give him for using Prefect that might not hurt his feelings. He didn't deserve that. So, she would use what he wanted…this time.

He pointed at the chair, so she sat. "What can I do for you, Rogatus?"

"I need to meet Bellicus, and I'd like to do that the first time in a way that doesn't feel threatening"—one corner of his mouth lifted—"to either of us."

He rubbed under his jaw, like Father always did after so many years wearing a helmet with cheek shields.

"So, what's the best way to do that? Maybe you or Sulio could show me where his farm is. Or is there a particular time when he's at the council house so tribal members can bring issues to him? Is that the better place to do it?"

She clasped her hands atop the table and fixed her gaze upon them to avoid looking into Rogatus's eyes. Uncle would not be happy if she showed up at his farm with a Roman officer in tow. Even if he didn't bring any of his men with him. And if Albiso was there, could her cousin keep from saying something to make Rogatus angry enough to do something? And if he did, would it stir up Uncle's younger workers to do something foolish? On the other hand…

"You've picked a good time to ask. One morning a week, Uncle makes himself available for any of our clansmen at the council house in Isurium. He should be in town today. It's much better to meet him there rather than simply showing up at his farm."

"Then I'll go there right now." He leaned back in his chair. "Where is the council house?"

Go now? Did he mean alone and without his helmet so it wouldn't feel threatening? But any of the clan might be there, and many would wish him harm.

"Atto will show you." She wrinkled her nose. "It might not be the wisest choice to go to town to look for it alone."

He snorted a laugh. "I'm not that foolhardy. I don't plan to be alone."

She drew air between her teeth before she thought to stop it. "It might not be best to take too many with you. It could look like a show of force to intimidate."

"If I take two soldiers and Germanus, would you call that too many? Two cavalryman from his turma would stay outside with the horses."

"That should be fine."

He stood. "I'll return to the fort for the other three, and we'll be right back. Should I bring a horse for Atto?"

Riding a cavalry horse? That would make Atto look like he was deliberately helping the Romans.

"No. He'll ride our mule, and after he's shown you the building, he'll pick up some butter for Veldicca."

Rogatus's brow furrowed. "Butter?"

"Maybe I shouldn't have told you." Her light laugh flipped his slight frown into a smile. "It's one of Veldicca's secret ingredients that makes what Minconus serves taste so good. I know you Romans prefer to use olive oil in your cooking, but there are times when nothing less than butter will do."

He licked his lips. "Whatever she does, I'd like her to keep doing it."

"I'll tell her you approve. But she'd keep doing what she thinks best whether you did or not. Sometimes she uses olive oil…from now on you can try to guess which."

"I will, but will you tell me if I guess right?" He raised his eyebrows and put on the smile that reminded her of Lucania's.

"Of course." She tipped her head back and looked down her nose as a smile played on her lips. Just like she did with Sulio.

But that made his eyes light in a way that Sulio's didn't, and she kicked herself for being too playful with a man she didn't want to like her any more than he did already.

She wiped the smile from her lips. "Well, maybe not. Veldicca might not want me revealing her secrets."

His eyes only laughed more. "I give you my word that her secrets are safe with me. I'll be back within the quarter hour."

"Atto will be ready, Prefect."

He waggled his finger at her before his hand swept the empty room. "Rogatus. I might be in uniform, but that doesn't matter when it's just the two of us."

"I'll try to remember…Rogatus."

He strode into the street, and she returned to their prayer room.

"He wanted to know how to find Uncle so he could meet him today. I told him Atto would show him were the council house is." She turned to Atto. "You'll need to saddle the mule right away. He'll be right back with the decurion you met the first time he came and a couple of cavalrymen. But I don't want you to stay with them after you've shown him where Uncle is. Buy some butter before you come back so people will see there's a reason for you to be in Isurium other than helping the Romans."

Atto took a step toward the doorway, then paused. "Did you want me to stay in town while they're in the council house to make sure no one looks like they're planning to start a fight? I could come tell you or maybe Bellicus if it looked like trouble was brewing."

Veldicca's vigorous headshake was the first answer. "We don't want you to do anything that would put you in danger. The wisest thing we can do is to pray for them here while they're up there."

Lucania still sat on the bed, and Narina rested a hand on her shoulder. "We'll definitely do that. The prefect said he'd be taking his top decurion and two men to watch their horses. Those two will be staying outside, so he won't be able to go into town without a lot of people knowing he's there. But once he and his decurion are inside with Uncle, they should all be safe enough."

"I'll go saddle the mule and be waiting when they get here." He disappeared into the kitchen.

Lucania looked up at Narina before placing her hand atop Narina's. "Why do you think it's so dangerous for Rogatus to go into town to meet with Uncle Bellicus? Why wouldn't four soldiers be safe there?"

Narina wrapped an arm around her shoulders. "Because most of our tribe would like to have the Romans leave us alone to rule ourselves, and it's Rogatus and his men who are supposed to make sure that doesn't happen. Our uncle isn't one of them, but many of our tribe would willingly fight the Romans if they thought they might win. Uncle and Father talked enough about how Rome fights for him to believe only suffering and death would come from rebelling."

"Is Uncle right?" Lucania chewed her lip.

"Father would have said so. He fought for Rome in Dacia, and the end of that war meant death or slavery for most of the Dacian people. We don't want that to happen here. I wish everyone around here lived like Apostle Paul told us. 'If it is possible, as far as it depends on me, live at peace with everyone.'"

Lucania traced a stripe on the blanket. "Father earned us the farm by fighting for Rome. Did he regret it after he did that?"

"I don't think so. He told me he was proud of most of what he did. But he didn't like being part of what happened to the innocent people who weren't warriors fighting against him."

"What about the prefect?" She looked up at Narina, worry in her eyes.

"He told me he wants to keep anything from starting so our people won't have to suffer like those Dacians. He mostly agrees with what Apostle Paul said, even though he didn't know Paul said it. Remember that Iesu said, 'Blessed are the peacemakers, for they will be called children of God.' We should always try to help people get along better."

"Like Cousin Sulio and the prefect? Sulio doesn't like him. I've heard him say such mean things to him."

"Yes, and the prefect mostly doesn't let it anger him. That's part of being a peacemaker. Ignoring it when someone tries to start a fight with us. Forgiving what they do instead of striking back is part of being a peacemaker, too, and it pleases God when we do that. It's how He expects His children to act, like Iesu told us to."

Lucania gave a sharp nod. "So, I'm going to pray that the prefect has a good meeting with Uncle and they figure out how to keep the peace together."

Narina sat beside her. "Let's do that now."

Veldicca joined them on their bed. Then all closed their eyes and bowed their heads.

"Father, we lift up to you Uncle and Rogatus and all his men. Let their meeting be a peaceful, even friendly, one where each feels good about what is said and what might be done. Let them both try to be peacemakers, and give us all peace. In Iesu's name, we ask this."

Veldicca and Lucania echoed her amen before heading back to the kitchen.

Narina remained on the bed. Rogatus wanted to be a peacekeeper, not just for Rome but to spare everyone from what war did. But would Uncle see that when they talked? Would he see they both wanted the same thing and be willing to work together to keep the peace? And what if her cousins were with Uncle when Rogatus came?

Even Sulio, who had as kind a heart as any man and a clear-thinking head on his shoulders, didn't want any Romans in Isurium. Albiso would gladly go to war to get them out of the Brigantian lands.

God, please don't let anyone do something stupid that might light the fire of a war that could consume us all.

Town of Isurium, morning of Day 15

With Germanus at his side and two men behind them, Rogatus followed Atto into Isurium. The town wasn't laid out with Roman-style right-angle streets, but he'd been in Britannia long enough to expect a meandering set of paths that never went straight where he wanted to go. As Atto passed a larger wattle-and-daub building with a hitching rail in front of it, the youth pointed at it without raising his arm and rode on.

Rogatus reined Boreas toward the rail and dismounted. He chose the dark tan dun over Zephyrus so the horse wouldn't draw the attention of every man who passed. But maybe it wouldn't have mattered. The four-horn military saddles made all their horses stand out in a Brigantian town, and having two men in chain mail waiting near them would draw unfriendly gazes no matter what they rode.

Germanus opened the council-house door, and Rogatus entered the local center of Brigantian power.

One large room with a hearth on one wall held an assortment of benches and stools. Shafts of light passed through small windows near ceiling level and made rectangular islands of light on the slate floor. At the far end, an open door let more light in from a room beyond.

Germanus tipped his chin toward that door. "Do you think someone might be through there?" He'd whispered his question as his hand settled on the hilt of his sword.

Rogatus had chosen a shorter gladius for both of them instead of the longer spathas they used on horseback. This should be a day for only talking, but the horse he had tied outside proved it unwise to assume anything was safe.

He pointed toward the second room as quiet Brittonic words drifted through its doorway. Then he started toward the door. When they had almost reached it—

"It's a good day to finally meet the chieftain of the Brigantes of Isurium." He spoke loudly enough for his voice to reach whoever waited in the next room. "I've had the pleasure of meeting his son Sulio, and I've been looking forward to this meeting because of it." He spoke the Latin slowly and clearly.

He stepped inside with Germanus right behind him and moved three feet into the room. Germanus stopped beside him, close enough to his right side to provide cover but not so close as to inhibit his sword arm.

Bellicus sat in a throne-like chair behind a table with Albiso standing at his right hand. and Sulio sat to his father's left on the front edge of the table.

As the chieftain crossed his arms, a scowl grew. Without taking his eyes off Rogatus, he spoke Brittonic. "Sulio, who are these and why are they here?"

Sulio slipped off the table and let his hand hover near his hunting knife.

"The new commander of the fort and a junior officer." His reply was Britton-ic, then he flipped to Latin. "Rogatus, why have you come?"

"To introduce myself to your father, chieftain of the Brigantes, and to exchange greetings with him."

Sulio looked at his father and raised his eyebrows. Bellicus rested clasped hands on the table. "I am Bellicus, chieftain of the Isurium clan of the Brig-antes. And who are you?"

Bellicus's words were heavily accented Latin, and that triggered Rogatus's subdued smile. Communicating with the chieftain wouldn't require a trans-lator.

"Prefect Trebonius Rogatus, commander of the Ala Tungrorum, which is now stationed in the fort by the river."

He placed a closed left fist against his chest, moving it slowly so it wasn't a salute but an expression of respect.

"And this is my second in command, Decurion Germanus. I sometimes go to Eboracum to meet with the legate of the Ninth Legion. So, if you ever need to speak with me when I'm away, Germanus will be in charge of the fort and will stand in for me."

"Hmph." Bellicus leaned back in his chair. "But why have you come?"

"I want to let you know of our desire to live peaceably with your tribe, to get along in this land. The legate thought it would be good to move some of his units farther from the legion town to better serve in keeping things peaceful in the region. I have heard you are as interested as we are in helping Romans and Brigantes live peaceably together."

Bellicus tipped his head to look down his nose at Rogatus. "That is my desire as well."

Rogatus directed a smile at Sulio before returning his gaze to Bellicus. "I believe we have made a good start. I want to thank Sulio for his help as we settle in, especially for showing me enough good grazing that does not cause undue problems for the members of your clan. I hope we can continue to live as good neighbors."

Bellicus rubbed his jaw. "If you do nothing to earn our anger, I will con-tinue to urge the men of my clan to accept you being here."

"I am glad we agree on this."

Rogatus extended his right arm to Bellicus. Except for an angry inhale by Albiso, silence filled the room. Then Bellicus slowly extended his hand to grasp Rogatus's forearm.

"If there is nothing else you want to discuss today, I will return to the fort."

Bellicus flicked his hand toward the door. "We have said enough for to-day."

Rogatus raised his left fist to his chest and tipped his head toward Bellicus and his sons. After a parade turn, he led Germanus from the council house.

After he mounted Boreas, he turned to Germanus. "That went as well as I hoped."

Germanus's mouth twitched. "If he meant what he said, I'd call it a victory for you, Prefect."

"I believe he does, and we've made a good start here for ensuring peace in this region."

Rogatus led them back through the maze of streets and down the hill toward the fort.

Narina was in the corral brushing Bena when he rode by. He reined in.

"Narina Lucana, I want to thank you for lending me Atto to show us where the council house is. My first meeting with Bellicus went well."

"Atto was glad to show you as he was going to town anyway to get supplies. I am glad your visit with my uncle was what you hoped."

Enough formality. He gave her the smile her help deserved. "I'll be back for dinner and for my first lesson in Brittonic."

She crossed her arms and leaned on Bena's back. "Lucania and I will be ready to instruct you."

After a crisp nod, he nudged Boreas into a trot and headed for the fort with Germanus beside him and the two cavalrymen behind.

Satisfaction surged through him. The day had begun with a good first meeting with the local chieftain. It would end with a good dinner and some pleasant conversation with the woman who'd made that possible. What more could a man ask?

Chapter 24

Watching over Narina

The Isurium council house, morning of Day 15

Sulio sat once more on the edge of Father's table and listened for the closing of the door to the street.

Albiso strode to the doorway and leaned against the doorpost. After a creative curse directed at the departed prefect, he turned toward Sulio and their father. "The nerve of that man. How dare he come uninvited into the clan's meeting house?"

Palms up, Sulio spread his fingers in front of him. "What did you expect? The ala isn't going to go away because we don't want it there, and from everything I've seen of Rogatus, he decides what he needs and does what he can to get it. Meeting our chieftain…he sees Father as the closest thing to his equal here. Of course he'd want to meet sooner rather than later and make sure it happened."

Father leaned on the table and steepled his fingers. "I'm surprised at him showing respect like one chieftain to another. You've been watching him. Can you tell when he's lying or acting to get something he wants?"

"I haven't caught him in a lie yet. He's careful about what he says, and sometimes his words might be taken two different ways. I'm not always certain what he's thinking. But he's a man who says nothing instead of lying if he doesn't want you to know his thoughts."

Albiso's snort echoed in the room. "You sound like you admire him, maybe even like him. I can see him fooling a soft-hearted woman like Narina, but you should see through him."

"I don't like him, but I respect him. When he says he wants to keep peace among us, he's speaking truth. He could have just taken what pasture he wanted for his horses instead of asking Narina and me to find some for him that the clan could be comfortable with."

Father's brows lowered. "He asked both you and Narina? Why would he ask her?"

"He bought her silver dun stallion, and he's been eating at her taberna that's near the fort. Minconus opened it because he knew the ala was coming here with officers who would pay money for good food. You know how nice she is to everyone. She can't stop herself. He's the only elite Roman out here. A man so far from his own kind misses having someone to talk with that knows his world."

"Is she encouraging him?"

He scrunched his nose. "Not really. She's no nicer to him than she is to me or Albiso."

Father fingered his lip. "I promised my brother I'd watch over her. Since you're watching the Roman for me, make sure he doesn't do anything that could hurt her."

A knock on the door announced the arrival of the first clansman with a problem. Sulio raised his hand in a silent farewell and left the room.

As he strolled down the street, he kicked at a pebble, sending it flying into the nearby wall.

He'd told Father Narina wasn't encouraging the Roman, but that wasn't entirely true. She did nothing deliberate, but that man found her just being herself more attractive every day. Despite her big nose and square jaw that made her the plainest woman Sulio knew, the Roman had started looking at her as if she was as pretty as Lucania.

Whether Rogatus would try to do anything beyond eating and talking with her—that remained to be seen. But Father expected him to make sure the Roman didn't, and he'd do whatever it took to protect his cousin from the danger she refused to see.

Narina's taberna, evening of Day 15

When Rogatus entered the empty taberna and took his usual seat, he reached into a small satchel. He pulled out a thin wooden sheet with his first list of words and set it on the table.

It might be getting dark when he returned to the fort, so he'd come in armor. But Narina already knew it didn't matter what he wore. She could call him by name whenever it was only her people around them. Maybe she'd remember this time without his reminder.

He cleared his throat, and Lucania popped out of the storeroom.

"It's good to see you, Prefect. I think you'll love what Veldicca made tonight. We can start on your word list as soon as I tell her you're here."

As quickly as she appeared, she vanished.

He stretched out his legs beneath the table and blew out a slow breath. A good dinner and a relaxing conversation awaited him. Could there be a better ending to an already good day?

It took only a few moments before Veldicca brought his stew and bread. Lucania came behind her with his mead.

The girl seated herself across from him and silently watched him eat. It felt awkward in a way it never did with Narina. He stopped the sigh before Lucania heard it. She wouldn't understand it was only her sister's absence, not her presence, that disappointed.

If only the older sister sat across from him now. But a man must make do with what he had, and the pretty little sister could fill the silence with Brittonic words if he asked for some.

"Let's begin."

Lucania blinked several times, then bit her lip, as if unsure how to start.

He held up the spoon. "What's the word for this?" He tapped the edge of the bowl and then the bread plate. "And for both of these."

He knew them already, so none were on his list. But sharing easy words for everyday things should take the edge off her first attempt at teaching.

Her shoulders relaxed, and she began, pronouncing each word slowly and waiting for him to repeat it.

In no time, she'd told him the words for most things in the dining room. What to ask next?

"Who are your local gods?"

Her eyes widened. She turned pale, and then she rose. "Please excuse me."

Before he could ask what was wrong, she disappeared into the storeroom.

◆

Narina, still wearing an apron, stepped through the doorway and sat across from Rogatus.

"Lucania isn't quite feeling well, so she asked me to take over talking with you."

"I hope she feels better by tomorrow, but having you teach the first words is a good way to start." He traced the rim of his half-empty cup with his middle finger. "She's given me the words for most things in the taberna. I'd just asked for the names of your local gods when she dashed out."

"Hmm." Narina chose a smile she hoped looked natural and nodded.

God, please guide me as I answer this. Don't let him ask anything that leads him to suspect that we follow you.

He rubbed his jaw. "This is harvest season, so I expect there will be some festivals to celebrate a good one. Who are the gods of the harvest for your clan?"

"The one you'll hear most often is Sucellus. Maybe the closest you have to him is the goddess Ceres. But Brigantia is the patron goddess of the tribe, and any celebration might include her or the mother goddess Danu."

He took a sip from his cup. "What are the names of your gods of war?"

"Why do you want to know those?" She bit her lip. She shouldn't have asked that. Why wouldn't a military man want to know about the gods he thought would oppose him?

"Those are the most important to know. If I hear someone speaking their names, it could mean something dangerous is developing. I already know Camulos and Camulus are names for a Brittonic war god, but there might be others."

"That's the main one. Father used to argue with Uncle Bellicus about whether Mars or Camulus was the stronger god."

He tipped his head back to look down his nose, but the smile that played on his lips said he was planning a tease.

"You once told me you're both Roman and Brigantian, so which do you think is more powerful?"

She fingered a cut in the table where someone had once driven a knife into the wood. "I don't spend my time thinking about war gods. That's something for military men to worry about, not a horse-trading taberna keeper."

His deep chuckle made her tensed shoulders relax. "Then I'll ask about things that would matter to a horse-trading farmer." He picked up a thin sheet of wood with a column of words written on it. "I expect that's something I'll overhear many discussing, so I made them my first list."

He held it out to her, holding it longer than he needed when she grasped it, and his smile grew as he did.

"Pasture, cow, bull, oxen, horse, stallion, mare." She looked up from the list to find his gaze locked on her, and he looked like he was enjoying the view.

Her ears heated. Lucania would get those looks from men in a few years. How could he look at her that way now?

She turned her gaze back on the sheet. "Sheep, pig, chicken, rooster, hen."

"Did I miss any?"

"Maybe corral, pen, barn, and stable."

He reached into a satchel he'd hung from the chairback and pulled out a stack of wafer-thin sheets, a bottle of ink, and a pen. He handed her the ink and slid a blank sheet toward her. "Add them now. Then write each word as you say it by the Latin one so I can practice later."

She pulled the wax plug from the ink bottle and dipped the pen. "You came prepared. Do you always?"

"I try to. But no one I met before prepared me for you."

She drew her head back and scrunched her nose. "I don't expect flattering words from a man of truth and honor. The world is full of ordinary women like me. You're a man of experience. Surely, you've met many by now."

His eyes turned serious. "I don't flatter. I only spoke the truth as I know it. There's nothing ordinary about you."

Heat raced up her neck to the tip of her ears. Good thing Sulio hadn't heard his words or seen her blush.

She cleared her throat, then tapped beside the first word with the pen. "You have a long list. We'd better start or we won't finish this evening."

"As you wish, Narina. You're the teacher." He leaned forward and scanned the list as it sat between them.

A warm, woodsy smell teased her nostrils. If anything, she'd expect the smell of horses and sweat, but he must have bathed before he came. Was that for her or just something he often did, like Grandfather back in Moesia? Mother use to say the only thing she missed here in Britannia were the Roman baths.

She leaned back. What did she smell like herself? The seasoning in Veldicca's stew that she'd helped prepare?

She tightened her lips to stop a laugh. Why should she care what she smelled like? She was only trying to teach him her language, not get him to like her more than he should.

"It's a good list you made. I hope you hear these words much more often than any related to being a soldier."

"So do I."

◆

Heavy footsteps in the back room drew Rogatus's gaze and then his frown. Her cousin barged into the room, grabbed a stool from the other table, and sat with them uninvited.

"What are you two doing?" He crossed his arms and leaned on the table.

Narina tapped the list with her pen. "I'm giving Rogatus our words for farm animals and such."

Sulio peered at the list. "Writing them down for him to study later?"

"She is." Rogatus fingered the rim of his cup. "Practice is how we get good at anything."

"True. But it looks like you're missing some that you need to know. Ones about eating quickly and then leaving."

Rogatus took a deep breath and held it before the slow release, but he managed not to roll his eyes.

"Narina doesn't think I'll need those words, and I don't intend to use them. But you might like to use the one about leaving yourself."

Sulio's snort accompanied his wry smile. "I've just arrived, but it looks like you've already eaten. The sun's behind the hill now. It might not be wise to stay too much longer."

Narina capped the ink bottle and held it out to Rogatus. "He's right. But I think we made a good start this evening. I hope you'll have more words for us tomorrow."

"I will." He touched her fingers as he took it from her. "And maybe we can practice some casual conversation, too."

"We can." She set the bowl on the empty bread plate. "I want to check on Lucania, and then I'll be helping Veldicca. But we'll look forward to your visit tomorrow."

Rogatus returned the sheets, ink, and pen to his satchel. When she rose, he stood as well. "Until tomorrow, Narina."

She flashed him a smile. "Tomorrow." Then she carried the dirty dishes into the back room.

As she disappeared through the doorway, Sulio stood as well. "You might learn more if we make that a three-way conversation. Or maybe just the two of us. There are a few things I think you need to hear that she won't teach you."

Rogatus's teeth clenched before he forced a close-lipped smile. "I'll keep that offer in mind."

He donned his helmet, draped the satchel on his shoulder, and strode toward the door. As he stepped into the street, he looked back. Her cousin had followed her into the back of the house. He'd be telling her to stop spending time with him.

Why did that cousin have to come when he did? A few questions about the farm would have led to her talking about raising the horses. They both would have enjoyed that.

But Sulio had volunteered to practice Brittonic with him. That was progress, even if it was only to keep him from talking more with Narina. He could start figuring out whether the chieftain's son was a likely leader for a rebellion.

He'd seen Bellicus's respect for his younger son, but not the older one. How could any chieftain respect a grown man who didn't know how to control his tongue or hide his thoughts when it was wise not to let someone see them?

If he were a betting man, he'd bet Bellicus would put forward Sulio for the next chieftain, and his clan would be relieved to see the younger son chosen over the older one.

That might not be for many years, but if he was still commanding the ala when Bellicus died, he'd be relieved himself.

◆

Narina carried the dirty dishes into the kitchen, then returned to the courtyard. Sulio would be waiting for her there. He couldn't resist telling her to beware of the Roman every time he came. It was time for him to stop.

She met her cousin at the storeroom door. "Please go bolt the shutters while I bar the door. Then sit at the table. We need to talk."

Sulio settled into Rogatus's chair, and a smug smile played on his lips. She'd soon get rid of that.

She joined him at the table, crossed her arms, and leaned in. "I wish you would stop being so mean to Rogatus."

"Why should I?" Her cousin's smile broadened. "Nothing seems to bother him, and it's fun to try to get a normal reaction out of him."

Narina tightened her lips. "It bothers him. Somehow he's learned not to let it show."

Sulio's eyes narrowed. "So, how is it that you see it?"

"I've seen enough of him to know when his silence is because he's holding something in or because he's so comfortable with someone that he doesn't need to say anything."

She picked at her thumbnail. He'd definitely grown comfortable with her. Although she wouldn't tell Sulio, the feeling was mutual.

"He seldom says a word while we're eating. But he likes to talk afterward."

Sulio leaned back in the chair and traced the carved R. Like the prefect had done before telling her to use his name, not his rank. "He didn't say much to you when we were looking for pastures, but he looked too pleased as long as you were riding close to him."

"Lunch and dinner are like that. Companions in silence while we eat. It's quite pleasant, actually." She reached across the table and patted his hand. "But I'm glad that you prefer words to silence. We're all glad that you join us so often now."

"Your prefect isn't." One corner of his mouth lifted. "And that's part of why I'm dropping by. To keep him from feeling he belongs here." His smile vanished. "He doesn't, even with all of you being so welcoming to him that he might think he does."

Narina slapped his upper arm. "You act like he's an enemy. He's not. He's just a nice man who's stationed far from home right now, and sometimes he's lonely for someone who understands Roman ways. Apostle Paul told us to show hospitality to strangers, and when we get this taberna running well, we'll keep it a place where strangers can feel welcome."

Sulio placed his elbow on the table and rested his forehead on his hand. When he lifted his head, his gaze locked on her. "There's a fine line for a man between feeling welcome and feeling wanted. You're in danger of making him think you want him, and maybe not just as a friend."

With a flick of her fingers, she shoved that thought away. "Like I've told you before, the only man I'd want is one who loves God like I do. He doesn't. Just this evening he was asking about the gods of the Brigantes and how they relate to his. I'd told Lucania to get me if he started asking about such things, and she did. I could tell he assumed I worshiped the Roman gods."

Sulio frowned. "Which gods was he asking about?"

"First it was the gods of the harvest and then the war gods."

Her cousin's head drew back. "War gods? Why would he ask you that?"

"He wanted to know their names in case he heard them."

He straightened. "What did you tell him?"

"That Father and Uncle used to argue about Mars and Camulus, but I wasn't interested in war gods. He started asking for words for farm animals then. I was telling him those when you came."

"That sounds harmless enough." Sulio settled back in the chair. "He came to the council house this morning. He said it was to meet Father."

"Did the meeting go well?"

"Albiso wouldn't say so, but Father found it…interesting. He asked me if I thought your prefect was an honest man."

"He's not my prefect. But what did you tell Uncle?"

"That I hadn't caught him in a lie yet." He stopped tracing the R and tapped it. "Have you?"

"No. I think he speaks what he thinks is true. I'd call that being an honest man."

She glanced at the storeroom door. Did Rogatus really think she was more than an ordinary woman? Mother's mirror told her she was too plain for a man to be looking at her like Rogatus sometimes did. But she'd seen no other young women living near the fort, so maybe it was only the lack of comparison that made him think her more than ordinary.

"After meeting Rogatus, Father told me to keep an eye on how he's treating you. I was planning to anyway, so you'll keep seeing a lot of me as long as he keeps coming."

"You can tell Uncle that I appreciate his concern, but I don't expect any problems with Rogatus or his men."

Her cousin's lips tightened into a narrow, straight line. "I don't think what you're letting him do is safe, and I don't want him to hurt you."

She released a deep sigh. Once Sulio set his mind one way, he was a stubborn as she was about changing.

"I don't think he would ever try to, and I hope you'll change your mind as you get to know him. But for now, will you please not be so nasty to him? For my sake, not his."

After a shrug, Sulio's lips relaxed. "Maybe. That depends on what he does as much as on me. But I'm going to keep coming when I suspect he'll be here."

A playful smile curved his lips. "He expects it now, and I'd hate to disappoint him by being too nice."

"He'd be more surprised than disappointed, and I'd be delighted."

He leaned forward and took her hand. "I won't stop, but maybe I'll tone it down…for your sake. But promise me you'll be more careful with him."

She squeezed his fingers before she let go. "I'll be as careful as I need to be."

With her overprotective cousin, that was the most she could expect for now. But at least he knew it pained her to see it.

"It's always nice when you stop by. Veldicca and Lucania are as happy as I am that we get to see you so often." She stood. "You should go home before it gets too late, like you told him to do. I don't want anything bad to happen to either of you."

He followed her to the door and lifted off the bar. "I'm always careful, and he has five hundred men to protect him. You don't have to worry about either of us."

She hugged him before he stepped outside into the deepening dusk. After bolting and barring the door, she strolled into the courtyard.

Overhead, the first stars were appearing in the dark gray sky. But Sulio should get home before it was totally dark.

She closed her eyes.

God, I hate seeing Sulio pick at Rogatus like he does. Thank You that Rogatus mostly ignores it. He's become a friend, and I don't like seeing him hurt. Let him and Sulio become friends as well. Let Uncle see that he's a good man so they can work together to keep the peace.

She bit her lip. *And please keep Rogatus content to be friends and nothing more.*

Chapter 25

WORTH THE RIDE

The Isurium fort, late morning of Day 16

Rogatus stood by Zephyrus's stall, stroking the stallion's forehead. Already Narina's horse trusted him enough to welcome that and leaned into Rogatus's moving hand. Fortuna smiled on him in so many ways the day he met the warhorse trainer, and Zephyrus wasn't even the best part of it.

"The optio by your principia office told us we would find you here."

Rogatus turned to find Dexter and Plantus walking toward him. So, they'd come after all.

"Welcome. Did you have a good ride up?"

"Good enough." Dexter patted his stomach. "Minconus was pleased last night when we told him we'd be visiting you and getting lunch at his new taberna."

Rogatus answered with a nod. Even though Dexter had said they'd visit him the last time he saw him, it still made little sense that a man he'd barely met would ride for hours just to join him for lunch.

"It's not quite time to eat, so let me show you the fort while we wait."

Plantus raised an eyebrow. "We rode past some of what the extra two centuries Dexter had to send did to an infantry fort. We should both take a look at everything before we get our own ala assignments." He nudged Dexter. "Or maybe Dexter would rather have a repeat of a legate saying any man with an iota of common sense would know a cavalry fort needs to have housing for horses."

Plantus chuckled. "He has you to thank for that conversation."

Dexter flushed and looked away.

"No, he doesn't." Rogatus crossed his arms. Valentinus often accused him of things he didn't do in Deva, but he wouldn't put up with it here. "I told

156

the legate that a man who hadn't commanded cavalry before had no reason to know what had to be changed for an infantry fort to house five hundred cavalry. He listened, and I thought he agreed."

Dexter directed a scathing look at Plantus before giving Rogatus a friendly smile. "I appreciate your effort on my behalf, even if the legate made a point of it in front of everyone. He was telling all of us about things we could do better to earn his favorable recommendation for the next posting." The smile he directed at Plantus held no warmth. "He made some comments about your deficiencies, too."

A fleeting scowl darkened Plantus's countenance. He flipped it into a fake smile almost before Rogatus saw it. What had looked like friendship in Eboracum maybe wasn't. But like Narina with him and Sulio, he could try to be a peacemaker.

"There's not a legate alive who doesn't find something to criticize about his tribunes. They're supposed to ready us for the next command, and hearing what's wrong helps us do what's right the next time."

The tension between the two faded as they nodded.

"Soldier." With a curve of his fingers, he summoned the man cleaning Boreas's stall. "Go to the Taberna Lucani and tell them I'll be bringing two men with me in about a half hour."

The cavalryman saluted and left the stable.

Palm up, he directed them toward the road. "Let me show you some parts of the fort that an ala needs so you'll both know when you get one. I learned what I needed for horsemen from one of my equitata cavalry centurions. Without him, I wouldn't have had as successful a command there, and I'd be trying to figure out what to do now."

Dexter tipped his head back before giving his fellow tribune a condescending smile. "Plantus knows even less about cavalry than I do, so do inform us."

"This way." Rogatus led them to the road that ran to the right of the headquarters building. "It shouldn't take more than a half an hour to see how an ala fort differs from the cohort forts you commanded in your first postings."

Dexter lengthened his step to walk at Rogatus's side. "So, now that you've been here over a week, is commanding an ala as good as you expected it to be?"

Rogatus let a natural grin leak out. "Even better. And thanks to Minconus, I'm eating better than in Deva. Even better than in Eburacum."

"We'll be the judge of that." Plantus patted his stomach. "And I'm ready to start judging."

They passed the row of rooms that served as the fort's hospital, and as they walked toward the workshops, relief flooded Rogatus. It was so much better being a man in charge of an isolated garrison than a legionary tribune where even men who seemed to be friends were competitors who enjoyed another's discomfort. Maybe the Ninth Legion was no better than the Twentieth after all.

Narina's taberna, lunchtime of Day 16

When they reached the taberna, Rogatus rang the triangle and directed them toward his usual table. He grabbed a stool, leaving them to take the chairs, and set it on the side where he could watch the storeroom.

When Narina emerged, she wore her usual smile of greeting.

"Narina, these"—he held his upturned palm to one, then the other—"are Cornelius Dexter and Pomponius Plantus, tribunes from the Ninth Legion. They rode half a day to try out Minconus's new taberna. I've told them they won't be disappointed."

She stood across the table from him, hands clasped at her waist. "Welcome to the Taberna Lucani. We're serving one of the prefect's favorites today, and I think you'll find it worth the ride."

"I agree." Rogatus smiled up at her. "Bring us three servings and some mead."

"With pleasure, Prefect." After offering another smile to all of them, she disappeared into the storeroom.

Dexter leaned back in his chair. "Minconus's standards are much lower for this taberna than for the one in Eboracum. Only two chairs and a serving girl who borders on ugly."

Rogatus clasped his hands and leaned on the table. "What she lacks in beauty she makes up in gracious hospitality. And the food is even better. The cook in Eboracum is using the recipes of the one here, and the one here keeps surprising me with new dishes that are fit for a senator's banquet."

"But wouldn't you like a better-looking woman to serve you?" One corner of Plantus's mouth lifted. "I'd expect you to be as picky about women as you are about horses. Minconus should send one of the pretty ones up from Eboracum to replace her if he wants to keep Roman customers."

A headshake was Rogatus's first answer. "She doesn't belong to Minconus. She's his sister and part owner of this place. She's getting it started as a favor for her brother, and she's in charge of everything right now."

He tightened his lips to stop the appreciative smile that thinking of her often inspired. "She's also the one who trained both my horses. She may not be a beauty, but any man who sees her ride couldn't forget her."

"Maybe it doesn't matter what her face looks like. In the dark, all horses are gray." Plantus chuckled at his own joke. "The plainest ones are grateful to any man who treats them like they're desirable." Plantus tapped Rogatus's upper arm. "You're handsome enough any woman should feel honored by your attention."

Rogatus's jaw clenched, but only for a moment. They didn't need to know that an insult to her offended him, too. "Don't even joke about that. Narina is the niece of the local chieftain. If any soldier so much as touched her, that would give tribal hotheads the excuse of seeking justice for one of their women who'd been wronged. And I'd be left with trying to settle it down without it turning into full-scale rebellion and war. Remember what happened with Boudicca and her daughters?"

Plantus's lustful grin faded.

"The legate told us some history of the province when we first arrived." Dexter traced a cut in the tabletop. "Surely, they aren't that concerned about their brothel women. There is one out here, isn't there?"

"Not that I've seen." Rogatus shrugged.

Truth be told, he hadn't looked. That was an expensive waste that had no place in his budget.

Plantus whistled. "So, this is a hardship posting." He leaned over to slap Rogatus's arm. "Next time you're in Eboracum, we can go to the best one."

Rogatus nodded once without answering. Dinner and conversation with Narina was better than time spent with a woman for hire. Besides, being with her cost him nothing more than the dinner he'd eat anyway. But he'd willingly pay twice as much if she wanted to charge it.

◆

In the storeroom, every word they spoke reached Narina's ears. With what she'd just heard, she'd rather they hadn't. Bordered on ugly—she knew it was true, but it still hurt to hear it. Not because the stranger said it, but the way Rogatus agreed that she was no beauty.

But he did say her gracious hospitality made up for it. That restored her smile. She couldn't change how she looked, but making people feel welcome was both good for business and the way God wanted her to treat other people.

She filled the third cup and placed it on the tray with the others.

His friend was right that Rogatus was a handsome man, one who could attract any woman he wanted. He attracted her, even though she shouldn't let him. That he seemed to want her seemed strange. But the way he looked at her sometimes made her almost feel pretty. And Sulio was worried that he found her too attractive, even as plain as she was.

Mentally she shook herself. It didn't matter what any man who wasn't a Christian thought. That was the only kind she wanted, and she hadn't yet met a man who could meet that requirement. She sighed. Certainly not a Roman prefect, even if he overlooked her plain face and liked her company.

Veldicca joined her with three soup bowls and a plate of rolls.

Narina held up her hand, then placed a finger against her lips.

Rogatus was telling his friends who she was and that anyone hurting her could start a rebellion. It probably wouldn't, but it could provoke the hot-headed ones like Albiso to do something stupid to avenge her.

A slight smile curved Veldicca's lips as she raised her eyebrows.

Narina whispered in her friend's ear. "We heard it from his own mouth. Sulio doesn't have to worry about what Rogatus might do with me because he thinks it could start a rebellion. He'd never risk that, so I couldn't be safer."

With a roll of her eyes and a barely suppressed grin, Veldicca whispered back. "Even if it wouldn't, I'd never expect him to treat you like that. I still say your father would have approved of him." She tipped her head her head toward the dining room. "Heard enough?"

Narina scooped up her tray of drinks and nodded.

Veldicca put on her friendliest smile and strode into the dining room.

As Narina followed, she did the same. Maybe it was better not being a woman that men's eyes would follow. That kind of beauty faded so fast. Having the inner beauty that came from loving God and living to please Him was much better than the beauty of face and form that only lasted for a season.

If she ever met the right man for her, he would agree.

Evening of Day 16

The sun had set behind the hills, and dusk would soon turn to darkness. Narina stood in the taberna doorway, arms crossed, as she gazed down the street toward the fort.

Rogatus wasn't coming tonight. But why?

She stepped back inside and slid the bolt into its catch plate. It should have been the most profitable day yet with him buying three lunches and then a dinner, maybe even three if his friends spent the night.

But he'd neither come nor sent word that he wouldn't be there. And even though that shouldn't disappoint her so much, it did.

He was often busy at lunchtime now. But even when he'd eaten dinner with the garrison, he'd dropped by, like he was checking to see she was all right. Had something happened with his friends that made him decide not to come see her?

With a sigh, she lowered the bar into its brackets.

"No Rogatus tonight?"

She spun at Sulio's words behind her and placed her hand over her heart. "You startled me."

"Sorry. I know I'm late tonight, but I didn't want him to think I'd given up protecting you. Veldicca said he never showed for dinner."

A satisfied smile curved his lips. "Maybe he's finally getting the message that you're not for him."

She rolled her eyes. "He doesn't think I'm for him now, and he's not going to. He's often not here for a midday meal, but he brought two other tribunes with him for lunch today. They rode up from Eboracum to visit. Minconus serves them often, and they wanted to try his new taberna." She massaged her palm. "Rogatus might be with them this evening."

Sulio lowered himself into the chair Rogatus always used. "The last thing we want is more tribunes in Isurium. Veldicca said you waited on dinner to see if he came, so I asked her to bring something for you and me."

He leaned back and crossed his arms. "Atto hadn't eaten Rogatus's share yet, so she said there was enough."

"There's always enough for you. We could have split mine if that was all that was left." She settled in across from him.

Sulio tipped his head toward the storeroom doorway. "Lucania was saying she wished he'd come so she could be growing her dowry." His nose twitched. "She thinks he's a nice man."

He picked at his thumbnail. "But I warned her again to be careful. She shouldn't be getting too friendly with him. Romans aren't safe around Brigantian women, and she'll be one soon enough. A very pretty one. And with her looking Roman like her mother, she might tempt him."

As he turned his gaze on her again, his smile vanished. "She laughed. She said he doesn't care about pretty. It's you he comes to talk with, even though he's nice to her and Veldicca, too."

He leaned forward and rested his crossed arms on the tabletop. "Talking with him every night…it's foolhardy. I see how he looks at you now. What is he going to do if you keep encouraging him?"

She tightened her lips. "I'm not encouraging him. I'm no nicer to him than I am to everyone else."

With upturned palm, she swept the empty room with her hand. "He didn't come tonight, so clearly he can resist my charms."

She drew a deep breath. He made that clear when he talked with his friends. But how much should she tell Sulio?

"After I greeted his friends at lunch and went to draw some mead, one of them said I bordered on ugly. He agreed that I wasn't a beauty, and then he told them I was niece to a chieftain. He said any Roman who did anything to me could start a rebellion, and we know he doesn't want that. So, I think you can stop worrying about him doing something to hurt me."

A black scowl darkened Sulio's face as he cursed. "You don't border on ugly, and if I'd heard an arrogant Roman dog say that, I would have told him to apologize. I wouldn't have agreed like Rogatus did."

She rested her hand on his arm. "I have Mother's mirror. It doesn't lie. He's right that I'm not a beauty, but I don't need him or any other man to think I am. Only what God thinks matters, and in His eyes, I'm beautiful."

Sulio laid his hand atop hers. "I doubt any god thinks much about people like us, not even yours. But I think you're as fine a woman as the best in the clan, no matter what you look like. Whatever any Roman thinks…that means less than nothing."

Voices grew louder as Veldicca and Lucania approached the storeroom. They entered with two bowls on the tray, and Veldicca placed them before her and Sulio before they both took the stools to join the conversation.

Narina wasn't sorry. Surrounded by the people who loved her, what a handsome Roman tribune thought mattered less, even though she found herself missing him.

She squeezed the back of her neck. It was odd how quickly she'd grown to care about him, but only as a friend.

She'd been asking God to keep him from wanting more than friendship from her, anyway. So, why did God answering that prayer prick her heart?

Chapter 26

A Celebration?

Narina's taberna, midday of Day 17

When the triangle rang before its usual time, Narina swept the thin-ly sliced carrots from the cutting board into the soup pot. Rogatus had a particular way of moving the rod, and she smiled at the sound. After last night, she hadn't been sure when she'd see him again.

Thank You, God, that he's coming again. We need him here. She drew a deep breath.

Minconus wanted him to come and buy a meal every day. But it was more than that for her. She wanted him to come whether he spent money or not.

She nibbled her lip. Would he be alone or with the men who thought her too plain to serve Romans?

Veldicca nudged her. "It looks like Sulio was wrong about convincing your prefect to stay away."

"Good. We need him to come every day and to start bringing some of his decurions with him." She returned knife and cutting board to the counter. "And Lucania needs our first Brittonic student to build her dowry."

She pushed a strand of hair behind her ear. She'd been showing Lucania some fancier braids this morning, like Mother had once shown her. Her sister wanted to practice them, so she'd made a tiny braid on each side and clipped them together at the back to hold Narina's hair off her face.

Lucania said it made her look less ordinary. But her little sister had paused before saying the last word. She'd probably thought "homely" and changed it at the last moment. If his friends were still with him, would they think the same? Would they say anything if they did?

"I'll find out what he wants." She took a step toward the courtyard before looking back over her shoulder. "And he's not my prefect."

She entered the dining room to find Rogatus's helmet on the table and

163

him looking out the window. He turned, and the smile that made his handsome face even better looking greeted her.

He crossed the room to stand before her. "I want to offer my apology. I meant to dine with you last night, but I was prevented."

"None needed. You hadn't said you would. You missed a new dish, but Veldicca will make it again for you."

"My apology is not for missing Veldicca's delicious cooking." He glanced away as he rubbed his jaw. Then his gaze focused on her again. "For what Dexter and Plantus said. I didn't expect them to insult you like that. In the storeroom, I suspect you heard every word."

There was no good reason to blush, but she felt her ears warm.

"It's not the first time I've been called that." She shrugged. "Since it's true, it won't be the last."

"Only a small-minded man judges by what someone cannot help." He looked away again, then back at her. "Being of the noble orders can blind a man to how words and actions can hurt someone. Arrogance doesn't become the rich anymore than it does a slave."

It was all she could do not to stare at him. She hadn't met an equestrian yet who didn't think himself more important than she was. Most made sure she knew it.

"Pride can lead us into many evils. I suppose when you've spent your life being told you're special, anyone could come to believe it."

He took a step toward her. "But some people are special. Not for how they look, but for how they make a man feel."

She opened her mouth, but no words came.

The approval in Rogatus's eyes and his slowly growing smile brought heat to her ears again.

She cleared her throat and moved away from him. "Please take a seat. What would you like today?"

He settled into his chair. "My usual, and that includes some conversation. It's the best part of eating here."

She scrunched her nose. "I won't tell Veldicca that. She thinks you come for her scrumptious food."

"I do enjoy it, but garrison food isn't the worst I've had. I ate it most of the time in Deva."

She barely kept her eyebrows from rising. The tribunes of the Ninth didn't eat it. Minconus had counted on that when opening this taberna. So why had he?

"Dexter and Plantus should be commanding an ala soon. When we left here, they saw a turma drilling in the field south of the addition. Dexter wanted to watch some drills while I explained the purpose of each."

"Has he seen what Zephyrus can do?"

"Not yet. He should have seen the legion cavalry training in Eboracum, but maybe they don't practice near the fortress." A crooked smile tugged at his lips. "If he saw you riding, he'd be impressed."

Rogatus pointed at her chair and shifted the helmet out of their way. "He oversaw the century that was at this fort. The legate of the Ninth has already questioned his common sense for not knowing an ala fort must be able to house five hundred horses with their riders so they can mount and leave at a moment's notice. He needs to change that perception before the legate decides whether to recommend Dexter's promotion to his final command. And Dexter wants to know more before he risks showing his ignorance to the legate to whom that ala reports."

He fingered a cut in the tabletop. "So, I explained a few things. Then I told them their decurions would know how everything should be handled wherever they're posted. If asked, their junior officers would be glad to teach them. It's how I learned. Two of my centurions took me under their wings. One was a cavalry centurion like your father. I owe much of my success to them."

"Father always liked to teach, too."

How many times had Father calmly told her and her brothers how to do something better? She'd always listened, but her brothers…they mostly did, too.

He ran his hand along the horsehair crest. "By the time I finished, it was too late for them to ride home before dark. So, I invited them to dine with my garrison and talk with my decurions. Germanus and Adolphus would answer many of their questions, including things I hadn't thought to tell them. Plantus agreed it was a good idea. So, they stayed until this morning."

He rested his forearms on the table and leaned toward her. "But I would have preferred Veldicca's stew and your company. I prepared a list of words for this evening before I retired last night. I'll be back to learn more at dinnertime."

She slid her chair back and rose. "Then I'd better get your soup. And I'll let Veldicca know you'll be coming so she can plan something special."

She turned at the footsteps behind her.

Atto walked toward her with a large sack in his arms. "We might be getting some Brigantian customers soon."

"Why do you think that?"

He set the sack on the other table. "People are talking in the market about a small early harvest festival here and plans for a bigger one with several clans later. Bellicus invited the chieftains of some other clans to meet here to talk about it in two days."

From the corner of her eye, she saw Rogatus straighten. "How many are coming?"

Atto shrugged. "I don't know, but all the nearby ones were invited."

The prefect's eyes veiled. "Is it common to celebrate harvest together?"

"It's the first time I've seen it." After scooping up the produce sack, Atto carried it into the storeroom.

When Narina turned to face Rogatus again, she saw the face of a soldier, not a friend.

He rubbed his chin. "Do the other chieftains ask Bellicus to their celebrations?"

"I don't know. If he's gone, it's not on the day that Isurium celebrates. He's always here for the local rites and the feasting afterwards."

Her heart rate rose. Celebrating anything together—that wasn't something the clans usually did. But did it mean anything?

Rogatus leaned back and crossed his arms. "Fortuna smiled when I decided to eat lunch here today. This festival presents an opportunity to meet many of the other chieftains who live near your clan."

She blew out a slow breath. She should warn him, but would he listen? "It might not be wise to attend the festivities or to let any of your men attend. Often our men drink too much, and when drink goes in, sense leaks out. Someone might be tempted to challenge you being there, and it could turn into a fight between them and your men."

"Hmmm." He squeezed the back of his neck. "Perhaps it would be better to meet the chieftains at the council house with Bellicus to introduce me."

"You can ask Uncle, but the answer might be no. He shouldn't let it appear that you and he are friends."

Rogatus's snort ended with a wry smile. "I don't think there's any risk of that. At our last meeting, he was civil but not welcoming. I expect more of the same. We agreed that it was best for everyone if his men didn't do anything that would break the peace, and that was all. But even two enemies can do introductions. His fellow chieftains would see that we are acquaintances who respect each other and nothing more. It would give them an opportunity to become the same."

She traced a long scratch on the table. There had never been a joint harvest celebration since Father moved back from Moesia. Why had Uncle suddenly decided this was a good thing to do? Father always said his brother knew how to play power politics with his fellow chieftains and was a leader among them. Was this just an excuse for getting the leaders together for another reason?

Sulio would know, but would he tell her? And if he did, would he ask her to swear that she wouldn't tell the Roman officer he neither trusted nor liked?

"Some of them might not want to meet you, and forcing a meeting would only make them less likely to want to have anything to do with you in the future."

"A point well taken." His brows lowered, then relaxed. "But I can ask Bellicus to let them know I would be honored to meet with any of them who would like to meet while they're here."

"I suppose that won't hurt as long as they could decide whether they met you."

"I'll ask him to make sure they know that." A single nod declared his determination to do it.

"Atto!" Rogatus's call was loud enough to be heard in the courtyard.

Within moments, Atto stuck his head into the room. "Yes?"

"Is Bellicus in town?"

"I saw him with his sons going into the council house. They left their horses at the stable, so they might be staying a while."

"I want to catch him before they leave. So, if you'll excuse me…" Rogatus rose.

"Of course." She stood as well. "Lucania and I will be ready this evening. It's always a pleasure to see you."

◆

"As it is to see you." Rogatus placed the helmet on his head and strode out the door.

Bellicus might not stay long at the council house, and if he hurried, he shouldn't miss him.

Germanus had found two soldiers who spoke Brittonic well. As he passed through the gate, he told one of the guards which turmas they were in and sent him to tell them to mount up and meet him at the fort stable immediately. He would have Boreas saddled and be waiting for them.

Less than a quarter hour passed before the three of them rode up to the council house. He left them with Boreas after telling them to listen without letting anyone know they understood. Alone, he entered the council house and strode through the empty hall to Bellicus's office.

He knocked on the doorframe and waited.

Albiso stood at his father's right hand, glaring at him, hand on his knife. Sulio moved behind his father's left shoulder, and crossed his arms.

Bellicus slipped the wooden sheet he'd been reading under a stack of others. "What do you want this time?"

Rogatus approached the table and stopped three feet short of it. "Something that I believe will benefit both of us. I heard that you are planning a harvest festival, and some of the area chieftains will be joining you in the celebration. While they are here, I would like to meet them and discuss the mutual benefit of peaceful relations, as you and I have done."

"Hmph." Bellicus raised an eyebrow. "Peaceful relations, you say. Some might say Roman peace comes at the price of a Briton's freedom." He looked down his nose at Rogatus. "But I do not find your request unreasonable. However, I will have to discuss with them whether they want to meet with you. I cannot commit them. We Brigantes are a federation of clans, and each chieftain makes his own decisions about what they tell their men to do."

"I understand. That is why I am making this request to you before any arrive for the festival."

"And I accept the request. But if it's peace you want…" With thumb and middle finger, Bellicus smoothed the mustache that drooped on each side of his mouth. "You and your troops won't be welcomed by many who come to celebrate. I advise you to keep your men inside your fort while the clans gather."

"Your niece has already explained that to me. As long as the gathering is peaceful, my men will have no need to come near your celebration."

What he was about to suggest could be dangerous, but ensuring peace was worth the risk. "I'm willing to come alone and out of uniform for the meetings."

Bellicus's guffaw echoed in the room. "I would not have taken you for a fool who cannot understand risk."

Rogatus combined a wry smile with a shrug, as he'd often seen Sulio do. "Is any risk too great if it achieves our mutual goal of peace?"

Any trace of humor vanished from Bellicus's face. "Red crest or not, you look as Roman as you are, and some who have drunk too much could not resist challenging a lone Roman, uniform or not."

Sulio moved forward until his thighs pressed against the table. "He wouldn't have to come alone. I would be willing to escort him from Narinas's taberna and take him back if anyone wants to meet him."

"And I would gladly accept your escort." Rogatus tipped his head to Sulio. "Thank you for the offer."

He turned his gaze back on Bellicus. "Would that be acceptable to the chieftains?"

Bellicus watched him in silence. Finally, a wry smile lifted the corner of Bellicus's mouth. "Whether it will be, only they know. But if you are willing to take that risk, I will extend your invitations."

"Thank you. I'll look forward to hearing what they answer." After slowly moving his left fist to his chest, Rogatus made a parade turn and left the room.

◆

Sulio followed Rogatus to the chamber door and watched until he left the building.

The prefect had requested Father's help instead of demanding it. The last thing he expected from a Roman officer was that kind of respect toward any Briton, chieftain or not.

He jumped when Albiso hit his upper arm with the back of his hand.

"How dare you let that Roman dog think he would be welcome at a meeting of our chieftains? They're only coming so we can figure out why a battle group like his replaced a small garrison that was here to make the Roman road safer from bandits. You know we'll be discussing what to do about that, and letting him come where he might overhear something is stupid."

He hit Sulio again. "You shouldn't have offered to keep him safe so he'd think it was a good idea to come up here to talk with anyone."

When Albiso pulled his hand back to hit him one more time, Sulio caught his wrist midair and jerked his brother's arm down.

"If we want to get that ala out of Isurium, the only thing that will make it leave is if the legate of the Ninth Legion orders it out. That's only going to happen if he's convinced we'll stay peaceful under Roman rule. You should have listened to Uncle Lucanus. You can destroy one Roman army, and they just move a new one in to finish what the first one started. Father is right to be telling us not to start anything. Our women and children will keep paying for it long after we're dead."

He released Albiso's wrist. "You'd better hope nothing happens to Rogatus until things settle down. Any other officer would be demanding, not asking, and he'd use his troops to make sure we did what he demanded."

"Stop it." Their father's growl turned both of them to face him. "I am more than willing to ask the others if they will talk with him. I hope most will. Maybe the hotheaded ones will finally listen to what I've been telling them for years. We don't want to start a fight with Rome that we can never win."

He pointed at Albiso. "And you had better not be saying or doing anything that will give the Romans an excuse to come after us. This Rogatus thinks before he acts, and he asks before he demands. We can live with the ala while he's in command."

"Yes, Father." Albiso spoke the words, but one glance at his eyes told Sulio he didn't mean them.

"If you don't need me, I'll leave now."

With a flick of his fingers, Father dismissed his angry son. After the great hall door opened and closed, he turned to Sulio. "I won't be long finishing this. Catch up with your brother and keep him from saying or doing something he shouldn't. I'll meet you two at our usual taberna shortly."

"Yes, Father." Sulio tipped his head and strode into the meeting hall.

He would try to keep Albiso from doing anything stupid, but if his brother refused to listen, how could he succeed?

Chapter 27

Worth the Risk

Narina's taberna, evening of Day 17

The sun had not yet slipped behind the hills when Rogatus rang the triangle, but it soon would. He was later than he'd wanted, but even a short conversation was enough to make a good day even better.

He'd already seated himself and hung the satchel with his word list on the back of the chair when Narina entered the dining room.

"Welcome, Prefect. How did your meeting go?"

He spread his arms and made a point of scanning the room. "It's no one but us here."

"You're right. It's Rogatus while that's true." She settled into her usual chair. "So, did it go well?"

"It did." He rubbed his palms together. "Bellicus agreed to extend my invitation to meet with the other chieftains, but he was skeptical that any would want to."

"I warned you that might be the case, but at least he's going to ask them."

He moved his helmet to the side and out of their way. "And that's half the battle." He patted the satchel. "I brought my words from last night, but I have something more pressing to learn. Can you teach me how to offer a greeting in Brittonic that a chieftain would consider appropriate?"

She sucked air through her teeth. "I'm not sure what to tell you. I've never been where I heard one chieftain greeting another. I'm not even sure what someone of the clan who's meeting Uncle for the first time would say."

Heavy footsteps in the storeroom drew Rogatus's gaze and turned into Sulio. "Veldicca said you hadn't eaten, so I'll join you tonight."

He grabbed a stool and claimed his spot between them.

Rogatus let a slow smile form. "You're just the man I need to answer a question."

Sulio squinted at him. "What question?"

"How does a Brigantian chieftain greet another chieftain he doesn't know well?"

"That's easy." He rattled off Brittonic words too fast for Rogatus to catch all of them. But he did hear the word servant, and that seemed odd.

Narina slapped Sulio's arm. "You know very well no chieftain would tell another chieftain he was his servant. The prefect doesn't want to insult them, and he doesn't want to tell them they can tell him what to do. He needs something that a powerful man would say to his equal."

Sulio shrugged. "Then he should stick to Latin. They all know it well enough." He tipped his head back and scratched under his chin. "The way you introduced yourself to Father should work well enough for any who want to talk with you. Anything you say in any language will offend the ones who don't want to meet you."

"I expect that." Rogatus leaned back in his chair and crossed his arms. "I've never spoken with your brother, but we don't need to exchange words for me to know what he thinks. You don't approve of me being here any more than he does, but at least you're willing to talk to me. I respect you for that. I appreciate your honesty, too." He didn't even try to stop the wry smile. "And sometimes your sense of humor."

He clasped his hands and leaned on the tabletop. "Your father…he's a man whose respect is worth earning. I hope there are others among the chieftains who care as much about the welfare of their clans as he does."

Sulio's brow furrowed, but he said nothing.

With a tray holding stew for three, Veldicca entered the dining room. Her gaze bounced between him and Sulio, and her lips straightened. Then her usual smile returned.

"I think you'll all love this one tonight. I changed one of Narina's favorites a little, and I think it made it better. But you can tell me after you eat if I should do that again."

She set a bowl in front of each.

Narina cleared her throat. "The prefect and I usually eat without talking, then chat for a while. Let's do that tonight."

"As you wish, Narina." Rogatus drew the bowl closer and picked up a spoon.

Perhaps it was best to stop talking for a while. Bellicus was a man who thought before he spoke or acted. Albiso seemed like a hotheaded fool. What Sulio was…he'd made the offer to provide escort if the chieftains would meet with him. That took courage since the Albisos of the clans wouldn't like that.

But if words failed and the time for action came, would the second son still choose the way of his father over that of his brother?

Narina's taberna, midday of Day 18

Narina sat in Rogatus's chair, elbows on the table and forehead resting on her clasped hands. Veldicca's soup had been ready for almost an hour, and he still hadn't come.

Today was the last day before the festival, and she needed to warn him. Atto had gone to the market in Isurium. He returned with news that several chieftains had come for Uncle's festival, and most brought a dozen or more young would-be warriors with them.

Maybe it was only talk, like Albiso was prone to do, but Atto had heard too many mumbling about what should be done to the Romans who went where they weren't wanted. That promised trouble before the last of them went home in two days.

She closed her eyes.

God, where is the prefect? I don't want him coming here tonight if it puts him in danger. If he comes for lunch, I can warn him. But what if he doesn't? What am I supposed to do?

"Narina?"

She jerked back as she opened her eyes. The man himself stood across the table from her. How had she not heard him come in?

"Are you all right?" Quiet words spoken with concern.

"I am now that you're here."

Her hand flew to cover her mouth. His eyes warmed as her favorite of his smiles appeared. Why had she used words that could seem like she wanted more that his business and a casual friendship?

He seated himself in her usual chair and placed his helmet to the side. "I was discussing tomorrow with my decurions and lost track of time."

She leaned back in the chair he always used. With its clear view of both front door and storeroom entrance, no wonder a cautious man in hostile territory chose it. "That's what I've been waiting to talk with you about. Atto went for supplies, and he said there were already dozens of strange tribesmen in Isurium. Even more will be arriving this afternoon for tomorrow's festival."

She clasped her hands again and rested her chin on them. "Of course, you're always welcome when you come, but it might not be wise to come alone for dinner or at any time during the celebration. We might get out first Brigantian customers, and I'm afraid they won't like sharing the dining room with you."

His smile had faded, and serious eyes proclaimed him the officer of Rome, not the man who'd become her friend. But even if he didn't like what she said, she wasn't through.

"Maybe it would even be best to stay away at lunchtime the day after until all the visitors leave. With the Brigantes, words often end with fists, and if others join in…"

With crossed arms, he leaned on the tabletop. "Is that for my safety or yours? If mine, you don't need to worry about that. If yours, then I don't want to put you and your people in danger."

"For yours."

His intense gaze caught and held hers. Heat spread across her face. Why did this man make her blush so easily?

He settled back in his chair. "I'm hoping to do something much riskier than walk from the fort to the taberna for dinner. Bellicus will be extending my invitation to the chieftains who are coming. If any of them agree to meet with me, Sulio will be escorting me to the council house without my armor to do that."

Narina's hand flew up to cover her mouth. "But that puts both of you in danger."

"It surprised me when he suggested it, but I truly appreciate it. He's like his father, wanting what's best for protecting the clan, and brave enough to do something about it. He should be the next chieftain. Too bad he's not the oldest."

"Being chieftain doesn't have to pass to the oldest. It's just that it usually does. But it's not as rigid as how the oldest Roman son always becomes the new paterfamilias. Minconus is my oldest brother, and Father made him my guardian. But I think he would have done that even if he was second-born. He's wiser in money matters than Dubnus." She traced the carved R like he often did. "Are you the firstborn son?"

Rogatus stared at his hand as he rubbed his palm with his thumb. "No."

Why didn't he look in her eyes as he answered? Why did his whole body seem to tense at such a common question?

Trotting hoofbeats in the street turned Rogatus's face toward the doorway. A mounted soldier rode past. Then his gaze returned to her.

"I told Bellicus my men would have no need to come near his celebration as long as the gathering remains peaceful. But staying inside the fort would appear weak and cowardly to men wanting to challenge Rome's rule. Nothing is further from the truth, and it's best if anyone contemplating rebellion knows that. I'll keep my men out of the hilltop town if nothing gets out of control, but they will be doing what they normally do at the fort, including drills in the field next to it."

He pushed back from the table. "If some want to come watch the show, they are welcome to do it. The close-order drill of the turmas should convince anyone they don't want to face them in battle."

As he rose, he donned his helmet. "That was a courier from the legate. I need to go find out why he's come." He smiled down at her as he fastened the chinstrap. "I'm not afraid to come tonight, but I'll eat at the garrison so no one who would take offense at you hosting me has a reason to threaten you. After Sulio escorts me back here tomorrow, perhaps the three of us can share one of Veldicca's creations."

"I hope so." She walked him to the door and leaned her shoulder against the inside surface as he stepped through. "Thank you for caring so much about keeping the peace here, even though many don't appreciate it."

"Doing what's right is reward enough in itself." He paused, and one corner of his mouth turned up. "But knowing you approve…that's important, too." His mouth twitched, and the smile vanished. "You be careful."

"I will."

As he strode toward the gatehouse, her gaze remained fixed upon him.

God, please protect Rogatus. Thank You for making him commander here. Bless his efforts to keep peace among us.

A deep sigh escaped. Veldicca was right. Father would have approved of the prefect. But as long as he didn't share her faith, he could never be the man for her.

Evening of Day 19

Rogatus slipped the scabbard strap over his head, then donned his helmet. It was not what he'd hoped to wear when he walked to Narina's taberna today, but what a man hoped for and what actually happened were often not the same.

He'd expected Sulio to come for him, so he watched his men drilling from the fort's wall-walk. From there, he could see the intricate maneuvers below him while watching for Sulio to come to her taberna. A few times, he'd seen small clusters of men watching from a distance. They lingered awhile before returning to the town, but none came closer than a quarter mile.

Wearing his armillae told his ala that he was an accomplished soldier. Drilling his horsemen told the watchers that he was prepared for action against the enemies of Roman rule.

As he told Bellicus, he'd planned to leave his armor in his chambers and join Sulio wearing his tunic with only a dagger. He had yet to see a Brigantian man without a knife, so it would seem strange if he had none. Sulio was supposed to send Atto for him at the fort, and he wanted to be ready to leave for the council house without delay.

But Sulio never came.

When he reached the gatehouse, Germanus stood, arms crossed, staring toward the town.

"Prefect." His second-in-command struck his chest. "I have the third and fourth turmas ready to ride if needed, but so far it looks peaceful up there."

"Keep two turmas on alert until midnight. If the drinking gets heavier when the sun goes down, there still might be a problem."

Germanus glanced at the gladius hanging at his side. "Going to dinner?"

Rogatus nodded. "The chieftain's son was going to escort me to the council house if any wanted to meet. If he shows up at the taberna tonight like he usually does, I might find out why he never came." He squared his shoulders. "I'll be back before dark."

One corner of Germanus's mouth turned up. "I'll have someone on the wall-walk watching for you…just in case."

With a nod and an appreciative smile, Rogatus strode out the gate. Dinner with Narina was always a pleasure, whether Sulio was there or not. But for the first time, he hoped her cousin came.

When he reached the taberna, the door was closed, but a gentle push with his hand opened it. He stepped inside and closed it before ringing the triangle.

As he settled in at his table, Narina came from the storeroom. But instead of coming straight to him, she first bolted the door.

After a disappointing day, satisfaction surged through him. She'd only left it open for him.

She came to the table but didn't sit. "I had Veldicca prepare one of your favorites in case you could join us. Atto stayed ready to go get you all day, but since Sulio never came…" She sighed. "I'm sorry."

She rested her fingertips on the back of his hand. "I'll go get our dinner."

Too bad she lifted her fingers after only a moment. It was the second time she'd touched him like that, and he wanted more.

She had barely disappeared through the doorway when Sulio stepped out of the storeroom.

Rogatus stopped the sigh before her cousin could hear it. He had wanted to speak with him, but not as much as he wanted to relax with only her across the table. She was the only person with whom he felt safe sharing his disappointment with the failed attempt to promote peace beyond the Isurium clan.

Something about her invited trust like no one he'd known before.

Sulio grabbed a stool and took his usual place to Rogatus's left. "I wondered if you'd come tonight after I didn't come today."

Rogatus gave him a fleeting smile. "I'm not easily discouraged. What happened?"

"None of the other clan leaders wanted to talk with you. When they learned that you were only the commander of the troops in Isurium and not in their territories, they saw no reason to talk with you. You probably don't want to hear their exact words." A short chuckle accompanied his usual shrug. "Some of the curses were quite creative, but I won't repeat what they said where a lady like Narina can hear."

"I regret they all felt that way. I had hoped some were as wise as your father about protecting their people from harm."

"Hmph." Sulio put his elbow on the table and rested his jaw on his palm. "I'm not surprised none wanted to be seen meeting with the enemy."

Rogatus's mouth curved down. "I'm not their enemy. I won't be unless they do something themselves that declares them to be one. I don't think of Bellicus as my enemy nor any of the men in your clan, even if your brother seems to think of me that way."

Sulio opened his mouth, then closed it without a word.

Narina returned with their mead and took her seat. "Veldicca will bring dinner shortly."

"I haven't eaten since breakfast, but even a man with a full stomach would welcome any chance to eat what she prepares." Rogatus turned his gaze on her cousin. "But I assume you shared in the feasting on the hill top."

He traced the rim of his cup with his middle finger. "What was done at the celebration?"

"I can't tell you." Sulio waved one finger back and forth. "The secret rites of the Brigantes are not something a Roman needs to know."

◆

Narina's brow furrowed. Before Father's death, she'd gone with him to each harvest celebration. Nothing involving a secret rite was part of it. So, if it wasn't for the open worship of the Brigantian gods that the chieftains gathered, what was it?

Before she could ask Sulio, Veldicca came with the tray of food.

Sulio lifted his cup of mead. "To eating in silence, the better to enjoy a great stew."

She stirred the stew, then lifted a still steaming spoonful to her lips. As she blew on it to cool it enough to eat, she watched Rogatus. He seemed unaware of the lie Sulio had just spoken. Should she press Sulio for the truth? Would he even tell her?

Did some other clans have rites they didn't want Romans to know about? Did her own clan? Rites that Father or Uncle Bellicus would never have told her about after she became a Christian at twelve. Rome claimed it had ended human sacrifice in Britannia, but had it?

She glanced at Rogatus and found him watching her. As he lifted a spoonful to his lips, he raised it enough to proclaim his pleasure in eating it…with her.

And even though Sulio would scold her for it later, she rewarded him with a smile.

Chapter 28

Cattle Thieves

Isurium, morning of Day 20

Rogatus was at the desk in his quarters when he heard trotting footsteps. One of the gate guards paused at the door to knock on the doorframe.

"Enter." Rogatus set down his stylus.

"Prefect." The man's fist hit his chest. "The cattle guards just returned. One is injured, and someone stole ten cattle last night."

Rogatus scrunched his face and rubbed his forehead. It had seemed too good to be true that so many Brigantian men could gather and nothing bad would happen.

"Tell Germanus and Adolphus to meet me at my headquarters office."

After another salute, the guard left.

Just like the raiders in Moesia, but here he had no one who would tell him who did it and where they took his cattle.

He squeezed the back of his neck. He could ask Sulio, but might her cousin be the one who told the thieves where the cattle would be?

Maybe not. They had been in that meadow since the ala came, and many from Bellicus's clan would know they were there.

And the thieves didn't have to be from Bellicus's clan. Almost anyone who came for the celebration could have seen where they were.

But with no evidence that pointed to any of the visitors, someone from the Isurium clan was probably responsible.

The deepest sigh drained his lungs. Someone to guide where he looked— if he didn't have that, how was he ever to get the cattle back?

That herd was only meant to feed his men, so he could easily buy replacements. But if he let someone steal his cattle, would they go after his horses next?

He rose and donned his bronze body armor. As he latched the final side clasp, he gritted his teeth.

At their first meeting, he'd told Bellicus of his desire to live peaceably with the clan. Bellicus had agreed that he wanted the same. But he also said he would keep telling the men of his clan to accept the Roman presence only as long as they did nothing to earn Brigantian anger.

With no choice but to ask Bellicus to turn over his cattle and the men who took them, he was about to do just that.

He draped the strap of his spatha scabbard across his chest. Afoot, he preferred the gladius. But on horseback, the half-foot-longer spatha gave the reach a cavalryman needed. With his helmet tucked under his arm, he headed for headquarters. His first and second decurions would be waiting for him to tell them what to do. He would meet with them first, then a visit to Narina was in order while Adolphus readied his turma for action.

From her, he needed two things. If Bellicus wasn't at the council house today, he'd need a guide to show him where her uncle's farm compound was. Atto should do for that.

The next was harder. He should ask her who was most likely to have stolen his herd. But even if she suspected someone, she might not reveal who they were.

She'd told him she was both Roman and Brigantian. But to which was she more loyal? If she helped him, would that put her in danger with the clan?

And if he forced her into that hard place of choosing, would she end their friendship before it grew into what he wanted it to be?

Narina stood at the kitchen counter, preparing to knead the dough that would become today's rolls for her best customer. Rogatus loved her usual recipe, but today she had substituted tarragon for the rosemary. She loved the variety, but would he?

"Narina."

She startled and spun to face the door. Rogatus stood there in full armor with a grim look on his face.

"I didn't mean to frighten you. But no one heard me knocking, and I need to speak with you right now."

Her hair was down, and she tucked some behind her ear before she remembered the flour on her fingers.

"You didn't. I just never expected you to come in where Sulio does." She reached for her hair again but stopped just in time. "What's so urgent that you have?"

She dusted the flour off her hands. "You look like something's wrong."

"Someone stole ten cattle from my herd after breaking the guard's arm and knocking him out." He drew a deep breath. "I'm going to Bellicus to demand the return of the cattle and the men responsible. I can't let theft from my herds go unpunished."

Her hand shot up to cover her mouth. "Oh, Rogatus. I'm so sorry."

He rubbed his palm with his thumb. "I was hoping to borrow Atto for a while. I need someone to show me where your uncle's farm is."

She lowered her hand to her chest. "There could be more than a dozen men at Bellicus's compound, and none of them would be pleased to see you there." She bit her lip. "You're not going alone, are you? And you shouldn't let anyone know Atto helped you."

His mouth twitched, as if what she'd said was funny. But the danger to him, to both of them, was real.

"I'm taking thirty soldiers with me to make sure nothing happens on the way. What happens after I get there will depend on what Bellicus does. But you shouldn't have to worry about Atto's safety. I'll send him back to you once he's shown us where the farmhouse is. No one needs to know that he guided us there."

He glanced away, then focused his eyes on her again. "I'm leaving Germanus in charge of the fort. If you need to, you can take all your people to him and ask to stay inside the fort until I return. He'll put you in my quarters. You'll all be safe there."

She stared at him. When had she become so important to him that he'd make that offer?

"I don't think that will be necessary. These are my people. I'm perfectly safe here. But I want you to let me know as soon as you get back so I won't worry about what happened."

His straight lips curved into his warmest smile.

She bit her lip. Without intending to, had she just told him he was as important to her?

"I need to know that Sulio, Albiso, and Uncle are all right."

His smile dimmed, and the warmth in those dark brown eyes cooled.

She hadn't mean to hurt him. Of course she cared about him, too. Sulio would be scolding her if he knew how much she'd grown to care.

"And after you come, I'll know that nothing bad happened to you, either." She pointed at the dough on the counter. "I'm making something different for you, and I hope you'll like it. I hope you'll be back in time for dinner to try it."

She lifted her hand to tidy her hair again before remembering the flour.

He moved closer and reached out to push back the hair that had fallen forward along her too-large jaw. He did it slowly, tracing an arc around her ear before lowering his hand.

She'd never known a man's touch could make her shiver.

He stepped back and cleared his throat. "I hunted raiders many times in Moesia. This is no different. I'm hoping Bellicus will help me resolve this quickly so only the ones who took my cattle are punished. I'll do my best to keep any of us from getting hurt."

She hugged herself. "I suppose that's all I can ask."

One quick nod, and he turned and strode out the door.

Oh, God! Please protect Sulio and Uncle and Albiso from Rogatus's men. But protect Rogatus, too.

She touched the place where his fingers had traced around her ear. Sulio was right. Rogatus liked her as a woman. A shiver coursed through her, and this time it wasn't from unexpected pleasure.

He was a Roman prefect, a man who served their god of war. The last kind of man she should consider for herself. And yet, she couldn't deny how fond she'd become of him. How much it would hurt if anything happened to him.

And the scary part was he'd grown to feel the same.

God, I know I should only want a man who loves you like I do. Rogatus will never be that. So, please let this go back to just friendship without me having to push him away.

Bellicus's farm, late morning of Day 20

With Adolphus leading the Second Turma, Rogatus stopped just short of the crest of a hill overlooking Bellicus's farm.

Then he turned to Atto, who rode beside him on Narina's mule. "Thank you for your help. You need to return to the taberna now. Cross the river on the old road by the fort. I don't want anyone who sees you to suspect you led us northeast of Isurium to Bellicus's farm. Do not tell anyone you brought us here."

Atto grinned like a youth of fifteen who only saw the adventure, not the danger of what they were doing.

"I'll be careful." He reined the mule away and rode back along the line of soldiers. Rogatus watched until the youth disappeared into the woods.

He dismounted and removed his helmet. After hanging it on one of the four horns of Boreas's saddle, he crept forward to survey the compound in the valley below. A helmetless Adolphus joined him.

"I think we don't want to ride in on their road to town." Rogatus pointed toward a narrower pathway that left the compound on the side opposite the wider road to Isurium. "We'll come in that way. It's a shorter distance to the house from where we'll leave the trees."

A fleeting smile accompanied Adolphus's quick nod. "A good plan, Prefect." He pointed at a path that ran along the base of the hill and into the trees. "It looks like that should lead where we want to go."

They slipped back to where the horses waited and remounted. With silent hand signals, Adolphus told the men to reform their column of twos and follow him down the hill to the path that might take them into danger.

When they rode into the compound, a woman ran into the main house.

Rogatus reined in before the porch. Adolphus faced away from the house, and the thirty men of the Second Turma fanned out into a half-circle behind Rogatus, each facing outward with a shield in his left hand and his right hand resting on his sword.

The door swung inward, and Bellicus stepped out to face him. "Why have you come here?"

His hand swept half the cavalrymen. Then he stood with legs spread, arms crossed, and a scowl on his face. "And why all these men?"

"You are chieftain of the Isurium clan, and we agreed it was important for the safety of all to keep your young men from doing something stupid."

Rogatus straightened in his saddle and rested his hand on his spatha's pommel. "But they have. Some men of your tribe are cattle thieves. One of my men had his arm broken before he was knocked out. I want the cattle returned and the ones involved turned over to me."

"Hmph." Bellicus's hand swept Rogatus's words aside. "You claim the ones who stole them are of my clan. You cannot know that. More than a dozen clans live close enough to be the raiders. The men who took your cattle could be from any of those. I have been telling my young men to ignore you Romans as much as possible. I know of none who are doing otherwise. So, what proof do you have that they are thieves?"

With chin raised, Rogatus met Bellicus's glare with a steady gaze.

"I don't know which men did it. That is why I have come to you first. I want to make certain the guilty are punished as an example for others who might think about stealing from the Ala Tungrorum. I have no desire to punish the innocent just so I can tell the legate of the Ninth Legion that someone paid for their theft."

Bellicus recrossed his arms. "I will remind my own men that they are not to do anything against your ala's herds. But the loss of ten cattle"—he shrugged—"what is that for an empire that rules so much of the world? It is best for both sides to let sleeping dogs lie."

Rogatus's jaw twitched. "Neither you nor I want to unleash the dogs of war. I would prefer we settle this quickly between ourselves before the legion must get involved. I doubt they would take the time to find out who is really guilty and stop with punishing only those. The totem animal for the Ninth is the bull. The men of the Brigantes would be wise to consider what can happen if they anger one and then stand in its way."

He relaxed in the saddle. "I know several chieftains with their escorts came to your festival. Many had opportunity to see my herds. Perhaps the thieves are not of your clan." His hand dropped away from his sword to rest on his thigh. "But you are a leader among the chieftains. So, I ask you to pass my demand on to them and urge them to tell their young men to make wiser choices. I am asking you to make it clear to them that I'm not looking for trouble, and it would be to the benefit of all if they would keep their men from starting any."

He donned a grim expression as he shook his head. "But I cannot let an attack on my men and the stealing of my cattle pass as if nothing happened. I want my cattle back, and I must punish the ones who hurt my herder. But I want to be certain I am punishing the guilty, not the innocent."

With thumb and middle finger, Bellicus smoothed the mustache that hung along both sides of his mouth. "I will pass on your message, but I can give no promise of what that might cause. What you demand will be seen as a threat, and the Brigantes do not back down from a threat."

Rogatus blew a quick breath through his nose. "It is not a threat. It is a promise that I will act if my stolen animals are not returned and the guilty ones punished."

He tapped his own chest with his index finger before pointing it at Bellicus. "We both understand the difference between influence and authority, and I believe you are a leader whose influence reaches far beyond those under your authority. I hope other chieftains are as wise as you in putting what is best for all their people first. And even though none chose to meet me when you hosted the gathering here, I am always willing to meet with men who are as concerned about the future of their clans as you are."

Bellicus's scowl relaxed into a frown, and he shrugged. "It would take a few days for your message to reach all of them. And you should know that young men act impulsively without consulting their chieftains. Most of us are not like you as a commander who can give orders that they must obey without question or die."

A single quick nod was Rogatus's reply. "I am willing to wait for you to speak with the others, but I want an answer within a week."

"I will see what I can do." Bellicus tucked his thumbs in his belt and tapped his stomach with his fingers.

"I thank you for your help in keeping the peace. It is in the best interest of all of us."

Rogatus slowly moved his left fist to his chest and nodded once before turning Boreas toward the main road to town and nudging him into a trot.

Adolphus fell in beside him as he passed, and the turma formed a column of twos behind them with each horse peeling away from its quarter-circle position to pair with its match, like couples in a dance.

When they entered the trees that blocked the view of the compound, Adolphus turned toward Rogatus. "Masterfully played, Prefect."

Rogatus accepted the compliment with a nod and a quick smile. "Now we wait to see if Bellicus can deliver. It might not be over yet."

He quickened the trot. In Moesia, he'd excelled at the strategic boardgames of tabula and latrunculi. He'd challenged his centurions to play without betting, only for the honor of winning. They didn't know that his savings goal didn't permit gambling losses. They'd thought it strange, but they'd enjoyed the games as much as he had.

But this negotiation with Bellicus was no game. If he got what he demanded, they both won. And if he didn't…too many innocents might be the losers.

◆

Sulio wanted to stand beside his father confronting Rogatus, but Father had ordered him and Albiso to remain inside out of sight. But he'd grabbed his hunting bow and quiver of arrows before standing against the wall just inside the door. From there, he heard every word and suspected every concealed emotion those words conveyed.

Albiso stood across the door from him, fingering his knife, obeying the command but fuming.

The rhythmic thuds of trotting hooves hadn't faded to silence when Father entered the house and slammed the door.

Many times Sulio had heard Father curse, but his eyes widened at the passion behind each word. Everything was directed, not at the Romans who'd invaded their compound, but at whoever put the whole clan at risk for a few head of cattle.

When the tirade ended, Father ground his teeth. "I'll kill them myself if they're from this clan. Many times I've told our men what my brother said. I had Lucanus himself describe how Roman armies march through a land, killing and enslaving those who never even opposed them. The cattle thieves have put all our people at risk of that."

Father's shoulders drooped as he lowered himself into his favorite chair, laid his head back, and closed his eyes.

"It could be worse." Sulio never expected to speak well of the Roman who wanted Narina, but truth was truth. "At least Rogatus is trying to keep a single stupid act from being the spark that could burn it all down."

Albiso hit Sulio's upper arm with the back of his hand as curses poured from his lips. "The Romans have no right to order a chieftain of the Brigantes around. If they don't want to lose their cattle, they should never have brought them here."

Bellicus's eyes popped open, and he glared at his son. "Did you have anything to do with it?"

"No." Albiso raised his chin and mirrored his father's glare. "But I wouldn't have told them not to do it if they asked me."

Bellicus's arm shot out, finger pointing. "You are never, ever to be part of any thieving or attacks on Roman soldiers. Do you hear me?"

His brother lowered his gaze. "Yes, Father. I won't do anything to put the clan in danger."

Father settled back into his chair and closed his eyes again.

Albiso left the room quietly, but as soon as he thought himself out of earshot, he muttered something and kicked at a pebble that lay in his path.

As Sulio slowly rubbed his jaw, he watched his brother mount his stallion and ride out of the compound.

If someone asked Albiso to take part in something Father had just forbidden, would he even try to keep that promise?

Chapter 29

Keeping the Peace

Narina's taberna, evening of Day 20

Narina kept glancing out the kitchen door to see whether the sun had dropped behind the hills. It was getting late, and Rogatus hadn't come yet. Then the ringing triangle announced his arrival, and she hurried through the courtyard to find him seated in his chair.

"You're smiling. So, it went well?"

She stood beside the table, and he tipped his head back to gaze at her.

"Maybe. It's too soon to tell. But it didn't go badly. No one got hurt, anyway."

She slipped into her chair. "I suppose that's worth smiling over."

He blew a breath out his nostrils as his smile broadened. "Just sitting here with you can make me smile, even when matters are still unsettled."

She looked away. Sitting across from him was enough to make her smile, too, even though she shouldn't let it. Thank goodness Sulio hadn't heard him say that.

With elbows on the table, she clasped her hands. "What happened? Atto said he left you on the backside of the ridge overlooking the compound."

"We came in the back way, and Bellicus came out on the porch to talk with me. He claimed it wasn't done by men of your clan, but he couldn't or wouldn't tell me who did it. He did agree to pass my demands to the other chieftains who came to the festival."

"What did you ask for?"

"The return of the cattle and the men who stole them."

She drew back. "You might get the cattle, but why would anyone turn some of their men over to you to punish?"

"I told Bellicus I only wanted to punish the ones who stole from me as an example for others who might be tempted. I threatened them with the legion.

I pointed out they wouldn't be willing to investigate to make sure only the guilty pay for the crime, like I will."

He rubbed his jaw. "I think he understood why I must make sure the thieves pay so others won't try the same thing and expect to get away with it. He sees the value of keeping the peace for all his people, and he's willing to try to convince the other chieftains to do it my way before the legion gets involved."

"Was Sulio there?"

"I didn't see him or his brother. But I always expect to see Sulio here. I'm sure he'll have something to say about it. Depending on what that is, I might have a clearer idea of how it really went."

"He hasn't come yet this evening." She rose. "You must be hungry, and it's getting late. I'll fetch your stew right away so you'll have time to enjoy it."

"You take good care of me, Narina. I appreciate it." He turned in the chair to face her, and admiration filled his eyes. "I appreciate you."

She flashed a smile and hurried into the storeroom. As she hastened through the courtyard, she bit her lip.

Maybe he just meant as a friend, but the curve of his lips and the gleam in his eyes suggested much more.

God, I'm not doing anything deliberate to make him say such things. What should I do to stop it?

By the time Veldicca ladled stew into two bowls, God's answer was still silence.

At least in this matter of the heart, He was leaving her on her own.

Late afternoon of Day 22

Rogatus sat at his desk in the headquarters office, massaging his temples as he stared at the blank wax tablet. It had been two days since he visited Bellicus. He'd given the chieftain a week to contact the other clans with his demands. It was too soon to expect any answer, but the uncertainty gnawed at him.

What should he do if no one admitted taking the cattle? He hadn't reported the theft to the legate yet. He needed to, but he'd seen in Moesia that a legate preferred hearing about a problem when he could report how he'd solved it at the same time.

He pressed the stylus into the wax and began to write. First about the gathering of chieftains for a small harvest celebration while planning a bigger one. He knew how many chieftains came, but not which ones. The legate would want those names.

He massaged the back of his neck. Would Sulio tell him who they were? If not, did Atto know? Or Narina?

The celebration was peaceful, but had one of the clan escorts seen his cattle and decided to take them?

Whatever he wrote, he must make it clear that the Isurium clan was not the problem, that Bellicus was willing to help, that any punitive action should not target the Isurium clan.

A knock on the doorframe drew his attention. The optio who served as his aide stood beside a soldier holding a thin wooden sheet.

"Enter." Rogatus closed the tablet and leaned back in his chair.

The solder approached and saluted. "Prefect. I just came off guard duty with the cattle. Two men delivered ten to us an hour ago. They also gave me this and said Bellicus sent it to you." He offered the sheet, and Rogatus leaned across the desk to take it.

"Did they say anything else?"

"No, Prefect."

"Were they the same cattle as were taken?"

"They might be. I can't be certain."

"You're dismissed."

The solder saluted again and followed the optio out the door.

Rogatus held the sheet with both hands and took a deep breath before he read.

> I have returned your cattle to your herdsmen. As I told you, they were not taken by men of my clan. But since you have them back, you do not need to know who took them. So, do not ask. But I can tell you that the guilty ones have been punished as if they stole cattle from men of their own clan. They will never do it again.
>
> Bellicus

He closed his eyes, and a deep sigh of relief drained his lungs.

Then a smile started small and grew into a satisfied grin. What could have meant disaster for Narina's clan had been settled in the fairest possible way. Without her uncle's help, that would have been impossible.

He reached into his drawer and picked up a wooden sheet. Then he exchanged it for a fresh wax tablet, some twine, and a wax seal box. What he wrote to Bellicus should be for his eyes only. Not because he wanted to conceal anything, but because Bellicus might not want others to know what he wrote.

Sulio lounged in the Roman's chair, waiting for dinner. Or more accurately, watching out for his brother and the Roman who'd earned his grudging respect.

When he left home, Albiso was still complaining about Rogatus forcing his way into the family compound and telling Father what to do. But after a few cups of mead, he'd also made threats about what he'd do if the Roman tried anything with Narina. After several attempts to talk sense to his fired-up, drunken brother, he'd given up and come early to Narina's in case Albiso decided to show up here as well.

They were both half a foot taller than the short Roman, but if Sulio had to bet on who'd win a fight, Albiso wouldn't be his choice. Rogatus wouldn't start a fight, but he'd know how to win it. Albiso could end up badly hurt or worse.

When Rogatus entered and saw Sulio in his good chair, the Roman's brows lowered, but only for a moment.

"Sulio. I'd hoped to see you this evening."

Sulio's head drew back. The Roman sounded like he meant it.

As Rogatus walked toward the table, he reached into the satchel that held his word lists. But he pulled out a sealed wax tablet instead and placed it on the table in front of Sulio.

"What's this?" Sulio tapped the tablet.

"The cattle were returned this afternoon, thanks to your father's efforts, and the thieves were punished as if stealing from their own clan. I can report to the legate that the matter of the theft of our cattle has been settled in a satisfactory way for all."

Rogatus removed his helmet and set it on the table. "So, it's a letter of appreciation for him being a peacekeeper." He settled into Narina's chair. "And a request that he extend my thanks to the chieftain who took action to keep the peace. It's what's best for all of us, both Roman and Brigantes."

He relaxed in the chair, as if they were two friends meeting for a drink.

"I would deliver my thanks in person, but I suspect Bellicus would rather I not."

Sulio fingered the twine sealing the tablet. "I'll pass it on."

The Roman returned to the triangle and rang it to announce his arrival.

"I expect Veldicca will have an excellent stew for us tonight. It's a fitting way to celebrate."

Sulio fingered his mustache. Although the ala should never have been stationed in Isurium, it was good that this man was in command.

Who would have thought overlooking insults and minor offenses could be a strength, not a weakness? But when it came to keeping swords sheathed and innocent ones unharmed, perhaps it was among the most important.

Chapter 30

A New Emperor

Morning of Day 23

Rogatus had just filled his spoon with the final scrapings of porridge when a commotion at the entrance to the dining hall drew his gaze. His optio stood just outside, pointing toward him. When two soldiers strode toward him, he returned the spoon to the bowl.

Legion couriers. Why two of them? They would have started before dawn, as soon as it was light enough to follow the road to reach him this early.

He pushed back his chair and stood, as did Germanus and Adolphus.

The couriers paused in front of him, both striking their chests and saying in chorus, "Prefect."

"You have something for me?"

The older spoke. "Yes, Prefect. The Legate sent us to bring you to him as soon as possible."

His stomach clenched. An urgent summons by your commanding officer never signified something good.

He wanted to ask, but with his decurions beside him, that was too risky until he had some idea of what it was about. Maybe word of the cattle theft had reached the legate but the news of how he'd solved it hadn't? Or maybe the legate disapproved of what he'd done, even though it worked even better than the heavy-handed approach most would have taken.

He pointed toward the cook's helper who was dishing out porridge. "Eat if you're hungry. I'll be returning with you to Eboracum in half an hour."

He turned back to his decurions. "Have Zephyrus saddled. I also want four men ready to escort me to Eboracum. Make sure they ride horses that can make the trip twice today, in case I need to return immediately.

His men left to fulfill his orders, and he headed to his chambers for his armor and weapons.

As far as he knew, he'd done everything needed to lead his ala well. He could explain his handling of the cattle thieves, and the legate would approve...if he was a reasonable man.

He drew a deep breath and blew it out slowly. The last time a legate summoned him unexpectedly, he got an early promotion to a command where he was truly needed. He'd impressed his new commander from the beginning. He had no reason to expect that had changed.

He fastened the side latches on his cuirass and draped the strap holding his gladius over his head. If he were going into battle on horseback, he'd take the longer spatha. But that hung down too low and made him look as short as he actually was when he wore it while walking. After those two and a half years in Deva, he'd heard more than enough snide remarks about boys wearing their father's swords.

In battle what you looked like didn't matter, only how well you fought. He could fight like the best of his men in Moesia, and Rome had rewarded him for his dedication and skill. If war came, she would do so again.

But fighting here could hurt Narina and her people, and that was the last thing he wanted to do.

He fastened the helmet's chinstrap and headed for the stable.

In three hours, he'd know why he was summoned. Whether for praise or condemnation or some other reason entirely, only Fortuna knew.

Eboracum, late morning of Day 23

Rogatus rode through the stone arch of the gatehouse and reined in at the stable. The stableman who'd given him Boreas approached.

"Prefect." His fist hit his chest, and he held out his hand to take Zephyrus's reins when Rogatus dismounted.

"I might be riding back to Isurium later today. Take care of our horses and make sure they're fit for the return journey."

A quick nod, and the stableman led Zephyrus toward a grass-filled manger and water trough.

Rogatus turned to his men. "I won't need you this morning, but check back here right after lunch. I should know by then if we need to head back today or can wait until morning."

They rode past him to tend to their mounts, and he strode toward the principia.

What waited for him inside?

He was halfway across the courtyard within the principia walls when—

"Rogatus."

He turned to find Dexter and Plantus leaving Dexter's office to join him.

"Have you heard the news yet?" Plantus bounced his eyebrows once.

That earned Rogatus's frown. "No."

"The legate told us last night that Trajan is dead, and Hadrian is the new emperor. He said the change of emperor sometimes led to unrest in the frontier provinces." He started to grin, but turned it into a subdued smile. "That means we might be seeing action. The locals are fools if they think they can stand against the legions of Rome, but he thought they might try."

Plantus opened his mouth to say more, but Rogatus's deepening frown silenced him. "Action can mean your death or the death of the men you command. Don't underestimate British tribesmen. In Boudicca's rebellion, the infantry cohorts of the Ninth were ambushed and wiped out on their way to relieve Camulodunum. Only the legate and some of his cavalry escaped."

Plantus's mouth straightened, but a slight shrug betrayed his naive optimism concerning what might lay before them. "But the tribunes escaped with him, and Boudicca and her rebels were soon crushed."

Rogatus's snort was what that answer deserved. "That doesn't always happen. Three legions with all their officers and the auxiliaries with them were ambushed and completely destroyed by Arminius's Germanic warriors. Don't be wishing for battle. You can't know who will die before it's over."

Plantus narrowed his eyes. "But you've seen action and came through fine."

It was all Rogatus could do not to roll his eyes. "I hunted raiders, not an army set on killing me."

Dexter stepped closer, and Rogatus shifted his gaze to the wiser of the two. "Before you go back to Isurium, please stop in and tell us what the legate said you would be doing. We'll soon be ala commanders, and I want to know how one fits in with how the legion is preparing for battle if a rebellion breaks out."

"I can." Rogatus tipped his head toward the legate's office door. "But first I must find out myself."

In silence, they watched him as he strode the final distance toward the optio's desk. Before he reached it, the optio stuck his head into the office, then stood holding the door open for Rogatus to enter.

The legate sat at his desk, tablet open before him, stylus in hand.

"Rogatus. You made good time getting here. Excellent. I'll want you back with your ala before day's end. Trajan has been replaced by Hadrian, and that could mean trouble."

He leaned back in his chair. "Unrest in the frontier provinces is common when imperial power changes hands. Have you seen any signs of rebellion yet?"

Even as he squared his shoulders, Rogatus relaxed inside. The summons was nothing personal after all. "No. The chieftain over the Isurium area does what he can to keep the men of his clan calm under Roman rule. There was a harvest celebration where men from some other clans came, but that stayed peaceful. Some of the visitors stole a few of the ala's cattle, but they were thieves, not rebels. The Isurium chieftain arranged for the return of the cattle, and the chieftain over the thieves punished them like he would anyone stealing cattle from his clansmen. I expect no more problems."

The corner of the legate's mouth twitched up, then settled back to a straight line.

"It's not thieves I'm worried about." With his silver stylus, he drummed a few times on the desktop. "Whenever there's a change of emperor, some think that weakens Rome's control. As the news of Trajan's replacement by Hadrian spreads, I expect some who would throw off Roman rule if they could will think this gives them a chance of success. Your job is to prove them wrong."

As he rolled the stylus between thumb and middle finger, he stared at his hand. Then his gaze turned back on Rogatus. "There's already unrest in some of the eastern provinces because they see the loss of a strong emperor as an opportunity to gain freedom. Any act of rebellion that goes unpunished could ignite a full-blown revolt. So, I want an immediate response to anything that challenges or even seriously questions our control of the region. No matter how small, crush it quickly and harshly. Make an example of any rebels that will scare others into submission."

The legate set the stylus down and leaned back in his chair. "I expect Hadrian will be as strong a ruler as Trajan was. It shouldn't take more than a few months for that fact to sink in, even for hotheaded Britons."

Rogatus barely stopped himself from staring at the legate in disbelief. Did the legate really expect the Brigantes to act happy about Roman rule? To stop saying what they thought even though they probably would never do anything about it? He'd never talked with Sulio without her cousin questioning Rome's right to control. But he was no more a rebel than Bellicus right now. Would what the legate commanded push men like him into the rebel camp?

As Rogatus delayed responding, the legate's lowered brows and start of a frown sent a warning. "Is that clear enough, or do you have questions?"

"It's clear, Legate. I have no questions."

"Then you're dismissed for now. But I want you to join my tribunes for lunch in my quarters. I want to talk with all of you about what I expect and answer any questions. Then you can return to your ala."

"Yes, Legate." Rogatus struck his chest, executed a parade turn, and strode from the office.

Once he moved far enough past the optio's desk that it wouldn't be noticed, he closed his eyes and rubbed his forehead. Both the fort centurion and Narina spoke of generals in the past who thought they'd conquered the Brigantes, even though the Brigantes didn't think so themselves.

He'd succeeded in getting Bellicus to help keep the peace because he showed respect for his rank in the tribe. Had he just lost the power to enlist a useful ally, however reluctant, because the legate demanded total submission from a conquered people, not a reasonable response from a proud man?

Through pursed lips, he released a deep, slow breath. He'd sworn his loyalty to the emperor and to Rome. That meant obeying the legate's commands. But where the lines were between questioning, seriously questioning, and challenging…that was up to him to define. He would respond at once to open challenges, but most of the questioning…that was only talk he could let slide.

Chapter 31

For Safety's Sake

Narina's taberna, late evening of Day 23

When Rogatus finally turned off the Roman road onto the street that went past her taberna, only the moon lit his way. It was far too late for dinner, but he sent the soldiers on to the fort before he dismounted and approached the taberna's front door. He needed to tell Narina about the change in emperors and what that might mean for her safety.

After first knocking, then pounding on the front door, he waited in vain for someone to come. So, he remounted Zephyrus and rode around to the back.

After a few blows to the kitchen door, Veldicca's voice came from behind the wood.

"Who is it?"

"Prefect Rogatus, and I must speak to Narina immediately."

She opened the door partway and peered into the darkness. She drew back when Zephyrus snorted a few paces behind him.

Worry filled her eyes. "In private?"

"That would be best."

She stepped back and pointed to the side. "Go back around front and Narina will come let you in."

He retraced his steps, putting Zephyrus into her corral on the way. As he waited for her to come, he stood with his back to the door, watching for any movement in the street and gazing at the town atop the hill. Had anyone there heard the news, and were they preparing to act upon it?

◆

Narina was in her sleeping tunic and had just turned back the sheets when Veldicca stepped into her bedchamber.

"I heard the prefect knocking on the kitchen door, and he said it was urgent he see you. He's waiting for you at the front door now."

Narina's eyebrows rose. "Why?"

Veldicca took her cloak from its peg and held it ready for her to put on. "He didn't say, but he looked deadly serious and wanted to speak with you alone. I think he'd just come from somewhere since Zephyrus was standing behind him."

Narina wrapped the cloak around her and made it snug with a belt. She picked up the candle from the night table and led Veldicca out the door. She looked back over her shoulder. "You don't suppose something's happened to Uncle or Sulio?"

Veldicca tightened her lips and shook her head. "He didn't look like he felt guilty about anything."

She touched Narina's shoulder when they reached the storeroom. "He said alone, but I'll stay just inside the courtyard where I can hear if you call me."

Narina placed her hand on Veldicca's. "I don't expect to, but thank you."

As she approached the front door, soft knocking broke the silence. After setting the candle on the shelf by the front door, she put her lips near the crack. "Who's there?"

"Rogatus. Please let me in." He didn't sound different, but she'd seen how well he could mask what he was feeling when Sulio goaded him.

She lifted the bar, slid back the bolt, and pulled the door partway open.

He slipped inside and closed it behind him.

She picked up the candle holder and took a step toward their table. "Shall we?"

"I've just come from Eboracum." He didn't move. "I can't stay, but I wanted to tell you before anything happens."

Her breath caught. "What's going on?"

The bronze cheek pieces covered his jaw, so he rubbed under his chin. "The legate summoned me to legion headquarters this morning. Trajan has died, and Hadrian is the new emperor. There's unrest in some other provinces among groups wanting to get free of Roman rule, and he expects trouble in Britannia."

He drew a deep breath. "I've been ordered to respond immediately to anything. I've lost the power to choose the best way to deal with something like I did when the cattle were stolen."

His gaze rested on their table. "If attacks on Roman settlements start, I will be taking most of the ala away from Isurium to deal with the rebels."

Deep concern filled his eyes when he looked at her again. "I'm afraid for you if the fort is left with only a skeleton force while I'm away. That could lead to an attack on the fort, and your taberna is so close that it might be a target as well. I won't be able to protect you."

He stepped close enough to touch her, but he didn't. "Lucania might be in special danger because she looks so Roman, and anyone who wasn't from her clan might kill her or take her as a slave. I won't be here to prevent that, and Sulio might not be able to, either."

She covered her mouth with steepled fingers as the full meaning of his words struck her. He might be going to war, but his first concern was her protection and that of her little sister. She'd denied it so many times, but Veldicca might be right. He was her prefect, even though she'd never encouraged him.

She lowered her hands and gripped her left thumb. "You don't have to worry about us. I'll close the taberna for a while and return to the farm tomorrow. It might be too dangerous for Lucania here. She could be seen by men who don't know she's Brigantian and our chieftain's niece. But I can keep her safe there. We're well off the roads, so no one should see her while passing by."

"Tomorrow." His smile was sad. "That's for the best, even though I won't be seeing you every day. I'll certainly miss Veldicca's cooking." His jaw clenched. "When things settle down, I hope you'll open the taberna again." He rubbed his palm with his thumb, then focused once more on her eyes. "I would still like to learn more Brittonic."

"Perhaps we will. Only time will tell whether that might be. You can study the word lists I made you in the meantime." She forced a smile. "I'll expect you to know them perfectly the next time I see you."

His nod was silent, but his eyes declared deep regret. As he had once before, he pushed a loose strand of hair behind her ear, but he left his palm on her cheek when he finished. "Zephyrus will miss seeing you, but I'll take good care of your horse."

He pulled his hand away as if he'd touched something too hot. "I'm sorry. Don't tell Sulio I did that."

"I won't." She gave him the smile that always got his best one in return. "I know you'll take care of him, but take care of yourself as well."

She felt the tears start to build, but none had escaped…yet. Prolonging goodbyes only made them hurt more, and the last thing she wanted was for tears to be his final memory of her.

She opened the door. "We'll be gone before lunchtime tomorrow. So, goodbye…for now."

"Goodbye, Narina."

With squared shoulders and a final longing glance, he stepped out into the darkness.

She bolted the door.

Then she pressed her forehead against the wooden plank and let the tears flow.

God, I know there's no future for us together. I would never fit in his rich pagan world, and he wouldn't want to fit into mine. I've tried so hard to keep us just friends. So why does this hurt so much, as if it's a final goodbye?

Chapter 32

Returning Home

Early morning of Day 24

The sun was three hand-breadths above the hills when Narina put the last crate in the cart and closed the tailgate. With the cart so heavily loaded, they would go down the Roman road instead of the tow path. She surveyed the cart. The expensive mead and wine were right behind the seat. They'd managed to load all the foodstuffs from the storeroom and Veldicca's favorite pots. Her treasured herbs and spices sat at her feet. They hadn't planned to stay more than a few weeks, so they hadn't brought many clothes or personal items. Veldicca had taken their weavings off the looms, and those lay atop the rest of the crates.

Narina had moved the Latin signs inside and put them face down on the floor under her bed and back by the wall. If there was looting, maybe the thieves wouldn't find them. At least the new chairs hadn't been delivered so she'd only lose two.

All looked ready. There was no reason to tarry. Prolonging a goodbye only made it harder.

"Let's go."

Lucania, Veldicca, and Atto climbed aboard the cart.

Her gaze swept the dining room one last time. It paused on the comfortably padded chair Rogatus always chose. He loved that chair. When she closed her eyes, she could still see him, smiling as he traced the R someone carved in the tabletop. Maybe someday he'd sit across from her again, and she'd watch his finger follow the curves of the letter once more.

She pulled the front door shut for the final time and started to put the key in the lock. Then she paused. There was a good chance someone would break in and whatever was left would be stolen. She wrapped her hand around the key. She wouldn't have to pay for a new door or replace a broken lock if she didn't lock it. The thieves could just walk in. Nothing would keep them out, anyway, and maybe they wouldn't break everything she left behind. If they were on horseback, they might even leave the chair Rogatus had claimed as his own.

God, please protect this place. Please don't let all our hard work be for nothing. Please let there be peace so we can return and have things go on as they did before.

She glanced toward the fort. Was that him looking over the parapet, watching the maneuvers of a turma below him?

God, please protect Rogatus. He's a good man. He wants peace for everyone. Don't make him go into battle where he has to choose to do what's wrong because he thinks his oath of loyalty to the emperor demands it. Bring him back safely.

She wanted to add "to me," but that wouldn't be true. He was a rich pagan nobleman. She was only the daughter of a centurion who was more Brigantian than he'd ever been Roman. But even if Rogatus could overlook that, her loyalty was to Christ, not Rome or her gods. They had no future as long as that was true.

Her vision blurred, and she wiped the starting tears away. Then she draped the chain around her neck and tucked the key inside her shirt.

It was time to go.

◆

Rogatus stood on the wall-walk watching a turma drill, but he was really waiting to see her leave. They were loading the cart. She had dressed for riding, but not in the long plaid tunic she pulled up to reveal pants the day he met her. She wore a shirt and trousers like the day they found his pastures, when she rode Zephyrus beside him and life seemed full of possibilities.

Her glowing eyes and beaming smile when he told her they were trading horses, her whispered promise to see her favorite soon. She found pleasure in the simplest things.

If the rebellion came and he survived to reach the other side of war, would he ever have her mounted beside him as his warhorses enjoyed a friendly race?

Her storm-cloud eyes could make a gray Britannic sky seem brighter than a cloudless summer day in Rome ever had. How long before he saw them again?

Then Lucania climbed aboard the cart and moved to the middle. Veldicca settled in to her right. Atto handed the reins to Lucania before he checked the wheels one last time and took his place beside the girl.

Narina led Bena out of the corral and latched the gate.

She mounted and turned her mare to face the fort.

He raised his hand in farewell, but at that distance, would she see it?

Then she lifted her hand, mirroring his motion. She kept it there for a long moment before lowering it.

Then she turned Bena and moved ahead of the cart. His gaze remained locked on her. Would she look back and wave one more time?

But she looked straight ahead until she reached the Roman road and turned south. If she glanced his way then, he couldn't see it. But even if she had, she didn't wave.

He turned his attention back to his galloping men as they wove around and between each other. But he couldn't stop glancing toward the first woman he'd cared for until the trees lining the road finally hid her from view.

Narina's farm, afternoon of Day 24

As Narina led the cart into her farm compound from the west, the first thing she saw was the paddocks for her stallions. She reined in Bena, and her steepled fingers covered her mouth and nose.

Both the two-year-olds were gone, and the three-year-old bay she'd tried to sell Rogatus was missing as well. Past the stallion corrals, in the field where she should have a dozen mares with their foals, only three grazed. None of their foals were more than three months old.

She clutched her throat. The missing mares had all bred with Father's magnificent stallion who died this summer. He'd sired Zephyrus, and she'd hoped for another colt at least as good as the bay. Only two of the three remaining mares might be carrying one of his foals now.

Father's beautiful herd, the one he'd spent years refining to have the best horses for at least fifty miles, was gone.

Tears trickled down her cheeks, and even though she flipped them away, they kept coming.

Her gaze swept the buildings of the compound. Where were all the people who worked for her? Had they been kidnapped? Or killed?

Veldicca climbed down from the wagon and came over to place her hand on Narina's thigh. "Are you all right?"

"No." The word came out a whisper. Then the sobs hit.

Veldicca leaned her head against Narina's side and wrapped an arm around her waist. "I'm so sorry." Then she patted Narina's thigh. "Let's get everything we brought home put up, and then we can figure out what to do next."

Narina nodded, and Veldicca climbed back into the cart. Narina nudged Bena into a walk, and they traveled the final distance to the house.

As Atto reined in the mule, the front door cracked open. Then Bikka's head peeked out, followed by the rest of her scurrying over to meet them.

"I'm so glad you're home."

Veldicca climbed down, and the two women exchanged lingering hugs.

Narina dismounted and tied Bena to the wagon. "What happened here?"

"Raiders." The male voice behind her made her jump.

Narina spun to find her steward, Trenus, standing on the porch, leaning heavily on a crutch. Fresh bruises on his face drew Narina's gasp.

She hurried over to him and guided him to the nearest bench.

He settled heavily onto it.

"Who did this to you?" Anger like she'd never known before surged within Narina.

"Ten or so men. Not of our clan. They came to take your horses. When I told them they had no right to them, they beat me up and took them anyway."

He turned fond eyes onto his wife Bikka. "They would have taken all the mares and left the foals that still need their mother's milk to starve. But my Bikka ripped into them, telling them you were Bellicus's niece and what he'd do if they left your foals to die." He shrugged. "They decided three more mares weren't worth risking what the chieftain of the Isurium clan would do to them."

"Where are the rest of our people?"

Trenus tightened their lips. "After they saw what the raiders did to me, they were afraid to stay. With the wheat and barley crops already harvested and the spring crop planted, I told them they were free to go for now. Some went home to their families. Some went to Eboracum since Minconus will help them there. It's two or three weeks until the broad beans have to be planted, and I figured I'd be well enough by then that Bikka and I could do it if no one had come back yet."

"Back yet?"

"They all promised to return when it was safe. Maybe I won't have to plant beans after all. But we do have to pick the apples now and dry them."

She released a deep sigh. "Safe...I don't know when that will be. The prefect of the ala told me I should bring Lucania back here for her safety. The old emperor is dead, and there's a new one taking over. The legate in Eboracum is expecting some of the clans might rebel. Rogatus thought Lucania looked too Roman to be safe if Brigantes who don't know we're Bellicus's nieces saw her."

Trenus leaned his head back against the wall. "So, they took our horses for mounting warriors." He shrugged and offered a wry smile. "Since they already took every horse worth taking, they shouldn't be back. She should be safe here."

Narina rested her hand on Trenus's shoulder. "With the four of us picking the apples and Lucania out of sight in the courtyard cutting them up to dry, we can do what needs to be done. You just rest and get better fast."

She summoned the others with a curl of her fingers. "But first we're going to ask God to hasten that healing and keep you from hurting too much while He does."

The women and Atto gathered around Trenus, and each placed a hand on him.

Veldicca cleared her throat. "God, we ask you to heal Trenus. Please give him relief from pain as he heals. Please hasten his healing so he can soon be completely well. Protect us all from the evil actions of men who don't know you. We thank You for loving us and caring for us. We ask this in the name of Your only son, Iesu."

All joined in the amen.

Narina turned to Atto. "Let's get everything moved from the cart into the house."

As they carried the crates and baskets inside, Bikka directed where they should go. In no time, the mule and Bena were in the paddock that had belonged to Zephyrus, and the cart was parked by the stable with the wagon.

Narina stood, gazing to the northwest at the hills she could see from her taberna. It was almost the time when Rogatus came for dinner. He'd place his helmet on the table, and they'd eat Veldicca's stew in silence. Then he'd take out his word lists, and after she gave him the Brittonic words, they'd chat about something so he could practice.

Was he missing that as much as she was?

She shook her head. It was silly to think about a man she could never marry. But it still warmed a place deep inside her when he looked her as if she was a pretty woman whose company delighted him.

Sulio was right that Rogatus had grown too fond of her. It was probably a good thing that they'd been separated before it went further than fondness. But that goodbye left a hole in her world, at least for now.

God, please protect him and Zephyrus, too. Let any war end quickly, and spare the innocent ones from suffering.

Lucania's voice made her jump. "Veldicca said to get you. The stew is ready."

"I'll be right there." Narina gazed one more time at the distant hills. Whatever might happen, God would watch over His children. But since Rogatus wasn't one of God's own, would He watch over her prefect as well?

Chapter 33

WHY DID SHE LEAVE?

When Sulio rode past the taberna with a rabbit for Veldicca, he reined in. The sign inviting people to enter in Brittonic and Latin was gone. The windows were shuttered, and the front door was closed. When he turned past the corral on the way to his favorite tree, neither Bena nor the mule watched him. Where the cart usually sat by the stalls was only trampled grass.

He put his stallion in the corral and went to the front door. When he pushed on it, it swung freely into the room.

With his hand resting on his knife, he entered. "Narina?" His voice echoed in the dining room "Veldicca? Lucania?"

No smiling girl skipped through the storeroom to give him a hug.

Where was everyone?

As he passed through the storeroom, he froze. Except for some empty baskets, nothing was there. He ducked into room where Narina had stored the fine mead and wine that Minconus thought tribunes deserved. Only a few jars of the cheaper mead remained.

As he checked each room around the courtyard in turn, his heart rate rose.

What had happened? Were they all right?

When he'd dropped in for dinner yesterday, everything seemed normal. Better than normal since the Roman wasn't eating with her. When he asked where Rogatus was, she didn't know.

His jaw clenched. That Roman must have had something to do with her vanishing.

He left through the kitchen and strode down the street to the fort. Narina often went to the farm to train her horses, but Rogatus better have a good explanation for the others being missing.

Before he reached the gate, the guards drew their swords and blocked his path.

"Out of my way. I need to see Rogatus." He held his hands away from his body to show he was no threat, but they didn't move.

The taller one pointed up the road with his left hand while aiming the tip of his blade at Sulio's chest. 'Go back where you came from. There's no admittance to the fort for Britons."

"I'm Sulio, son of Bellicus, and I need to see Rogatus right now."

Another soldier stepped out of the gatehouse. A fountain of horsehair rose from the tube atop his helmet and hung down to his back. It was the decurion Germanus that Rogatus had introduced to him when Albiso got so offended over being ignored.

"I know this one. I'll escort him to the prefect."

Sulio followed him to a large stone building straight ahead of the gate. With guards by its door, it must be their headquarters.

Germanus led him across an inner courtyard to a desk by a door with an eagle carved on it.

"This one needs to see the prefect."

The soldier sitting at the desk rose, opened the door, and disappeared inside. When he came out, he held the door open for them to pass.

Rogatus sat at a desk, writing on a thin sheet of wood.

Germanus saluted. "Prefect, Sulio, son of Bellicus, is here to see you." His gaze raked Sulio. "Do you want me to stay?"

Rogatus set down his pen. "No. Sulio is a friend."

Sulio clenched his teeth. Friend? That wasn't a word he'd use for this Roman. Not an enemy, but certainly not a friend.

Another salute followed, and the decurion left the room.

As soon as the door closed, Sulio strode forward until he reached the desk. He glared at Rogatus. "I came from the taberna. Where is Narina?"

Rogatus leaned back in his chair. "She decided to go back to her farm."

With a snort, Sulio tipped his head back to look down his nose at the Roman. "What did you do to make her leave?"

◆

Rogatus set the wooden sheet aside. "Nothing. She decided it was safer for Lucania."

Should he tell Sulio that Hadrian was now emperor? He'd learn soon enough even if he didn't, but the time might come when he needed to ask Sulio something. With Narina gone, her cousin was the only Brigantian whose answer he might trust. Or at least be able to tell if he was lying and the truth was the opposite of what Sulio said. If he didn't reveal what made her leave now, how could he expect Sulio to tell him anything in the future?

"Emperor Trajan has died, and Hadrian is now emperor. We thought it was safer for her Roman-looking sister not to be in a Brigantian town if angry words turn into unsheathed swords."

Sulio's eyes widened, but only for a moment. Then they narrowed.

Rogatus massaged his palm. "I would have offered her protection within the fort, but if rebellion breaks out, especially if the Roman towns near here are threatened, I'll be taking the ala to stop it. I can't know when or even if that might happen. But I couldn't promise to be here to protect her."

A puff of air through Sulio's nostrils spoke more than words. "Lucania would be safest at my father's house. It's only you and your soldiers being here that put Narina and her people at risk. It's good she saw the danger and left."

"I agree." Rogatus stopped the sigh before Sulio heard it. "Please tell your father about the new emperor. The change means nothing in terms of the power of Rome. Hadrian has served with Trajan for many years, and Trajan picked him as the next emperor. He is as good a general as Trajan was, and the replacement of one by the other doesn't mean Rome is any less capable of defending what is already hers."

"What you Romans think is yours. There are many who don't agree with you."

"I know, and too many innocent ones will suffer if the rights and might of Rome are tested in battle. I hope your father will continue to warn how short-term victories don't mean winning the war. I would hate to see Britannia and her people become another Dacia."

Sulio tightened his lips. "You sound like Narina's father. He tried for years to scare the clan with his stories of the undefeatable armies of Rome."

"I do because what he told you is true. No matter how bloodied a legion of Rome might be, even if most of its men are killed, another comes in to take its place. Your Boudicca destroyed the infantry of Ninth Legion almost sixty years ago, yet here it is in the fortress in Eboracum."

Sulio rubbed his lip. "I'll tell Father, but he'll decide what's best for the clan, not you."

Rogatus crossed his arms. "As I would expect him to. And since I think he is a man of wisdom and honor, I expect he'll urge restraint, not rebellion. I hope you'll do the same."

With a snort, Sulio spun on his heel and walked away.

Rogatus rubbed his forehead as her cousin disappeared from view. What if Sulio proved as foolish as his brother and both died at Roman hands? Would he lose the future he wanted with Narina because she blamed him for what he had no power to stop, even though he wanted to?

Bellicus's farm, night of Day 24

In the flickering light of a campfire kept small enough to seem harmless, dozens of men of the Isurium clan milled around, speaking in low voices. Sulio had told Father about the change of emperor, and Father dispatched all the men at the compound to gather the clan for this discussion of what it might mean.

Sulio stood with the other young men outside the circle of elders who were close to the flames. Albiso and his impulsive friends stood apart, muttering among themselves.

Father approached the fire pit, gripping a short stick with his left hand.

"Clansmen." Bellicus raised his hand, and the group grew silent. "I learned today that the Roman emperor is dead and has been replaced by another man. The rise of a new man to power brings confusion as men of ambition expect shifting alliances and new chances to move up themselves. But this Hadrian was hand-picked by Trajan after serving him many years. Like Trajan, he's experienced in war and should be ready to take the reins of Roman power."

Bellicus scanned the group of elders, catching the eyes of each. "It is tempting to think now is a good time to rise up against Roman rule, that the response will be weaker than before this change, that we can easily win and drive the Romans out of Brigantian lands."

A murmur of assent rippled through the gathered men.

"But history tells us differently. Winning some battles does not mean winning the war. We saw that with Boudicca. She had great early victories, with her warriors killing every Roman and pro-Roman Briton in Londinium, Camulodunum, and Verulamium. Her warriors even wiped out the Ninth Legion except for its cavalry."

He hurled the stick into the fire, and a swarm of sparks flew upward. "But even that didn't drive the Romans from our land. With less than two legions, their governor defeated her army. That legion her warriors destroyed was brought back to full strength, and today it is in the fortress in Eboracum."

The gathering grew silent.

"Many here have heard my brother Lucanus's stories about what happened in Dacia. How many warriors the Romans raised to fight there. How the Dacian defeat led to most of the people of that land being killed or made Roman slaves. They were shipped away from their homeland, never to return."

Silence lay so thick around Sulio that the crack of a branch breaking in the fire made him jump.

"We must not bring down the wrath of the Romans upon the clan. Brigantian men have no fear of battle. Win or lose, we would soak this land with Roman blood, and our valor would be spoken of for generations."

A ripple of agreement spread through the crowd.

"We are not afraid to die a glorious death in battle. But..." His hand swept in a circle, taking in the many building of the compound. "Our women and children, our sons and daughters, would die in misery as Roman slaves."

He tightened his lips and slowly shook his head. "I think of the future of our clan. What I want in this moment...I must weigh that against the cost to all of our clan, from our babies to our honored elders. I am going to choose what protects the ones I am responsible for. I urge you all to join me in standing back and not taking part in any rebellion that others might start. Their failure to see what must happen to all they love if they strike against Rome...I will not make that mistake myself. I will not make all the ones I hold dear pay that terrible cost."

He spread his legs and crossed his arms. "I will not force my family and you, my clansmen, to sacrifice everything and gain nothing in the end. That is all I have to say. If any want to stay and talk with me, I will listen. But we all should return to our homes before the Romans realize we have gathered."

As the clansmen stepped back into the darkness away from the dying fire, Sulio glanced at his brother. With lowered eyebrows and the deepest scowl, Albiso and his friends turned and walked away as a group.

Had his brother listened? Had he heard a single word that Father said? Was he still burning with excitement, thinking Rome couldn't hold on to what she thought she'd conquered now Trajan was gone?

Sulio squeezed the back of his neck. Would his brother remember the promise he gave Father not to do anything to put the clan in danger? Even if he remembered, would he keep his word?

Chapter 34

What Loyalty Demands

The Isurium fort, morning of Day 25

Rogatus sat at his office desk, eyes closed, rubbing the bridge of his nose with his middle finger.

He'd awakened with a headache. Or more accurately, he'd risen with one after a miserable night with little if any sleep.

It was his own fault, but he'd really had no choice. He told Narina that Lucania might be in danger. Of course she'd take her sister somewhere that should be safer. Sulio was right that the ala being in the fortress put anyone living as close as she did in mortal danger if a rebellion started.

But the trace of tears as she told him to take care of himself, the last, lingering wave before she turned and rode away...each time he closed his eyes, he'd see those or some of a hundred other little things from their evenings together.

His optio hadn't felt well that morning, so he'd told the man to leave the door open and go rest for a while. He always found the sounds of a fort soothing, but not today.

He'd just picked up his pen again when the faint metallic clattering of a soldier sprinting on a stone floor reached him.

Then it grew louder. A soldier burst into his office, breathing hard.

He snapped to attention and saluted. "Prefect. You're needed at the hospital. A horse herd has been attacked, and only one man made it back alive."

With his jaw clenched as he swore silently, Rogatus rose. It should take more than a single day before the first rebel attack called him into action. "Tell Germanus and Adolphus to meet me at the hospital."

The man strode away to fetch his two lead decurions, and he headed for the hospital himself.

Strange at it seemed, Fortuna had smiled on him when Narina left yesterday. No matter what he had to do now, she and her people should be safe.

When he reached the hospital, the soldier lay on the treatment table, pale but conscious. The *medicus* had removed an arrow from his upper arm, and it lay on the metal tray beside him. The arrow seemed delicate, like you'd use hunting rabbits or birds. It lacked the arrowhead used for a stag or a wild boar...or a man.

He fingered the red dogwood shaft that had been sharpened to a point. Like Sulio used. Probably what Albiso used as well.

Rogatus stood at the soldier's bedside. "What happened?"

The soldier saluted with his uninjured right arm. "Prefect. I and four others were watching the sixty horses in the meadow east of here between the Roman road and the towpath. The two across the meadow from me fell from their horses, then before we could do anything, a half dozen men rode out of the woods. They started firing more arrows, killing the others. But I only took an arrow through my arm, so I retreated to come warn the fort. A couple of them chased me, but I lay low in the saddle, and my horse was fast enough that they gave up on catching me."

Rogatus glanced behind him to find Germanus and Adolphus listening to the report. Their faces were as grim as his must be.

He laid his hand on the man's chest. "Rest now. You're in good hands here."

With a curl of his fingers, he summoned his decurions to follow him out of the room. When they were out of earshot of the injured man, he planted his feet and crossed his arms.

"Your thoughts?"

Germanus sucked on his lip. "Word of a new emperor might be what caused this, but it's been such a short time. The legate only heard of Hadrian's rise to emperor three days ago. It only takes a couple of days for a message from Londinium to arrive by the military relay service. By regular military dispatch, maybe five days. Did the men in the fortress know when you got there?"

"The tribunes knew the night before we did, but I don't know if more than the officers knew."

"Something this big, they would." Adolphus rubbed under his chin. "And they'd talk about it at the tabernas. But someone might have heard about it in the capital and come up to Petuaria by ship. That takes four days. Word could already have spread from there even before the legate knew. But I wouldn't expect too many to know before you told the Isurium chieftain, though I could be wrong."

"So, we can't be certain it's related to Hadrian, but it might be." Rogatus blew out a slow breath. "That was a rabbit-hunting arrow in our soldier's arm. So, it might have been a hunting party that saw the horses and decided to take them for their clan or to sell themselves." Rogatus furrowed his brow and rubbed his forehead. The mild headache had turned into a nagging one.

"I wouldn't expect a war party to arm itself that way. So, it might be a crime of opportunity, where they expected that killing our men would keep us from discovering the theft until the replacement guards went out this evening. They could have been too far away by then with the herd split into smaller groups so we'd never find them." An appreciative smile curved his lips. "They didn't think the guard could reach the fort. They had no idea how determined a wounded Roman can be to fulfill his duty."

He drew a deep breath and huffed it out. "I know where that meadow is, and I know how to track stolen horses from my time in Moesia. With only six of them, I'll take the Third Turma and go get our horses back."

He scrunched his eyes. "Germanus, you're in charge of the fort, as usual. Adolphus. I want you and the Second Turma here and ready in case something else needs an instant response while I'm away."

Rogatus tapped his bronze cuirass. "Impressive for military parades, but when I'm fighting on horseback, I want chain mail."

Germanus opened his mouth, then cleared his throat. "I can look for one that will fit you."

"With an auxiliary of Tungrian men, I don't expect you'd find one my size." A wry smile curved Rogatus's lips. Sulio would make some snide comment about his shortness if he heard Germanus. "I led Britons and Germans in Moesia, so I had my own made. I earned the armillae wearing it. Get Zephyrus saddled, and tell the decurion of the Third to get his men mounted and ready for action. His *draconarius* won't carry the standard today. We might need to sneak up on the thieves."

After two "yes, Prefects" and two chest thumps, the men who were his second and third in command left to summon thirty men and their decurion to inflict Rome's retaliation.

In his chamber, he lifted the leather strap holding his gladius and scabbard over his head. He hung it on the hook beside his cavalry spatha. Next, he removed the brass cuirass and placed it on its rack. Then he knelt by his trunk and took out the chain-mail shirt that had served him so well. After removing the belt that held his dagger, he lowered it over his head and tightened the belt over it.

He fingered the red horse-hair strip, then released it from the bronze helmet and laid it on the night table. He never wore it hunting raiders. It made him too obviously the commander, and it was better if his enemies didn't know who to target.

He pressed his fingertips against his eyes. If only his head would stop throbbing. Then he draped the spatha strap across his chest and donned his helmet.

His dead mother's uncle had arranged his first post commanding an equitata, even though they'd only met once. Father had no interest in his military successes. No interest in him. So, Rogatus wrote about them to the man who'd taken pity on a neglected, rejected youth. He always wrote back of his pride in every accomplishment of his great-nephew. Rogatus's next letter would report how hunting raiders was the first action he saw in Britannia, and he'd thank him once more for getting him that equitata that made all he'd become possible.

He adjusted the scabbard strap and squared his shoulders. It was time to go hunting. Narina's cousins better not be part of this. He'd do what loyalty to Rome demanded, but the last thing he wanted was to harm anyone she loved.

But surely her cousins wouldn't be foolhardy enough to steal his horses. At least Sulio wouldn't, but Albiso.... Had her angry cousin seen where his horses grazed and told the ones who'd killed his men?

As he strode toward the stable, determination filled him. He'd get his spare mounts back, and what he did with the horse thieves would send a message to others not to try that again.

Zephyrus stood saddled and waiting. Head high, ears cocked, he knew something was going on, and he radiated alert enthusiasm as he watched the activity around him.

Rogatus mounted and leaned forward to slap Zephyrus's neck.

The stately silver head turned to look at him, and an eagerness for what lay ahead filled the stallion's eyes.

Through the south gate that opened into his extension of the fort, the Third Turma came toward him. When they reached him, the troops fanned out to form three lines of ten, awaiting his orders.

Rogatus sat tall in the saddle. "Today we ride out for the glory of Rome and the honor of the Ala Tungrorum. Six raiders killed four of our comrades and stole sixty of our horses. Those men were fools. No one who attacks this ala can expect to get away with it."

Zephyrus tossed his head and snorted, as if disgusted by what the raiders had done.

"In Moesia, I hunted raiders like these many times, and the men who have attacked us will learn what all of those learned. When Rome pursues them, their death is assured. Today we will find these thieves and take back what is ours. No one will steal from the Ala Tungrorum and live to use what they stole."

He turned Zephyrus toward the main gate and nudged him into a trot.

An enthusiastic cheer erupted from the troops as the decurion and dra-conarius fell in beside him. A column of twos formed behind them, and the cheer faded away, replaced by the rhythmic thuds of dozens of hooves. In silence, they passed under the stone arch of the east gate.

As they rode past her taberna, Rogatus gave it the briefest glance. With her gone, it was nothing more than an empty building. But when the unrest was over, perhaps she would return, and it would feel like home again.

South of Isurium

Rogatus led his men into the meadow where the horses had been, and his anger burned. He'd had men injured but never killed before. As they approached two of his fallen, he reined in. The men of the turma formed their three lines of ten, and he turned Zephyrus toward the dead.

"As Horace has written, 'It is sweet and honorable to die for one's country.' Decurion Germanus will send men to bring our fallen home. But in this moment, I salute them." He struck his chest and raised his hand as if saluting an emperor. The men of the turma did as well, and all held the salute until Rogatus lowered his arm.

"It is also sweet to avenge the death of our own, and we shall." He turned Zephyrus and signaled the troop to move forward.

Several paths headed out of the meadow, and he approached each one at a slow walk. The passage of a herd of horses always left signs, and he knew every one of them. The first two they passed showed nothing, but the third had broken stems and trampled grass from the passage of many hooves. He pointed down the path, then led his men onto it, still watching to make sure the horses had gone on before them instead of turning off into the trees.

They followed the trail into a wide meadow, and near the far side, his horses walked at a leisurely pace, grazing as they went, with six Britons driv-ing them.

With silent hand signals, he split his men into two groups, with each going single-file along the trees on opposite sides of the meadow where they wouldn't be obvious until it was too late.

Satisfaction settled in his gut. He'd be getting his horses back quicker than he expected. His troops would soon kill or capture the thieves, and the example he'd make of any living ones would convince others to leave his herds alone.

When they were only a short distance from the riders trailing the herd, he signaled, and his two groups of men headed toward the raiders, riding fast.

One group aimed for the two in the lead and the one on their side and the rest for the rear guard and the other side guard.

But before they could reach them, the raiders abandoned the herd and raced toward a path into a dense wood. Rogatus fell back and yelled at the leading men. "You five stay with the herd."

Then he led his decurion and twenty-five cavalrymen into the woods.

The path entered a ravine as it threaded through the trees. They started out two abreast, but some distance in it narrowed until they had to ride single file. The hairs on the back of Rogatus's neck stood up, and he raised his hand for a silent stop. He held his breath, listening. The normal sounds of a wood had grown silent, and he couldn't hear the men they were chasing. Something was wrong up ahead. It was probably a trap.

He raised his hand for the troop to see, making a circle with his first and second fingers before pointing behind them. Each man turned his horse and started back toward the meadow, with Rogatus riding at the rear.

Would they make it back to the meadow where there was room to fight before whoever had been ahead of them got close enough to attack?

Rogatus was the last in line as his troop emerged from the woods.

The five he left with the herd lay scattered on the ground, killed by archers.

Two arrows hit his back, knocking him forward. He felt the pricks as the tips of the arrowheads pierced his skin, but his small-link chain mail kept them from killing him.

His men were falling around him, picked off by a volley of arrows from archers spaced out among the trees.

The six had lured them into a killing field of too many archers, and nothing his men did could save them.

Some mounted Brigantes were moving the herd away at a walk. They were in no hurry as their pursuers died behind them.

He bent low over Zephyrus's neck, then shifted to hang off the side away from the woods concealing the archers.

He charged into the center of the walking herd. The horses spooked and bolted, reaching a gallop alongside him as Zephyrus carried him away from certain death.

The hail of arrows had stopped. They wanted the horses unharmed.

He centered himself on his horse again, staying low in the saddle to make a poor target. He drew his sword.

Two mounted Britons angled toward him, aiming to cut him off. When they'd almost reached him, his knees commanded Zephyrus to stop, and a single slash of his sword took the first one down as the pair rode past him. Then Zephyrus spun and surged forward, and a single stroke claimed the second one.

But most of the herd had moved past, exposing him to the archers' aim. Another arrow hit his back, then one pierced the side of his knee. He tumbled, losing his grip on the sword.

He lay face down on the ground with the two Britons' corpses not far behind him. A cascade of Brittonic curses washed over him as a third Briton dismounted and approached to finish him.

He slid his hand across his stomach and tightened his grip on the dagger. He'd have one more chance to take another with him, but only if surprise was on his side.

When the man was two feet away, he summoned what little strength remained to propel himself upward, driving the dagger under the ribs, aiming for the heart. The man staggered back, dragging Rogatus with him. He pulled the dagger free, but it was all he could do to balance on his good leg and stay upright.

When the man crumpled, Rogatus stood alone, awaiting his own death. The world started swirling, and he fought to stay upright. Then an arrow hit his arm, and he dropped the dagger. Another hit his thigh, and he fell again. But he still had one good arm, and he reached as far as it let him to pick up the dagger. He wrapped his fingers around the hilt.

His eyes closed, but he forced them to open. He'd heard stories of the sparkles that a man saw before death took him.

A sigh drained his lungs. He'd never get to tell anyone that the stories were true.

But as long as he could hold the dagger, he would fight.

Zephyrus's prancing legs came near him, then froze.

The stallion's warm breath caressed his face, followed by a soft nicker.

"Sorry, boy."

If only he'd bought the bay...or ridden Boreas today.

He'd lost the herd. He'd lost all his men. He'd soon lose his head.

But maybe she wouldn't lose her horse.

"Go to Narina."

With his voice scarcely above a whisper, the stallion ignored the command.

He raised a hand to shove her horse away. His fingertips rested on the stallion's cheek.

Then everything faded to black.

Chapter 35

The Best Warhorse

Near the Isura River

Sulio sat his horse atop a low hill, scanning for small game. But movement at the edge of the meadow caught his attention.

Three horses trotted out of the path that came in from the north. Then six more. Then a steady stream, and maybe a third of them carried Roman military saddles. Spread out along the moving herd were a few mounted men, all Brigantes.

Maybe a hundred head total. Someone was stealing a Roman herd, but where had all the saddled horses come from?

His stomach clenched when the next rider to appear was Albiso.

At a canter, Sulio rode off the hill and over to his brother.

He reined back to a trot and matched his brother's speed.

"What are you doing? Those are Roman saddles. Where are the men who own them?"

Albiso snorted. "Where all Roman soldiers belong."

Sulio reined back to a fast walk, and Albiso slowed beside him.

With a roll of his eyes and shake of his head, Sulio glared at his brother. "What have you done? You didn't listen to a word Father said, and you may have just killed us all."

"I did listen. I don't agree, but I did what he said. I came across these men after they stole a Roman herd and used it to lure a whole turma into an ambush. The saddled horses are theirs." Albiso's feral grin lit his eyes. "I didn't kill anyone, but I watched the end of it from the hilltop. It was beautiful the way our archers took care of every last one of them." He chuckled. "That tribune you can't stand was leading the Romans."

He scrunched his nose. "They got him last. He killed two of our horsemen with his sword before an archer unhorsed him. He was on the ground with arrows in his back. Our man who was going to finish him and take his head—that Roman rose up and killed him. A few more arrows and he went down again. Last I saw, he had four arrows in his back. If he wasn't dead then…"

Sulio pressed his fingertips into his temples. How could his brother be so stupid? If the Romans discovered he'd been part of it, they'd blame the whole clan.

Albiso tapped his upper arm. "Hey, I didn't help with the killing. But some riders had to bring home the ones he'd killed, so they were short of horsemen. I saw which path they were taking the horses down, and I met them in the woods to offer my help."

Sulio scanned the mix of brown and tan horses the raiders had stolen. No gray or silver among them.

"What was Rogatus riding when you saw him?"

"Narina's favorite, that silver dun. She should never have sold it to him."

"Is he with the herd?"

"I haven't seen him."

Her beautiful horse that she loved so much. Sulio's shoulders slumped. Her prefect had promised to take good care of him. He rode him to his death instead. Or even worse, Zephyrus was now injured, maybe horribly, dying slowly in great pain.

"Where did they set the ambush?"

"In the meadow south of where the Romans had them grazing. Why?"

With a sweep of his hand, Sulio took in the Roman herd. "Zephyrus isn't here. If he's dying slowly, it will break Narina's heart when she finds out. I've got to find out what happened to him. If he's not already dead, I'll end it."

Albiso nodded his approval. "I'm going with them to help get the horses to their warriors. They're planning to ford the river where no one will see. I'll come home after I help with that." His eyes narrowed. "Don't tell Father where you saw me. He's been telling the Romans it's not his clan that's causing trouble. None of these are Isurian, so for the most part, it isn't. He can keep saying that if he doesn't know better."

"I won't say anything if he doesn't ask. Don't you ever tell him I saw you."

With an appreciative grin, Albiso nudged his horse into a canter to catch up.

Sulio reined in and rubbed his forehead as his brother disappeared around the bend in the path. Then he nudged his horse into a trot in the opposite direction.

He knew where the herd had been. He should find Zephyrus somewhere near there. Alive or dead, his silver coat would be impossible to miss. If his injuries might heal enough for him to stand at stud, he would take the stallion home for her to nurse back to health.

His mouth set to a grim line. If Narina was with him, she'd be asking her god to protect her horse and telling him nothing was too hard for the Christian god to do. But if her god was that good at protection, Zephyrus and his rider wouldn't have been where they could get hurt in the first place.

When Sulio reached the meadow, he found at least thirty corpses, stripped of their armor and weapons. Farther into the meadow, Rogatus lay face down in the grass, still wearing a chain-mail shirt and a bronze helmet with no red crest. Four arrows in his back had taken him down. Three more had pierced his arm and his leg. His long sword lay near him, and blood-stained grass within a few feet of him revealed where he'd killed at least two before the archers got him.

But Zephyrus stood guard over the body. He moved to block Sulio's approach to the Roman, and as far as Sulio could see, her stallion was unharmed.

A wry smile joined Sulio's headshake. Zephyrus had been left behind because he refused to leave Rogatus or let anyone get close to his master.

Normally, that sword and the chain-mail shirt would belong to a Brigantian now. Someone would have taken the helmet to wear or to melt down for the bronze, and a Roman officer's head would have been taken as a trophy.

But Sulio wasn't some stranger. The horse had seen him often when he stopped at the farm for some of Veldicca's cooking, and Narina had even let him ride the animal a few times. Would Zephyrus remember that and let him take the horse home to her?

His gaze settled on the Roman's body. The blood stains on the ground showed he'd bled some from his arm and leg, but maybe not enough to kill him. She'd be upset when he told her the tribune was dead, but she'd be more upset if she learned he'd left Rogatus without checking to be sure.

"Zephyrus."

The horse cocked his ears toward Sulio.

"I'm going to check your master, but I'm not going to hurt him more than he already is."

Explaining to a horse. Sulio rolled his eyes. It wouldn't understand the words…but maybe his tone of voice was enough to convey that he only meant to help.

He rode close to the silver dun and dismounted on the side away from him. But when he stepped past his own horse toward Rogatus, an angry neigh broke the silence. Zephyrus spun and moved between him and the body before rearing and striking out.

Sulio moved back behind his mount, but that proved pointless when his own horse bolted away from the angry stallion.

Sulio raised his hands as if in surrender. "Zephyrus. You remember me, Zephyrus. Narina let me ride you more than once. I only want to help Rogatus. You need to let me try, Zephyrus."

Each time he spoke its name, the stallion's ears relaxed a little more. When it no longer looked ready to kill him, he moved forward.

With hands still raised, he took slow steps toward the fallen Roman. With ears back, Zephyrus watched him.

But the stallion let Sulio slowly lower himself to one knee beside Rogatus. The arrows meant to kill him had hung up in the chain mail, only pricking the man inside it. Whatever unhorsed him might not have killed him.

Zephyrus snorted when Sulio reached toward the fallen man, but the horse didn't attack.

He lifted an eyelid, then felt for a pulse by the jaw. Slow and weak, but still there.

He sat back on his haunches and stared at the man he'd been doing his best to keep away from Narina. A senior officer of the occupying army. A man who'd just killed three men of his tribe, even if not of his clan. Loyalty to tribe and clan demanded that he walk away and let the enemy die. Maybe even hasten his departure.

But Rogatus was a decent enough man who was trying to keep the peace, just like Father was. The respect he'd shown all the chieftains, the restraint he'd shown over the stolen cattle—it was nothing like the stories Uncle Lucanus told about how Roman armies behaved in Dacia.

If Albiso was here, he'd slit the Roman's throat. If Father was here…would he try to help him or leave him to die?

Sulio rubbed his forehead. Father would help him. The enemy you didn't know might be much worse than the one you knew. Would the next prefect show anywhere near the same respect and restraint?

Narina's voice played in his head. Love your enemies. Do good to those who hate you.

He drew a deep breath and blew it out. She'd say he wasn't their enemy. She liked the Roman, and it would grieve her kind heart when she heard he was dead. If she ever learned he could have saved Rogatus and didn't…

And Rogatus wasn't a bad man…for a Roman. He wasn't entirely arrogant with the way he showed Father respect and asked for his help in keeping the peace. And even though he had no right to ask anything of Narina, Veldicca thought he was harmless, at least as far as his cousin was concerned.

A steel dagger lay nearby. Engraved as it was, someone important to Rogatus probably gave it to him. Sulio wiped the blood off it before slipping it into its sheath.

"He's not dead yet." Sulio stood. It was less than a mile to Narina's farm. "And you're going to help me get him where he might not die. Let's get you and him home to Narina."

Zephyrus's ears perked up at Narina's name, and he snorted.

"That's a good boy. Help me take Rogatus to Narina."

The stallion tossed his head as if he understood and agreed.

Was it better to drape the injured man across the Roman saddle on Zephyrus or across the saddle pad on his own horse? Would his own mount even stand still long enough to let him hoist the body over and tie it in place?

He rubbed his mouth. Getting him loaded was only part of the problem. What should he do to keep those wounds from opening and Rogatus bleeding out before she could start tending him?

He broke the three arrow shafts a few inches from the arm and leg. He'd bleed less with the arrows filling the wounds than if he took them out. But he left the others stuck in the chain mail. It would look like he was moving a corpse if any Britons saw him. If they knew he was helping a Roman officer, he'd have some fresh arrows in his own back.

From the bottom of the Roman's tunic, he cut strips to tie above the wounds. Tight enough to slow fresh bleeding, but not too tight.

Then he hoisted Rogatus to his feet and draped him across his shoulder before carrying him toward Zephyrus. It was good the Roman was short, but the chain mail made him heavier than he looked.

"Stand." The command he'd heard Narina use froze the stallion in place long enough for him to hoist the limp body across the saddle and tie hand to foot on the uninjured side to keep it there.

He mounted his own horse and led Zephyrus and his human cargo into the woods. To avoid being spotted, weaving between the trees was better than taking the path.

If the Romans saw him, they might think he'd killed one of their own and return the favor. If Britons stopped him, they might finish off Rogatus and then kill him as a traitor for helping the enemy.

But if he reached the farm, Narina would think this the best gift he'd ever brought her. Having her stallion come home would delight her. What having the Roman come with him would do…he'd have to wait and see.

Narina's farm

Narina pulled the last basket of apples to the end of the cart. With Veldicca, Bikka, and Atto helping, they'd picked enough of the ripe ones today to keep Lucania busy in the house's inner courtyard tomorrow.

Brigantian men who didn't know who lived there had already come once. Rogatus had warned about Lucania being in danger if anyone like that saw her. So, for now at least, her little sister had agreed to stay out of sight and cut up everything for drying while the others harvested the crops.

The concern he'd shown for Lucania, for all her household...he was a good man. When she remembered the sadness in his eyes when he told her they should leave, it warmed her heart. Evenings would feel incomplete without him coming to eat silently with her, telling her she was important to him simply by how he looked at her.

God, please let his worries about rebellion be proven wrong. Please let us be together again soon.

She'd just bent her knees to let her slide the basket onto her shoulder when movement in the trees past the stable caught her eye. Trenus had insisted they take the ax "just in case." It lay on the floorboard under the seat, and she moved forward to get it.

But she froze before reaching it. Sulio rode into the farmyard leading Zephyrus. Her hands shot up to cover her mouth. Draped across her favorite horse was a soldier with a bronze helmet with no red crest and too many arrows stuck in his back.

Rogatus.

She bit her lip as her vision blurred. Tears dribbled down her cheeks as she walked toward them. She'd been praying for his protection. He wasn't supposed to die.

When Sulio reined in, he dropped the lead. Zephyrus kept walking toward her. The horse didn't stop until he pressed his forehead against her chest. She wrapped her arms around his neck and closed her eyes.

"I brought you two presents." Sulio stood beside her. "You've only looked at one."

Her gaze shifted to Rogatus. Only Sulio would call bringing her dead friend to her a present.

She swept the tears from her cheeks, but a new set rolled down. "Who killed him?"

Sulio felt behind Rogatus's jaw. "No one. He's not dead yet. That's why I brought him here."

He wiped the fresh tears from her cheek. "I thought you might help me keep him alive."

Her head drew back. "But those arrows…"

"Stuck in his chain mail. The archers were fooled by those, too. They didn't get through far enough to kill him. He's got a couple more in his leg and one in his arm, but Veldicca knew how to fix us when we got hurt as children. I expect she can do something for him."

Atto came through the front door and stopped midstride. Then he trotted over to join them.

Sulio tapped Atto's shoulder. "You and I need to get him inside before someone sees him here."

He squatted and untied the cloth strips that held hand to foot. Then he stood and slapped his own shoulder. "Help me get him on here so we can."

When Sulio got his shoulder under Rogatus and straightened so he could bear the whole weight, Atto led Zephyrus away from them.

"Let me help you take him in." Narina placed her hand against Rogatus's side to keep him from slipping off Sulio. "We can put him in Father's old room. Atto, please put Zephyrus into the stable before someone sees him. I don't want him stolen like the other stallions were. Then come help us. We need to get him out of this armor and into something less Roman. You two men can take care of that."

Narina kept her gaze on her wounded friend as they carried him through the narrow hallway into the courtyard.

Thank You, God, for protecting both of them and having Sulio bring them to me. Please let Rogatus make it through this and get better quickly.

A duet of gasps came from Veldicca and Lucania when they looked up from slicing apples. Lucania started to rise, but Veldicca pressed down on her shoulder. "Stay here with Bikka. I'll help them."

"But I want to help, too." Lucania wiped at the corner of her eye.

"You can after we get him tended." Veldicca set her knife aside and rose.

Sulio grunted. "He's heavier than he looks. Show me where to put him."

Narina opened the door to her father's room. "I need to make the bed. No one has slept here since Father died."

She took a clean sheet and a pillow from the cabinet and covered the straw-filled mattress.

After Sulio knelt beside the bed, Veldicca helped him move Rogatus onto it, face down.

"We can take these out now." Sulio pulled the first arrow out of the chain mail. "I left them so any Briton would think I was only moving a corpse. I didn't want to become one myself."

As he removed the remaining ones, Narina wrapped an arm around his shoulders and gave him her biggest hug.

He eyed her as if suspicious, but his smile declared he wasn't. "What was that for?"

"For saving him. For loving your enemy like Iesu said we should."

"I don't love your Roman. I don't even like him." He wrinkled his nose. "But I've gotten to know him well enough that I wouldn't call him my enemy. For a Roman, he's not as bad as he could be."

She rested her head against his shoulder as they stood looking at Rogatus. "You know that's not the kind of love I'm talking about. The way Iesu told us to love is a decision, not a feeling. It's doing what we can to help, even when we don't want to. It's taking a risk to save someone, even when it might get you killed. That's what you just did."

His nose scrunched. "I didn't do it for him. I did it for you. I didn't want you sad all the time, mourning for a dead Roman who thought you were friends." He massaged the shoulder he'd carried Rogatus on. "Besides, it wasn't me who saved him. It was Zephyrus."

"Zephyrus?"

"I found him standing over what I thought was a corpse, defending it. A whole troop was ambushed by archers. The rest of them were stripped and left in the field. Zephyrus didn't let anyone get close enough to discover he wasn't dead."

"I knew he was the best warhorse I've ever trained." She hugged him once more. "But you're the best cousin to bring Rogatus so we can help him."

Veldicca bent over to inspect his arm. "After we get the arrow out and bandage this wound, we can get him out of the chain mail. But I'm not sure how to do that. Do we just pull? And then there's the ones in his thigh and his knee."

"Leave all those to me." He placed his hands on Narina's shoulders and turned her toward the door. "You don't want to watch. But you can go boil some water and bring it back here with some soap and clean cloth strips. Bring some wine or vinegar as well. We'll need to clean his wounds well and pour one of those into them before we bandage them. Loss of blood hasn't killed him, but an infection still might."

Narina paused in the door to look back at the Roman she'd grown too fond of and the cousin she loved more than her own brothers.

Thank You, God, for Sulio finding him. Thank You for making him help instead of leaving Rogatus to die. Please make Rogatus well again. I know You can heal anything, but Sulio doesn't. Please show him Your power and mercy at work by healing Rogatus as if he'd never been hurt.

Chapter 36

A Safe Haven

When Narina returned with clean rags, cloth strips, and the vinegar, Atto had come. They'd already turned the bed so they could reach Rogatus from both sides. They'd taken off his helmet, sandals, scabbard, and skirt of leather strips. His sheathed dagger lay in the corner with the rest.

"Lucania is watching the water. She'll come tell me as soon as it boils."

Sulio was down on one knee beside Rogatus's shoulder, where the broken shaft of an arrow stuck out just below the short chain-mail sleeve.

"It missed the bone, so it's better to push it on through. We can clean it better as well."

She handed the cloths to Veldicca and set the vinegar on the bed table.

Push it on through. She closed her eyes, and swallowed hard to control her stomach. How could it be better to make two bleeding holes instead of one?

Rogatus's sun-bronzed skin was like Grandfather's at the end of summer, but somehow he seemed paler as he lay there, his eyes closed.

She turned away before the tears started again. "He'll need something other than that bloody tunic. He can wear one of Father's so we can get to his thigh and knee to clean the wounds for a few days. Besides, the red stripes on white...anyone seeing those would know what he is."

From the trunk in the corner, she took out a short-sleeved, knee-length, tan tunic.

She clutched it to her chest. How many arrow wounds had Father seen treated? If only he were here to tell them what was best to do.

"At least he's still unconscious." Sulio sounded so calm, but when she looked at his face, the nervousness showed. "Let's get it all done before he wakes up. Then I'll leave him to you."

When her cousin prepared to push the arrow through, she shuddered.

"I'll go check on the hot water."

As she left the room, she glanced back at the two most important men in her life.

Thank You, God, for protecting Rogatus today. Please let him be all right when this is over. And thank You for Sulio. I don't know what we'd do without him. Protect him, too, until peace returns.

Pain was a welcome companion when a man thought the darkness that surrounded him meant death had come.

Rogatus's upper right arm ached, his thigh throbbed, and his knee...he had no word to describe how that hurt.

But even with his eyes closed, he saw light on his eyelids. He opened them slowly. Above him were wooden beams and rafters and a thatch roof above that. Light came through an open door, and it lit the end of the bed where he lay. A light sheet covered his lower body.

A movement to his right drew his gaze. Lucania sat in a chair, watching him. Her smile started slowly and grew into the biggest grin he'd seen on her yet.

"Where am I?"

"At our farm. Narina asked me to watch you until you woke up. Would you like me to get her now?"

Nothing he could think of would please him more.

"Yes. Is Zephyrus here?"

"He's in the stable. Narina thought it best if no one saw him. All but the mares with nursing foals were taken by the rebels. She didn't want to lose him again."

Lucania touched his forearm. "And she didn't want anyone to come after you. Many of our clan know you ride Zephyrus. If someone hunting for you saw him, they'd search the house. She didn't want to risk you getting killed here. She said they might kill us for helping you, too."

"She's right."

"But we all think you're worth the risk." She patted his good leg. "I'll get Narina."

The last thing he remembered was Zephyrus standing above him, nuzzling his cheek. He'd ordered the horse to go to Narina. Maybe she came back with her horse and got him, but why hadn't the raiders killed him before she could?

Soft footsteps approaching the door turned into the smiling woman standing at his bedside. "It's good to see you awake again. It's been too long."

"Too long since I saw you last. But how did you find me?"

"I didn't. Sulio did. Then he brought you here."

His head drew back. "I thought him more likely to kill me than help me."

"He's not that kind of man." She wrinkled her nose. "He's seen enough of you to know you're not as bad as he thought all Romans were. He came across you when he went looking for Zephyrus. He saw some men who were not of our clan driving horses with many having Roman saddles, but Zephyrus wasn't among them."

She bit her lip. "He thought he must be dead or badly hurt. He couldn't leave him suffering, so he went looking for him. He found him in the middle of a meadow, defending you where you lay. When he checked and you weren't dead, he brought you both home to me."

He rubbed his forehead with his left hand. Sulio. He'd hoped her cousin was more like his father than his brother, and this just proved it.

"Lucania said he's in your stable now. Did he get hurt at all?"

"Not even a bad scratch. You took good enough care of him for me."

"It sounds like he was taking care of me instead. Like he would have defended you if I'd tried to hurt you that day we met." He lowered his arm to rest on his chest. A newborn baby would be stronger than he felt.

"I didn't expect to earn his loyalty so quickly."

She moved to Lucania's chair and sat. "Horses are good judges of character. He could see you were worth defending, like I can. What happened to you?"

"I went hunting the ones who stole my horses and killed all but one of the herders. He made it back to the fort to report six men had stolen the herd, so I took a turma out to get it back and punish the thieves. Thirty should have been more than enough for only six. But now I think they let him get away so they could set the ambush. Cavalry can't defeat archers in the trees." He blew out a heavy sigh. "I'm the only one still alive."

Without lifting his arm, he rubbed his cheek. "Germanus is my second in command. He'll lead some out looking for us. When he finds the others, he'll think I'm dead as well or taken captive. He'll report that to the legate. I'll lose my command if he thinks I'm dead and replaces me."

She touched his right hand where it lay on the bed. "I can take care of that. I'll ride to Eboracum to tell the legate I have you recovering at my home."

A vigorous shake of his head was his first answer. "I can't let you do that. You said that road's not safe to ride alone."

Her eyes laughed at him, but what she proposed was more than he could allow.

"Not safe for a Roman officer. Look at me. I couldn't look less Roman if I tried. I've ridden it alone many times."

"But you weren't alone when you brought the stallions."

"I only brought someone along to watch the rest of the horses while I left to show you what they could do. I've ridden down to see Minconus and his family many times, and I've never had a problem."

What she said was probably true, but that was before Trajan died.

"But what if someone wants to take your horse? They stole most of your herd already."

"I'll ride Bena. Anyone on that road is likely to be from my clan, and all I have to do is tell them they'll be in trouble with Bellicus if they steal her. The ones who took my horses weren't of our clan, but even those were afraid to take the mares that were still nursing their foals after Bikka threatened them with what Bellicus would do."

Bellicus had been his ally in keeping the peace, but her uncle had no friendly feelings toward Rome or her soldiers. Was he friend or enemy now?

"Does he know you have me here?"

"Sulio didn't say whether he'd tell him. But I'd be surprised if he did. He knows the only way to be certain something remains secret is to tell no one. But even if Uncle does know, I don't think you need to worry. He can keep secrets, too. Some might be angry enough to kill Sulio if they knew he'd helped you. They'd be at least as angry at me. I don't think his father would risk that any more than Sulio would."

She patted his hand again. "Uncle knows I came home to protect Lucania until this is all over. He wouldn't want anyone showing up here who might think she was Roman and hurt her. All three of you agree on that."

More tension drained away. She had that effect on him every time they were together. "I've seen how Sulio loves you two and Veldicca. I'm alive because of that."

"Probably, and we're all glad of it." Narina stood. "So, it's decided. Tomorrow morning I'll go tell your legate that you'll have a safe haven here until you recover enough to ride the distance, and then you'll return."

She leaned over him to adjust the sheet. Like he'd imagined his mother would, if she'd been with him as a child. But the fondness he had for this special woman was nothing like a child's emotion.

"Bikka said some of my people went to Eboracum after the horses were stolen. Minconus will be taking care of those, and I can check on them while I'm there. I'll let Minconus know what's going on and that we're safe here. He shouldn't try to come up to the farm, either. He looks too much like Grandfather, not Father." She took a step back. "Are you hungry?"

Inexpressible tiredness swept over him. Hungry? Not really, but she and Veldicca liked to feed him.

"Not yet. But maybe one of your special rolls and something to drink?"

Her soft laugh washed over him. "You're out of luck today. We've been harvesting apples, so I haven't baked. But I can bring you something Bikka made, and it tastes good enough to me."

"Sounds fine." His voice had grown quieter. He shook his head slightly. It was getting harder to stay awake.

"I'll be right back with the drink. After that you can rest. I'll just leave the bread on the chair for later."

"Thank you, Narina...for everything."

She glanced over her shoulder as she moved away. "We're all happy to do it. We love to take care of our friends."

As he watched her walk out the door, his smile grew. Her warhorse had saved him. Her cousin had brought him here. He'd have a safe haven with her until he could ride again. Everything good since he came to Isurium he owed to her. Nothing he could say would ever thank her enough.

But what he hoped to do someday should be enough...for both of them.

Chapter 37

Past and Future

Early morning of Day 26

Rogatus had been awake for some time when Narina entered with two bowls of porridge.

"I thought we could eat together so you won't feel lonely. Then after we tend your wounds, I'll ride down to the legate to deliver your message."

"I'd like that."

They ate in silence, like they always did, but it was the best meal he'd had since she closed the taberna.

They'd barely finished when Veldicca came in with the tray holding vinegar, honey, and clean strips of cloth. He scrunched his nose. The next few minutes would be unpleasant at best and miserable at worst, but healing never started without pain.

First, they unwrapped his arm, and he clamped his jaw as they poured the stinging liquid into the wound from both sides. Then Veldicca applied some honey before wrapping it back up.

One done, two more to go. When they exposed his thigh, it was no worse than he expected. Two open wounds again because whoever removed the arrow pushed it through instead of pulling it out. But without the ladle-like cup of Diocles or the special forceps his medicus used to pull arrows back through the entrance hole, they'd done the best thing.

While Veldicca treated both wounds on his thigh, Narina kept her eyes averted, even as she held the basin that caught the vinegar.

He stopped himself from smiling at her modesty and kept his gaze off her caring face. She'd blush even more if she thought it amused him. Even though a blush always became her, enjoying how her eyes brightened as her cheeks reddened wasn't worth causing her embarrassment today.

But when they moved to the knee and unwrapped it, fear surged within him, and he fought to mask how much what he saw shook him.

The arrow had pierced the knee itself, not above or below it. It had swelled to twice its normal size, and the reddish purple hue of the whole area around the joint made his heart rate rise.

He tried to bend it. It barely moved, and that effort made him close his eyes and grit his teeth until the explosion of pain settled back to a steady ache.

He stayed on his back, eyes closed, until Veldicca finished and touched his arm.

"That's all I need to do for now. I'll be back later with your lunch." Compassion filled her eyes. "I'll make something you like a lot, in case you're hungry."

"Thank you." His voice was quieter than he intended, but it was the best he could do.

He expected Narina to leave as well, but she brought the chair over to sit beside his bed.

"I'll stay a while if you like."

He nodded, then looked away.

"Is there something you want to talk about?"

He started to shake his head, then stopped. He wasn't a man to share his fears with anyone. But if he were, she'd be the one he'd trust with them.

"It was the arrow to my knee that unhorsed me. The thigh, the arm... they'll heal well enough, but my knee..."

His breaths came too fast, and he willed them to slow down.

"Will I be able to ride well enough to lead cavalry? The only thing a Roman son owns is his military pay. I can't afford to lose my command until I've earned another 25,000 denarii."

"I expect you will. Things always look their worst when you first hurt them." She scooted the chair a little closer. "Grandfather was laid up for a month when he was hurt in the Dacian war, and he didn't lose his command. I can't see how the legate would want to replace you after you've done so well."

"I got promoted early because he thought he needed someone who knew how to lead cavalry immediately, much quicker than he could get an experienced ala prefect from a mainland province. He won't want to wait while I heal."

"Does it matter that much if he doesn't?"

"I need to earn 100,000 denarii of my own to be equestrian. That arrow put my whole future in jeopardy."

She leaned closer. "But you're equestrian already, so why must you earn 100,000 to be one?"

He drew a deep breath and held it before letting it out. Revealing a hidden truth was always risky. If he told her about his past, would it change everything? But maybe it was better if she knew it sooner rather than later. If it was going to drive her away, it was better to find out now than when he asked her to be his wife. He'd have to reveal the truth before he did.

"I never told you my first name. I haven't told anyone here. I've signed things P. Trebonius Rogatus. Most will assume that's Publius, but it isn't."

He kept his gaze fixed on those compassionate eyes. But was he brave enough to watch how his next words might change them?

"It's Proculus. My grandfather saddled me with it. It means 'born while his father was away.'"

She tilted her head, and confusion filled her eyes. "So? My brothers and I were all born when our father was away with his cohort. We lived with Grandfather in Viminacium while he was gone. Minconus was twelve when Father retired and we came here. So, Grandfather mostly raised him, and he's always thought of himself as Roman, not half and half like me."

For a moment, Rogatus turned his gaze away from her. He could trust her never to tell anyone, but could she look at him the same once she knew?

"But your father never questioned whether you were his. I was a big baby when I came almost a month early. So, Grandfather wondered whether I was fathered before his son was home on leave. He kept me and named me because he didn't want the embarrassment of admitting my mother was unfaithful."

Concern for a friend still shone in her eyes. It felt safe to tell her what only his great-uncle had heard of his past.

"But when Father returned home, he accused her of adultery and divorced her. Grandfather banished her then, and I never got to meet her before she died. Before I was ten, Father and Grandfather treated me no better than the household slaves." He glanced at her still-caring eyes. "I know what it is to go to bed hungry."

He stared at his hand as he rubbed his palm. "After I was ten, Grandfather had me educated like my brothers because he was worried about what his friends would think if he didn't. But he died when I was eighteen. Father shipped me off to the family villa more than fifty miles from Rome and left me there." A wry smile tugged at his mouth. "That's where I learned to ride so well. There was nothing else to do." The smile faded. "More than once after Grandfather died, my father said he'd probably disinherit me because I wasn't his."

Narina's brows dipped as her frown deepened. "How could he do that to a little boy? It wasn't your fault how you came to be a Rogatus."

"My nanny swore Mother was faithful, that I was just big when I came early. I think I believe her. Father and my two brothers never let me forget I wasn't a real Rogatus. Father refused to do anything to help me start the usual equestrian career. He said he'd be ashamed to ask one of his friends to find someone like me a post. It was my mother's uncle who recommended me for the tres militiae. He's the one who used his influence to get me an equitata for my first command. He's the one I write when something good happens."

He glanced at her. Her smile had returned.

"I expect you make him proud every time you do."

"That's what he tells me. He's one of the finest men I know. He's certainly the kindest. But I expect Father to disinherit me. If I don't earn that 100,000 before I leave my last command, I won't be equestrian anymore."

Narina rested her hand on his arm, and the warmth of it spread from his arm to his heart. "It doesn't matter whether you're equestrian or not. What matters is the kind of man you are, and you're one of the finest men I've ever known."

A wry laugh escaped before he could stop it. "Then you probably haven't known many men."

"I don't need to see hundreds of horses to know when I have a truly superior one. I could name your many fine qualities, but I'd probably embarrass you." The smile he liked best appeared. "Veldicca would agree with every one of them."

Rogatus placed his hand atop hers. "Sulio says you're too kind-hearted to see the flaws in people. That you only look for the good."

She touched the back of his hand. "I see people's flaws clearly enough, but I choose to see the potential instead of the limitations."

She rose. "We can talk later. I need to leave for Eboracum if I'm going to get there early enough to come back before evening."

She touched his foot. "I hope you'll want company for dinner."

"I will."

Two quick pats, and she stepped back. "I'll take the note you wrote to the legate, and I'll see you soon."

His nod sent her out the door.

Would he want her company for dinner? He rolled his eyes. He'd rather have a crust of stale bread with her than Veldicca's best stew without her, but he wouldn't say that aloud. Still, it felt so good to have shared his past and what might be his future, only to discover neither mattered to her at all.

Narina reached Eboracum late enough that Minconus would be at the taberna with the lunch guests. Normally, she would let him know she had come before taking her mount to his town house. But today she went straight there and left Bena with his stableman.

It was a short walk to the front gate of the fortress. As she approached, the guards eyed her with suspicion. One drew his sword.

She stopped three feet from them. "I would like to speak with the legate."

"No Brigantians are allowed within the fortress." A wave of the sword added a threat to his words.

"I have a message for the legate from Prefect Rogatus."

"Leave now." The second guard stepped forward, sword drawn.

Her hand tightened around strap of the purse that held the report. How was she going to deliver it if they wouldn't even let her in? Maybe...

"Would someone please find Tribune Dexter and tell him Narina Lucana needs to speak with the legate about Prefect Rogatus. The tribune has met me, and he knows you can safely allow me to see your legate. What I have to tell him is urgent."

One narrowed his eyes, then called out a Roman name. A soldier came out of the gatehouse.

"This one is asking for Tribune Dexter. Let him know a Narina Lucana is here for him."

The new man scanned her, then walked off, muttering something under his breath about not meeting tribune standards.

As she watched him go toward the headquarters building, she tried not to blush. But the words were too close to what Dexter and Plantus said when they didn't know she could hear them. It didn't matter what any of them thought, but it still hurt.

It was only a few moments before Dexter, wearing his helmet, came out the principia doors and strode toward her.

His face was grim. "Narina Lucana. I regret to tell you that Rogatus is dead. He was killed by Brigantian rebels. You've ridden here for nothing."

"I've ridden here for him. He's not dead, but he almost was. He's at my farm, and he hasn't recovered enough to ride yet. I have a message for the legate that he said was urgent, so I offered to deliver it for him."

Relief filled Dexter's eyes before he turned to the guards. "I'll escort her to the legate myself."

They saluted as he led her under the stone arch and into the fortress.

They passed saluting guards at the entrance to the principia. More guards saluted Dexter by a pair of doors carved with an eagle, its wings spread and its talons reaching out to attack.

An optio who sat at a desk by the doors rose and saluted Dexter.

"This one has a message from Rogatus for the legate."

The optio nodded and opened the door for them.

It was brighter inside than Narina expected, and they approached a desk that sat where light from the windows lit it. The man who sat behind it looked so much like how she remembered Grandfather.

Dexter stopped four feet from the desk and saluted. "Legate, this is Narina Lucana. She's come with a message from Prefect Rogatus."

The legate's eyebrows rose. "Rogatus isn't dead?"

"No, Legate." Narina cleared her throat and spoke in her best Latin. "He was ambushed, and his injuries are enough that he can't ride to Eboracum yet. But he wanted you to know that he wasn't dead and would be returning as soon as possible. He asked me to tell you the ambush wasn't by men of the Isurium clan, but he's not sure yet which of the other clans was involved. He wanted to urge restraint toward the Isurium clan until he can resume his duties and find the ones truly responsible for the theft of his herd and the attack on his turma."

A patronizing smile curved the legate's lips. "Was there more to the prefect's message?"

"Yes, Legate. Punishing innocents makes enemies and rebels of those who were willing to live in peace under Rome's rule. The chieftain of the Isurium clan understands what happens when a tribe rebels against Rome, and he's dedicated to keeping the peace so his people won't suffer the consequences."

"Is that all?" His lips had straightened.

"Rogatus is very eager to return so you won't replace him." She bit her lip. She hadn't meant to say that. "He's deeply committed to serving Rome well."

She reached into the purse hanging at her side and withdrew the thin wooden sheets of Rogatus's report. In her nervousness, she'd already told the legate almost everything that was there.

She held it out. Dexter took it and gave it to the legate.

Silence filled the room as the legate read the sheets. When he finished, he set it aside and clasped his hands on the desktop. His eyes narrowed.

"He chose a messenger who spoke what he wrote almost word for word. Did he write it...or you?"

Narina's heart skipped a beat. What was he accusing her of? "He took two arrows in his leg and one in his right arm, so it was too painful to write. I volunteered to write down his words as he spoke them."

She raised her chin. "My grandfather was a cohort prefect in Moesia, where I was born. I received a good education from my mother. My father served as a cohort cavalry centurion in the Dacian war under Grandfather. Father won personal armillae before he retired and returned to Britannia. I am a citizen of Rome."

The legate stroked his cheek, and suspicion faded from his eyes. "Rogatus chose a capable messenger, if an unconventional one."

He leaned back in his chair. "Tell Rogatus he can rest easy about his command. He's already demonstrated his skill at leading it. I don't want to risk getting someone less capable who'll lose the whole ala. You can tell him I don't hold losing the horses and a turma against him this time. His assumption that he was riding after a handful of raiders, not into an archers' ambush, was reasonable, given what his injured man reported."

Relief surged through her, but she managed to stop at a subdued smile instead of a beaming one.

His brow furrowed. "But how was it that the archers didn't kill him as well?"

"He bought one of the warhorses I trained. He had four arrows in his back that hung up in the chain mail."

"Chain mail? That's not tribune armor."

"He had a shirt made when he led cavalry against raiders in Moesia." She shrugged. "I guess it's easier to fight with a cavalry sword in that. With three more in his leg and arm, the raiders assumed he was dead and left him."

The legate's head drew back. "And yet he's still alive. Why didn't they take his head?"

"My horse wouldn't let them get close enough."

A chuckle was the last thing she expected to hear.

"It's an old saying that the right horse can make the difference between victory and death. Maybe I should buy one from you."

"The day before the ambush, raiders who weren't from the Isurium clan stole the bay I had ready and the two-year-olds I was training. Maybe it was the same men who stole your herd." She put on her best horse-trader smile. "But I should have some trained in three years."

"Hmph." The legate leaned back in his chair and crossed his arms. "I hope not to be here that long. Do you need anything to care for Rogatus right now?"

"No. One of my people knows what to do, and we're happy to do it until he recovers enough to return."

"Good. You have my thanks and that of Rome for doing so." His gaze shifted from her to the tribune beside her. "Dexter."

Rogatus's friend squared his shoulders. "Yes, Legate?"

"Escort her back to the gate."

Dexter's fist hit his chest. "Yes, Legate."

He turned and pointed toward the door.

Narina walked at Dexter's side with silence between them until they were out of the office and almost back to the main gate.

"Tell Rogatus Fortuna certainly smiled on him when he bought that horse." He glanced at her, then looked straight ahead as they walked. "It appears that good fortune includes meeting you, too."

She gave him what Mother had called a social smile. Fortuna had nothing to do with anything, but God had blessed him for sure.

"I'll tell Plantus and the other tribunes what happened. They'll be glad to hear he didn't die." His face turned solemn. "I hope none of us do."

Her next smile was genuine. "I hope you don't, too. Thank you for helping me see the legate."

His friendly smile was untinged by condescension as they reached the gate. "Give him my greetings, and tell him I hope to see him soon."

"I will."

With a single nod, he turned and strode back toward the headquarters.

She watched until he disappeared inside.

God, please don't let rebellion bring war on this land. Make it safe for Rogatus's friends to come see him again. Make it safe once more for us all.

Chapter 38

Praying About It, Too

Minconus's taberna, midday of Day 26

Narina's first stop after leaving the fortress was the taberna. When she entered, the tinkle of a silver bell announced her arrival. Minconus turned from a conversation with two well-dressed merchants, and his eyebrows rose. Then he turned back to his customers.

She seated herself at an empty corner table. In the shirt and trousers she wore training horses, she drew more than one questioning glance from diners at the other tables.

When Minconus approached, smiling broadly, she stood. She tipped her head toward the stairs that led to the second story lodgings.

"We should speak in private."

He looked into her eyes, and stopped. His smile faded as he nodded slowly. Then he pointed at the stairs.

She went up ahead of him and turned into one of the rooms that he hadn't yet rented for the night.

He closed the door. "How is Trenus doing? When he sent some of your people to me, they thought he'd get better, but they didn't know what was happening with you and Lucania in Isurium. I have your two women helping out in the taberna, and I helped your men find work as dock laborers until things calm down."

"Thank you for doing that. He's getting better. Two days ago, I took Lucania and the others home to the farm. Now that Atto is there, he's not trying to do things he shouldn't. There are enough of us to bring in the apple crop, too. But I've shut down the taberna, and I don't know when I'll open it again."

What remained of his smile turned into a frown. "Was that necessary? Wasn't the prefect about to start bringing his decurions to eat? He'll get used to not eating Veldicca's cooking while you're gone, and maybe he won't start again."

"I'm not worried about that. He was sorry to see us go, but it was his suggestion. If he has to take the ala out to deal with a problem, he thought the fort might be attacked. With the taberna so close, someone who wasn't of our clan might think Lucania was only a Roman. They might kill or kidnap her."

Minconus sucked in a breath through pursed lips. "He's right. She has a full share of Roman beauty, just like Mother did." He put on the smile he always used when she used to let being homely bother her. "But you got Father's skill with horses, and that's much more important."

It wasn't much of a consolation then. And after losing Father's herd...

"That's not worth much now." She hadn't meant to cry, but when she thought about what might happen to Father's beautiful horses, she couldn't help it. "Father spent years building our herd. We had one of the finest around here." She swept the first tear aside. "Beside Bena and the mule I had in town, all I have left is three nursing mares and their foals. There's only one colt among them. Two might be carrying the last of the old stallion's foals. The one who just gave birth...maybe I can breed her with Zephyrus."

"Your silver dun? I thought you sold him to the prefect."

"I did, but he's in my stable right now."

Minconus made a circle with his hand like he used to when he wanted the rest of the story.

"Rogatus has become a good friend. He offered to let me bring the mares up to breed with him when they were ready."

Minconus's smile returned. He sat on the bed and patted the spot beside him. "Tell me more."

"It's not our clansmen, but someone was after more than my horses. They stole one of his horse herds yesterday and used it to set a trap for whoever came for them. He chose to lead the turma hunting them himself, and archers killed all but him. He's at the farm now. He's only alive because Zephyrus wouldn't let anyone near him after he fell."

"And now you're looking after him while he heals?"

"Yes, and I rode here to deliver an urgent message for him to the legate."

He rubbed his lower lip. "This presents an opportunity. While you're looking after him, maybe you can get him to decide to marry you. There isn't anyone who gets to know you who doesn't like you. He should be grateful enough after you nurse him back to health. It wouldn't be the first time that's happened."

She rolled her eyes. "I don't want a man to marry me out of gratitude. Besides, Zephyrus and Sulio saved him. I'll just be taking care of him until he recovers enough to ride."

Minconus's eyes widened. "Sulio?" He snorted. "I never would have expected him to help a Roman soldier."

"Yes, but don't tell that to anyone, or he might be killed as a traitor. He heard about the ambush, and he went looking for Zephyrus. He was going to bring him home to me if he wasn't hurt too badly to breed. Sulio found him defending Rogatus, and none of the raiders got close enough to kill him. So, he brought both of them."

"Hmm." Minconus tapped his lips with one finger. "So, Rogatus owes a big debt to the two of you. A rich equestrian would bring a great deal of money into the family if he'll marry you. Do you think you can get him to stay in Britannia, or does he want to move on to a warmer province when his time as ala prefect ends?"

She slapped his arm. "How can you only be thinking of the family fortune? We're on the edge of war breaking out, and only God knows what that will mean for all of us."

"I have no control over that, but Father made me responsible for you. It's you I'm thinking about. You deserve a husband and children. Here's your chance. Who else is interested in you?"

She stared at him. He might as well have told her no man ever would be.

"Sulio tells me there are many who would be. He's offered repeatedly to find me one, but I don't want just anyone. I want someone who loves my God, too."

Minconus mimicked her eye roll. "It's easy for him to say that because he knows you won't ask him to produce one. And how many young Christian men do you know? Do you know even one? Have you even heard of one anywhere in the neighboring clans?"

"Veldicca knew many of them in Isca Silurum. There were groups who gathered every *Solis* to worship together."

"But that's hundreds of miles away, and you're never going to live there. So, what you're really saying is you'll never marry because you can't find what's impossible to find here. If you ever want to have children of your own, you'll have to settle for a man who doesn't care what you believe, but who's not going to change what he believes."

He crossed his arms. "Mother and Grandfather worshipped the Roman gods. So did Father. My wife and Dubnus's wife do, too. I haven't seen anything to convince me we've made the wrong choice. But if you're ever going to marry, you'll have to settle for a man who worships either the gods of the Britons or the gods of Rome. You might as well pick Rome when that could make you rich."

She felt her anger rising, but she drew a deep breath and blew it out slowly. Minconus had no idea what it was like to know and follow the God who loved her more than any man could, and she loved Him in return. Before she spoke again, the anger was gone. Her brother didn't understand her, but he did love her.

"If all I wanted was to marry, then what you say is true. But even if I didn't care about what he believed, I don't want a man who wants me only because he feels he owes me something. I want a marriage like Father and Mother had, where they truly loved each other."

"You don't find Rogatus repugnant, do you?"

"No. He's a very nice man. Father would have approved of him."

"You couldn't find a handsomer one. Maybe some of the other tribunes are richer, but none of those owe you their life. Some of these young tribunes make their choices according to what's the most honorable, and only an ingrate wouldn't see you as deserving that if you asked for it."

"I don't know why we're even talking about this. Neither of us will be changing our minds."

The deepest sigh escaped her brother. "Not today anyway. But you're not getting any younger, and you might never get a chance at an equestrian like him again. Be so nice to the man that he'll think he can't do without you before he's finished healing."

"I'm not going to try to manipulate him into liking me."

She would never tell Minconus, but she wouldn't have to. It was clear he already did.

"I want you to promise me you'll at least think about whether he'd make a good husband for you."

She thought about him all the time. That wasn't the problem, but Minconus would never understand. At least not until he discovered that following Iesu was what he needed to do as well.

"All right. I won't do anything to drive him away, and we'll see what happens. But I won't just think about it. I'll pray about it, too."

"Good girl." He drew her into a quick hug. "There's still time to get home well before sunset, but don't wait too long to leave. I don't want to see you ambushed and kidnapped."

"You'd be at much greater risk than I will. I look like Father and blend right in. You look Roman, and that could get you killed right now. Please don't try to come visit the farm until things get more settled."

She stood. "I left Bena at your house, and I'll visit a little with your family before I leave. Please tell Gavo and Lanuccus I'll let you know when it looks safe for them to come back. I'll speak with Vinda and Minura here, and then I'll go."

"Good. I don't want to lose you. You don't need to worry about them or the men. I'll keep taking care of all your people, and I won't do something stupid like riding up to see you with the roads unsafe for travel."

She gave him a quick hug. "I'd hate to lose you, too."

As she headed downstairs to find her workers who were also good friends, she breathed a sigh of relief. Dubnus lived south of the Brigantian lands, so the unrest shouldn't affect him at all. Minconus's family and her people here couldn't be much safer since they lived in the legion town.

But Rogatus...the legate valued him enough to wait for his return, but would returning to duty to earn that last 25,000 denarii end up costing his life?

A deep sigh drained her lungs.

Whether he died in action or made all he needed and returned to Rome, she'd be losing her friend someday. She'd be praying for the second. But even as fond as she was of him now, either would end up breaking her heart.

Narina's farm, early afternoon of Day 26

Lucania lounged in Father's wicker chair, watching Rogatus sleep. She'd spent the morning inside the farmhouse, slicing apples and arranging them on drying racks under the covered colonnade of the inner courtyard. So, she'd already been bored half to death when Veldicca left her soup pot to go tell the ones in the orchard that lunch was ready.

Narina and Veldicca had told her why it was so important to stay out of sight since the raiders came and stole the horses. She didn't want to be kidnapped or killed for looking like Mother. But it wasn't fair that she couldn't go roaming in the fields or riding one of their horses, like she used to.

She'd expected another long afternoon with an endless supply of apples to cut when Veldicca asked her to take some soup to Rogatus. Then he'd asked her to stay for a while to practice Brittonic, and Veldicca had said yes.

They'd gone over maybe two dozen words about the farm and talked in Brittonic for a while when his eyelids started drooping. Then, after an unusually long blink, they didn't open. The soft sounds of his slow, steady breathing pronounced him asleep.

Veldicca had warned her not to wake him if that happened. But if she went back to the courtyard and all those apples, wouldn't he wake up when she left?

He looked so peaceful, but she'd overheard something this morning that didn't bode well for him.

Narina and Veldicca hadn't heard her soft footsteps or seen her when she entered the kitchen behind them.

Veldicca's words had been quiet, like she didn't want anyone else to hear. "That knee—I've never seen one look that bad. I don't know what will help it. The look on his face when he saw it...he knows how bad it is."

Then Narina had replied, "But he doesn't know how much God can heal. We'll just keep asking God to spare him."

So, Lucania had asked God for healing many times that morning. Right now, in the silence of his room, was a good time to do it again.

Veldicca said God knew every thought, so just thinking a prayer was the same as speaking it. But this was too important to not speak the words. She closed her eyes and spoke to Him in softly whispered Brittonic.

"God, I'm asking again for You to heal Rogatus's knee. Please make it as good as new, as if the arrow never hit it. In Your mercy, please let him feel how Your love surrounds him, and help him not to be afraid until You do. I ask this in Iesu's name. Amen."

When she opened her eyes, his uninjured arm had moved onto his chest, but his breathing was still that of deep sleep.

◆

The distant sounds of a legion fortress pulled Rogatus from the painless darkness of sleep into a waking nightmare. In the fortress hospital, he lay on a cold metal table. Straps across his chest and thighs, more around his wrists and ankles held him in place. He struggled against the bindings, but he couldn't break free. In the hallway, the legate stood, arms crossed, facing the legion physician.

"That's all we can do now." The physician's voice was flat, emotionless.

"Then cut it off. I'll request a replacement today." The legate turned and walked away.

With a bone saw in hand, the physician came and stood over him.

He opened his mouth to forbid it, to ask for more time, but no sound came.

Then a young girl's whisper reached him. "Heal Rogatus's knee...as good as new...in your mercy...your love surrounds him...in Iesu's name."

Through half-opened eyelids, he saw the rafters above him. No physician, no legate stood near him. In the hazy world between sleep and awareness, the men in his dream had only spoken his own fears.

He reached up and tapped his cheek. He was fully awake now. He forced his breaths to slow and deepen until he breathed like a man asleep. Since childhood, he'd done that to calm himself when he awoke in the dark, alone and afraid.

He was that child again, with no one to depend on but himself and fears that soon might be reality.

Something stirred in the room, and he turned his head to find Lucania still in the chair beside him. Had she spoken the whispered words, or were they only part of the dream?

Iesu. A name spoken in a Brittonic prayer, but it wasn't the name of any Brigantian god he'd heard before. And her words sounded more like a conversation than the formal petitions to gain a god's favor or the priest-led rites in the public worship of the Roman gods.

Iesu—that sounded a lot like Iesus, a name he'd heard used for a dead Jewish rabbi. The man had been crucified almost a hundred years ago for claiming to be a king in a defiant province. No emperor tolerated that. Some Jews then decided he was their god in human form, and his followers had been accused of setting the Great Fire during Nero's reign. But Nero had been suspected himself, so any accusation could just be a cover up for his own selfish cruelty.

He didn't know enough about them to have his own opinion.

Words in two languages often sounded similar but had nothing in common. But if Lucania prayed to that god, did Narina? Did Veldicca?

He opened his eyes, but she'd already stopped speaking.

It only lasted a moment, but the look of a child who'd been caught doing something they shouldn't crossed her face before being replaced by her usual bright smile.

"Did you want to hear some more Brittonic words?"

He fingered his lip. "Not at the moment, but I heard one today that I'm wondering about."

"What is it?"

"Iesu."

Her eyes saucered as the color drained from her face.

She swallowed hard. "That's one you'll have to ask Narina about. I'm going to see if Veldicca needs some help for a little while." She stood. "I'll be back later."

As she always did, she patted his foot as she walked past. But she walked faster than normal, and then she was gone.

His mouth curved into a deep frown. From relaxed and friendly to afraid of him. She'd run off once before when he asked about the local gods. Narina had taken her place. But she hadn't said whether Roman or Brigantian gods were more powerful when he asked her. She'd changed the subject, and they never returned to it.

What did that name mean that Lucania couldn't tell him? When Narina returned, would him knowing her little sister prayed to it frighten her as well?

Chapter 39

The Power of a Name

Narina's farm, midafternoon of Day 26

No one passed Narina as she rode up the tow road from Eboracum to the turnoff to her farm. With the grains and some other crops already harvested and still more being harvested now, that was odd. There was a mix of Brigantian and Roman families who owned farms along the river. Maybe others had been raided like she had or were not yet shipping, wary of losing what they still had before the Roman troops made things safe again.

If they even could.

As she rode by the orchard, Bikka waved. All but Trenus and Lucania were spread among the trees, filling baskets and carrying them to the mule cart she'd brought back from Isurium. Tomorrow she would help Lucania with slicing and drying. It was good they'd come home. Trenus needed their help.

She put Bena in Zephyrus's old paddock and carried the saddle and bridle into the stable. Zephyrus's nicker called her to his stall, and he closed his eyes as she worked her fingers into his forelock and drew them through.

"It's so good to have you home." She hugged his neck. "Thank you for keeping Rogatus safe for both of us."

"Narina?"

Narina jumped when Lucania spoke behind her.

"You scared me." She chuckled. "Please don't do that. What are you doing out here? Tired of cutting up apples?"

She expected at least a roll of Lucania's eyes, but her sister stood grim-faced, rubbing her palm.

"Yes, but that's not why I watched for you."

Narina placed her hand on her sister's shoulder. "Is something wrong?"

"No...maybe. Rogatus asked me to give him more words and talk with him a while. Veldicca said I could, but not to wake him up if he went to sleep."

She glanced away, then turned her eyes back on Narina. "He dozed off, so I stayed ever so quiet in the chair so I wouldn't wake him by getting up. You know how he sounds when he's asleep. Well, I thought he was, so I was praying for him, like you said we should. I was whispering, and I didn't use Latin. He should never have heard me or understood if he did."

Lucania looked down at her feet. "But he wasn't. I don't think he heard everything, but he heard me finish."

She bit her lip and looked up. "He asked what Iesu meant. I told him he'd have to ask you and left."

She closed her eyes. "Veldicca reminds me that God knows all my thoughts. But I heard you and Veldicca this morning. You said his knee was bad, and we needed to keep asking God to spare him. It seemed too important not to ask out loud for God to heal him. He shouldn't have heard my softest whisper."

Her trembling smile didn't match her worried eyes. "I'm sorry I wasn't more careful, like you said I had to be."

Narina's stomach clenched. What Sulio feared most had happened, and where would that lead? Rogatus wouldn't forget he'd heard it, and he'd be asking her for an explanation that she'd hoped she would never have to give.

She spread her arms, and Lucania stepped into her embrace. There was no point in her sister worrying about what couldn't be undone.

"It's all right. What exactly did he say?"

"Only that he'd heard a Brittonic word today that he'd been wondering about. Then he said Iesu, and I told him I needed to go help Veldicca. I left him alone and haven't gone back."

"So, maybe all he heard was 'in Iesu's name,' but maybe he heard more of your prayer?"

Lucania nodded. "That's all he said, but maybe."

Narina placed her hand on her sister's cheek. "Don't worry about it. I won't bring it up, and maybe he'll have forgotten. But if he does, I'll ask God to tell me what to tell him. There's no need for you to worry now."

She wrapped her arm around her sister's shoulders. "I hear those apples calling to us. Let's go back to the house. You can work on those again, and I'll check on how he's doing. I think he'll feel better after I tell him what the legate said."

Lucania rolled her eyes. "More apples." She faked a shudder before they strolled toward the house.

Narina looked heavenward, and drew a deep breath.

God, I hadn't planned to tell Rogatus about our faith in You. But after hearing what he did, I guess I might have to. It's not like we're in a province where the governor hunts Christians right now. But he said he'll do his duty whether he likes what he has to do or not. Is it safe for him to know? Please give me a sign. Tell me what I should do.

As she took her next step, peace flowed over her. She'd tried many times to tell Sulio about Iesu, but he'd never wanted to hear it. Was Rogatus going to listen? Was he going to understand?

God, guide my words so he won't be put off by what I'm telling him. Let him want to learn more.

When they entered the courtyard, she drew a deep breath, then squared her shoulders. After putting on a smile, she knocked on his open door.

"I'm back. The guards didn't want to let me into the fortress, but I asked for Tribune Dexter. He was glad to hear you weren't dead. He escorted me in to see the legate. I delivered your message, and I have his reply."

His jaw twitched. "What did he say?"

She lifted his shoulders and slipped a couple of pillows behind his back. "He was also very glad to hear you weren't dead. He said you can rest easy about your command. He's in no hurry to risk getting someone less capable than you've shown yourself to be. He asked me to tell you that he didn't hold losing the herd and one turma against you this time. With what your herder reported, he said it was reasonable to assume you were only chasing some raiders, not riding into a planned ambush. He's fine with you staying here until you've recovered enough to ride."

A smile curved his lips as his shoulders relaxed. "I couldn't have asked for better. I sent the right messenger." His smile turned teasing. "But I suspect your horse-trading skills helped you bring him to those decisions."

Her horse-trader smile was what she gave him in return. "After he heard how Zephyrus saved you, he did say he wanted one of my warhorses for himself. I was sorry to tell him he'd have to wait three years until I had another one trained. He said he'd be gone by then." She shrugged. "But maybe the next legate will want one, too."

She adjusted the sheet across his legs. "It's obvious that he sees you're a man worth keeping. You said I didn't see your flaws because I was too kind-hearted. I doubt he has too kind a heart, but he doesn't see you as having too many flaws, either."

"He might if he knew what they are." His smile had faded.

"Perhaps, but he only sees with a Roman man's eyes. We worry too much about what we think people see. Or what they think of us. I do see people's flaws. I see my own, too. But I don't have to worry about what men think, only God."

She drew a deep breath. If she said the next words, there was no taking them back. He'd ask what she was, and where would that lead? But she felt God's nudge to proceed.

"I serve a God who sees us for what we truly are, flaws and all, and loves us anyway."

"About that…" His eyes narrowed, and her heart beat faster. "I overheard Lucania praying to a god when she thought I was sleeping. She called him Iesu. Is that the god you mean?"

"It is."

"I haven't heard of a Brigantian god by that name. What is he god of?"

"You might have, but you didn't know it. In Latin, you'd call him Iesus."

He inhaled deeply and held it. Her stomach clenched again. Had she misunderstood what the peace she'd felt meant?

"You're both Christians. Veldicca too?" His eyes were questioning, but not threatening.

"Yes." He was curious, not condemning, and relief surged through Narina. "It was she who first introduced me to Him. She came from Isca Silurum. Many people follow Iesu there."

"How did you get to know her?"

He'd told her his story, even the painful parts. That he wanted to know more of hers made her smile.

"Mother died shortly after Lucania was born. I was only twelve then, too young to be a mother or the domina of a household. Father needed someone to care for her, and a prefect who'd served as tribune with the Isca legion was going back to Rome. He sold her to Father before he left."

"So, she's your slave?" He shifted a little, and that triggered a grimace. "You seem more like good friends."

"She's not, and we are. Father hated how the Dacian families were separated and sold, so he didn't keep slaves. Once he knew he wanted her to care for Lucania and me until we were grown, he freed her and made her our housekeeper. He had our farmhands work for a share of our profits. I kept doing that after he died."

"What a man does when serving Rome…it can change how he views things but not his duty to obey while he still serves. A soldier doesn't have the luxury of saying no to something he doesn't want to do. Each one swears an oath of loyalty to the emperor and Rome when joining, and then every year. With Hadrian replacing Trajan, the legate had me swear the new oath. I had my men swear their new loyalty as soon as I returned with the news."

She didn't let him see it, but inwardly Narina cringed. She could never swear such an oath to anyone but God.

His jaw twitched, and he pressed his hand against his injured thigh.

She sat to put herself at his level. "I wish we had something to make it hurt less."

"It could be worse. At least I'm still alive."

He held his breath before blowing it out slowly. "So, the legate said I should stay here while I recover?"

"Not exactly. I told him that we were caring for you until you recover enough to ride. Then you'd return. He said you could stay here, and I told him we were glad to keep you. He asked if we needed anything to do that."

She bit her lip. "I said we knew what to do for you, and we're glad to do it. But maybe it would be better for you to be with the fort's physician. He'd be an expert on arrow holes and stab wounds."

Rogatus shook his head. "I saw what my cohort physician did in Moesia, and Veldicca did everything he would have." His mouth twitched, like it often did before his best smile. "And he wouldn't care enough to pray to his favorite god, like Lucania did."

A teasing smile curved his lips. "Since you're all Christians, can I assume you pray for me, too?"

Narina's heart beat faster. *God, is he about to ask about You? Please give me the right words to say.*

"You can. I've prayed for you for some time now."

His eyes changed from teasing to intense, and her neck warmed as his gaze stayed locked on her eyes. Did he think she meant that she thought of him often? She did, but not in the way he was thinking. He was a good friend. Nothing more was possible for a Christian like her and a pagan like him.

Then his gaze shifted to the doorway for a long moment. The blush had faded before he turned it back on her.

"I like being here." One corner of his mouth lifted. "Veldicca feeds me much better than any garrison cook, and as long as I can't do anything, I'd rather have you and Lucania to entertain me."

"I don't know how entertaining I'll be. I'll mostly be harvesting apples or getting them ready to dry."

His smile faded. "Whatever time you can spare me, I'd like that."

She leaned forward and rested her hand on his shoulder. "When the fruit's ready for harvest, it can't wait. But we won't neglect you." She slid back in her chair. "Lucania will be eager to take breaks from slicing them up, and she'll gladly spend those talking with you."

"I think you'll need breaks, too." He raised one eyebrow. "Perhaps you can spend some with me as well."

"Perhaps." After she stood, she wrinkled her nose. "Probably. But the apples piled up while I was your messenger, and I need to be filling the drying racks for a while."

She tipped her head toward the doorway. "If you need anything, just call. We're working in the courtyard, and one of us will come right away."

The last of his smile disappeared as fatigue and pain dulled his eyes. "Thank you...for everything."

When she walked past his feet, she patted one. "It's our pleasure. Rest now."

As she passed through the doorway, she glanced over her shoulder. His eyes had closed. His jaw clenched, then relaxed.

God, please take his pain. Please heal him quickly.

She turned into the courtyard where he could no longer see her and leaned against the wall. She looked up and tipped her head back before closing her eyes.

God, I like him being here, too. If he believed in Iesu, he'd be the right man for me. As You heal his wounds, will You please open his heart and mind to see it's only You, not Rome or the emperor that he should want to serve? Please don't let him die before he discovers that, even if he's not meant for me.

A deep sigh escaped as she walked toward the table where Lucania was working. It was good he'd heard her sister's prayer. But what could move him from curiosity about the name of their god to wanting to know Him and follow Him as well?

Late afternoon of Day 26

Rogatus lay on his back, staring at the roof. A few heavier beams rose at an angle from the wooden bases atop opposite walls. At the top, they were nailed to make an upside-down V and notched to support a roof pole. Between those beams, more poles ran from the bases to the roof pole. Between those poles were lath strips, and atop those the thatch.

As he pondered the finished structure, each piece seemed obvious and well-suited to its task. But if he'd been told to make a thatched roof when he'd never seen one, would it look like this when he finished? Even if it looked different, would it still keep the rain out and the warmth in?

For the last five and a half years, he'd known what he needed to do, and he'd done it well. The next three and a half should have been the same. And after those, he'd have more than enough to keep him equestrian in his own right.

But what that arrow did to his knee...

He shuddered. If it didn't heal well, what lay ahead? Rome's military had been the only place he felt he belonged. And it was the pathway to freedom from the father who hated him and wanted him to fail. But after his military career was over, everything new he earned, every business he built, would become Father's until that man died. And it might become his brothers' if Father's will declared it so.

Unless he could get himself disinherited sooner rather than later. That would make him *sui iuris*, his own man instead of his father's son, and all he earned would be his.

The voices of two women grew louder. Narina and Veldicca were coming to tend his wounds.

He massaged his temples. He'd awakened with the headache he knew too well. He'd borne with the throbbing and aches from his wounds all day. But they'd be bringing vinegar to pour into the five open holes left by the arrows.

He steeled himself for what was coming and smiled at them when they entered his room.

Veldicca set the tray of clean cloths, a jar of honey, and the pitcher of vinegar on the chair. "Time to clean those wounds. I know it will hurt, but if we do this for a few days, you should heal fine."

"Just do it fast and get it over with." He scrunched his nose.

"Arm first, then thigh, then knee." Veldicca patted him on the shoulder.

"Are you going to pray for me like Lucania did?"

Narina's eyes widened, triggering his wry smile. She thought he meant it. His smile faded. At some level, maybe he did.

"We have been." Veldicca loosened the bandage around his arm and set it aside. "But it's good that you asked so you can take part in our prayers."

She placed a towel under his arm before placing her palm on his shoulder. "God, please help Rogatus as we care for him. Lessen his pain, and let him heal quickly. We ask this in Iesu's name."

Narina's soft "amen" drew his gaze to her face. Her eyes were closed, and a strange smile curved her lips. He thought he'd seen every one of her smiles. He'd been wrong.

Veldicca dribbled the vinegar into both holes. It stung enough to make him suck a breath between his teeth. But it wasn't as bad as the last time.

After applying the honey and rewrapping his arm, she moved on to his thigh.

Almost the same prayer, but the words were a little different. Same cleaning procedure. Same impression that it hurt but not quite as much.

But when Veldicca unwrapped his knee, he turned his eyes away. When he summoned the courage to look, what he saw was as bad as before. Still red, still swollen. Maybe still damaged beyond repair.

He startled when Narina's voice replaced Veldicca's.

"God, please heal all Rogatus's wounds. We pray especially for his knee. It looks bad now, but You can fix anything. Let it heal so he can still do all that he needs to. Please ease his pain while it does. Thank You for bringing him to us so we can help him get better. In Iesu's name, we pray."

Veldicca joined her in saying amen. Then she finished treating it and wrapping it before pulling the light sheet over his legs.

"We'll leave you now. Narina still has piles of apples waiting for her, and I'm making one of your favorites for dinner."

"Will I also get Narina's special bread?"

"You'll have to settle for mine today. Narina started the dough, but she didn't have time for the kneading and baking before she left for Eboracum this morning."

Narina came to the bedside. "Maybe tomorrow I'll make the rolls you like best. It's time for you to rest until dinnertime."

Veldicca picked up the tray, and the women left him alone with his thoughts.

It was odd how the pain had lessened when they prayed. Or had it?

A man could shut out pain in the heat of battle. He had himself during the ambush. He hurt much worse when he awakened than when he passed out.

So, had he somehow convinced himself that it didn't hurt as much right after they prayed, but it really did?

He rubbed his temple. He often had headaches. He'd had one most of the day. That seemed to be gone, too.

His lips tightened. Over the next week or two, he'd have way too many chances to observe whether their prayers did anything or not.

He blew out a heavy breath as a memory from years ago resurfaced.

When he lived in Rome, Grandfather had taken him to the games in the Flavian Amphitheater a few times. There were executions during the lunch-time break between the animal fights in the morning and the professional gladiators in the afternoon. Twice he'd seen Christians and other criminals forced into the arena for lions and leopards to kill.

The common criminals ran and screamed and struggled with the beasts before dying. It had struck him as odd how the Christians just stood there and let the animals come. Some screamed, but it sounded more like screams of pain, not sheer terror.

When they stood, arms raised, were they calling on their god to save them? He didn't. They all died, savaged and then eaten by the ravenous cats. But the way they faced pain and death... Were they asking their god to rescue them or only to make it less painful as they died?

He shook his head. Some things were impossible to know. The dead don't come back to tell you what dying was like.

As the sparkles surrounded him and everything faded to black, he sensed death was close. So, he could tell anyone that part was true. But no one had come back after death itself to tell the living what lay ahead.

Chapter 40

The Best Way Forward

Early evening of Day 26

Sulio put his own stallion in the stable in the stall farthest from Zephyrus. But with no mares ready to breed nearby, the horses exchanged casual glances and focused on the hay in their mangers.

He crossed the farmyard and entered the house unannounced. Along the walls under the roofed colonnade, racks of sliced apples filled the air with a sweet, fruity aroma. It made his mouth water. It was a long time since lunch. But a good dinner was not why he'd come.

The absence of anyone who would see him triggered a smile. He'd come to check on how Narina was doing now her prefect was stuck here. But before he did that, he wanted some words with the man who'd wormed his way into Narina's affections.

Just because she was looking after him while he healed was no reason for him to assume he had a right to her special attentions. Warning Narina had done nothing. She had no wish to tell Rogatus to back off. She might claim that was for the sake of the family taberna. But it went far beyond that, whether she admitted that to herself or not.

Making the Roman see how he endangered her...that seemed more likely to succeed.

He strode to the room where he carried Rogatus. The Roman was unconscious the last time he saw him. But he shouldn't be now. Before anyone realized Sulio had come, they'd have that conversation about Narina's future and how a Roman officer had no place in it.

Rogatus still lay where he'd put him, eyes closed, breathing slowly.

Sulio stopped at his bedside, and a frown grew as he stared at the tanned face and tousled hair of the wounded man. Handsome enough to attract any woman, even a level-headed one like Narina. Then he placed his fingertips

255

on Rogatus's shoulder and pushed, first gently, then harder when his eyelids failed to open.

After several hard pokes, the eyes popped open and widened with surprise. The Roman's head drew back into the pillow. Then recognition replaced confusion, and his whole body relaxed.

"Sulio." A slow smile curved Rogatus's lips. "It's good to see you. Narina told me what you did. My deepest thanks for that."

"Thank Zephyrus. I only draped you across his back and brought him home to her." Sulio crossed his arms. "You're looking better than the last time I saw you. But with Veldicca taking care of you, that's to be expected."

Rogatus's smile broadened. "She and Narina are doing a fine job. Lucania as well."

"You'd be better off at the fort with your cohort physician. When are they sending you there?"

"They aren't. Narina told the legate I was here, and he told her they could keep me until I was well enough to ride."

Sulio scrunched his nose. "Why would he do that? He should be afraid to leave you in a Brigantian house. Too many might want to finish what the raiders started. Does he want to get rid of you, too?"

Rogatus chuckled as if Sulio was joking. He wasn't.

"Narina wondered whether the physician could tend me better. For some things, he could, but arrow wounds aren't among them." Rogatus smiled as if they were friends. "But the food and the company are much better here. Your cousins and Veldicca are up to the task, so I don't want the change."

"You should. If anyone who's not Roman sees you here, that's dangerous for them."

"I'll be going no farther than the courtyard for some time, much like Lucania." Rogatus shifted on the bed, and a fleeting grimace dimmed his smile. "She's tired of cutting and drying apples, so teaching and talking with me gives her something more enjoyable to do."

"She shouldn't be talking too much with you, either."

Rogatus's eyebrows lowered, and his eyes turned unreadable. "I know why you don't want Narina to talk with me, but why shouldn't Lucania?"

Sulio drew back at that question. An eleven-year-old could too easily reveal they were Christians, but that wasn't something he could tell an officer of Rome who might be ordered to arrest such people.

"There are Brittonic things a Roman has no right to know. A child who likes you might not remember what she shouldn't say. You shouldn't spend too much time with Veldicca, either."

The Roman fingered his lower lip as silence stretched between them. "Things like the god they worship?"

Sulio barely stopped the inhale that would confirm Rogatus's suspicion.

"You don't need to know about Brittonic gods. You have enough Roman ones."

One corner of Rogatus's mouth lifted, and Sulio tensed. The Roman was taking their conversation in a dangerous direction. But how could he stop it without arousing suspicion?

"Not all Britons worship Brittonic gods. When I asked Lucania for some names of your gods, she left and sent Narina."

Narina trusted this man too much. What had she told him? Surely, not the truth about the three of them.

"After so long in your army, Narina's father worshiped Mars. Her mother had a shrine for a few Roman gods that women like. You're not likely to learn about Brittonic gods here."

But Sulio hadn't seen that shrine for years. Had he just revealed something that might lead to dangerous questions when Rogatus could get around and found it missing?

"Children don't always follow parents when there's a reason not to." Rogatus looked at his hand while he massaged his palm, but he fixed his gaze on Sulio when he stopped. "Lucania was talking Brittonic with me right after lunch. She taught me a new word, and I think it's one you don't want me to know. I suspect you know what that is."

Sulio leaned his thigh against the bed and glared down at Rogatus. "Not likely. I don't care what Brittonic you learn or what you know already, but Lucania and Narina don't need to be teaching you more."

"She thought I was asleep when she said it."

Sulio's heart beat faster. Had she let slip the most dangerous secret about this family? He didn't want to ask, but he had to know. "What was it?"

"Iesu. I overheard her whispered prayer for me."

The worst thing a tribune could possibly have heard. But maybe he didn't know who that was.

"There are many Brigantian gods." Sulio shrugged. "You already know about Camulus, our god of war. If it weren't for Zephyrus, your head would have been an offering to him."

"I asked Narina about it when she got back from Eboracum. She told me that's Iesus. Him I've heard of, and he's not Brittonic. And I think you've been trying to keep me from finding out they worship him."

Rogatus blew a short breath out his nostrils. "I can understand why. I've seen Christians in the arena in Rome. But this is Britannia. What happens in Rome doesn't happen here, and I'm no threat to any of you."

Sulio couldn't stop the frown. "But that's only part of why I don't want you getting too close to Narina."

Rogatus tipped his head. "Why else?"

"You can't honestly tell me you don't know. You've been treating her like a woman you're interested in for something lasting."

Sulio's gaze raked the Roman who hid what he was thinking better than anyone he'd ever known. "But I don't see how a rich Roman like you could be. What does she have that attracts you? She's not pretty, she's not wealthy, she doesn't flirt to attract a man's attention. She doesn't even know how."

He pointed at the Roman's face. "You'll only be around here until you move on to another command. Are you just looking for a woman to satisfy your needs, and then you'll leave her behind when you go? If a man is at an outpost like this long enough, even a homely woman who shouldn't appeal to him can look good. But she's not someone to be used and cast off just because you think you can."

Anger like Sulio had never seen flamed in Rogatus's eyes. "Stop saying she's homely, because she isn't. There's a beauty inside her that lights her eyes and warms her smile, and any man with an iota of wisdom would choose her over the prettiest women with the largest dowries." He jabbed his finger toward Sulio's face. "Only she has the right to decide whether we belong together, not you."

Sulio raised an eyebrow. The Roman's last words had revealed the surest way to get rid of him. "You're right. She does, so you may as well stop pursuing her. You're handsome and rich, but she'll tell you no."

Rogatus snorted. "Because I'm Roman? She's half Roman herself and comfortable with that."

"No. Because you're not Christian, and she won't marry anything else." Sulio shoved his fists into his hips. "And she won't give herself to any man she's not married to, so you can forget about that, too."

Rogatus opened his mouth, then closed it without speaking

Sulio pushed out his cheek with his tongue. He'd found Rogatus's weak spot at last. "If you care about her, you won't ask her to join you in your Roman world. It would mean her death. She'd never deny Iesu and worship Caesar just to save her own life. Don't take her where she'd be forced to make that choice."

Rogatus's eyes turned thoughtful. "How do you know so much about what she believes? Are you one, too?"

"Hmph." Sulio rolled his eyes at that accusation. "She's tried for years to persuade me, but I don't plan to risk my life for something I can't see. But I'd risk everything to protect her, even from herself."

He rubbed his cheek. "You said you heard Lucania pray for you. You should ask Veldicca and Narina to pray for your healing, too. They think their god listens and answer their prayers. The sooner you get better, the sooner you can go back to your fort and leave her alone before you break her heart."

The sound of someone humming grew louder until Lucania came through the doorway.

"Sulio! We didn't know you were here." She looked down at the tray she carried. It held two bowls of stew and a plate of rolls. "I've brought Rogatus his dinner."

Sulio put on the smile he usually gave his young cousin. "Where is Narina going to eat?"

"I'm not sure. I'm eating with Rogatus in case he needs help with something."

He rested his hand on her shoulder. "Then I'll join her and Veldicca in the kitchen." He glanced at Rogatus and found the alert eyes and social smile that hid what the man was thinking.

"It's good to see your patient looking so much better. It won't be long until he can go back where he belongs."

As he stepped through the doorway, he looked back. An odd smile played on the tribune's lips. After what he'd just told him, why did that man look so pleased with himself?

◆

As Lucania piled some pillows behind him so he could sit up enough to eat, Rogatus watched Sulio look back as he left to join Narina. Her cousin thought he'd shown him why he could never be with her because she'd reject him herself.

But it was more like the day they found the pastures, when Sulio tried to make him feel guilty about buying Zephyrus when she needed him as her stud. Her cousin had revealed the best gift he could possibly give her, and her delight when he offered the use of Zephyrus proved it.

Now her cousin had opened the door to Narina saying yes when he asked her to marry him. But first he had to learn what she believed and why. Only then could he find the best way to make a Christian woman willing to say yes to a man like him.

Chapter 41

So Different

Narina's farm, morning of day 27

Rogatus scraped the last bite of porridge from the bowl and licked the spoon. Eating with his left hand was still clumsy. But when he'd tried to use his right, it hurt too much to lift his arm.

Lucania slipped off the chair and took his bowl. "There's still way too many apples out there, but Veldicca said I could take some breaks to talk with you."

"I'd enjoy that." He gave her the smile she deserved, but he'd much rather have Narina come.

The voices of two women grew louder. The person he most wanted to hear was almost there.

When she stepped into the room behind Veldicca, his smile broadened. "Coming to torture me with vinegar again?"

Narina's fake glare didn't dim her smile. "We're coming to help you, and you know it. Sometimes the things that are best for us have to hurt for a while to do their good work."

Lucania picked up the tray that held their bowls. "I'll be back after a few hundred apples."

He raised his eyebrows. "A few hundred?"

She flashed him a smile. "It seems like that many." She balanced the tray against her hip, freeing a hand to pat his foot as she passed, then disappeared into the courtyard.

Narina set her tray on the chair. "Are you ready?"

He blew out a slow breath. "Yes. Are you going to pray again to make it hurt less?"

Veldicca felt his forehead and smiled. "Of course. There's no better medicine than asking God for healing."

260

She placed her hand on his shoulder. "God, we thank You that Rogatus is feeling stronger today. Please make each of his wounds heal quickly and hurt less each day. In Iesu's name, we pray."

As Veldicca poured vinegar into the holes in his arm, it still stung a lot, but one thing was clear. It hurt somewhat less than yesterday afternoon when he first asked them to pray. Then came the honey and rewrapping. When she finished, he blew out a deep breath. His arm looked no worse than he expected. A few more days of this, and he'd have nothing worse than a scar.

She moved down to his thigh and unwrapped it.

He gritted his teeth. This one hurt as he expected. No, not quite as he expected. Less. And no streaks of redness ran out from either side of the clean-looking wound.

But what he really feared was the next thing he'd see. He stared at the rafters and worked to slow his breathing as Veldicca unwrapped his knee.

"Hmm." The lightness in Veldicca's voice pulled his gaze from the network of poles and laths above him.

His knee was still swollen, still purple, but at least the discoloration wasn't getting bigger. Neither was the swelling.

Narina rested her hand on his foot. "Thank You, God, that Rogatus's knee doesn't look any worse. Please guide us as we care for our friend. Show us what to do so he'll get better as quickly as possible. Make the pain lighter for him to bear. Please heal his knee so he'll be able to ride. When he's well again, please protect and guide him. Thank You for Sulio bringing him here so we can help him. In Iesu's name, we pray."

He closed his eyes. This time did hurt less. He was sure of that, but why were a few words spoken to an invisible god far from any temple working?

"We'll let you rest now. Call if you need anything." Someone patted his foot, just like Lucania.

When he opened his eyes, her sister stood there. That triggered his smile. "Can you stay for a moment? I have some questions."

"Of course." Narina handed her tray to Veldicca and moved the chair closer.

As Veldicca took the tray away, she paused in the doorway to bounce her eyebrows once at Narina. Then she left with a satisfied smile.

"What's your first question?" Narina relaxed in the chair, her eyes inviting him to speak freely.

"You seem to expect something will happen when you pray. But it's different words each time, so how do you know whether the prayer should work?" He scrubbed his face. "Certain exact words are spoken every time a rite is performed in a temple in Rome. The same is true when the many festivals are celebrated in the legion fortresses. And there are special places where the prayers are offered. If the rites aren't performed exactly, they might not work."

She nodded, but didn't speak.

"In every legion fortress or cohort fort, there's an *aedis*. It's the sacred room at the back of the principia. The legion's eagle or the ala's draco is kept there. The century standards and turma banners are as well." He rubbed his mouth with the back of his hand. "Small statues of Jupiter Optimus Maximus, Mars Ultor, and Hercules Magusanus are in mine, and an image of the current emperor. My men can enter to venerate them at any time. But when the rites are performed where we ask the gods for something, each man doesn't choose how to worship. It must be done the proper way. If there's a mistake, we start over. There's also an offering of something to gain the god's favor."

He raised his chin. "That's why the favor of the gods goes with Rome's armies, and our enemies rightly fear that." He locked his gaze on her eyes. "So, why do you just talk with your god like you would with me?"

Narina's slow shake of her head wasn't what he expected. "Father told me it was the superior training, total devotion to duty, and unyielding courage of Rome's soldiers that gave them victory. You don't need the help of any gods when you have that. And the Roman gods did nothing to save the Ninth Legion when Boudicca's army killed every legionary and only the legate and his cavalry escaped." She straightened in her chair. "Father told me how Varus lost three whole legions in the ambush by Arminius during Augustus's reign. Wouldn't the proper rites have been performed before those losses? Where were your Roman gods then?"

Silence hung suspended between them before he finally answered. "I don't know."

His admission made Narina smile. "I used to believe in the Roman gods. Grandfather said the morning rites in Moesia, and Father had a *lararium* built here for Mother's Lares and Penates so he could do the rites with her."

Rogatus shifted on the bed to face her better. "What did your father say?"

"I stopped taking part when I decided to follow Iesu twelve years ago, and no one has used the shrine since Father died. I don't remember exactly what he said. But he asked the gods to watch over and protect his wife, children, and grandchildren."

"My grandfather did the same, asking for protection for his children and grandchildren without naming them. As far as anyone knew for sure, I was his grandson. I felt included."

Rogatus stared at the lathwork above him before turning his eyes back on her. "But when Grandfather died, Father changed the ritual. He asked for protection of his two sons and their children, his daughter and her children, and that was it. I was the third son. I had to stand there every morning and listen to him deny me in front of the whole household. And when Father sent me to the villa, I should have been the one leading the rites there. But the steward kept doing it, like before I came. When I asked him why he did and why he only asked for Father's two sons, he said that was what my father had ordered him to do."

She leaned forward to touch his hand. "I can see why that hurt, but you should know that it made no real difference. The Lares and Penates aren't gods with any power to do what a paterfamilias asks."

Her head tilted. "Haven't all the good things that have happened to you come after your grandfather was no longer alive to include you? Your great-uncle helped you because he cared about how his niece and you had been treated. You did well in Moesia because you asked your centurions to teach you what you needed and were good at doing it. The legate thinks you've done a fine job here, and you have."

She patted his hand. "But it's what you've done that made you successful. It's not some words, either for or against you, that your father spoke to gods who aren't real."

She withdrew her fingers, and he wished she hadn't.

"But our prayers aren't just part of a ritual." She slid forward on her chair. "God wants us to share our thoughts and requests with Him, like I can with you. And He has the power to do something about them in a way that's best for us."

He fingered his lip. "So, you just ask your god, and everything goes how you want it to?"

"I didn't say that. God does what's best for me, but sometimes what I want isn't what would be best. I can't know what the future might hold, but He does. What I think would be good now might keep me from a better future."

"Fortuna frowns now so she can smile brighter in the future." He shrugged. "I suppose that's possible."

"Not really." She shook her head, but her eyes still invited his words. "Fortuna neither smiles nor frowns. She's no more real than Mother's Lares and Penates. None of the Roman gods are real. They're only stories made up by someone long ago."

Her eyes softened as she looked away, but it was only a moment before they focused on him again. "But I serve the God who created everything we see and everything we can't see. He formed us before we were born to be what He knew was best for us. And He wants us to know Him and love Him, like He loves us. That's why we can talk with Him like I do with you."

Rogatus narrowed his eyes. "And you think he answers you?"

"I know He does."

He waved his index finger from side to side. "I've watched Christians praying in the amphitheater in Rome. Your god didn't answer their prayers."

"You can't know that because you don't know what they were asking for." She swept the room with her hand. "What you see around us, that's not all there is. This all gets left behind when we die, whether from old age or because someone kills us. Right now, those people you watched die are joyous in the presence of God, and someday I'll join them."

His breath caught. He'd do anything to make sure that didn't happen. "I'll keep your faith secret. I don't want you to die that way."

"I don't mean I'll die in the arena. I probably won't in Britannia. But because I believe in Iesu, I will join them with God when I die. And that's the best thing that could ever happen, even if I suffer before I get there."

He found himself staring at her. She was raised in a Roman household, like he was, except she knew love and acceptance in hers. Her father and mother taught her Roman ways and worshiped Roman gods. How did she get to this strange way of thinking, especially when it could get her killed?

She rose. "I need to go work for a while."

"Will you come back when you take your first break? I want to hear more."

The most beautiful smile he'd ever seen lit her face. Why did her eyes almost glow? The closest he'd seen to this was when he offered her Zephyrus in the first pasture.

"I will." She took his hand. "I'm so glad you overheard Lucania. I'd love to tell you everything."

"And I want to hear it."

After a gentle squeeze, she released it. "Until later, then."

She paused in the doorway and raised her hand before stepping out of sight.

He scrunched his eyes and rubbed his forehead.

The Roman gods weren't real, but there was one who is. One with real power who wanted to give you what was best for you, whether it was what you wanted or not. One you could be with after you died. So different from anything he'd heard before.

But there was nothing in what she said that would keep him from marrying her. Or keep her from marrying him. So, why did Sulio think he had no chance if he didn't believe in her Christian god?

When Narina entered the apple orchard, she looked first for Veldicca, her dearest friend, the closest thing to her earthly mother, and her mother in the faith. Veldicca had introduced a grieving girl of twelve to God the Father and Iesu His son, who loved her more than anyone else could.

Rogatus had just opened the door to what she longed to tell him, but how was she to do it?

She joined Veldicca at the tree she was picking. "I just had the most wonderful conversation with Rogatus." She plucked an apple and placed it in the basket. "And the most terrifying."

Veldicca's eyebrows plunged. "What did he do?"

"He asked about the way we prayed and why I expected God to answer us."

Veldicca's worried face relaxed into her happiest smile. "Good. That young man needs to know God's love more than anyone I've ever met. What did he say?"

"He'd noticed how we pray differently from what he's used to. He told me about how he and his troops worship the Roman gods and what's supposed to make the rites he leads them in work."

Narina laced her fingers and rested them above her heart. "I told him I hadn't worshiped the Roman gods since I was twelve, that they weren't real. But we worship a real, living God who hears our prayers and answers them. He was surprised that we simply ask for something, expecting that God might do it just because we asked. I told him God gives us what's best for us, even when that might be different than what we ask."

She glanced back toward the house. "He didn't believe me at first. He pointed out how the Christians he watched being executed in Rome prayed, but they still died."

Veldicca massaged her throat. "How did you answer him?"

"That he didn't know what they were praying for. Maybe God actually gave them what they asked for if it wasn't to be spared that day and set free."

After setting an apple in her basket, Veldicca straightened. "Go on."

"I want to tell him how you told me about Iesu and why I wanted to become a child of God by believing in Him. How Iesu's sacrifice removed the things that kept me separated from God. Until you told me, I never understood about sin and how it puts a barrier between us and God." Narina shook her head. "He was taught to worship the Roman gods, like I was. I'm sure he's never heard about sin and what it does to us. So, Iesu's blood covering our sins so we're clean in God's sight won't make any sense to him right now."

Narina glanced heavenward before returning her gaze to Veldicca. "Neither will God loving me even more than Father or Mother or anyone ever has. Father always loved me for just being me, not for what I looked like or what I did. It wasn't hard to imagine God loving me like that, but even more."

Veldicca touched Narina's upper arm. "Your father was one of the best men I've ever known."

"But I can't talk to him about the love a father has for his children. His father has treated him terribly his whole life." Narina bit her lip. "It broke my heart to hear his family story the day after Sulio brought him here. The way his father always treated him, still treats him...it's horrible. I can't tell Rogatus how God loves us like a father, enough to give His only son up to the cross so we could become His children. He'd say letting your child die was what his father wanted to do to him, and that wasn't love at all."

A sigh drained her lungs. "How do I explain the love of the Father when he's never been loved by anyone? His grandfather sent his mother away when he was too small to remember her, so he didn't even have that. His brothers were cruel, too. How can he understand love when he's never had it in his life?"

Veldicca turned her gaze on the house and rubbed the back of her neck. "I think you've opened his eyes to what love is. In his own way, I think he loves you already."

With her hands placed atop her head, Narina sucked a breath between her teeth. "That's what I'm afraid of. What if he tells me he loves me before I can let myself love him back?"

She stared at her feet, then back at the house. "Sulio's right to be worried. I didn't see the signs because it didn't seem possible." She blew out a slow breath. "He's so good at hiding what he's thinking until he suddenly says something you don't expect. He's surprised me so many times."

She picked another apple and stroked its smooth skin before placing it in the basket. "If he did ask me to marry him, I'd want to say yes. But I can't marry a pagan officer like him. I can't follow him back where my faith is a death sentence if I'm found out. I can't deny Iesu, but I don't want to die."

With a gentle push by her foot, Veldicca moved the basket to a new place under the tree. "Then we'll just have to pray that he'll decide that he wants to follow Iesu like we do and that he can get free of what's chaining him to the Roman way of life."

That earned Narina's eye roll. She always prayed for him. She always would. "But how do I start getting him to see he needs that? How did you start telling me?"

Veldicca put her arm around Narina's shoulders. "Well, it wasn't long after your mother died giving life to your baby sister. Your father had just bought me, and..."

Chapter 42

What He Needed?

Late afternoon of Day 27

As Narina and Veldicca passed through the courtyard on the way to treat Rogatus's wounds, Narina gave thanks for her dear friend and sister in Christ. It had been twelve years since Veldicca came, but to Narina, sometimes it seemed like yesterday. Mother thought she was too old to bear more children, but joy filled her days as the delivery drew near. Father tried to mask it, but his worry was obvious, even to a twelve-year-old girl.

On the day of the birth, Father paced the courtyard and cringed as Mother's cries grew closer and more intense. When he heard the first high-pitched cry, she'd never seen his smile bigger. For the first day, they'd been thrilled with the precious girl who seldom left Mother's arms.

But the second day, joy turned to worry as the headaches, fever, chills, and vomiting grew worse. Three days later, Mother was gone.

They buried her with Roman rites. Father spoke the words and lit the funeral pyre. When all had burned, leaving only ashes and memories, he put what remained of the love of his life in the urn he'd had made for his own funeral and placed that inside the small mausoleum he'd built with his own hands.

Then he mounted a young stallion and headed for the tow road. He didn't say a word to Narina or her brothers. She figured Father had gone back to work at their taberna in Eboracum. Soldiers buried their dead and kept marching forward.

But she was no soldier. Every time she heard that baby cry, her tears flowed, too. She should have helped the farmhand's wife who'd been told to care for the baby, but she couldn't bear to look at what had taken Mother from her too soon.

Then Father returned with Veldicca mounted behind him. He told her that Veldicca was in charge of Lucania and, if she proved worthy, would be in charge of the house like Mother had been.

The first time Veldicca found her sobbing on the stone bench by the mausoleum, she sat beside her and wrapped an arm around her shoulders. When Narina turned and buried her face in Veldicca's tunic, a second arm enveloped her. Wrapped in those arms, Narina cried until no more tears were left. Then they sat there in silence until a strange peace filled Narina.

She knew now that Veldicca had prayed the whole time. But she hadn't only prayed for Narina's grief. She'd prayed for an open heart to hear God's call and decide to follow Iesu, too.

Now she was offering the same prayers for Rogatus as they approached the doorway to Father's old room. Veldicca was praying, too.

In her mind, it had become Rogatus's room, and within its walls, she would explain how much God loved him and what He had done out of that love.

But what was the best way to begin?

"How's our best patient?"

Rogatus opened his eyes at Veldicca's greeting. "You can tell me after you're through."

His smile lacked enthusiasm.

Veldicca set the tray on the chair and placed her hand on his shoulder. "God, we thank You for the healing Rogatus has had so far. We ask You to continue his healing until all is as it should be. In Iesu's name, we pray."

Narina echoed the amen.

After Veldicca treated his wounds, she patted his shoulder again. "Your arm and thigh are looking very good. I'll only be putting some honey on them starting tomorrow morning. Your knee...it doesn't look infected, but the bruising and swelling haven't changed much."

He closed his eyes for a moment, then focused them on Veldicca. "When will I be able to get up for a while?"

"Well..." Veldicca scrunched her nose. "Trenus has a crutch he used for a while after the beating, but that was mainly for balance. He's not using it now. You can try that tomorrow." She wagged her finger at him. "But you can't put any weight on that knee."

"One of my centurions in Moesia said two crutches instead of one let a man move around better than leaning on a single crutch. The two together act like the leg I can't put weight on."

"Two?" Veldicca nodded. "I'll send Atto in to talk to you later about what you would need. Trenus made one, so between the two of them, they can make another to give you a pair."

She picked up the tray. "I have stew cooking, and the apple trees are calling Narina, but we'll be back later."

Rogatus raised his eyebrows and offered a pleading smile. "Can I have a little of Narina's time now? We haven't finished a conversation we started."

Veldicca's laughter filled the room. "If I were Narina, I'd choose talking with you over harvesting apples anytime. Trenus is helping some today, so we can spare her for a while."

As Veldicca left the room, Narina pulled the chair close enough that she could touch him if she leaned forward. Sometimes a single touch made so much difference in how someone felt.

He cleared his throat. "You didn't come back when you said you would."

"I came by twice on my breaks. You were sleeping, and I figured that was what you needed more for your healing."

"You can always wake me. I prefer your conversation to sleep. You said earlier that you'd like to tell me everything about what you believe, and you now have me curious."

"Everything...hmm." Narina stroked her jaw. "God is the biggest of all topics, so that could take a while."

He placed his hand on his bad thigh. "I'm not going anywhere. I think we'll have more than enough time."

"I suppose you're right." She flashed him her warmest smile. The more he heard, the more likely he'd hear God calling him.

"So, I guess I'll begin at the beginning when God created everything, all that we see and everything we don't see. As He finished creating each thing, He pronounced it good. Last of all, He created people. A special man named Adam and a woman named Eve. Even though He created the earth, the sky, the sea, and every living thing, Adam and Eve were special to Him. He spent time with them each day."

"Spent time with them?" His eyes narrowed. "Why would a god who could make everything spend time with two people he'd just made?"

"He loved them. We want to spend time with people we love. Being with Mother and Father...I never grew tired of that."

Rogatus fingered his lip. "It wasn't that way in my family. Grandfather ignored me until I was ten. He took me some places after that because his friends expected it, not because he wanted me with him. And Father made it very clear every day until I left for Moesia that he wanted me out of his sight."

Her fingers covered her mouth before she thought to stop them.

God, how do I explain Your love to someone who never had any?

"Did you ever have someone who cared about you? A good friend, maybe? They can love you, too."

"Aprio." Rogatus's jaw clenched, and he looked away. "Until I was ten, I ate with the servants and slaves. Aprio was the son of a gardener. Before he started helping his father, we played together. Then, since Grandfather didn't care what I did, I helped him with garden chores. We were like brothers."

A smile curved his lips as his eyes seemed to look at something she couldn't see. Then it flipped into a frown. "Father stood watching us one day when I was eight. The next thing I knew, Aprio was gone. Sold. Father let it be known it was for stepping out of his place and playing with me. After that, none of the slave children had anything to do with me. I didn't understand at the time why some who'd been friendly avoided me like I had the plague. Now I think their parents forbade it. They were afraid anyone who let me get close would share Aprio's fate."

The frown relaxed into a sad smile. "And they were probably right. So, I learned to make do with my own company. After a while, I was fine with that. When Grandfather sent me to tutors and *rhetors*, I knew equestrian boys my age, but I didn't want them to see what happened at home. So, I didn't make close friends. I got along well enough without one."

His eyes turned serious as his gaze locked on her. "Until I met you."

"Oh, Rogatus. I'm so sorry." She felt her eyes moisten, but she willed herself not to cry. "I wish your father had been like mine. He was so good to me and my brothers. Lucania, too, even though her birth cost my mother's life. He grieved Mother's death until he died himself, but he loved Lucania as much as any of us."

She twisted the filigree ring that Father had given Mother when he asked her to marry him. When she breathed her last, he'd taken it from her finger, and he wore it on a neck chain until the day he died.

"But even he fell short of how wonderful God is as my heavenly father. When I decided to follow Iesu, God made me one of His children, and I feel His love for me every day."

"Made you one of his children? What does that mean?" He snorted. "Are you telling me you're a demigod like Hercules with Jupiter as his father? Or how Romulus and Remus were fathered by Mars?"

She didn't try to stop the chuckle. "Of course not. I learned all those stories when I was a child. But those gods aren't real, and none of that ever happened. I should have said God adopted me as His daughter, but that gives me all the privileges of a natural-born one."

"Then what do you mean?" One raised eyebrow declared his skepticism.

How was she to explain what she only partly understood herself to someone ready to challenge what she said?

God, help me!

She took a deep breath, and her heart beats slowed.

"Iesu is God's only begotten son. He was born of Mary in Israel, but it wasn't after God lay with her like a man. God has no body like you and me. He made both time and everything that's around us, and neither of those limit Him. He can be here with me at the same time as He's in the orchard with Veldicca. He can answer any prayer because He can do anything, but He loves us and gives us what's best for us, even when we ask for the wrong thing because we don't know what's best."

Narina slid the ring up and down her finger. "It broke my heart when Mother died. But Father would never have brought Veldicca to us if she hadn't, and she's been both mother and sister to me. God knew Lucania and I needed her. He knew she would tell us about Him."

She clasped her hands in her lap. "So, He's as far above my understanding as I am above an ant. But He spoke through his prophets to reveal Himself to those who follow Him, and He came to earth as Iesu to give us the way to become His children. Now He guides us when we ask for that, and He listens when we pray."

Rogatus's eyes remained skeptical, but despite that, he nodded.

"Anyway, He sent an angel as His messenger, and the angel told Mary that the Holy Spirit would come upon her and the power of God would overshadow her. He said that the holy baby that she would bear would be called the Son of God. I don't know exactly what happened, but Iesu was born as a mortal man who was also the Son of God. After I became a child of God, the Holy Spirit came within me, too."

Rogatus raised a hand to stop her. "Is this Iesu the Jewish rabbi that Rome executed for claiming to be a king?"

She drew a deep breath. How was she ever going to explain what Iesu did in a way he'd understand?

"Yes, but that's not really why he died. God himself planned that execution."

Rogatus's head drew back. "He planned the crucifixion of his own son? Hmph. And I thought I had a bad father."

"You won't understand until I explain why Iesu really came and what that sacrifice did."

He started to cross his arms, but a shot of pain from his bad arm triggered a wince. He lay it back on the bed. "Tell me that part of the story."

She closed her eyes. *Thank You, God, that I haven't doused his interest by doing this poorly. Please help me find the right words.*

"Iesu came as our savior, and I need to explain what we needed to be saved from. But I have to go back further than his birth to do that."

Curiosity had replaced skepticism in Rogatus's eyes. "I like history, and we have plenty of time."

"God gave us all the ability to choose what we do. Iesu reminded his first followers that God's greatest commandments were to love God with all their heart and soul and mind and strength and to love their neighbors as themselves. God had given those commands to His people hundreds of years earlier, and they were written down in the Jews' holy scrolls." She drew her thumbnail along the filigree. "But when we choose not to do that, we're sinning. Sin builds a barrier between us and God, one that we can't remove and that God, by His very nature, can't simply ignore. Each sin, no matter how small, has to be paid for to remove its part of the barrier."

He was looking at her with those impossible-to-read eyes that Sulio hated. But since he hadn't said stop, Narina continued.

"But God knew no one would actually be able to do that, so He gave a way to make up for their sins using animal sacrifices. He gave instructions for special sacrifices in His temple that would cover their sins once a year. The animals had to be as close to perfect as possible. Then His people could approach Him because their sins had been covered for a while. But they had to do it again every year."

Rogatus's eyes narrowed again. "But that temple was razed when Titus took Jerusalem. It hasn't been rebuilt. If their god is so powerful and his people needed that temple for those sacrifices, why did he let Rome destroy it?"

"That was after Iesu had already made the perfect sacrifice to not just cover sins but to erase them. When he was crucified, he took all our sins on himself and paid for them in full. He ransomed us with his blood by his death there. He came from heaven to earth knowing he would do that, and he did it out of love for each of us. And now, because I believe in what he did for me, I have become a child of God. God is my father, and a child can always approach a good father. That's why we pray as if we're having a conversation. It's because we really are."

With tightened lips, Rogatus slowly shook his head. "It sounds good, but how do you know any of this is real? How can you tell it's not just a story like those about the gods of Rome?"

At last, something that was easy to answer. Thank You, God!

"Because Jesus told us that the Holy Spirit would come live with us and even be in us when we believed. What Iesu did paid for any sins I confessed, so I wouldn't have to pay for them. When I confessed and told God I believed in Iesu, I felt the Holy Spirit come. When we pray for you, the Spirit is here with us as we pray. When I don't know what to pray, I ask Him to pray for me, and I feel Him doing it."

She paused, giving him time to form the question she could see coming.

God, don't let it be too hard for me to answer.

Rogatus scrubbed his face. "Is that all there is to it? You confess what you call sins, claim you believe Iesus paid for them, and you become a child of your God?"

Relief surged through her. Despite her fumbles, he understood the essence after all.

"That's the most important part and a good start, but there's so much more I can tell you."

"Hmm." Rogatus scrunched his nose and rubbed the spot between his eyebrows. "I want to think about this a while, and I'm sure I'll have more questions."

"I'll look forward to those. I love talking about God. I love talking to Him." She rested her fingers on the back of his hand. "And I love telling you about Him."

She stood. "I'm going to help Lucania cut up apples for a while. I think you'll like dinner, Veldicca is making one of your favorites."

His eyelids drooped with fatigue, but he mustered a smile for her. "I think I'll take a nap before I think about this more."

"You do that. As you say, we have plenty of time."

As she left the room, she heard him shifting on the bed behind her.

God, did I really tell him what he needed to hear? I've never done this before. I care so much about what he decides. Not just for him, but for me, too. Please guide his thoughts and claim him as Your own.

Chapter 43

Not Ready to Return

Narina placed the last apple slices on the mesh tray and stretched her back. It was full enough now to place on the drying rack. With Trenus, Lucania, and her cutting, they were almost keeping up with the pickers. It was a plentiful crop this year, and she'd have plenty for both farm and taberna, if she ever got to reopen it.

But she was still disappointed. When she left Rogatus to take his afternoon nap yesterday, she was sure he'd have questions for her after dinner or maybe this morning after Veldicca tended his wounds.

But he hadn't.

She carried the now-heavy tray over to the partly-filled rack across from his doorway. Standing on tiptoes, she slipped it into place. Then she turned to watch the special man who lay sleeping in Father's old room.

She bit her lip. When she took her midmorning break, she could ask him if he had some questions to start the conversation. But was that the best thing to do? Mother used to say she could lead Father to her way of thinking by the end of any conversation, but only if he started it himself. Then she'd laugh and say, "Don't tell your father that." Was the same true of Rogatus?

She closed her eyes and drew a deep breath. *God, please let him start the conversation again. There's so much more he needs to know, and I don't know how much longer he'll be with us.*

She crossed the courtyard and listened at his door for the sounds of someone awakening, but there were none. So, it was back to the cutting table and another empty tray. Maybe by the time she filled that one...

Isurium, morning of Day 28

Sulio sat on the council house table, watching his father rub his forehead. Albiso stood by the window, looking out, but that was probably to keep Father from seeing the guilt in his eyes.

Father's sigh was deep and long. "One of the nearby clans is planning to do something stupid. I'm almost sure of it. First someone steals Narina's horses. Then they take almost a hundred from the ala, counting the horses of the soldiers they ambushed. There are others who've had horses disappear, too. Someone is getting the mounts for an attack on the Romans, and they'll unleash destruction on all of us."

Albiso kept his gaze focused on the street outside.

Sulio squeezed the back of his neck. "Maybe it wasn't one of the local clans. It would be worth traveling some distance to get horses already trained for battle, like Rogatus's herd was. By setting that ambush, they got thirty more and enough weapons and armor for thirty men at the same time."

At least none of the men he'd seen Albiso helping were ones who'd come to Father's harvest gathering. So maybe it was some distant clan that stole them. But if they brought the fight here, Rome's soldiers would blame the Isurians anyway. With Rogatus laid up, there was no one to argue against that.

"Father." Albiso turned from the window. "A decurion and four cavalrymen just stopped outside, and the decurion is coming in."

Father leaned back in his chair. "I wonder what he wants."

It was only moments before the clicking of hobnails on a stone floor announced the approach of the Roman. He cleared his throat to announce his presence before stepping into the room.

He took off his helmet with its flowing horsehair fountain and placed it under his arm. "Bellicus, chieftain of the Isurian clan, I come with a request. I am Germanus, decurion of the Ala Primae Tungrorum and acting commander in Prefect Rogatus's absence."

He didn't salute, but he stood at attention, waiting for Father to speak.

Father clasped his hands and rested them on the tabletop. "What is your request?"

"I have received word from the legate of the Ninth Hispana that Prefect Rogatus is recovering from wounds at Narina Lucana's farm. I request a guide to take me and the ala's physician to her farm to check on our prefect."

Father rubbed his mouth. "I have also heard that he is there. I find your request reasonable, and I will provide you with a guide. I wish your commander a speedy recovery."

Sulio stood. "Germanus. I'm willing to guide you there this morning. My horse is in the stable, and I can be ready to go with you as soon as I get him saddled."

Germanus's cool expression relaxed into an appreciative smile. "I gladly accept your offer, Sulio. We'll swing by the fort and collect the physician, and we can be on our way."

"I'll meet you where the street to the fort runs into the Roman road as soon as I've saddled."

Germanus's smile faded before he tipped his head to Bellicus. "I thank you for your help, Bellicus."

Father's nod acknowledged the thanks.

The decurion donned his helmet, turned on his heel, and strode from the room.

"It's good you're going with them." Father leaned back in his chair. "I want a report as soon as you get back. I'll be going to the compound as soon as I finish with whoever comes today."

"Yes, Father." Sulio had taken several steps toward the door when Albiso appeared at his side.

"I'll help you get your horse."

With some effort, Sulio kept his eyebrows from rising. No help was needed, so why was Albiso so eager to accompany him?

They had barely entered the street when Albiso hit his arm with the back of his hand. "Thank you for saying nothing to Father about the horses. But why are you always so eager to help the enemy?"

Sulio rolled his eyes. "Rogatus is not our enemy. You'd better hope he recovers enough to stay as the leader of that ala. No other Roman I've heard of has the patience and openness to compromise of Rogatus. With a man like him in charge, we've got someone there who might be more friend than enemy when it matters most. If they get a new prefect...who knows how he might behave."

Albiso snorted. "If I didn't know better, I'd think you've turned into a Roman-loving weakling who's afraid of fighting for what's ours."

They were out of sight of the council house, so Sulio wrapped his hand around Albiso's throat and shoved him against the building's wall. "And if I didn't know you'd promised Father you wouldn't do something to endanger the clan, I'd think you were a battle-hungry fool who didn't care how many people die as long as you can call yourself a warrior."

He let go and took a step back. "For once in your life, don't just act without thinking about how bad it could end. Then stop before you do something stupid that can destroy us all."

Sulio left Albiso rubbing his neck and turned into the stable.

He didn't have to like the Romans to recognize they were here to stay. The cost of trying to get rid of them was higher than any sane man would want to pay.

His anger faded as he tossed the saddle on his stallion's back and tightened the girth.

Even though he still acted as if he disliked Rogatus and would as long as he might pose a threat to Narina, he had to admit the short Roman was a decent man...and maybe even a good one.

Narina's farm, late morning of Day 28

At a trot, it took less than half an hour to reach the turn-off to Narina's farm. Germanus had doubled his escort from four to eight, and Sulio didn't blame him. He had thought Rogatus an unusually quiet man, but not a word was spoken by any of the ten Romans.

He'd chosen the Roman road over the tow path, even though it was longer. It was less likely Brigantian warriors would be using a road built for Roman troops.

As they entered the farmyard, Atto set down a basket full of apples and trotted over. "Sulio. Germanus." He smiled as if greeting a customer at the taberna. "What brings you out here?"

Sulio pointed at the physician. "Germanus brought the fort physician to look at Rogatus."

Atto pointed at a pair of benches under an apple tree, then at the paddock that used to hold Narina's bay stallion. "Your men can rest there while you do. I'll put some fresh water in the trough for your horses."

Atto's helpfulness almost made Sulio's eyes roll. But growing up in Uncle Lucanus's household made all his people less Brigantian. He turned his stallion in with Bena and the mule. He'd be staying longer than the Romans, of that he was sure.

"Where's Narina?"

Atto started pouring water into the trough. "Inside cutting apples."

"This way." With a curl of his fingers, he invited Germanus and the physician to follow him in.

When they stepped into the inner courtyard, only Lucania was visible. She looked up from the cutting table and waved, but she didn't stop working.

Sulio pointed to Rogatus's room. "He's in there."

The decurion and physician entered ahead of him, and with his back against the wall, Sulio stood just inside the room. That was the best place for a man who wanted to watch and listen.

Germanus strode to the edge of the bed and saluted. "Prefect. The legate told me you were here, and I've brought the physician for you."

"I expected you'd be coming." The smile Rogatus directed at his decurion looked almost human. "Considering I was left for dead with Zephyrus defending my corpse, I'm feeling quite well."

Germanus's official frown appeared. "How did you get here?"

"Someone who recognized Zephyrus as Narina's brought us both here. It doesn't matter who, only that they did."

Germanus stepped back to let the physician reach Rogatus's side. "Let's take a look and see how you're doing. Then we'll know when you'll be able to return to the fort."

"Proceed." Rogatus relaxed his body, but his eyes stayed fixed on the physician's face. Sulio's stayed fixed on Rogatus.

When he finished the examination, the physician crossed his arms. "You're healing well, even faster than normal. I expect in about a week we can return to get you."

"Bring the cisium when you do. I expect to be able to drive myself by then."

The physician's nod came with a smile. "I expect so, too."

"When can I use crutches? One of the farmhands is making me a pair."

A scrunched nose was the first response. "Normally, I wouldn't recommend that for at least two weeks and usually four after the injury. Using that wounded arm might put too much stress on the healing wound and cause something to tear. But with the way you're healing, by the time we come back to get you, I think you'll be able to use them. Maybe even a day or two earlier if you keep healing as you have been."

The physician scrubbed his face. "I would like to talk with whoever's been tending you. They've done something unusually effective, and I'd like to know what. I might use it in the future."

"That would be Veldicca. She's the housekeeper and many other things here. Lucania." Rogatus curled his finger, and a sheepish looking girl slipped into the back of the room. "Would you take this man to Veldicca to talk about what she's been doing to care for me."

Sulio stood just inside the door, leaning against the wall with his arms crossed. When Rogatus's gaze shifted to him, the Roman's wink without smiling said more than words. Narina's prefect was thinking about all their prayers, but neither Rogatus nor Veldicca would be telling the physician about those.

Lucania slipped out, but before the physician passed, Sulio tapped his arm.

The man stopped, but his head drew back. "Yes?"

"He's not a man who does well doing nothing. If you take him back in a cart, he'll do fine at overseeing what's going on around him."

The physician's eyes narrowed. "How do you know this?"

"I've seen him more than a few times. Narina is my cousin, and I check on her for my father, Bellicus. He's the chieftain of the Isurians, and she's his niece.

Sulio shrugged. "Even if Rogatus can't ride for a while, you Romans seem to keep records on everything. He can do that even like he is, and that should keep him busy until he can ride."

"The prefect will decide what he's ready to do, based on my advice, not yours."

With tightened lips and a shake of his head, the physician followed Lucania toward the front door.

"Sulio." Rogatus's commanding-officer voice pulled Sulio's gaze from the physician.

"What is it?"

"I need to talk with my decurion now. Alone."

Sulio gave him what he hoped was an irritating grin. "I'll go help Narina put some trays on the tallest racks. They were built for Brigantian men." He looked back over his shoulder as he stepped out of the room. "Call me when I'm needed again."

◆

Rogatus watched Sulio cross the courtyard to the far set of drying racks, then her cousin turned toward the kitchen before vanishing from sight.

"I'm not sure I trust that one." Germanus's words were scarcely above a whisper.

"I do. A lot of what he says is a game he plays with me. He's done it since I met him. But he's like his father in wanting to keep the peace here so the members of his tribe don't suffer."

Rogatus cleared his throat to end Sulio as their topic of discussion. "Are there any signs of problems that would require me to return to the fort immediately?"

"No." Germanus's lips twitched, his equivalent of a fleeting smile. "All seems peaceful. The chieftain Bellicus was friendly enough when I went to the council house to ask for a guide to bring me here. He wished you a speedy recovery." The twitch turned into a wry smile." "I think he even meant it."

With his hand placed on his injured thigh, Rogatus smiled back. "I do seem to be recovering quicker than normal under Veldicca's care, so I'm not in a hurry to give that up. Medicus is better for treating serious wounds, but now that I'm recovering well, that's not as important."

Germanus licked his lips. "The food is definitely better, and that alone could tempt a man to prolong his recovery here." Germanus glanced into the courtyard where Narina was stretching to put a drying tray into a rack. "The view and the conversations might be more satisfying as well."

Rogatus smiled at the remark. While other tribunes might find it impertinent, he considered it a sign that Germanus was comfortable with his commander. They had mutual respect, and that was better than faked deference. "You're right on all three counts."

His officer's laugh echoed in the room as Germanus looked into the courtyard at Narina.

"So, when you come for me in a week, bring the *cisium*. I'll drive it back to the fort myself. It's not a horse, but it can travel as fast as long as there's a good road to go on. If there's any reason I need to be there earlier, come get me. Otherwise, I'm sure you will do a fine job of overseeing the ala while I recover more."

"As you wish, Prefect."

◆

Sulio took the loaded tray from Narina and put it in the highest position on the drying rack directly across from Rogatus's open door. He would have preferred to listen to everything the decurion said to Rogatus, but they were conversing in near-whispers. So far, there was nothing new to tell Father. Then a peal of laughter broke the near-silence, and from the look on the decurion's face as his gaze raked Narina, it had something to do with her.

He ground his teeth. He'd be coming to check on the prefect's recovery every day now that Veldicca's care had closed death's door. He'd be pushing for that prefect to go back to his fort as soon as possible. He'd wondered about the wisdom of it as he'd done it, but he really had no choice but to bring Rogatus here after finding Zephyrus guarding him. But he didn't have to leave Rogatus here unchaperoned. Letting that man live in the same house as Narina, where they could spend many hours talking with each other—it was a calculated risk. And maybe he'd calculated wrong.

When Germanus came out of Rogatus's room, Sulio approached him. "Do you need my escort back, or can you find your way home? Narina is short of male farmhands, so I'll stay and help if you don't need me."

Tightened lips and a single shake of the head was Germanus's answer. "I thank you for showing us where this place is, but we don't need you to go back. Or to find it when we return to get the prefect."

Sulio tapped the decurion's upper arm, and got a raised eyebrow in response. "Then I'll wish you a good ride back. You'll find your physician in the orchard, so you won't need to come back in here."

Germanus's eyes turned suspicious. "I'll remember what you've said and done today." He tipped his head and left the courtyard.

Sulio strolled into Rogatus's room. The crutches Narina's farmhand had made leaned against the wall. He lodged the armrests in his armpits and took a step, swinging one foot as if he couldn't use it.

"Did Atto make these?"

"Trenus and Atto. One helped Trenus with his balance after the beating, but he doesn't need it now. Atto made the other to match."

"He's going to have to cut a few inches off the post. He made it for a man his height, and there's at least a four-inch difference between him and you, even though he's not fully grown yet." He placed them against the wall again and shrugged. "But if you give them back to Trenus when you're through needing them, they'll have some if one of the women needs a pair in the future."

Rogatus's laugh was quieter, but it sounded as genuine as his decurion's had. "Let's hope they never have need of them." Rogatus ran his left hand through his hair. "Weren't you going to help Narina's farmhands? There are a few hours left today for doing that."

Sulio clenched his jaw, but relaxed it before the prefect should have seen it. Rogatus had no right to tell him what to do, but he wouldn't let the man see it bothered him.

"You're right. I'll go help in the orchard with the high-up apples. But I'll be back for dinner." He grinned. "I've missed our conversations."

Without waiting for a response, Sulio left the courtyard.

He'd be watching Narina tonight to see how it lay between her and the prefect. Then he'd know what his next move should be.

Chapter 44

What God Demands

Dinnertime of Day 28

Rogatus had dozed off and on that afternoon, but during each period of wakefulness, he'd heard Sulio's voice. Sometimes near, sometimes far, and often exchanging words with Narina.

He sighed. Perhaps she would choose to dine with him instead of in the kitchen, where Sulio would certainly join them. It wasn't by his choice that Lucania ate with him more often than she did.

But it was Narina's voice that made him open his eyes with the words, "Are you ready for dinner now? Veldicca made one of your favorites."

She carried a tray with a plate of rolls and two bowls of something with an aroma that made him lick his lips.

"Do I get my favorite dinner companion tonight?"

Narina shook her head, and he suppressed the sigh.

"No. You'll have to settle for me."

When the smile he liked best lit up her eyes, it was the highlight of his day.

"So, the answer is yes, and I couldn't ask for better."

"But since I haven't dined with you two since the taberna closed, I can't miss this chance to do so." Sulio carried a second chair into the room and set it next to Narina's. "This is almost like old times. I'll be back with my stew."

Rogatus sucked in a breath and held it as he counted to ten. He didn't want to curse in Narina's presence.

Worry swept the laughter from Narina's eyes. "Are you all right."

"Yes."

He couldn't tell her Sulio had spoiled what he'd hoped for all day.

She had placed the pillows behind his back and handed him his bowl and spoon when Sulio returned with a full bowl and more rolls.

Before her cousin could sit, she bowed her head. "Thank You, God, for how well Rogatus is healing. Please continue to heal him until he's completely well. Thank You for bringing Sulio in time to find him and bring him to us. Bless this food and our time together. In Iesu's name, we pray."

Sulio settled into the second chair. "You look better each time I see you. Seems to me like you're well enough to go back to leading your men. I can let Germanus know you want him to come sooner than a week. Your physician said you were healing unusually fast."

Sometimes her cousin made it hard, but Rogatus managed a social smile. "He also said that he and I would decide when it was time."

Sulio took his first bite of stew. "Hmmm. This is good enough to tempt any man to shirk his duty to keep eating like this."

Narina flicked his upper arm with the back of her fingers. "You know very well he's not shirking his duty. He was close to death when you brought him to us. He certainly can't walk with that knee, and he can't even use crutches yet until his arm heals more. We're all glad to have him here, and he's welcome for as long as he needs our help."

Rogatus's irritation faded when the eyes she turned on him declared him much more than welcome.

Sulio bit a chunk off his roll. "I wonder what Veldicca told that physician. I bet she only told part of what she did, and he's still wondering what worked so well."

He leaned forward and nudged Rogatus's hip. "But you didn't say anything about them praying for you, either."

Rogatus rubbed his jaw. He didn't, and he never would.

"It would do him no good to know. He can't do that himself."

Narina tightened her lips and turned to her cousin. "You kept telling me how dangerous it would be to do anything that let Rogatus know we're Christians. After all that, you know he wouldn't put us at risk that way."

She turned warm eyes on Rogatus. "He asked us to pray out loud for him, and we're all glad to do it. I'm sure that's why he's doing so well. And we'll keep doing it until he's completely better."

Rogatus didn't speak the words, but he held her gaze as he nodded once. When she and Veldicca asked him, the Christian god did seem to have some power to make him heal faster.

She picked up a roll. "Now, I suggest we all eat what Veldicca made us before it gets any colder. We can talk afterwards."

As Rogatus took his first bite of the lentil and who-knew-what stew, he wasn't sorry Narina had silenced the conversation, at least until they'd eaten. Maybe Sulio would go home right after they ate, and he'd get some time alone with her. But if her cousin stayed too long, his questions about her god would have to wait until tomorrow. No soldier lets an enemy see his doubts or his weakness if he can help it. Especially if that enemy could reveal them to a man's commander to get rid of him for good.

Morning of Day 29

Rogatus watched as Veldicca treated his wounds, and he listened to their prayers for his healing. It was finally time for the conversation she'd promised and Sulio had prevented.

When Veldicca picked up the tray and they both turned to leave—

"Narina, can we talk for a while?"

She settled into the chair. "Of course." She scrunched her nose. "I'd rather talk with you than cut apples. But I can't stay long."

"This won't take long, but I want you to know something."

She tensed, but why would she? What did she think he was going to say?

"I think your prayers to your god in Iesu's name make me hurt less."

He stared out the door, then turned his gaze back on her. "I've had more than my share of headaches for years. Before Father banished me from Rome, I tried going to the Sanctuary of Asclepius on the island in the Tiber. But Father let me have almost no money, and what I could give as a votive offering wasn't much. The priest I gave it to had me take a ritual bath and gave me a slip of papyrus with a prayer to use when my head hurt."

He glanced at her, and the tension was gone, as if they were practicing Brittonic at their table in her taberna.

"I got to sleep one night in the special dormitory where Asclepius or his daughters were supposed to visit me in a dream. The priest said he'd interpret it and tell me how to get better. Except I didn't dream. I went home with just the prayer that didn't work. Father found out. He accused me of wasting his money since I deserved the headaches. Then he ordered me to move to the villa that's a hundred miles from Rome."

"So, you learned that Asclepius couldn't heal you."

"I learned that Father hated me enough to try to keep the gods from helping me. But I tried again later. There's always an altar for Asclepius in the hospitals of legion fortresses and cohort forts. Over the years, I've made votive offerings at different ones to get rid of the headaches. But they never stopped, so I quit asking that god for anything."

He shifted a little. Moving hurt, but lying in one spot too long wasn't comfortable, either. "But when you spoke your prayer over me that first time after Lucania had revealed who you worship, the headache left. It hasn't returned."

Rogatus gave her an appreciative smile. "So, next time I have one, I'll ask your god instead of Asclepius to take it away in Iesu's name. It's good to know one god who will actually do something to help. Did you make an offering to him before you came in and prayed for me?"

The breath she drew in was almost a gasp. What had he said that offended her?

He expected her to draw back, but she leaned closer instead.

"That wasn't a ritual prayer like you'd use in a Roman rite. Iesu told his followers to ask in his name when we pray, but not like it's something magic. I was simply asking God, my heavenly Father, to heal my friend. I don't have to buy His favor with some offering. He gives us all the good things you see around us because He loves us, not for some price we pay. I give Him my love and try to do what pleases Him. That's what He wants from any of us."

She touched the back of his hand where it lay on his chest. "When Iesu told his followers that God's greatest command was to love Him with all our heart, mind, soul, and strength, that didn't leave room for any other gods in our lives. God gave His people ten commands that were the most important, and the first two make that clear."

She raised one finger. "The first is 'I am the LORD your God, who brought you out of the land of Egypt, out of the house of bondage. You shall have no other gods before Me.' He's not saying He'll be the greatest god among the gods you worship. He's the only one. That's why we Christians will choose death over worshiping Jupiter or any of the other gods that Rome decrees we must. It's why I stopped taking part in what Father and Mother did each morning at their shrine."

A second finger joined the first.

"The second is 'You shall not make for yourself a carved image—any likeness of anything that is in heaven above, or that is in the earth beneath, or that is in the water under the earth; you shall not bow down to them nor serve them.' He couldn't have made it clearer, and what happens at the shrines and temples every day goes against this command."

"There are dozens of religions around the Empire. Except for the Jews and Christians, they all make idols and then worship them."

"God knew people were especially prone to do that. That's why he gave that command to make sure his people knew they shouldn't."

He blew out a slow breath between pursed lips. One god to the exclusion of all others?

She'd said before that none of the gods of Rome were real, just stories made up by the ancestors. If a man could be sure that was true, it would only make sense to follow the one real god. But what if it wasn't true? Should he ask her that question? Would revealing his doubts about what she was telling him drive her away, like Sulio claimed?

"Before being here with you, I never spent time thinking about whether the gods of Rome are real and have the power to change what happens. I'd been told all my life that they do, and I've been told what to do to get them to look favorably on me."

He stared at his bandaged knee.

"But they never have. Until my great-uncle helped me get into the tres militiae, I'd decided Fortuna began frowning on me from the moment my mother lay with the man who really was my father. She mostly frowned until I was ten. For the next eight years, she smiled a few times after Grandfather started treating me like my brothers when he thought his friends might be watching."

He looked at her again, and her lips had straightened. Was it sympathy or pity he saw in her eyes? He didn't want her pity. He wanted her friendship... and her love.

"But when he died, my father's hatred for me closed all the doors he held open for my brothers. I couldn't even petition the gods because it takes money for big enough offerings to get the gods to help." He snorted. "But a man has to have hope, or he might as well give up and die."

The trace of a smile had turned into one of his favorites. It wasn't from pity. It was only the look of someone who truly cared.

"So, I looked for a way out. I learned where my mother's uncle lived, and it was only a couple of hours ride from the villa. So, I went to him and asked him to help me. I didn't expect he would, but I had to try something. When he sponsored me as if he'd known me all my life, I thought the gods were finally smiling on me."

He rested his hand on his bad leg. "And now what I've worked for so hard, what I hoped I'd achieve, it's all at risk because of one arrow."

Narina touched the back of his hand. "But maybe what you've been after isn't what's best for you. Sometimes the best things come out of what only seems bad at the time. If Mother hadn't died when Lucania was born, Father would never have bought Veldicca. I would never have learned how much God loves me, and I wouldn't know the joy of following Iesu. Without those arrows, I wouldn't be talking with you right now about how wonderful it is to be a child of God."

She bit her lip as their gazes locked. "All you have to do is turn away from the gods of Rome, confess the sins that are keeping you from God, and believe that Iesu paid for those sins so you can be a child of God like me."

His stomach clenched. *All* he had to do?

"But that would be giving up everything I've ever wanted."

"But if what you've wanted isn't God's best for you, are you really giving up anything?"

He couldn't stop himself from staring at her. Did she realize what she was asking of him? If he told her he couldn't do what she said, would she'd reject him herself, just as Sulio said?

He tipped his head back and stared at the rafters before she might ask what was wrong. If his knee didn't heal quickly enough or well enough that he could ride again, had he already lost what he'd committed his life to gaining?

"I don't know what's best. It's too soon to make any decision like you're asking for."

She meant for the smile she gave him to mask her disappointment, but he knew that feeling too well himself to be fooled.

"You don't have to. God is so patient with us. He wants us to believe and follow Iesu with our whole hearts, but that can take time. I didn't start out loving Him completely, but over time, I've grown to love Him more and more. I think that's what happens for most people once they take that first step toward belief."

She rose. "I need to work on apples for a while, and you need to rest. We can talk more about this when you're ready."

"I'll look forward to that."

He would, but his eagerness was lessoned by the fear of what saying the wrong thing might do.

As she entered the courtyard, she looked back at him. In those storm-gray eyes, disappointment had been replaced by hope.

But if he couldn't do what she asked of him, would they ever look at him with love?

Narina found Veldicca in the kitchen, packing dried apples into large clay jars for storage.

"I'm worried about him." She lifted an empty jar onto the counter and placed the first dry slice in the bottom.

Veldicca glanced at her and kept packing. "What happened?"

"He told me it hurts less when we pray, so he's going to add praying to God in Iesu's name to his worship of the Roman gods. I tried to explain to him how God had said he couldn't do that, how God commanded we not split our loyalties and serve other gods. But I'm not sure I convinced him. When I told him he had to turn away from the gods of Rome, confess the sins that keep him from God, and trust Iesu has paid for them, he said that would mean giving up everything he ever wanted."

"I've seen that before when I lived in Isca Silurum. For a noble Roman with obligations like Rogatus has...they take those very seriously. They swear absolute loyalty to the emperor, and they'd rather die than betray their oaths. They know what loyalty demands, and they're willing to live up to that. For men like him, what they'll lose if they leave what they've been raised to follow is obvious. It's only after we decide to believe that the benefits become as obvious as those losses appeared before."

Veldicca put an arm around her shoulders. "Be patient with him. He already knows God has real power. You only know what he's asking, and you know he's a man who keeps things inside until he suddenly surprises you with them. I think when he finally faces that choice between accepting the truth and doing what loyalty demands, he'll choose truth."

She squeezed and then released Narina. "Is it picking or cutting for you today?"

"Storing and cutting. Lucania's too short to reach the empty part of the racks."

Narina glanced at the door to the courtyard. "And I want to be close so I can answer any questions he wants to ask. He might not be with us much longer, and I might never get to share with him after he leaves."

She blinked a few times. Even the thought of that could start the tears.

A chuckle made Narina's head draw back.

Veldicca patted her arm. "Rest assured, he's not going to let that happen. He's frustrated every attempt by Sulio to get him to stay away. I think the only thing that would work would be telling him you didn't want to see him ever again."

A knowing smile curved Veldicca's lips. "But I think he's already in love with you, and you'd break his heart if you did that."

Narina sucked air between her teeth. "I've been asking God to keep him from asking me to marry him. All his life, he's been treated so badly by his father and grandfather. He never got to know his mother because of what they did, and the only person he thinks cares what happens to him is his dead mother's uncle. If he would only believe, I could say yes the moment he asks me."

She wiped the corner of her eye. "Telling him no would break his heart. It would break my heart, too, but if he's going back to noble society, he can't have a Christian wife."

"Never forget that God can work all things for good for those who love Him. I'll be praying that happens soon." Veldicca placed the lid on her jar and set it aside. "I'll go help pick a while."

Narina kept placing slices in hers.

Oh, God. Please help him see past what he's always believed to the truth he'll find only in You. And please let us be together after he decides to follow You.

Chapter 45

Duty Calls

Narina's farm, morning of Day 30

When Sulio rode into Narina's farmyard and put his stallion in the bay's old paddock, he was already later than he intended. He'd told Atto he would come early to help get the fields prepared for planting the broad beans.

But Germanus had come to the council house to see how he thought Rogatus was doing. When he told the decurion that Rogatus was almost ready to try the crutch, Germanus asked if Sulio was going to the farm and could deliver a message. Then he wouldn't have to send it with a courier and escorts.

Sulio had no good excuse for saying no, so he'd become the decurion's messenger boy.

He entered the house and went straight to Rogatus's room.

The prefect was dozing, so he flicked his foot with his fingers.

Rogatus awoke with a jerk, then grimaced. "Sulio." His eyes narrowed. "Why did you wake me?"

"Your legate sent a courier with a message this morning, and Germanus asked me to bring it to you so he wouldn't have to."

Rogatus sat up so quickly he had to put his good arm out to get his balance. "What's the message?"

"Let's see..." Sulio tapped his lips. "I think I'll remember." He looked up at the rafters and opened his eyes wide. From the corner of his eye, he caught the end of Rogatus's exasperated eye roll.

"Ah, yes. Apparently, there's been unrest to the northwest. Nothing specific has happened yet, but if you're up to returning to duty, you should do so. Germanus will be coming tomorrow morning with the physician and a cisium to see if you can return. Even if you aren't up to doing everything, your legate wants you there keeping track of what's going on and making any decisions about troop movements that won't cause a problem that didn't exist before they did something."

He shrugged. "It would seem he thinks a cavalry officer who can't ride can do more than keep records up to date."

Rogatus scrunched his face as he rubbed his forehead. After releasing a deep breath, he gave Sulio a wry smile.

"Is that all?"

Sulio reached into his pocket, pulled out the wooden sheet that the legate sent, and scanned it.

"Yes."

Then he handed it to Rogatus.

"Thank you for bringing the message." The Roman's mouth twitched. "You didn't have to recite it for me, but I suspect you enjoyed telling me I have to leave Narina's house sooner than I'd planned."

Sulio's chuckle almost made Rogatus smile. "We're starting to understand each other so well that someone watching us might think we were friends." He shrugged. "But some people are easy to fool that way."

He tipped his head toward the door. "Atto is waiting for me to help get some fields ready. I'll be working through lunch, but I'll join the two of you for dinner. It could be a long time before I can do that again."

He gave the frowning prefect a parting wave and headed for the fields to find Atto. It would be good to have the Roman out of Narina's house, but he would miss trying to get a rise out of the man whose self-control was almost unlimited.

◆

Rogatus's arm had scabbed over and so had his thigh. The knee was still purple and swollen, but there was no sign of infection. But Medicus had said it would be weeks or a few months until it healed as much as it would.

He couldn't ride, but he'd be able to handle a team. He could test sitting up in the chair that afternoon. If that went fine, driving a cisium the few miles to the fort tomorrow should be easy enough. It would be good to be doing something again instead of lying on a bed dwelling on what ifs and maybes.

A movement caught his eye.

Narina stood in the doorway. "Lucania said Sulio just came and talked with you, but he left right after."

"He came to help Atto. He said he'd be back for dinner."

"I'll let Veldicca know. Atto is getting the fields ready for planting the broad beans. They'll both be hungry, so she'll need to make extra."

She turned to leave, but she couldn't go before he asked her.

"I've been wondering. What was your father's name when he served in the Brittorum and after he became a citizen?"

"Lucanus, son of Catus. He became Marcus Ulpius Lucanus when he retired. Why?"

Why? He couldn't tell her. Not yet.

"I was wondering if Minconus shared it."

"No. Father wasn't a citizen when he was born, so he and Dubnus have Brigantian names. So do I, but Lucania got a Roman one."

"Is Bellicus also a son of Catus?"

"He is. He was the second son, but the eldest died. So, he became chieftain. Father was the fourth son. He wouldn't inherit much, so he enlisted in the new auxiliary that was being formed."

Rogatus kept his smile from looking too satisfied. She'd just revealed everything he needed to know. But he hoped she would never learn why.

"He made a good choice. Otherwise, I wouldn't have met you, and that's the best thing that's happened since coming to Britannia."

Pink spread across her cheeks and up to her ears. "I'm glad I met you, too. I miss Zephyrus, but I'm glad you bought him. He kept you alive, and I thank God for that."

He cleared his throat. Unwelcome news didn't get better with waiting.

"Sulio just told me that Germanus and Medicus will be coming with a cisium for me tomorrow. The legate wants me back at the fort to watch over things and direct troop actions to keep things peaceful."

Narina came deeper into the room. "Duty calls. That was Father's life, too. But we'll miss you."

"I'll miss being here. I'm sorry to be leaving so soon, but I've learned a lot from our discussions. I'll be thinking about what you've said."

Those words triggered her smile. He'd chosen the right thing to say.

"You know we'll keep praying for you. We think of you as family now."

Family. Not yet, but soon he'd ask her to make that reality. But would she say yes? How much did it matter that he couldn't yet worship only her god?

He looked at his hand as he rubbed his palm with his thumb. "As part of that duty, there are rituals that are required of soldiers, and as prefect, I lead them. But after our talk yesterday, I'm going to change some things. Germanus has been leading them while I've been here. I'm planning to use the crutches as an excuse for having him still do the rites. A sacrifice doesn't count if the animal struggles, and I couldn't do a quick, clean kill like I am." He didn't look at her as the corner of his mouth lifted. "A man on crutches can't work quickly enough for a healthy animal not to struggle. He'll accept that as a good reason to continue."

He glanced at her face. What she was thinking, he couldn't tell.

"All my men take part in formal camp worship. But when my men are off-duty, they can enter the shrine room in the principia and venerate the draco and banners of the turmas. There are statues of three gods there and an image of the emperor. Some do it often. Some never do it."

He didn't mean to let it, but a sigh escaped.

"Now that I know your god's command not to worship images, I won't be doing it. I haven't done it often in the past, so no one will think it odd that I'm not doing it now."

In her eyes, he saw compassion, but not condemnation. His next sigh was one of relief.

"Duty made Father do some things he didn't want to. You're at least taking a good first step. God is patient. You've only just heard about Him. Most people don't start out loving God as much as we should. I know I didn't. That comes with time."

What he was about to request...it meant more to him than she'd ever know.

"When I go back, will you come up sometimes for a meal at your taberna? You can tell me more, and I can ask my questions." He paused before speaking what he hoped wouldn't be needed. "Sulio could join us if you need that to protect your reputation."

"I'll be glad to, and Veldicca will be glad to come with me to give you a break from garrison food. How soon?"

"Maybe a week? We can figure out how often then."

Her smile dimmed. "That should work. I think we'll have the broad beans planted, or at least be far enough along that she and I can ride up for an afternoon and come home in the morning. Whether we'll need Sulio...Veldicca might be enough." She shrugged. "We'll have to wait and see."

Did that shrug mean what his often did?

She tipped her head toward the courtyard. "Apples are calling. We can talk more later."

He nodded, but his stomach clenched.

She hadn't offered to stay and talk. She was pulling back from him.

Was it because he was leaving? Or because he would still be doing what her god condemned?

If he were a betting man, he'd bet a week's wages that Sulio would make certain they didn't get to talk about anything important this evening. That was as close to a sure thing as he'd ever known.

As she vanished through the doorway, he closed his eyes. He wasn't tired, but if sleep would come, he could stop thinking about what duty demanded, what her god commanded, and how impossible it might be to satisfy both.

Chapter 46

What Love Demands

Morning of Day 31

Rogatus scraped the last bit of porridge from his bowl and licked the spoon before setting both aside. The rosemary Veldicca added gave flavor to a meal that would otherwise be too bland for his taste. But he'd seen none growing near the fort, so he'd have to be content with bland for the foreseeable future.

As usual, Lucania had eaten with him, but instead of her usual cheery self, she'd been quiet, almost sad. She knew he was leaving, and she was no happier about it than he was. She left as soon as she finished. To work on apples, she said, but she'd wiped at the corner of her eye on the way out. Was she trying to keep him from seeing her cry?

He swung his feet off the bed and put his weight on his good leg. Two hops, and he was able to turn and sit in the chair. He'd tried short walks with the crutches yesterday afternoon. It didn't hurt much to use them. Physically, he was able to return to the fort. But that didn't mean he wanted to.

Narina knocked on the doorframe, and he invited her in with a curl of his fingers. She looked no happier than Lucania. Only years of practice at not showing his thoughts kept him from looking the same.

"Germanus should be here soon. But I want to say a few things before he comes." He gripped the thigh of his bad leg and adjusted how he sat. There wasn't much time, so he'd use it carefully. "I want to thank you for your prayers for me. Your god seems to answer all of them. I've seen arrow wounds before, and my arm and thigh healed faster than any of them. So, I'm going to add God the Father and Iesu to the gods I pray to. I'd be a fool not to."

She said nothing, so he continued.

"But I still don't understand why the Christians I watched die didn't offer that one libation to the main gods of Rome and the genius of the emperor.

They didn't have to mean it. They didn't have to do it all the time. Just once to avoid the arena, and then they could worship how they wanted in the privacy of their homes."

Distress filled her eyes. "That would be a terrible sin. What loving God with all your heart and mind and soul and strength means is not giving any of that love and the worship that stems from it to another god. The emperors try to make everyone do exactly what God has forbidden." She placed crossed hands above her heart. "So, the ones you watched—to be faithful, they had no choice but to die. Since the only thing that would free them was offering worship in a temple to an idol that had been carved to represent another god, they chose death. They knew when we die, we don't stop living. We're children of God, and we live forever with Iesu in heaven."

She bit her lip. "Sometimes what love demands means giving up what we think we want most."

He was afraid of her answer to his next question, but he asked anyway.

"Would you make that choice if you faced it?"

"Yes."

He scrubbed his face. Exactly what he feared, but he expected it.

If he went back to the heart of the empire and took her with him, would that get her killed? Could she hide what she believed so no one asked her about her faith, like she'd done with him? Would his father somehow find out? He'd turn her in if he did and be the one cheering loudest as the lions tore her apart.

Narina was waiting for him to respond, but what should he say?

Her eyes narrowed. "When you asked if I'd come visit you...do you really want to keep learning about God, or did you just say it so I'd come?"

"I meant it. You've convinced me your god is real. I'd like to know more about who he is and what he does. I've already seen he has power to heal like no other god I know, and all you did was ask him."

Her eyes softened, and her usual smile returned. "Iesu said to ask whatever we want in his name. God loves us and will do what is best. One of the first things Veldicca taught me is God's promise that all things work together for good for those who love God."

"I'm not likely to benefit from that. I believe your god is real, but I don't love him. I'm going to pray to him, but I'm not ready to give him the kind of devotion you do."

His gaze locked onto her eyes. How she responded to what he said next mattered much more than she knew. "But a man and a woman don't have to agree on everything to be good with each other."

He counted to ten before she answered, and his heart beat rose with each number.

"That may be the case at the moment, but God isn't through with you yet."

Was that something to be glad about...or to fear?

The ala physician's distant voice reached his ear. "I hope the prefect is right that he's ready to return."

Closer still, Germanus spoke. "If the legate wants him on duty, he'll insist he is even if he isn't. He's a true Roman that way."

She'd turned toward the door, ready to leave him.

"Narina."

"Yes?"

"I can use Boreas when I start riding. I won't need two horses for a while, so I'm leaving Zephyrus with you. You can use him to restart your herd."

She came to his side and took his hand in hers. "Thank you. I'll take good care of him. Please take care of yourself. Don't do too much too soon. We'll be praying, and I'll see you in a week."

One squeeze, and she left to go work.

Whether he wanted to or not, it was time to get back to work himself.

While a frowning Germanus stood against the wall, Rogatus stayed in the chair as Medicus examined him. But he'd already decide he'd go back to the fort, no matter what the man said.

"Your arm and thigh healed as fast as I've ever seen. The knee...now it's about like I've seen in other cases. Slower than it was, anyway. The purple is less, but it's still swollen and I can barely bend it. It's likely to be another two months at least, maybe six before we can tell how much it will heal. In the meantime, don't try too hard to use it. That could make the damage worse."

He straightened and stepped away. "There is the possibility that riding will be difficult for you even after it heals. Especially in battle since you use your legs to give orders to your warhorse."

Rogatus's jaw clenched. He didn't need to be reminded of the obvious.

"Hand me the crutches, and we'll leave now."

Germanus came to the chair and scooped him up. "I'll load you, Prefect. It will be faster that way."

He was tempted to say he was no child, but Germanus was right. So, his decurion carried him out of the house and deposited him on the seat of the cisium.

After Rogatus unwrapped the reins from the rod next to him, he waited for Germanus to mount.

Medicus put the crutches and the sack containing all of his armor in the back and climbed up beside him. Then he reached for the reins.

Rogatus tightened his grip. "I'll drive for a while. I need to make sure I can do it before I go to Eboracum tomorrow."

His physician's brow furrowed. "Is that wise, Prefect?"

"Wise or not, I have urgent business there, and I need to meet with our legate to learn what's been going on while I've been laid up."

With a snap of the reins, he started the mules toward the fort that he used to call home. It shouldn't take long to feel that way again.

From the edge of the orchard, Narina watched Rogatus drive away.

She caught the tear that started to escape and wiped it on her tunic. She'd told herself she wasn't going to cry when he left, but she wasn't very good at following through.

Veldicca walked up beside her and wrapped an arm around her shoulders. "We'll all miss him. But I expect we'll see him again."

Narina gave her a watery smile. "He asked if we'd come to the taberna and have dinner with him sometimes. He said in a week would be good, and I told him you and I would be there."

Before lowering her arm, Veldicca gave her a good squeeze. "I'm sure he'll be counting the days."

"He said he would be praying to God, but he's not going to stop taking part in the camp worship. I thought he understood when I told him what God had commanded about not worshipping other gods. But I guess I failed there."

"You don't know that." Veldicca patted her arm. "He's the ala prefect. He can't just stop leading the ala, and that includes the camp worship. I think that's all he can do at the moment. It's a huge step forward for him even to know God is the one to pray to when he's barely even heard about Him. You can't know what God will reveal to him when he prays."

"I suppose you're right. He did say he wanted us to come up so we could talk more. He said he'd have questions for me."

"That's a good sign." Veldicca picked up her basket to move to the next tree. "Once a man of honor opens even a little of his heart and mind toward God, it's hard to keep resisting God's call."

Narina's last view of him ended as the trees by their road hid him from sight.

God, please let Veldicca be right. Help him see that he needs You more than anything. Then help him see he needs me, too.

The Isurium Fort, afternoon of Day 31

Back at the fort, Rogatus's arm and thigh were healed well enough that he could get around on crutches without too much pain. He'd walked from the cisium into his office in the principia under his own power. His orderly brought him his usual armor, and he now sat at his desk, scanning reports from during his absence. Each of the decurions had stopped by to welcome him back, and they seemed to mean it.

He leaned back in his chair, interlaced his fingers, and placed his hands atop his head.

It was good he could get around, but the physician had said the healing of his knee had slowed. Not slower than usual, but not strangely fast like it had been.

Was that because they'd stopped praying for him?

His future depended on that knee. He massaged his temple. The tightness that signaled the start of a headache was back. Was that from them stopping as well?

He put his elbows on the desktop and clasped his hands. With his forehead resting on them, he closed his eyes. Time to test whether him saying a silent prayer had any effect at all.

God of Narina, my head is starting to hurt. Please stop it now before it gets bad.

He straightened before he remembered the last part.

I ask this in Iesu's name.

He'd pulled another tablet in front of him when he noticed the tightness was gone. God had listened to his prayer and done it. Or was it because she was still praying for him from a distance? She'd probably laugh at that question and then tell him her God listened to him as well as her.

And maybe that was true.

He was attracted by her faith, and he'd seen how some of what he did was incompatible with being a Christian. But he wasn't ready to commit to something that might cost him everything he'd worked for. But if he didn't, would that cost him her?

He shook his head. When he said a man and a woman didn't have to agree on everything, she didn't flat out tell him they had to. What did she mean by "that may be the case at the moment?" Did that mean he could persuade her to marry him even if he wasn't willing to reject the Roman gods and worship only hers? And if so, how?

Germanus appeared in his doorway. "You sent for me, Prefect."

Rogatus pointed at the guest chair by the desk. "Yes. I need you to do something for me."

His lead decurion sat on the edge of the chair, but kept his back at attention.

"While I've been gone, you've been leading the rites for the ala, and I'm sure you've done them well with the precision required." He pointed at his crutches. "You've done them better than I could right now. So, I'm going to have you continue to perform the rites, both making the sacrifices and speaking the words."

A question formed in Germanus's eyes, but he said nothing.

"Moving with crutches makes it impossible to perform actions smoothly, and a fumble would negate the rite and make us do it over. I'd be doing them one-handed at best, and that not likely to be perfect enough. My leg isn't ready for killing any animal, let alone a bull if we're going into action. I can't move quickly enough to make sure there's no struggle, and any sacrificial animal struggling invalidates the sacrifice. So, it's best for you to continue."

Rogatus rubbed his mouth. "If the ala must go into action before I can ride, you'll be leading it. So, it's especially important for you to do this well."

"I'm glad to do that for you, Prefect."

"Good." Rogatus managed to rise, then tucked the crutches under his armpits. "I'm going to my quarters now. Have the cook send some dinner at the usual time."

Germanus moved over beside him. "Can I do anything else to help right now?"

"No. You've done enough for today, but I'm going to be relying on you more than I did until my knee heals."

"That will be my pleasure, Prefect." The decurion's normally stoic face relaxed as he smiled. "We thought you were dead. I'm glad we were wrong. We're glad to have you back here at all."

Rogatus moved the crutches and swung his good leg forward to complete a step. Germanus stayed beside him. At least he wouldn't have to worry about whether he'd make it to the praetorium today.

This time, he would count how many steps he had to take to reach his quarters. When something was hard, knowing how much more was needed to complete the task had always helped him finish.

With his future so unsettled until he knew if he'd heal, he needed at least one thing he could still predict. His career, Narina, what his father might do... there was too much uncertainty even for him.

She would tell him to pray about it, that her god could work all things out for the best.

Maybe tonight, in the solitude of his room, he'd try that advice.

Evening of Day 31

Dinner had been edible, but Rogatus would be lying if he told anyone he didn't miss Veldicca's cooking.

But there were two things that he could never do while he stayed at Narina's house, and he needed to do them as soon as possible. The first would be a gift that he hoped she'd never receive. The second might clear the way for the future he hoped they would have.

By the standards of anyone who wasn't of the noble orders, he was a wealthy man. As a soldier, he might die anytime without warning. The past week was proof of that.

It was time to make a will.

To be valid, a Roman will needed certain exact words. Seven men had to witness the signing and press their signets into the wax that trapped the cords sealing a stack of three wax panels. Many times, he'd been a witness for one of his soldiers, so he knew the legal wording by heart. He'd get the wax panels and cord in Eboracum. Seven citizen witnesses could be found there as well.

But for now, he took a thin wooden sheet and a pen from the drawer, uncapped the inkwell, and began to write.

> I am Proculus Trebonius Rogatus, prefect of the Ala Primae Tungrorum, and this is my will.
>
> I order that Narina Lucana, the sui iuris daughter of Marcus Ulpius Lucanus, deceased retired centurion of the Cohors III Brittorum Equitata, be my heir.
>
> Let all others for me be disinherited.
>
> You accept my estate within the next two hundred days after my death. But if you do not thus accept my estate, if you refuse to enter upon it, be thou disinherited.
>
> My personal property consists of all the money I have earned during my military service and all my property obtained while I have served in the tres militiae. This includes my warhorses, Zephyrus and Boreas.

He blew out a long, slow breath. When the tribunes read what he'd written, they would know the first name he'd concealed since his arrival. But protecting Narina was worth revealing the first name that had plagued him all his life. Protecting Narina was worth more than anything.

He took a fresh tablet from the desk drawer. The next problem was more difficult to solve. In fact, he had no idea what to do that had any chance of succeeding. So, it was time to ask the one person who might help him find out.

One deep breath, and he pressed the stylus into the wax.

> Proculus Trebonius Rogatus to Publius Visulanius Crescens, my esteemed great-uncle, greetings. If you are well, then I am glad. I write to ask you to help me. I cannot figure this out on my own.

Chapter 47

Legion headquarters, midday of Day 32

With four cavalrymen as his escort, Rogatus had driven the cisium to Eboracum. He drew some stares as he guided the team through the arched fortress gate and stopped in front of the stable.

As one of his escorts lifted him down, the other got his crutches.

By then, the stablemaster had reached him.

"Welcome back, Prefect." He rested a hand on the back of one mule. "Not up to your usual standard for mounts, but it's good to see you however you make it here. Sorry about you losing that silver dun."

"I didn't. He stood guard over me after I looked dead. I still have my head because of him."

The stablemaster grinned. "I knew you'd like a Lucanus horse. Looks like he liked you, too."

Rogatus tipped his head toward the principia. "I'll be meeting with the legate, and then I'll be back. I'll need the cisium for a couple of errands since I can't walk far today."

"I'll have your team fed and watered when you return."

His escorts stood by their horses, awaiting orders.

"I'll need two of you on foot to help me when I come back. You can choose which two. We'll be spending the night here and leaving tomorrow morning."

Four fists hit chests, and Rogatus started his slow walk across the street to meet with the legate in his office. Narina had protected her clan from being blamed when the ambush first happened, but keeping the peace long term might require more.

As Rogatus crossed the principia courtyard, Dexter stuck his head out of his office, then strode over.

"I didn't expect to see you here so soon. Your lady friend made it sound like you were at death's door when you came to her house. You look pretty good now."

"A week of three meals a day with the taberna cook can do wonders for a man's recovery. I've come to brief the legate on what I think happened and to find out what's going on here. But tonight, I'll be at Minconus's taberna. Can you make sure the other five tribunes come to dinner with you? I need seven citizens who know me to witness my will."

Dexter's head drew back. "A will? I suppose almost dying inspired that. What I have would go to Father if I die." He tapped Rogatus's unbandaged arm. "I'll tell the others, and we'll all be there."

"Thanks." Rogatus tipped his head toward the legate's door. "It's not easy standing, so I want to finish here quickly. I'll see you at dinner."

Dexter headed back to his office, and Rogatus continued his trek across the too-big courtyard toward the two steps that led to the legate's door.

Before he reached the optio at the reception desk, the man slipped into the office and returned. He opened the door and held it as Rogatus passed through.

"Rogatus." The legate stood and came from behind his desk to meet Rogatus half way. "I didn't expect to see you here for a while."

"The message I sent about the ambush didn't include everything I now think important for you to know."

The legate raised a finger to silence him, then dragged the guest chair over for Rogatus to sit.

As he lowered himself onto the chair, Rogatus blew out a breath. "Thank you."

With his arms crossed, the legate smiled down at him. "Continue your report."

"I've been thinking about who probably ambushed my turma. The raiders wanted military horses. They also stole the warhorses from the trainer of both Atilianus's horse and the silver dun that kept the raiders from taking my head. They don't seem to be from the local clans, but it's worth traveling some distance to get horses already trained for war. So, they could have come a long way. I think other cavalry units, both alas and equitatas, might be at risk of having a herd stolen and their men ambushed. It would be good if they were warned about what happened to the Tungrorum."

One corner of the legate's mouth lifted. "I heard that story from the trainer. An impressive woman. It's a good thing her father was a cohort centurion in Moesia so she's loyal to Rome." A full smile appeared. "And protective of you."

Rogatus returned the smile. "My first command was the same cohort he served as centurion."

"It's a small empire sometimes." The legate's smile faded. "There are more rumors of increasing unrest, but no reports of active uprisings yet. Perhaps one won't happen. The loss of an ala herd could just be thieves, but using it as bait to ambush a turma...that's military planning."

He rubbed his neck. "I have the legion on alert that we might need to go on campaign if something starts. Your ala would be part of that."

"My lead decurion has had the ala ready for action since the ambush. I can't ride yet, but he's capable of executing what needs to be done."

The legate's eyes almost matched his crooked smile. "Your most capable messenger said you were concerned about losing your command if I thought you were dead too long. She said you were very eager to return to duty."

He pointed at the crutches. "I didn't expect you to drive a cisium here while you're using those. Proof that she's right."

"I thought it important to come myself in case you had any questions."

"And I appreciate that." The legate rested his hand on his dagger. "The only province more likely to rebel than Britannia is Judaea, and there's nothing more likely to trigger a rebellion than the death of an emperor. But the Ninth and its auxiliaries are ready." He walked back to his desk chair. "You can spend the night in my guest quarters and return to the fort tomorrow. My chef will be serving something good for dinner."

"I thank you for the dinner offer, but I've made arrangements to dine with your tribunes at the Taburna Lucani. I need seven men to witness me signing my will so I can leave it here before we might go into battle. Minconus is a citizen, so that gives me seven."

The legate chuckled. "You're a man who looks ahead to avoid future trouble, Rogatus. That's why I'm leaving you in charge even while you can't ride."

"I'll try not to disappoint you, Legate."

"I expect you won't. Come back in a month, and we'll discuss how you're recovering. You're dismissed."

Rogatus managed to rise and balanced on his good leg as he saluted. Then he moved the crutches as quickly as he could to seem fitter than he was until he left the office.

When the door closed behind him, he slowed. He'd left the cisium with the stablemaster, and even that short distance seemed like a twenty-mile hike today. It was good he could drive it to the taberna. He'd never be able to walk there. He was already more tired than he could ever remember being. But making Narina's future secure if he lost his life for Rome...that was worth all the fatigue and pain of this day.

One of his escorts held the door for Rogatus, then followed him into Minconus's taberna.

Minconus turned at the tinkle of the bell and scurried over.

"Rogatus. Do you need help? Narina told me about your injuries. I'm glad to see you up and around so soon."

"I do need help, but not the kind you're thinking. Do you know of a lawyer who could come right away to the taberna? He would need to bring what's required to make a will."

Minconus's eyebrows lifted, then lowered immediately. "I do. He dines here often, as do several of his clients. I'll send one of my workers to fetch him."

Rogatus turned to his escort. "Take the cisium back to the stable. Two of you will return for me with it a half hour after sundown."

The soldier saluted and left.

Her brother pulled out a chair from a small corner table. "Sit and rest a while. Is there anything else I can do to help you?"

"I need to send something by horse courier to Italia. Can you, not one of your servants, take the letter to the courier and bring back the receipt?"

Surprise, then pleasure, then uncertainty played across Minconus's features. "I can do that right now."

Rogatus took the sealed tablet from his satchel and set it on the table. From his purse, he took more than he expected the courier to cost and set the coins beside it.

"Would you like a room to rest in while I do that?" Minconus swept the coins into his hand and picked up the letter.

Rogatus pointed at his knee. "I can't climb the stairs."

"I have a couch in my office. Would you like to rest there?"

Minconus was definitely her brother. Genuinely glad to see him and just as eager to help.

"Perhaps after I get the will drafted. And I'll be needing you and the other tribunes to witness it at dinner. Dexter said he'd make sure everyone comes."

"Of course. I'll send someone right now for the lawyer. Then I'll take your letter right away." Her brother disappeared into the passage that went to the kitchen.

Rogatus took off his helmet, set it on the table, and lay his head down on his arms.

It seemed he'd only closed his eyes for a moment when fingers pushed on his shoulder.

A man in a toga stood beside Minconus. "The lawyer you requested, Gaius Flavius Servus."

He tipped his head back to smile at her brother. "Thank you. That's all I'll need for now."

Minconus dipped his head and headed toward the kitchen. But as he looked over his shoulder at Rogatus, he almost walked into the doorframe.

When Rogatus pointed at the chair across from him, Servus sat. "I need you to make me a will. I drew something up last night. I think I have the wording right, but I want to make certain no one can challenge and invalidate this will."

The lawyer reached into a satchel and pulled out three wooden panels with fresh wax surfaces. "Show me what you have, and let's proceed."

Dinnertime, Day 32

"Rogatus?"

Two light taps on his shoulder started his awakening. Two more opened his eyes. Someone had draped a light sheet over him and partly tucked it in.

Minconus stood beside the couch in his office. "Dexter and Plantus are here, and he said the others are right behind them."

Rogatus swung his feet off the couch. He was still dog tired, but he could sleep later.

"Good. I want to take care of the signing as soon as everyone is here. Then we can eat."

He took the crutches Minconus handed him and made his way to the table where the tribunes always ate. All six had arrived, and Dexter rose to help him into the chair they'd saved for him.

As he pulled the set of three panels from his satchel, Minconus hovered beside him.

"Thank you all for coming. This won't take long, and then we can eat. I need you to read my will and witness it with your signets."

He set the two identical tablets beside each other. On each, he dropped some hot wax and pressed his signet into it. "Read both to be certain they match exactly."

As each one read, they mixed glances at him with nods. When it was Minconus's turn, his eyes widened, and he stared at Rogatus before the biggest smile split her brother's face.

When all had finished, he put one copy on the bottom, placed the blank panel on it, and put the second copy on the top so it could be read. Then he wrapped it with sealing cord and flipped it over. Each time he let three drops of hot wax fall on the cord, one of the men pressed his signet into the wax before it hardened. When all seven had completed their task, he put it back in the satchel.

"I'm sure some of you are wondering about my heir. Narina Lucana owns the taberna in Isurium with Minconus. But I don't want any of you to ever tell her what you just witnessed."

Plantus wrinkled his nose. "The plain woman who served us when we rode up to visit you. I know it's yours to decide, but why are you leaving everything to a taberna keeper you haven't even known a month instead of to your father and other people in your family? My father would be appalled if I did that."

Rogatus almost snorted. Give it to his father? If they only knew.

"My father has more than enough already to supply everything the family needs. I'd rather give it to a good friend who can use it than have it just become a small part of a much larger fortune."

Dexter tapped Rogatus arm. "Since she trained the warhorse that saved you and took you in to keep you alive, I think it's an appropriate way to thank her if you die in Britannia. A man can always change a will when he gets a family to support."

Dexter turned a frown on Plantus. "She may not look special, but she is amazing when you see her in action. I was there when she gave Rogatus's message to the legate. No one could have done it better. She certainly impressed him. He even wanted to buy one of her horses by the time she finished talking."

Several men laughed, and that broke the tension over his choice of heir.

Minconus signaled his serving girl, and she brought the cups and pitcher to serve the group.

As the conversation swirled around them, Minconus knelt beside him. "You can imagine how surprised and delighted I am by your choice. You couldn't have chosen a finer woman if you searched the entire empire."

Rogatus rubbed under his jaw. "I'm inclined to agree with you. But I want your word of honor that you won't tell her what I've done."

Minconus raised his right hand. "I swear I won't. But as her guardian, I'm responsible for her. Does this mean you're interested in her for your wife?"

Rogatus flexed his jaw. "That's between her and me."

If only he could say she wanted him, too.

Minconus raised both hands and rose. "Of course. And I won't say anything to her about what you've told me today."

He moved to the other side of the table. "A serving of the evening's stew for everyone?"

After the nods and yeses, Minconus headed toward the kitchen, humming as he went.

Rogatus leaned back in his chair and crossed his arms. The legate, the letter, the will. He'd accomplished all he intended today, and he was satisfied.

By the time his escort returned with the cisium, all but Dexter had finished dinner and left. But Dexter drove him back to the praetorium and helped him to the visitor quarters.

He opened the bedchamber door and held it as Rogatus entered. "Do you need help with anything else?"

"No." Rogatus was more than ready to collapse on the bed and sleep.

"Then I'll meet you for breakfast. I'll help you get the will filed with the legion records before you leave."

"Sounds good. Thank you."

As Dexter closed the door behind him, Rogatus sighed. If he'd been stationed with the Ninth, Dexter would probably have become the friend he never had.

He lay down on the softest bed ever and closed his eyes. It was time to pray, but only in a whisper.

"Thank you, God of Narina, for the legate being content to keep me a while longer. I know Narina and Veldicca are praying for me, even though I'm not with them. I hope you listen to their prayers for my knee. Thank you for listening to mine about keeping the headaches away. Keep them all safe." His mouth twitched. "Even Sulio."

It had been a good day, and thoughts of Narina made him smile as he drifted off to sleep.

Chapter 48

A Good Enough Dinner

Narina's farm, Day 33

With a crock of dried apples in her arms, Narina started for the storage shed. They would keep for next summer's meals. By the end of the week, they'd start putting uncut apples into the crop cellar for their winter and spring fruit. With the cut-and-dry work finished then, she and Veldicca could take a day off for the visit she was longing for.

She paused by Rogatus's doorway. Her gaze settled on the bed he'd used, and it stayed there. Was he all right as he tried to do his usual job with a body only partly healed? Was he healing or getting worse because he pushed himself to do too much?

Veldicca came back from the shed and stopped beside her. "Lucania is missing him, too."

Narina almost rolled her eyes. "It's not the same. She looks on him as a friend. My heart has moved far past there. I didn't want that, but it happened almost before I knew it was happening. And there are so many things I keep wondering about. Is he getting around easily enough? Is his knee still healing better than he's afraid it might? Is he still thinking about Iesu dying to save us? Is he thinking about God at all?"

Veldicca wrapped her arm around Narina's waist. "You're fretting about too many 'is he' questions. I know it's hard to do, but try not to worry that way. We're all praying for him. God hears us, but even more, He knows what Rogatus needs right now."

She released Narina and pushed a loose strand of hair behind her ear. "Our young man said he wanted us to come in a week. We'll get some of the answers you want then, and that's only five days."

"But that's five days too many." Narina shook her head.

Veldicca's chuckle drew Narina's gaze. "Remember, patience is one of the gifts of the Spirit."

"I know, and I am patient...about things that aren't this important to me."

Narina shifted the jar. It was getting heavy.

"The morning he left, he told me he was adding God and Iesu to the gods he'd pray to. He'd seen God had real power, and he'd be a fool not to. He also said he wanted to keep learning more from me."

She placed three fingers on her lips. What came next was the problem.

"But I sensed there was something he wasn't telling me. So, I asked him if he really wanted to keep learning about God, or did he just say it so I'd come?"

Veldicca's brow furrowed. "What did he say?"

"He said he did. We've convinced him God's power is real. He said he wants to know more about Him and what He does. But he's stopped at belief that God's real. Even the demons know that. He's going to pray to God, but he doesn't love Him now. He said he's not ready to be devoted to God like we are."

Veldicca bit her lip. "It sounds to me like he's a man who has started hearing God's call. It shouldn't be long now."

The small flame of hope Narina kept burning for him grew larger. If God was calling, surely Rogatus would hear. But would it be soon enough?

"He said something else. A man and a woman don't have to agree on everything to belong together. I'm afraid he has no intention of following Iesu, but he's going to ask me to marry him, expecting a yes."

A slow nod was Veldicca's first answer. "That might be his plan at the moment, but if he's praying to God, I think we'll see him respond to God's love by starting to love Him back. And I think that will grow over time." She rubbed her cheek. "One of the Romans in our fellowship in Isca Silurum said once a man of honor recognized what was true, he had to act on it. I have no doubt that young man is a man of honor, so I think it's only a matter of time."

The certainty in Veldicca's eyes—Narina wished she shared it. "I'll try to be patient."

"Good." Veldicca took the heavy jar from her. "We'll know when we go there in five days. I think I'll make his absolute favorite for dinner. But after a week of garrison food, anything I make will seem like a feast."

The Isurium fort, Day 34

It took two men to get Rogatus up to the wall-walk, but he needed something to do other than stare at the walls of his office. Watching a turma drill had always satisfied his love of order and precision. In Moesia, he sometimes joined his men in riding the intricate patterns and practicing the charges that mimicked real battle.

He hadn't yet done that here. Would he ever be able to?

He set the crutches against the wall and balanced on his good leg while he leaned against the cool stone.

One of the turmas he'd sent out on patrol was coming down Narina's street toward him. With their banner fluttering and the decurion's crest moving in their self-made breeze, the column of twos passed through the gate and out of his view.

He decided each day where patrols would go and what they would do there. In fact, he was doing everything he usually did except riding himself. Germanus and Adolphus both said it was working well. But if word came from the legate that they would be deploying with the legion to stop a problem in another tribe's land, where did that leave him?

The Isurium fort, Day 37

Rogatus was talking with Germanus when Atto was escorted into his office.

The youth stood at attention and even struck his chest, prompting a soft snort from the decurion.

"Narina sent me to ask if you still wanted her and Veldicca to come tomorrow."

"I do. Please tell her so, and give my regards to everyone in the household. Tell Veldicca I'm looking forward to her cooking again."

Atto's whole body relaxed. "You're in for a treat. She said she's planned one of your favorites, and Narina will bake something, too." With a quick smile and quicker nod, Atto spun on his heal and left.

When Rogatus turned his attention back to their discussion, Germanus was trying to keep the grin off his face.

"The taberna cook is excellent. I would think it worth going that distance to eat some of her food, even on crutches."

Rogatus's mouth twitched. "It is. You can take me up in the cisium and come back later to get me. But if you bring a bowl when you drop me off, I'll send some of my share back with you."

Germanus chuckled. "A fitting reward. I'll bring the bowl."

As Rogatus watched his lead decurion leave the office, Rogatus released the smile. The two centurions in Moesia had taught him how to command. He owed most of his success to them. But Germanus was everything a commander could want and more.

If he were Narina, he'd be thanking her god every day for giving him that Tungrian as his second in command.

He wasn't Narina, but maybe he'd do it anyway.

Narina's taberna, Day 38

When someone jiggled the latch, Narina's heart beat faster.

The front door swung open, and Germanus stepped in. Alone.

Her smile faded. Rogatus wasn't going to make it.

Then the clump clump of his crutches reached her, and the man she'd been waiting a week to see stepped across the threshold.

"I'll be back before sundown, Prefect." His decurion fisted his chest, then left, closing the door behind him.

She pulled out Rogatus's chair before walking to his side. "Welcome to the Taberna Lucani. It's so good to have you with us again, Prefect."

"I've missed our conversations." He grinned at her, and it was like the sun breaking through the clouds on an overcast day. "Don't you remember? It's Rogatus when no one else is listening." He lowered his voice. "And no one else is."

"I wouldn't say that."

Her shoulders slumped as Sulio came through the storeroom door. As much as she loved her cousin, why did he have to show up today?

Sulio scooped up a stool. "I stopped by to help Atto for a while. When I asked how Rogatus was doing, he said you looked much better when he dropped off Narina's invitation yesterday. I've missed our conversations, too, so I thought I'd join the party."

He tipped his head toward the storeroom. "I gave Veldicca a hare for tomorrow's stew. But I guess you'll miss that since she'll be making it for everyone at the farm."

It was all she could do not to tell him to go away. But her cousin only wanted to protect her reputation, and with so many grumbling about the Romans right now, having him there might be a good thing.

But she'd hoped Rogatus would ask about God, and no soldier would risk speaking dangerous thoughts in the presence of an enemy.

She stayed beside Rogatus as he made his way to their table. She moved the chair so he could sit without his injured leg getting in the way.

"I'll tell Veldicca we're all here. Then I'll be right back."

She caught Rogatus's gaze and smiled an apology that he read and received. But the smile he gave back was as stiff as any she'd seen. Above those frozen lips, his eyes smoldered.

Then he took a deep breath, and his face turned statue-like.

And Sulio smiled.

She stopped just past the storeroom and closed her eyes. *God, why didn't this turn out like I'd planned?*

She longed for their next talk about how God loved him and wanted him as His child. No chance of that this week with Sulio hovering. But maybe next week when they dined together again. God showed Himself to people who were seeking when they were most able to see Him. Maybe that wasn't quite yet.

It was so hard to wait, but she wouldn't pray for patience. That could mean having to wait until she learned to be patient. But she would pray for peace during the waiting because God's timing was always best.

◆

Rogatus had been looking forward to this for a week, and when Germanus helped him inside, the only person with whom he could let down his guard came toward him, as eager to see him as he was to see her.

Then Sulio arrived, grinning like he'd just won a tabula match.

He couldn't fault Atto for revealing they were dining. When Sulio asked how he was doing, the youth couldn't know that answer shouldn't include why he knew.

But it was deep conversation with Narina that he longed for, not verbal sparring with her too-clever cousin who took delight in baiting him.

He took several deep breaths, and the anger drained away. There was nothing to do now but enjoy the scrumptious meal Veldicca had made for him and let her smiles and glances be enough to tide him over until next week. And before she came again, he'd warn Atto not to tell Sulio anything.

When Germanus returned to get him, Rogatus was ready. Sulio still sat at the table with them, and he mostly kept Narina talking with him. The best part of the dinner had been eating in silence, watching her eyes as she returned his gaze.

"Germanus." Sulio turned on his stool to raise a hand in greeting. "I picked a good day to drop in. It's good to see you both. I've missed the good conversation to be had with the soldiers of the ala."

Narina hit her cousin's upper arm with the back of her fingers. "Enough, Sulio."

He smiled, then shrugged, then sat quiet.

Rogatus got up on his good leg. There was no point in staying longer. With one hand balancing him against the table, he held out the other.

Narina rose when Germanus handed Rogatus his crutches.

"It's been lovely being together again. I hope we can do this again soon." Her eyes said much more than her words.

"We will. Have Atto come by the next time he goes to Isurium, and we'll arrange it."

If he said one week aloud, Sulio would join them for certain. If he swore the boy to silence when he set the date, maybe her cousin wouldn't find out and spoil it.

He tipped his head toward the door, and Germanus escorted him out.

After the decurion lifted him into the cisium, he climbed aboard and snapped the reins.

"Prefect." He cleared his throat. "Would you like me to take that Brigantian away for a while the next time she comes to town?"

Rogatus almost said yes, but...

"No. I told her she could have Sulio join us if she thought that was needed to protect her reputation. I don't think she invited him, but that man has no qualms about inviting himself where she and I are concerned. It was a good enough dinner despite him being there."

A good enough dinner, but he wanted more. He still had so many questions about her god, and he couldn't ask them where the cousin who wanted him gone would overhear.

He was flirting with fire to even think about becoming a Christian. Quite literally. Nero used Christians as human torches in his garden after he declared they were the arsonists who started the Great Fire.

He didn't intend to light any emperor's garden or to feed his lions, either.

Chapter 49

GREAT-UNCLE PUBLIUS

A villa near Clusium, Italia, afternoon of Day 41

Publius Crescens had just handed his horse over to his stablemaster when a horse courier rode in. The man dismounted, took two wax tablets from his saddlebag, and strode toward them.

"I am looking for Publius Visulanius Crescens."

"And you have found him."

The courier held out the sealed tablet and opened the other. "Please sign here to show it has been delivered to you."

Publius took the offered stylus and traced his name into the wax where the courier pointed.

The man mounted his horse and rode back the way he came.

When Publius opened the leaf-shaped brass seal box, his head drew back. The signet he had given his great-nephew had been pressed into the wax that trapped the ends of the cords that kept the tablet closed. He pulled them free of the wax and opened the letter.

After a quick scan, he released the breath he'd been half holding. A horse courier almost never brought good news, and Rogatus had never used a courier service before. His frugal protege never spent that kind of money to share his news.

He closed the tablet with a snap and headed into the house to look for his wife.

He found her at her loom in the peristyle. He walked up behind her and wrapped his arm around her waist before kissing her cheek.

"You'll never guess what a courier just brought."

She turned and stroked his cheek. "What did he bring?"

"A letter from Rogatus."

Worry clouded her eyes. "Is he all right?"

314

He tipped his head toward a bench. "Let's sit, and I'll read it to you. I'll let you be the judge."

She settled in beside him, and he opened the tablet. After clearing his throat, he began to read.

> "Proculus Trebonius Rogatus to Publius Visulanius Crescens, my esteemed great-uncle, greetings. If you are well, then I am glad. I write to ask you to help me. I cannot figure this out on my own.
>
> After my studies with a rhetor, I was never allowed to study with a jurist like my brothers did. So, I do not know enough about Roman law to figure this out. I hope you can tell me how to get free from my father so he cannot hurt others just to strike at me. I need to get him to disown and emancipate me.
>
> I have saved most of my salary for the last five and a half years. I am 25,000 denarii short of the 100,000 that will let me stay equestrian if Father disinherits me, as my brothers claim he had been planning to do for years. I thought that would take eighteen more months, but I might no longer be able to reach that goal.
>
> I was almost killed in an ambush that killed the rest of the turma I was leading. I am recovering, but I took an arrow in my right knee. If it does not heal quickly and well enough, I expect I will lose my command and be put out of the army before I earn the rest. So, if I have to pay Father a bribe to get him to release me from his patria potestes, I can use some of what I have saved. Not all because I want to buy farmland in Britannia. The property I am looking at will cost a fair amount, plus I need to buy some quality horses and have enough to run it for three years until I have horses to sell.
>
> There is a woman who is the Roman citizen daughter of a Briton who earned his citizenship as a cohort cavalry centurion before returning to Brittania. Narina and her family do not worship the Roman gods. It was the warhorse she trained that kept the raiders from killing me and taking my head. Her cousin brought me to her house when he found me near death. Every time they prayed to their god, asking him to heal my injuries, I hurt less. Our ala physician said he had never seen arrow wounds heal that fast.

The headaches I have had since my youth...no matter how many offerings I made to Asclepius, they always came back. But when they prayed for my pain from the arrows, the headaches went away. They have not come back. I now ask that god to ease the pain and keep healing me, and even though the knee is still bad, that seems to help. So, she has convinced me the Roman gods have no real power to help a man like me, and hers does. But I am not ready to give up everything I have worked for when I might be wrong.

She has become a good friend, and I know she would be a fine wife. I intend to ask her to marry me and make a life together if I can get free of my father's control. If I cannot, then Father could take our children. From what he has done in the past, I believe he would do that to hurt me. I cannot ask any woman to risk that horrible fate.

I hope you can tell me what to do that would make Father willing to give up control over me. I cannot thank you and Priscilla enough for the help and encouragement you have given me these last six years. I hope you can help me with this most important thing of all.

Please give my warmest greetings to Priscilla. I hope all will continue to be well with you both. May the most powerful god guard your safety."

Publius closed the tablet. "I'll be leaving for Rome tomorrow morning. We have to help him, and I think I know how."

He handed her the tablet, and she clutched it to her chest. "Yes, we do. He's been through so much. I'll be asking God to free him from his father for good. It seems like yesterday he stood before us, asking for the help any good father should have given but not expecting anyone would." She opened the tablet. "When he told us all that had been done to him, I wanted to take him in my arms and hug him like I would our own sons. You told him you'd see what you could do, and I could tell he wasn't sure you meant it. He was afraid to expect anything would change. I'm so glad he came to us that day."

She scanned the tablet and pointed to a spot halfway down. "Narina. That's a pretty name. I think that young woman follows Iesus. Only God can answer prayers like Rogatus describes. And the way he signed the letter, I think he's almost ready to join her. I'll also be asking God to open our young man's eyes to see the truth and his heart to believe and become one of us."

He kissed her cheek. "Ask our fellowship to be praying as well."

He held out his hand for the tablet, but she held it close again.

"I want to put it on my dressing table. I'll pray for him, for them, each time I see it."

He rose and kissed her forehead. "I'll tell Primus to get things ready for us to leave for Rome early tomorrow. I'll take Victor to bodyguard as well. If we ride, we could be back in a little over a week."

"If anyone can free our boy, you can. We'll all be praying for your success."

Baths of Trajan, Rome, afternoon of Day 44

When Marcus Rogatus stood at the end of the *natatio*, he swept the water from his face and ran his hands across his still-full head of hair. He was no longer a young man, but he'd just outswum both his sons in their thirties. He could beat many of the men still in their twenties. Despite a few wrinkles on his face, he still drew the eyes of women his daughter's age.

He was toweling his hair when a voice came from behind him.

"Marcus Trebonius Rogatus?"

He turned to find an older man with a fringe of gray hair and a pleasant countenance. His eyes started to narrow, but he stopped them. He'd seen this man somewhere...

"I am."

"I was planning to come to your salutation tomorrow, but it's even better that I've run into you here."

Who was this man? Marcus racked his brain, but found no answer.

The old man chuckled. "I see you don't recognize me, but perhaps that's not surprising. You look much like you did fifteen years ago, but time has been crueler to me."

The man placed his hand on his chest. "Publius Visulanius Crescens."

"It's a pleasure to see you again."

It wasn't. He had no interest in talking with the uncle of his unfaithful wife. But the man was both wealthy and influential among the senators, so it might be worth meeting with him.

Two important senators that Marcus knew slightly came over. One tapped the old man's arm. "Crescens. It's good to see you here. It's been a long time since we've seen you in Rome. I hope you're in good health."

Crescens's smile declared them long-time friends. "I am. I rode down from Clusium to take care of some personal business, and I'll be riding home in a few days. I prefer a horse's back to a carriage bench, and it's still an easy ride for me."

He turned his attention to Marcus. "I heard your son Proculus was crippled when some cavalry he was leading were ambushed. I offer you my condolences on your youngest son suffering such a tragedy."

Marcus kept his surprise from showing. No one had told him of that yet. He hadn't heard from Proculus since he transferred to Britannia several years ago.

Three more senators were walking past as Crescens spoke his condolences, and they stopped to listen.

Marcus summoned a deep sigh. "We hope our sons will be safe serving Rome, but that's not always so. The whole family is grieved by what's happened to him."

He looked at his sons, and they had donned sad expressions already, even though they never liked their supposed brother any more than he did.

Crescens mouth tightened, and he nodded slowly. "I bear some responsibility. I never dreamed when I sponsored the young man into the tres militiae that this would happen."

He spoke his next words as if to the seven senators who were now listening to their conversation. "My brother is Proculus's mother's father, and he would like to provide the boy a small allowance to hire someone to care for him, one that's enough to live on, but since Proculus is still part of your family, he doesn't think he can."

Crescens rubbed his jaw. "But it's well known that you rightly questioned whether he was yours from the start, even though your father tried to hide what his mother had done by keeping and naming the baby."

The old man rubbed his palm with his thumb. "No one should expect you to deal with his needs since he's not really your son. But it would be good, even noble, of you to emancipate him so her father can take on the care of someone who sacrificed so much for Rome. The expense is rightfully his since there's no question that he's the grandfather, and he asked me to see if you were willing to let him assume it."

The listening crowd has grown to at least a dozen, and Marcus saw the approving nods and smiles of the powerful men who had gathered around to listen.

"I'm willing to do my part by emancipating Proculus. When he becomes sui iuris, there will be no bar to your brother helping him."

A murmur of approval passed through the crowd.

Emancipation would release Proculus from his direct control as paterfamilias, but he'd only be changed from son to a client freedman. As Proculus's patron, he could still make demands and set conditions to make life hard for him. And he wouldn't have to spend as much for the right to do it.

His sons had slipped back behind the senators, where a small crowd had gathered. Marcus saw one whisper to the other. Then they exchanged smirks.

He looked away quickly, lest any of the gathered senators glance back to see what had dimmed his smile. He'd taught his sons better than to discuss family business in public, but at least no one of importance was there to hear them.

Crescens clapped his hands once. "Excellent. I'm only in town for a couple more days, but I can bring the five citizen witnesses and a *libripens* with his bronze scale to your town house right after salutation tomorrow."

He scanned the assembled senators. "Who would like to be our witnesses?"

Seven men stepped forward.

"My thanks to all of you." Crecens beamed at Marcus. "I have one favor to ask. If my brother was in town and available to take part in the ceremony, he would want to be the third buyer who ends your role as Proculus's paterfamilias and lets him take care of his grandson. Then he would sell him back to you for the final manumission. But since he can't do that, I would like to serve as his stand-in."

Several expressions of what a fine idea that was passed among the senators.

"I agree." Marcus offered a smile all around. "It's a fitting way to make Proculus part of the familia that he should have been in all along. There's a papyrus vendor among the shops outside. I'll return with a map for each of you so you can find my town house tomorrow."

Before Marcus walked away, he scanned the approving faces of the senators who would take part in the ceremony.

He'd spent years hating Rogatus's mother for betraying him with some other man, and he'd taken great pleasure in letting her know how he made the son of that other man suffer. When she died, it was natural to keep disliking the boy that looked like another man's child. His own father's death made it easy to ship off the youth whose mere presence offended him to the villa he never visited.

But now important men were praising him for enabling that son of a woman no better than a prostitute to get an allowance from her family after almost dying in the service of Rome. He wouldn't have to waste any money supporting him. That was pleasant to contemplate. It was enough that Proculus was now crippled, so her son would keep suffering without him doing anything to cause it. Too bad she wasn't alive to know about it.

The Rogatus town house, Day 45

Marcus sat at his office desk with the sliding wooden screens that separated the *tablinum* from the *peristyle* garden left open to make the room feel larger. Two good friends who would make the first and second purchase in the three-purchase process lounged in the garden, waiting to be called to play their part in the ritual.

Since the early Republic, a father had been able to sell his son into slavery. But the Twelve Tables that were the foundation of Roman law only allowed a father do to it twice and still remain paterfamilias over a son. With the third sale, his power as a father was forever ended, and that son would be sui iuris until the son died.

That was still the procedure for emancipating a son under the emperors. But each sale and return to his father was acted out until after the third sale. The third buyer sold the son back to his father, who then set him free.

As soon as Crescens and his witnesses showed up, Marcus would act his part in the farce and turn Rogatus from son to slave to freedman, locked forever in the patron-client relationship that let Marcus keep telling Proculus what to do.

He smiled at that thought. When Proculus first heard he'd been emancipated, he might think he was free of his father's control. Cripple or not, Marcus would soon show him otherwise.

His house steward opened the door to the atrium and stepped inside. "Crescens and the senators are here, Master."

"Show them in."

His friends came from the garden and joined him by the desk.

Crescens entered first, followed by one senator holding a bronze scale. The other six volunteers filed in behind them.

"Welcome." Marcus came from behind the desk to join them. "I'm sure you all have other places to go, so let's proceed."

The first of his friends came forward, holding an as, the bronze coin worth one-sixteenth denarius, in his fingers.

He held up the coin and spoke in a solemn voice. "I declare that the man Proculus belongs to me by my right as a Roman citizen, and let him be purchased by me with this piece of bronze and bronze scales."

He then struck the scale with the coin and handed the coin to Marcus, completing the first sale. Then his friend spoke again. "I now free my bondsman Proculus, and he is again under your patria potestes.

Marcus nodded once to acknowledge completion of the first step.

His second friend came forward, and they repeated the process.

Then Crescens stepped forward and lifted the third coin for all to see. "I declare that the man Proculus belongs to me by my right as a Roman citizen, and let him be purchased by me with this piece of bronze and bronze scales."

He struck the scale and handed the as to Marcus.

It was done. Proculus was sui iuris and could never be under Marcus's authority as paterfamilias again. All that remained was to buy him back and free him to make him a client instead of a son.

But when he offered the coin to Crescens, the old man raised his hands and stepped back.

"No. Proculus is not for sale. Not to you. Not to anyone. My valet overheard your sons saying you intend to make his life as your client as miserable as you can. You've done that since he was born. But I own him now, and your power over him ended when you made the third sale to me. So, I will manumit him myself. He will be my client, not yours, and from this point on, he'll be treated as he deserves."

Silence filled the room, then one man began clapping. Another joined in, and another, until only Rogatus and his two friends stood motionless.

Crescens summoned his manservant, took two papyri from the satchel, and placed them side by side on the desk.

"Gather round. I'd like each of you who witnessed this emancipation to sign both of these declaring that Proculus Trebonius Rogatus is now emancipated from Marcus Trebonius Rogatus. He is now sui iuris and the bondservant of Publius Visulanius Crescens. He belongs to no other. I will be manumitting him tomorrow to make him henceforth my freedman and client."

The broadest smile split Crescens face, and he seemed suddenly twenty years younger.

"I thank you all from the bottom of my heart for helping me free a most deserving young man from a scoundrel who has never been worthy of being his father."

Marcus clenched his hands. He longed to smash Crescens's jaw with his fist, but with so many to witness the assault, he'd be an utter fool to strike.

"Get out of my house when they finish." Marcus hissed at the old man who'd outwitted him. "And never come back."

Then he stormed from the room, cursing Publius Crescens by every god he knew.

Chapter 50

CHANGE OF ASSIGNMENT

The Isurium fort, morning of Day 45

Rogatus closed the wax tablet and leaned back in his desk chair. Since his horses were stolen and a turma of his men killed, the soldiers on herding duty had been on high alert. But all had been peaceful, as if nothing had happened. Had the raiders settled for a hundred horses or were they coming back for more?

He rubbed his forehead, but not because it hurt. The headaches that used to bother him often seemed a thing of the past. Thanks to Narina's prayers... and maybe his, too.

A tap on the open office door drew his attention. The ala physician stood there, ready to check his progress. He summoned Medicus with a curl of his fingers and turned in the chair.

"It's not hurting to use the crutches now, but I'll be glad when I can use the leg."

He no longer had a bandage on his arm or thigh, so Medicus took a quick look at each, then nodded.

"Your arm and thigh wounds look completely healed. But don't be lifting anything heavy or swinging a sword for another month. You need to allow time for the full healing of the muscles.

"But your knee..." Medicus sucked air through his teeth. "It won't bend like I sometimes see after three weeks. Still, it's not worse than the worst that I've seen that ultimately healed."

Rogatus's jaw clenched. Not what he wanted to hear. "It's another ten days before I expect to meet with the legate again. I can take the cisium, but I was hoping to ride."

Medicus snorted. "Don't ride. You need to be patient and not force it to do too much too soon. You could injure it further, and it might never recover from that. It might get back to almost what it was in three to six months." He shrugged, and his optimistic mask slipped. "But it might not."

"I'll follow your advice, even though I don't like it." Rogatus squared his shoulders. "I'll keep using the cisium until you tell me I can ride."

"I'm glad to hear it. It sets a good example for your men. Too often they want to start doing things before they're ready as well. Let me know if anything changes."

Rogatus answered with a nod before opening the next tablet. The physician saluted and left.

He closed his eyes and squeezed the back of his neck. At least three months to get back to normal. Even three weeks was too long already. If the legion got the order to go on campaign, his ala would go with it. A legion on the march was several miles long, and the auxiliary cavalry provided the vanguard and many scouts at the front of the column. They protected the flanks from attack while the men were marching. They guarded the baggage train at the rear of the column as well.

If that order came, his men would go without him. He'd be left behind, and there was nothing he could do to prevent it.

Narina's taberna, late afternoon of Day 45

It was only a week since he'd last dined with Narina, but to Rogatus, it seemed much longer. He drove up from the fort alone. Atto would tend the mules and harness them to the cisium when he was ready to leave. And this time, the youth hadn't said anything to Sulio about their dinner. It should be a good evening.

But since his talk with Medicus, worry gnawed at him. If his knee didn't heal enough and even if it did but took too long, it meant the end of his military career.

The bell tinkled when he opened the door, and he hadn't even settled into his chair when she came through the storeroom.

"You're a little early. Veldicca's not quite ready to serve, but we can chat while she finishes."

She sat across from him and, with one elbow on the table, rested her chin in her palm. "How is my favorite prefect doing?"

He almost said fine, but that wasn't true. She would know he was lying, so it was pointless to hide his concerns.

"Medicus says my thigh and arm healed as rapidly as he's ever seen. The knee...when he first looked at it, it was doing better than normal. But not now. He said it's not doing the worst he's seen, but it's far from the best. Today he said at least three to six months...and maybe not ever."

He rubbed his mouth with the back of his hand. "I know you've been praying for me since the day it happened, and it seemed to be doing so well. But that stopped when I came back to the fort. Why isn't your god healing my knee, too?"

Narina reached across the table to touch his hand. "What have you done at the fort that you didn't do at my house?"

Not a question he wanted to answer, so he looked away.

"Are you leading the camp worship?"

He shook his head. "I'm present, but I've passed that off to Germanus. I told him I'm not steady enough on my feet with the crutches to do the sacrifices."

She withdrew her hand. "Do you remember what God told His people about worshipping other gods?"

"Don't do it. Although I am there, I'm not really worshiping them. But you're right that I can feel it putting a barrier between me and your god."

"He's not just my God. He's the only God that's real."

"Maybe. He's the only one I know with real power. But I can tell the knee isn't healing as fast as I think it was when you and Veldicca prayed every time she treated it. Maybe that does have something to do with it. But the physician tells me what it's doing is fairly normal and to be patient. It might get back to almost what it was in three to six months."

"But it might not. What then?" Her tone carried no accusation, but it didn't need to. He knew without her speaking it that her god didn't approve of divided loyalties.

"I don't know. I want to finish my three commands and earn enough to be equestrian, no matter what Father does. I only need seventeen more months, and I'll have it."

She leaned toward him again. "Maybe not getting what you think would be good now opens the way to a better future. You're already a wealthy man. Does it really matter so much that you save enough to be equestrian on your own?"

"It's been my goal since I was eighteen. I can't just give it up"—he snapped his fingers—"like that."

"Just because we've had a goal for a long time, that doesn't mean it's the right one. Is there a reason you shouldn't be in the military anymore? Would you be required to do things your conscience no longer allows? It's already making you take part in the worship of the Roman gods when you know God said we should have no other gods and only worship Him."

He turned his gaze from her face to his bandaged knee. If it weren't for the crutches it forced him to use, he'd be leading the rites, not just watching them.

"Will it make you kill a village of innocent women and children and even some men because a few from that place fought against Rome? That haunted Father, and he wasn't even a Christian."

He glanced at her face, then looked away. He didn't want to look into her eyes when he might see condemnation there.

"Have you considered that your bad knee is God's gift that will let you leave without anyone thinking less of you for it and without risking death for following Iesu?"

"I don't follow him."

Yet. But he felt her god call to him whenever she was with him, and even sometimes when she wasn't. And in the dark of his bedchamber when he spoke to her god, sometimes there was that feeling he wasn't alone.

As he massaged his palm, she reached across to touch his fingertips. "Not right now, but only God knows what the future holds."

Veldicca stepped into the room with a smile and a tray of stew and bread.

Narina sat back. "We have your favorites tonight, her best stew and my rolls." She inhaled deeply, then closed her eyes. "We thank You, God for this wonderful food and the pleasure of sharing it with our dear friend. Please keep healing him and give him Your peace. In Iesu's name, we pray."

They would eat in silence, and he was glad of it. He'd heard all he wanted about God and what he should be doing for the moment.

But when Narina and Veldicca spoke the amen, he whispered it, too.

The Isurium fort, evening of Day 45

When Rogatus drove the cisium through the gate, Germanus met him, looking grimmer than usual. He reined in, and his decurion climbed aboard for the short ride to the stable.

"There's a courier from the legate here. I told him you'd be back shortly, and I was in command of the fort until you returned. It's too late for him to return tonight without a fresh horse, and I didn't want to give him one of ours. So, I told him to eat dinner and ask Adolphus where to sleep tonight."

Rogatus's stomach clenched. "I'll go to my office. You can bring him to me there. Do you know what it's about?"

"I asked, but he wouldn't say." Germanus reined in the mule team by the main door to their headquarters. "I'll take the cisium to the stablemaster. That should give you time to get settled before I bring him to you."

Germanus jumped out and came around to help him down. An exchange of nods was all that was needed as their "thank you" and "you're welcome." As Germanus drove the cisium away, Rogatus climbed the three steps and went inside.

He'd barely settled into his desk chair when Germanus appeared with the courier. After escorting the rider to the desk, Germanus saluted and left the room.

"Decurion Germanus tells me you have a message from our legate."

"Yes, Prefect. He said you were to report to him tomorrow. There has been a change of plans, and he wants to tell you in person."

Report tomorrow? Rogatus's stomach clenched, but he let no emotion show.

"Is that all?"

"Yes, Prefect."

"You can spend the night and rest your horse. You'll be part of my escort tomorrow morning. We will be leaving early. Find Decurion Germanus and ask him to have four men ready as escort at dawn."

"Yes, Prefect." The courier fisted a salute and left.

Why was he being summoned so soon? The legate had said a month, and it wasn't even three weeks yet. Was he reconsidering whether a man who couldn't ride could command an ala?

With a weariness far beyond his years, he placed the crutches under his arms and made his way to the praetorium. His orderly helped him out of his armor, and he went to bed. Dawn would come early, and after the news of today, sleep might be slow coming.

He lay on his back, staring at the ceiling. Then he began his whispered prayer.

"God of Narina, please give me more time. At least until after I hear from Great-uncle Publius so I know what my next step should be to finally get free from Father. Narina says you can bring good out of bad for those who love you. I'm not one of those yet, and I don't know if I will be. But maybe you could do it for me this time anyway?"

He drew a deep breath. "Like she would, I ask this in Iesu's name."

Silence filled his room. He hadn't really expected otherwise. But there was something, almost as if someone was watching him. Many times, he'd felt unfriendly eyes in the Moesian woods when he led troops hunting raiders.

But this time, it felt more like a friend.

Eboracum, midmorning of Day 46

Shortly after dawn, Rogatus drove his cisium out the fort gate and headed south. Four hours later, he drove it across the bridge that led to the fortress gatehouse. He dismounted by the principia steps and told the escorts to take it and wait for him at the stable. They would all return to Isurium as soon as the legate finished with him.

What he didn't tell them was he might not be prefect when they returned.

As he crossed the courtyard, the legate's optio rose and entered the office. He wasn't smiling when Rogatus reached him. He only saluted and opened the door.

This time, the legate didn't meet him halfway, so Rogatus stopped four feet from the desk, shifted the right crutch to his left hand, and struck his chest.

"Legate, I've come as ordered."

The serious set of the legate's mouth relaxed into a subdued smile. "You have, and this time you're looking much better. That's good, because I must change your assignment."

Rogatus squared his shoulders and braced for the worst.

"The legion is leaving Eboracum in five days because there are serious problems near Coria and Luguvallium. I want it in place before a few attacks on Roman towns turn into full rebellion that tries to destroy the Roman cities. Your ala will be moving north with it. But I don't want an inexperienced man leading the Tungrorum. So, I'm assigning thirteen of your fifteen remaining turmas to one of my senior prefects. Petronius Honoratus is commanding the Ala Gallorum. He has five hundred men at the moment, and I'm enlarging the Gallorum to nine hundred during this action. He's very capable of leading a double-sized ala."

Rogatus froze his face. Thirteen of his fifteen given to another man. What was left for him?

The legate's mouth twitched. "It's not what you're thinking, Rogatus. I don't want to leave here to fight one rebellion only to return to put down another one that starts while we're gone. I want to keep anything that's simmering locally from boiling over. I think you are the man to do that, even if you can't ride. After the way you handled the matter of the stolen cattle, I expect you won't order your men to do something that would turn a pacified area into a rebellious one."

He clasped his hands and rested them on the desktop. "You're as much diplomat as soldier. So, I'm leaving you here to keep an eye on the area to make sure that doesn't happen. You'll remain prefect over the two turmas of the Tungrorum that will remain in the Isurium fort. I want you to keep the Isurium and adjacent clans calm."

Rogatus kept his shoulders squared, but all the tension drained out of him. "I accept that assignment with pleasure. The chieftain of the Isurians will do his best to keep rebellion from breaking out in his clan. He understands what can happen when Rome puts down a rebellion. He's a leader among the local chieftains as well. I think I can get him to help me keep the other clans out of any rebellion."

He let a subdued smile form. "You can tell Prefect Honoratus that he has an excellent second in Decurion Germanus. He can rely on him to make leading the extra four hundred as easy as possible. Germanus and I will decide which two turmas to leave behind, and the rest will be ready to join the column when it passes the fort in five days."

"Good." The legate fingered his lip. "I can't predict how long we'll be gone, but I expect a few months. When the legion returns to the fortress will be soon enough to make any decision about you resuming command of the whole Tungrorum. If unrest becomes full rebellion, it should be long enough for us to know whether you've been crippled for good by that arrow. It is possible you'll be able to ride like a cavalryman again. Rome will still need you as commander if that's the case. She needs you now to keep the peace here. Any questions?"

"No, Legate."

"Then you're dismissed."

He struck his chest. It was impossible to make a parade turn on crutches, but that wouldn't matter to this legate. He'd not only been spared forced retirement. His new assignment as peacekeeper was truly important.

As he worked the crutches to go down the steps into the courtyard, he barely stopped the grin. He'd even keep earning his 1500 denarii each month until the legate decided he didn't need him anymore.

He wouldn't risk even a whispered prayer here, but Narina said her god heard every thought.

Thank you, God of Narina. You worked this out for good, even though I'm not one of yours.

Not yet, but maybe he should be.

As he made his way past the principia, he glanced at the building across the street from the stables. Some of the best physicians in the Roman army would be in that hospital. It would take no more than half an hour to get one to look at his knee.

Then he rolled his eyes at how stupid that might be. The legate might learn his knee didn't bend as much as the ala physician thought it should after three weeks. But Medicus did say it was not as bad as he'd seen before with men who finally healed. It could be as little as three months before they knew if he could ride like a cavalryman again. The ala physician had said to be patient, and he'd promised to take his advice.

Besides, being able to march twenty miles in five hours was much more demanding than riding a horse. If the legion physician used that standard instead of what a horseman would need, his career would be over.

But neither physician knew what prayer to the right god could do. Narina and her family would keep praying. If he was supposed to keep leading his ala, God would make sure he could.

He reached the stable, and his escorts came over.

"Let's go home."

One helped him into the cisium. He snapped the reins, and they headed back across the river.

He found himself almost grinning, and he toned it down. A soldier shouldn't look too happy when his unit was going off to war. As soon as he told them, Germanus and Adolphus would get the ala ready to join the legion without his help. They were both more experienced than he was, anyway.

His smile dimmed further. But one thing was certain. He would miss his lead decurion more than that man would ever know.

Chapter 51

Leaving

The Isurium fort, Day 50

Tomorrow the legion would head north, so final preparations were underway. The draco would go with the troops that might see battle. The wagons were packed and ready to join the baggage train at the rear of the legion as it passed. The Tenth and Sixteenth turmas would remain behind, with the decurion of the tenth ready to perform any rites that were required for the gods of Rome.

Leaning heavily on his crutches, Rogatus watched Germanus at the fort altar as he stood beside the bull. Its sacrifice was meant to bring good fortune in battle, and Rogatus scanned the faces of the men who believed it would.

Germanus laid an arm across its back, and one hand stroked its neck until it stood calmly beside him. One quick slice, and the sacrifice was made. The men would feast on its flesh that night.

After help getting up to the wall-walk, Rogatus watched the galloping draconarius and listened for the last time to the hissing whistle of the draco as air passed through its hollow head and billowed its fabric tail. Each turma went through the series of shifting patterns as columns of two and four wove amongst themselves. Each one as it finished drew up in front of him and saluted.

With a mixture of admiration and regret, he returned each salute. How many of the men before him would he see again if war came?

Evening of Day 50

Rogatus sat on the chair in his bedchamber, and waited for the verdict.

Medicus was going with the ala, but he knelt by Rogatus's knee for a final examination before he left.

"I can't say for sure, but I think your knee might not heal well enough for precision riding. Whether you'll be able to ride at all...probably, but not well enough to be a cavalryman."

He stood, then shrugged. "But I won't tell the legate that. If he asks, I'll say it's too soon to tell. After seeing how fast you were healing at the start, I can't say for certain whether you'll end up like most men with your injury."

"Thank you."

"For what? I don't know anything to help you get over this."

"For your willingness to wait to say anything until we know for sure I won't heal."

Medicus snorted. "It's partly for my own sake. I don't want to be patching up men from battles both before and behind me. I think you're the legion's best chance that things will remain quiet in this region so that won't happen."

Rogatus got up on his good leg and moved from the chair to the bed. "I'll try to make sure you don't."

"Take care of yourself, Prefect. I hope to see you again in a few months. If Fortuna smiles, you'll ride out to meet us when we return."

"Take care of yourself and all my men. I'll look forward to that, too."

As the physician left, he closed the door behind him.

Rogatus lay back on the bed and closed his eyes.

God, please protect Medicus and Germanus and Adolphus. There are so many I want You to protect, but I can't name everyone. So, please protect them all.

The Isurium fort, Day 51

Rogatus sat on the cisium bench just outside the fort gate. With Germanus and Adolphus beside him, he'd been watching the legion pass for more than an hour. The men of the thirteen turmas waited beside their horses inside the fort. But since it took ten to fifteen hours for an entire legion with its baggage train to march past a single point, it could be a long time before his decurions led their men out to join it.

"It doesn't seem this big when you're moving with it." Germanus rubbed his jaw. "It gets hard to watch it after a while."

Rogatus nodded. Between the troops and the baggage train, they were watching a small city move.

Finally, a man dressed like himself turned from the moving column and rode down the street toward them. He reined in beside Rogatus.

"I'm Petronius Honoratus, prefect of the Ala Gallorum Sebosiana. I've come for your troops."

Rogatus pointed to his men. "Decurion Germanus of the First Turma and Decurion Adolphus of the Second. How do you want them to merge my men with yours?

"My decurions have left spaces between them that your decurions can fill for today's march. Tomorrow your ala will stay together as they spread out along the centuries."

Rogatus turned to Germanus. "Begin."

Germanus struck his chest and rode back into the fort. With the draco of the Ala Tungrorum beside him and the banner of the First Turma behind him, he led his men up the street past Narina's taberna. Adolphus's Second Turma came next, and one by one, the other eleven followed. Each waited at the Roman road until their assigned opening arrived, then joined the moving troops.

Honoratus remained beside Rogatus until the last man rode past.

"Honoratus."

The prefect turned to face Rogatus. "Yes?"

"While I've been laid up, I've found Germanus a very capable second-in-command for the Tungrorum. Whatever you ask of him, he'll excel at it."

Honoratus made a quick tip of his head. "I have a man like that myself. I'll make good use of both of them." A wry smile appeared. "Any commander who doesn't recognize it's his junior officers that determine his success is either arrogant or a fool. I'm neither."

He touched his temple with his finger and urged his horse into a trot.

Rogatus watched until the last of his men joined the moving army before driving back inside.

The legate had chosen well for the new leader of his men, but he still felt the loss of them all.

Narina's farm, afternoon of Day 51

Narina stood at her loom, weaving the shuttle between the warp threads. Tomorrow would be a week, so it was almost time for dinner with her favorite prefect.

Then Lucania scurried into the inner courtyard. "Sulio just rode in."

After parking her shuttle on the small shelf at the top of the frame, Narina followed her sister into the farmyard.

He had just turned his stallion into the paddock with Bena when she walked up behind him. He turned and gave her his usual hug.

"It's good to see you, Sulio, but why are you here?"

"I thought you'd like a report on the legion leaving. It's quite a sight to see one move. It stretches for miles." He wrinkled his nose. "But it's hard to imagine anything more boring. I stood on the hilltop with Father for at least three hours, watching the line of men trudge along the Roman road. The most exciting thing I saw was Rogatus's ala leaving his fort and joining the cavalry flanking the legionaries." He draped his arm across her shoulders. "So, I figured a visit to my favorite cousin would be more interesting."

"The legion is leaving today? The ala, too?"

She bit her lip. She hadn't heard from him since their last dinner at the taberna. Tomorrow would be seven days, and she'd planned to have Atto check today to see if he was ready for another dinner together.

But if the legion left and took his ala with it, had he gone, too, without even telling her?

"I saw them ride out of the fort with their dragon head and all the banners. Quite impressive if you haven't seen it before. They spread out along the marching men."

"Did you see Rogatus in his cisium?"

"There might have been one back by the fort, but it didn't join the parade. So, either he's riding now, or he stayed behind."

"Did everyone leave?"

"I don't think so. I saw some movement at the top of the wall. Maybe watchmen on the wall-walk." His eyes narrowed. "He didn't tell you the legion was going north?"

"No, but I haven't seen him for almost a week."

"You ate with him and didn't invite me?" He placed his hand over his heart. "I'm hurt that you'd do that."

She flicked his arm with her fingers. "I did. The last time you joined us, he and I hardly got to talk at all."

A smile curved Sulio's lips. "That was my intention, dear cousin. But I must admit, I do it more for the fun of irritating him now than to protect you from him." He shrugged. "He's a decent man, for a Roman."

"I think he'd consider that high praise coming from you."

"Maybe it is. Is Atto doing something I could help with today?"

"I think he's in the bean field."

Lucania came over for a hug, and he obliged her. "I'll go see what he's doing. If he wants help, you might need to feed me."

"I think we can manage that."

As Sulio walked away, Lucania snuggled against her side. Sad eyes looked up at her. "Did Rogatus leave without telling us?"

"I don't know, dear. It doesn't seem like he would, but I'll go find out tomorrow."

Isurium, morning of Day 52

When Narina rode up to the fort, two guards still manned the gate.

"I'm Narina Lucana, and I'm here to speak with Prefect Rogatus."

A decurion she didn't recognize came out of the gatehouse. "The Narina who ran the taberna?"

"Yes."

"Dismount and follow me."

She led Bena as she followed him to a stable by a large stone building. There a stableman took the mare from her. Then the decurion led her into the stone building, crossed a courtyard, and knocked on a door freshly carved with a dragon's head.

At a desk inside sat the man she most wanted to see.

"Prefect, I've brought you Narina Lucana." He escorted her to the desk, saluted Rogatus, and with a wink and a knowing smile directed at her, left the room.

"Come closer and take a seat." He pointed at a guest chair to the side of the desk. "I have a few things to tell you."

"Sulio told me the legion left, and it took most of your ala. I'm sorry."

"I'm not. The legion's gone north to deal with a rebellion, and the ala will be important for restoring the peace."

"But you lost your command."

Why was he smiling instead of sad?

"Yes and no. The legate left me as prefect of the Ala Tungrorum with two turmas remaining here. The rest are temporarily assigned to another prefect for the duration of the campaign. But he's given me a special assignment."

"What is it?"

"I'm to keep an eye on what's happening with the clans around here and do what I can to keep everything peaceful. I'll visit Bellicus this week to explain why the legion left for a while. I plan to ask his help in keeping things calm until it returns."

"Uncle will do that without you asking." She scrunched her nose. "But let me ask Sulio whether you should visit his father or not. I think it might be a better idea for you to meet on neutral ground where it won't look like he's being too friendly with Romans."

She settled into the offered chair. It wasn't comfortable like the ones in her taberna, but his company more than made up for that.

"I can serve dinner at the taberna, and you can talk for a while before eating at your separate tables. No one will think it disloyal to the clan if he lets his niece feed him a good meal now and then. You have the reputation of dining with us all the time because you don't like garrison food, so having a few words with each other whenever he joins me won't upset anyone."

He chuckled. "The legate said I was as much diplomat as I was soldier, but you're a better diplomat than I'll ever be."

With a soft grunt, he adjusted his leg. "I'm glad you plan to keep feeding me dinner. When you invite Bellicus, invite Sulio, too. He's the one your uncle can rely on when he wants good counsel, and someday he'll make a good chieftain of the Isurian clan."

She covered her mouth to hide the grin. "Can I tell him you said so?"

"No. I'm not sure he'd believe you anyway. But I think he knows how much I respect him without you saying it. And I think he respects me, although I don't ever expect him to say so."

"I'll see what I can arrange."

She wouldn't tell either of them yet, but what she'd been praying for had happened. The cousin she loved like a brother and the man she loved with all her heart would soon admit they'd become friends.

Chapter 52

WHAT TRUTH DEMANDS

The Isurium fort, Day 56

At the knock on his open door, Rogatus looked up. A gate guard stood there, holding a papyrus roll. Rogatus curled his fingers to call the man to his desk.

"Prefect, a horse courier just delivered this for you. Decurion Conradus signed for it."

The guard placed the scroll on the desk before him, saluted, and left.

He read the sender's name and blew out a slow breath. His great-uncle's advice on how to get free from Father had arrived.

God, please let him have figured out how I can free myself, and let it be something I can do from here in Britannia.

He broke the wax seal and unrolled the message that could help him reach the future he longed for...or not.

> Publius Visulanius Crescens to Proculus Trebonius Rogatus, my great-nephew, greetings. If you are well, then I am glad. I hope you will be pleased with some changes I have arranged for you. I think they are for the best.
>
> I went to Rome to get your father to emancipate you. Then I learned he intended to make your life miserable as his client after he bought you back from the third buyer and freed you.
>
> But he craves the admiration of others, so with the help of some of my senatorial friends, I persuaded him to let me represent your maternal grandfather as you were made sui iuris by the third sale. I told him the emancipation was so you could receive a small allowance from my brother after

336

being crippled in the service of Rome. My wealthy friends made him think they saw him as generous, even noble, for emancipating you to help you this way when you weren't even his son.

You can imagine his surprise when I told him he couldn't buy you from me to keep you under his control. I still smile at the thought of the look on his face.

So, I have now manumitted you. You are my freedman, and you will never find being my client a burden. Nothing in our relationship will change, but you will have a new name.

I know you have hated being Proculus all your life, so I gave you my first name. Publius suits you much better. To avoid confusion about your military records, I gave you two cognomens, Trebonius Rogatus. My nomen is now yours as well. So, henceforth you are Publius Visulanius Trebonius Rogatus.

Priscilla and I have regarded you as part of our familia for years. Now you truly are. Feel free to marry that fine woman who saved you. We look forward to hearing about your future children and the magnificent horses you will raise together.

We send our warmest regards to you and Narina. I hope all will continue to be well with you both. May the most powerful god guard you and your future wife's safety, as he has guarded ours.

Publius Visulanius Crescens

Rogatus rested his elbow on the desk and covered his mouth with his hand as he stared at the sheet. Great-uncle called on the most powerful God, just as he had. A man who worshipped the Roman gods never did that. The man who had been so good to him from the day he first asked for help was a Christian. That was why he took pity on a desperate young man with no hope of a future and chose to give him one.

And now he'd freed him to marry the woman he loved without fear of what the man who'd always hated him would do.

He leaned back in his chair, tipped his face heavenward, and closed his eyes.

Thank you, God, for Publius Crescens. Thank you for everything.

Narina's farm, morning of Day 57

After the departure of most of his troops, Rogatus took only two escorts when he drove to Narina's farm. He wouldn't stay long, but what he had to do couldn't wait. He left them on the bench by the stable, and made his way into the house.

Narina stood at her loom. He would have crept up on her and swept her off her feet to share his good news. But she heard the thuds of his crutches on the stone pavers and turned to face him.

"This is a surprise." She parked the shuttle and came toward him, smiling.

"I intended it to be."

She met him under the portico, close to the wall. "So, what is it?"

"I have a new name."

"A new name?"

"You're looking at Publius Visulanius Trebonius Rogatus."

She cocked her head, and her eyes narrowed. "Why?"

"My great-uncle got my father to emancipate me. But he kept me as his own instead of giving me back to Father. I'm his freedman now. Father gave up his power as paterfamilias, and that frees me to do something I've wanted to do for a long time."

"That's wonderful."

With the way her eyes sparkled, it was hard not to tell her right then, but he'd planned exactly how he would do it. He'd go through with the plan.

"He shared a secret with me by the way he signed his letter. 'May the most powerful God guard your safety.' It tells me he's a Christian. That's probably why he's always been so good to me. He and some of his friends tricked Father into making him the third buyer, the one who ends the father's control of his son. I suspect a lot of people were praying for it to happen, and not even my father could resist what God wants for one of His own."

She perked up. "One of His own?"

"Yes. I've spent a lot of time thinking about it. Praying, too. I've decided to leave the service of Rome when the legion returns. I'm praying any fighting doesn't last too long. I hope the legion returns sooner than I need to reach 100,000 denarii. I already have enough."

He shook his head. "I can't keep living with my loyalty split between what God commands and what Rome requires. My knee will provide the excuse for retiring from the tres militiae without me needing to explain my decision."

Narina crossed her hands on her chest as her most beautiful smile lit her face. "God can always bring good out of what seems only bad."

"Yes. That raider's arrow was His blessing in disguise. I have you to thank for helping me see that. It might be some time before the legion returns. I'll stay prefect until then. A new commander might do something stupid that could trigger a local rebellion. Too many would be hurt in the suppression of the rebels." A smile curved his lips. It was almost time for the best part of the surprise. "God can use me here as a peacemaker in a time of war. It's what the legate ordered me to do, and I couldn't ask for a better final assignment."

"What will you do then?" She bit her lip. "Where will you go?

"I thought I'd become a farmer. I have my eye on a good farm near Eboracum. I paid you full price for Zephyrus, but I won't have to for the farm. Last time I ate with the tribunes, Minconus introduced me to the owner. He's a Roman who's afraid to stay where there are constant rumors of rebellion. With the legion gone, I can get a good price that's still fair to both."

"I never thought of you as a farmer."

"I can do many things. I think I'll raise horses, too. I can buy top-quality mares, and I have Zephyrus and Boreas for studs. But I'll need the right partner. One who can ride and train stallions since my knee won't allow that."

He leaned one crutch against the wall and pushed a loose strand of hair behind her ear. "One who knows the one true God with real power to answer prayers. One who can teach me all I need to know so I'll love God with all my heart...like she does." He took her hand and drew her toward him. "I was hoping you'd marry me and be that partner. I'd like to raise horses and children with you. Now that I'm my own paterfamilias, Father can't take them away from us. He has no power to hurt me again."

She slipped her arms around him and rested her cheek against his shoulder. "I think that sounds like a wonderful plan."

"I love you, Narina."

"I love you, too...Publius."

He kissed the back of her neck before easing her away from him. Her eyes closed as he started the kiss that would be the first of many as their love grew stronger and deeper.

When their lips parted, she snuggled in. "When can we marry?" Then she pulled back and bit her lip. "And how?"

"We're both citizens, so simply living as husband and wife makes it a legal marriage that protects the rights of our children. Did you want something more?"

Her smile reappeared. "Of course. I want to be married in the eyes of God, not just Rome, before our wedding night. Veldicca can figure out how we declare our union before God. I won't consider us married until then." With two fingers, she caressed his lips. "But for now, shall we seal our engagement with another kiss?"

The second crutch hit the floor as he pushed it away, wrapped both arms around her, and drew her close.

He didn't yet know all it would take to live as a Christian, but he was ready to confess what he knew were his sins and to believe Iesus's death paid for them. Then Narina and Veldicca would teach him how to love and serve God.

But he already knew what he thanked God for, and some would make people laugh if he told them.

Thank You, God, for the arrows. Without those wounds, I might never have seen You're the God with real power. Thank You for Zephyrus. Without him, I would have died before I could learn about You and what Iesus did to make me a child of God. And thank You for Narina, who showed me how to love and guided me to Your truth.

He'd always done what loyalty demanded. He still would. But his loyalty was no longer to Rome. It was to the truth she had taught him and to the one true God, who loved them both. Loyalty demanded obedience and devotion, and God would have his for the rest of his days.

Finis

I'D LOVE TO HEAR FROM YOU!

If you enjoyed this book, it would be a real gift to me if you would post a review at the retailer you purchased it from. A good review is like a jewel set in gold for an author. Other great places to share reviews are Goodreads and BookBub. If you've read others in the series, it would be great if you post a review of those, too.

I'd also love to hear from you at carol-ashby.com/newsletter/ or directly at carolashbyauthor@gmail.com.

Want to hear about upcoming releases in the Light in the Empire series and free gifts only for newsletter subscribers?

For free gifts and other special offers, advance notices of upcoming releases, and info about my latest writing adventures, please sign up for my newsletter at carol-ashby.com/newsletter/.

Light *in the* Empire Series

What Loyalty Demands is the fifteenth volume in the Light in the Empire series, which follows the interconnected lives of several Roman families during the reigns of Trajan and Hadrian. Each can be read stand-alone. The novels of the series will take you around the Empire, from Germania and Britannia to Thracia, Dacia, North Africa, Roman Egypt, Judaea and, of course, to Rome itself.

Although each can be read stand-alone, here are some groupings based on the appearance of some characters in more than one story.

Drusus family: *The Legacy, True Freedom, Second Chances, Forgiven*

Lentulus family: *Blind Ambition, Faithful*

Crassus family: *Blind Ambition, Faithful, Honor Bound*

Sabinus family: *The Legacy, Honor Bound, More Than Honor, What Matters Most*

Glabrio family: *What Matters Most, Truth and Honor*

Titianus family: *True Freedom, More Than Honor, What Matters Most, Truth and Honor*

Brutus family: *Faithful, True Freedom, Honor Bound*

The Dacians: *Hope Unchained, Hope's Reward, True Freedom*

The Britons: *What Loyalty Demands*

Coming in in 2026 and 2027: Please Help Me Choose!

Who would you like to see in a future story?

I grew to love several of the characters in *What Loyalty Demands* while I was writing. That usually happens, and sometimes a future story takes shape in my head even before I finish. But more often the next hero or heroine is chosen because readers tell me who needs to come back as a story lead.

Readers who loved Galen as a teen in *Blind Ambition* wanted to see him as a grown man, so he became the hero in *Faithful*. People who asked for Brutus and Africanus to have their own story found out what happened to them in *Honor Bound.*

Since people kept asking what happened to Leander's beloved but long-lost sister in *True Freedom,* it was clear Ariana would need her own story in *Hope Unchained.* People who met Ursus in *Hope Unchained* asked what happened to him, so he returned with his childhood name of Matti in his quest to know God better in *Hope's Reward.*

In *What Matters Most,* Septimus, who was rather like a Great Dane puppy in *Honor Bound,* comes back four years older, and Tribune Titianus from *More Than Honor* and *True Freedom* faces the most dangerous assignment of his life. I'm SO glad people asked for still more of them after the earlier books.

For those of you who asked for more of Titianus's apprentice Glabrio, I hope you've enjoyed his story in *Truth and Honor.*

But there are many more characters in the books of the series that I would like to spend more time with, and I hope there are some for you, too. Who would you most like to see in a future story? What was it about them that made you want more of them? I'd love to hear what you think. It will guide what I write next.

Some possibilities:
Aulus of *True Freedom?*
Septimus or Manius of *Honor Bound, More Than Honor,* and *What Matters Most?*
Someone from *What Loyalty Demands*: Sulio, Dexter, Lucania?
Someone else I haven't mentioned? (I can't wait to see who shows up here!)

Please tell me who you'd love to see again as a comment at carol-ashby.com/newsletter/. While you're there, I'd love to have you sign up for my newsletter to find out what's going on in my writing life, for background on what's coming next, and for some freebies I'd love to share with you.

The Power of a Roman Father and How Emancipation Freed a Son

When we hear the word "emancipation," our first thought might be the freeing of an enslaved person. But in Roman times, the power of a father over his sons and daughters was vastly greater than that in modern families. Emancipation could also mean a son being freed from the absolute power of a *paterfamilias* over his life.

Ordinarily, the oldest male would be the paterfamilias of an extended family (*familia*) consisting of himself, his sons and daughters regardless of age or marital status, his son's children, and his slaves. He exercised *patria potest*es (power of the father) over them all.

Any property or money acquired by members of the familia belonged to the paterfamilias. He provided an allowance (*peculium*) to his grown sons so they could live independently and establish and run businesses. But that allowance could be changed or stopped at any time, and anything created or earned using the peculium was his as well.

The emperor Augustus made one exception to the paterfamilias's total ownership of the family resources. The property gained by a son during military service (*peculium castrense*) belonged to the soldier, not his paterfamilias. That included his wages, gifts, spoils of war, inheritances left by other soldiers, and any property he acquired using money that was part of his peculium castrense. He could leave his property to others in a will, but if he died without one, it would all belong to his paterfamilias.

The paterfamilias had absolute control over members of the familia, including the right to kill them and the right to sell them into slavery. He also had the power to remove someone from his familia through the emancipation of a child at any age and the sale or freeing of a slave. Because the children of the familia were officially his, not their mother's, he could refuse to let a mother have any contact with her child after a divorce.

Only two things would free a son from his father's control, making him *sui iuris* ("in one's own right"). The usual way was the death of his father. The second was emancipation. But the emancipation process usually changed his status from son under his father's control to client freedman who still had legal obligations to the father who emancipated ("freed") him. Emancipating a son still left that son's children under the control of their grandfather if he didn't also emancipate them.

A slave who was freed was no longer under the total control of his former paterfamilias. But as a freedman, he owed certain obligations of his time and/ or treasure to his former owner, who was now his patron. Failure to perform the duties of a client could lead to the freedman becoming his patron's slave again.

A son who was sold to someone else as a slave still remained subject to the power of his paterfamilias if he was freed. A father could sell his son twice and still keep control of him. But upon the third sale, his son was no longer under the father's control. He was an independent man (*sui iuris*). If the father bought him back from the third buyer, he could then free him, making him a free Roman citizen again and a freedman of his former father. The emancipated son was free to own property in his own name. But he'd lost the normal rights of a son that he had before his emancipation. As his father's freedman, he still had the obligations of a client to his patron.

Sometimes a son was emancipated to let him take advantage of being *sui iuris*. Receiving a gift or inheritance from his mother is one example. If she wanted to give something to her children while their father was still alive, it would belong to their father or grandfather, not them. He could decide not to give it to her children, and she had no way to make him. The best way to ensure that didn't happen was to have her children emancipated. Once they were *sui iuris*, her children would own whatever she gave them. Their father could still include them in his will as beneficiaries but not as heirs.

Another reason for emancipation was to disown a son who had displeased his father for some reason. The emancipated son had no automatic right to inherit from his father since he was legally no longer part of the familia.

In both cases, the emancipated son became a client freedman of his father.

Emancipation required a formal ceremony that dated back to before the Twelve Tables, which laid the foundations of Roman law around 450 BC. They established that a son would become *sui iuris* if his father sold him a third time. So, a series of three fake sales and returns were used to remove the son from his father's power.

The ceremony required five citizen witnesses and a sixth citizen to hold a special bronze scale. Three friends of the father would play the part of buyers using an as, a bronze coin worth one-sixteenth denarius. As each friend spoke the words, "I declare that this man belongs to me by my right as a Roman citizen, and let him be purchased by me with this piece of bronze and bronze scales," he struck the scales with the bronze coin before giving it to the father. The son was then the bondsman of the buyer. But unlike an ordinary slave, he remained a Roman citizen.

Then the buyer freed the man, who returned to his father's power. This was repeated by the second friend. When the third friend spoke the words, the son was made *sui iuris*. It was customary for the father to buy his son back and then free him, making his former son his freedman.

But if the third buyer refused to sell the former son back to his father, the son remained his bondsman until the third buyer freed him. Then he became the client freedman of the third buyer. Like any slave that was freed, his name would change to reflect the name of the third buyer.

During the Empire, a married woman remained part of the familia of her father, not that of her husband. So, if her paterfamilias was alive, she didn't own any property. If her paternal grandfather and father were dead, she was *sui iuris*. She owned the property that she inherited when the paterfamilias died and any income earned from it. But she had a legal guardian (*tutor*) who had to approve any business transactions. The guardian was often a male relative, but could be another man approved by the court. To encourage childbearing, Augustus removed the requirement of a guardian after a freeborn woman had three children.

A legitimate child of a married woman belonged to the paterfamilias of her husband's familia. An illegitimate child of a married woman would belong to the familia of the mother, not to her husband's familia. But every newborn baby was presented to the paterfamilias for him to decide whether to keep the baby or abandon it to either die or be picked up by another person to become a slave. If the husband or his paterfamilias chose to claim the child as if the husband was the father, the child was legally in the father's familia.

In *What Loyalty Demands*, Rogatus's grandfather had chosen to keep him and name him even though he was uncertain of the father. So, Rogatus was legally under the control first of his grandfather and then of the man who used him to hurt the ex-wife he thought was an adulteress. With a paterfamilias who kept threatening to disinherit him, Rogatus looked for a way to ensure a future if that happened.

As the son of an equestrian family, Rogatus entered military service as a senior officer, and everything he earned during his three postings in the *tres militiae* would remain his. Nine years of earning between 1000 and 1500 denarii a month would exceed the 100,000 denarii required to become or remain an equestrian. If he gained his independence by his father death, he would still be equestrian in his own right, even if his father gave him little or no inheritance. But when he found the woman he wanted to marry, he couldn't risk what his father might do after claiming ownership of any child born to them. So, he decided to try for emancipation instead of waiting for his father to die.

For more about life in the Roman Empire at its peak, please go to https:// carolashby.com. You'll find more articles about the Roman family: "The Roman Family: Power of the Father, Rights of the Mother, Fate of the Children;" "Paterfamilias: The Absolute Power of the Roman Patriarch;" and "Roman Marriage, Divorce, and Dowry During the Early Empire."

The characters in *What Loyalty Demands* are fictional people who don't have specific historical people among their ancestors. But the story is set in Britannia in AD 117, and I have tried to remain true to known history whenever possible. That meant careful research into which military units were in Britannia at the time of the story and the historical figures mentioned as the characters talk about real people and events.

Two men, Trajan (ruling AD 98-117) and Hadrian (ruling AD 117 to 138), were emperors during this story. When Trajan died in August of 117 and Hadrian succeeded him, unrest turned to open rebellion among the Brigantes. While there are no detailed descriptions of what happened that were written by Roman historians, there is a section of an ancient letter that refers to the event.

Marcus Cornelius Fronto had served as tutor to Marcus Aurelius. In the 160s, he wrote his former student, now emperor, to encourage him during the Parthian War. Fronto wrote, "Indeed, when your grandfather Hadrian held imperial power, how many soldiers were killed by the Jews, how many by the Britons!"

The Bar Kochba rebellion between AD 132 and 135 led to major troop losses for the Romans (several thousand), the enslavement, massacre, and dispersal of the Jewish population, banishment of Jews from Jerusalem and its surroundings, and the end of the province of Judaea as it became part of Syria Palestina.

In Britannia, AD 117-119 wasn't the first time the Brigantes had battled Roman troops. After the legions of Claudius invaded the island in AD 43, the Brigantian queen Cartimandua allied with the Romans, and Brigantia remained independent. During the Boudican rebellion of AD 60-61, the Brigantes, who were a northern tribe and still allied with the Romans, did not join the Iceni and Trinovantes, who lived in the south.

While the Roman governor Suetonius was occupied with conquering the Druids in what is now Wales, the Iceni queen Boudicca, after being flogged and her daughters raped, mobilized an army to drive out the Romans in AD 60.

Camulodunum (Colchester) had been the capital of the Trinovantes before being made into a Roman colonia for its veterans. Boudicca's army attacked that city. The IX Hispana Legion was coming to help Camulodunum when it was ambushed and its infantry wiped out. Only its legate (Cerialis), some mounted senior officers, and some of the cavalry escaped.

Cerialis retreated to Londinium (London), but knowing he was unable to defend it against the advancing Britons, he invited as many as could to leave with him. Boudicca's army killed all who were left behind and burned Londinium to the ground. They also killed the Roman population of Verulamium (modern St. Albans) and burned the city. In the combined cities, between 70,000 and 80,000 Romans and Romanized Britons were killed.

Suetonius returned with his troops from Wales and put down the rebellion. After an army of more than 200,000 Britons was defeated by Suetonius's 10,000 highly disciplined troops, Boudicca committed suicide, and the rebellion ended.

As a group, Cartimandua's Brigantes stayed out of this rebellion. That soon changed. During the turmoil of AD 69, when four different men were Roman emperors, Cartimandua lost her kingdom during an uprising led by her ex-husband, Venutius. That led to war between Venutius's Brigantes and Rome.

Cerialis was now governor, and the Roman armies under him put down the rebellion between AD 71 and 73, when Agricola was legate of the XX Victoria Victrix. By AD 79, the entire territory of the Brigantes was annexed by Rome into the province of Britannia. Agricola was governor from AD 77 to AD 85, during which time the annexation of Brigantia was completed. He then went on to conquer the lowlands of present-day Scotland before leaving Britannia.

But the Brigantes were not content under Roman rule, and rebellion broke out after the death of another emperor. *What Loyalty Demands* is set when Trajan died and the rebellion began that led to the major losses that Fronto mentioned.

HISTORICAL POLITICAL CHARACTERS

What Loyalty Demands is set in Britannia in the late summer/early fall of AD 117. Trajan died August 8, and Hadrian received the letter telling him of his adoption as son and successor on August 9. On August 11, he received the letter telling him that Trajan was dead. The Syrian legions proclaimed him emperor in Antioch, where he was governing the province of Syria. It took some time for official notice to reach Rome and to spread to the other provinces.

The following were real people who lived during the Roman era who are mentioned in *What Loyalty Demands.*

EMPERORS:

Vespasian: emperor from AD 69 to 79.

Domitian: emperor from AD 81-96, second son of Vespasian .

Trajan: born M. Marcus Ulpius Traianus, adopted name Caesar M. Ulpius Nerva Traianus, emperor of Rome AD 98 to 117. Died August 8, 117.

Hadrian: born P. Aelius Hadrianus, adopted name Caesar Traianus Hadrianus, emperor of Rome, AD 117 to AD 138. Received notice Aug 11 of Trajan's death and became emperor.

GOVERNORS AND LEGATES

G. Suetonius Paulinus: Governor of Britannia AD 52-61. After the destruction of the IX Hispana infantry, he returned from defeating the Druids in present-day Wales and used the XIV Gemina, some cohorts of the XX Valeria Victrix, and the available auxiliaries totally about 10,000 men to defeat Boudicca's army of over 100,000.

Q. Petillius Cerialis: legate of Legio IX Hispana when Boudicca destroyed its infantry AD 60, governor of Britannia AD 71-74. Put down a Brigantian rebellion during his governorship.

Sextus Julius Frontinus: engineer, author, legate of the Legio II Adiutrix on the Rhine under Cerialis, legate of the Legio II Augusta while he was also governor of Britannia AD 74 to AD 77.

Cn. Julius Agricola: military tribune when Suetonius was governor of Britannia, legate of the Legio XX Valeria Victrix AD 70-73 when Cerialis was governor, governor of Britannia 77-85, during which time he finished conquering Brigantia and expanded north to conquer the Scottish lowlands.

Cn. = Gnaeus, G. = Gaius. L. = Lucius, M = Marcus, Q. = Quintus, P. = Publius

(There were only 20 common first names in use at this time, so abbreviations were often used. Only family and close friends addressed a person using only their first name.)

HISTORICAL MILITARY UNITS

LEGIONS

XX Valeria Victrix: a legion headquartered in Deva (Chester). Rogatus served the XX as equestrian tribune from AD 115-117.

IX Hispana: a legion headquartered in Eboracum (York) in AD 117

II Augusta: a legion headquartered in Isca Silurum (Caeleon)

AUXILIARY COHORTS

Cohors III Brittonum equitata: mixed infantry/cavalry auxiliary cohort with 480 infantry and 120 cavalry. Narina's father enlisted in AD 75 and served as cavalry centurion AD 85-100. Rogatus commanded it as prefect from AD 112 to 115.

Ala I Tungrorum: auxiliary cavalry unit of 500. Rogatus became prefect August, AD 117, when it was attached to the IX Hispana in Eboracum. Archeological evidence shows that it was stationed at Deva (Chester), Eboracum (York), and Pexa (Mumrills) on the Antonine Wall during its time in Britannia.

For more about life in the Roman Empire at its peak, please go to carolashby.com.

Discussion Guide

1. Rogatus was disliked for something that wasn't his fault and used as a pawn to hurt another person. With a father who hated him, what did he do to seek a better future? What kind of man was he at the beginning of the story? How do you think his past influenced that? Have you ever known someone who faced a similar challenge?

2. Narina was raised by her mother to worship the Roman gods. How did she come to be a Christian? How did that affect her relationships with her extended family? How did it affect what she expected as her future?

3. Sulio was the second son of a chieftain who both loved and respected him more than his first-born brother. Why didn't he try to take advantage of that? When his father asked him to spy on the Roman prefect, he was willing but only as he protected his cousin, too. Why was that?

4. When Narina's father Lucanus was planning to enlist in the Roman army to have a better financial future, his father, who was a Brigantian chieftain, threatened to expel him from the clan if he did. Why? When her father returned 25 years later with enough money to be considered well-to-do and as a Roman citizen, how did his brother Bellicus, who was now the chieftain of their clan, respond? Why the difference? Would you have responded like Lucanus's father or like Bellicus? Have you or someone you know ever faced something like this?

5. The story is filled with tension since Britannia had been a province of the Roman Empire for more than eighty years, but the Roman forces were still viewed as an occupying army by the native Britons. Narina's relatives were divided between the two groups that were hostile to each other. She loved people on both sides. What did she do to be a peacemaker between them? Have you ever found yourself in that situation? How did you deal with it? Were you able to be a bridge between the two?

6. Narina's uncle Bellicus didn't like being ruled by Romans, but he put the safety of his clan above his personal feelings. How were his sons similar to and different from their father? How did the three of them change during the course of the story? What do you think might have happened after the story ends?

7. In the beginning, Narina had no interest in more than a casual friendship with Rogatus as he came to her taberna as a customer. How did that change and why? What did that lead her to do?

8. Rogatus came to Britannia as a loner who seemed content with his own company. He had no intention of building close friendships or settling down until he could be free of his father's control. What changed his mind? Why was he open to that?

9. Sulio was worried that Rogatus was a threat to Narina from the moment he met him. Why did he think that? What made his opinion change?

10. With a single-minded focus, Rogatus had pursued the accumulation of 100,000 denarii during his military service. Why did he do that? What put his goal at risk? How did he respond? Would you have responded as he did? Have you or someone you know had to adjust to not being able to reach their most valued goal? What helped with doing that?

11. *What Loyalty Demands* is a story of difficult beginnings, conflicting loyalties, unlikely friendships that open doors to new ways of thinking, and courage to accept the truth and whatever that brings. What touched you most? What made you think about what your own choices would be?

WHO WOULD YOU LIKE TO SEE IN A FUTURE SHORT STORY OR NOVELLA?

I grew to love several of the characters in *What Loyalty Demands* while I was writing. That usually happens, and often the next story for a character takes shape in my head even before I finish. Sometimes it's requests from readers that reveal who should be the focus of a future story. There are many people in *What Loyalty Demands* and all my other novels that I would like to spend more time with, and I hope there are some for you, too. Who would you most like to see in a future story? What was it about them that made you want more of them? I'd love to hear what you think.

Please go to my website, carol-ashby.com/newsletter/, and share your thoughts in the comment box. Sign up for the newsletter, and you can get some free things I'd love to share. Looking forward to hearing from you!

Glossary

GENERAL TERMS

as: in Imperial times, a copper coin worth 1/16 denarius

aureus: (pl. *aurei*) a gold Roman coin worth 25 denarii

Brittonic: a Celtic language spoken in Great Britain during the Iron Age and Roman period

caupona: an inn that also serves food and drinks

cisium: two-wheeled cart with forward-facing seat located above the axis

client: one with obligations to a patron; could be of same or lower status as patron. When slaves were freed, the former owner became their patron.

cognomen: the third name of the 3-part Roman name, the surname or family name

demigod: a child of a Roman god and a mortal who has divine abilities but remains mortal, ex. Hercules.

*denarius: (*pl. *denarii*) silver Roman coin worth about one day's living wage

emancipatio: a legal process that ended the authority of the paterfamilias over his son, making the son legally independent (*sui iuris*)

equestrian order: 2nd highest class of Roman citizens; required personal wealth greater than 100,000 denarii

familia: the Roman family unit consisting of the paterfamilias, his married and unmarried children regardless of age, his sons' children, his slaves, and sometimes his freed slaves

freedman: a freed slave who owes support and service as a client to his former owner

lararium: household shrine for morning ritual honoring the household gods (Lares and Penates)

libripens: the "scale-holder" who held the brass scale used to signify each completed sale in an emancipation ceremony

mead: a fermented honey beverage that blends honey sweetness with a mild wine-like flavor

natatio: a large swimming pool at a Roman bath complex meant for lap swimming

paterfamilias: (plural *patres familias*) oldest living male of an extended Roman family, the patriarch who owns everything except his son's military earnings

patria potestas: the absolute authority of a father over his children and their descendants

peristyle: a continuous porch formed by a row of columns around the perimeter of a courtyard

procurator: official (not a magistrate) in charge of the financial affairs of a province.

rhetor: a teacher of rhetoric or oratory as used in court, public speeches, and writing

senatorial order: highest class of Roman citizens; required personal wealth greater than 250,000 denarii

Solis: Sunday

sui iuris: under one's own authority, no longer under a paterfamilias's control, most often through his death, also through emancipation

taberna: tavern or shop selling prepared food and drinks

tablinum: the main office and reception room for the Roman master of the house

tabula: a two-player board game that is the ancestor of backgammon

MILITARY TERMS

ala: auxiliary cavalry unit of about 500 men

armillae: armbands or wristbands awarded as military decorations for bravery and valor

auxiliary cohort: a large Roman military unit of soldiers (500 to 1000) who were usually not Roman citizens; often attached to a Roman legion for use by its commander (legate) as needed

centurion: 1st level officer over 80 men (a century); rises through the ranks based on merit

cohort equitata: auxiliary cohort of 6 infantry centuries of 80 men commanded by a centurion and 120 cavalry forming 4 turmae commanded by decurions

decurion: a cavalry officer commanding a 30-man unit (turma), similar to a centurion commanding an infantry century

draconarius: standard bearer of a cavalry unit whose standard had the head of a dragon with an attached tube of fabric

gladius: short (18 to 24-inch blade) thrusting sword used by the Roman military and some gladiators

legate: commander of a legion

legion: a military unit of Roman citizens consisting of about 6000 men, including 120 citizen cavalry

medicus: medic or physician

optio: Roman junior officer ranked below centurion

palisade: a row of closely placed, vertical stakes used as a defensive wall

phalera: a sculpted metal disc awarded for distinguished conduct in action. Units mounted them on the staffs of their standards. Individuals wore them on their chests during parades.

praetorium: residence of the commanding officer, legate for legion, prefect for auxiliary cohort or ala

prefect: a Roman officer of tribune rank who commands an auxiliary infantry cohort of noncitizens or cavalry ala of noncitizens

principia: headquarters building within a fort or legionary fortress

spatha: longer sword used by cavalry that is good for thrusting or slashing

tres militiae: "three military posts" Roman military career progression for men of the equestrian order: infantry cohort prefect, then tribune of a legion, then cavalry ala prefect

tribune: officer rank below the commander of a legion (legate)

equestrian tribune: one of five tribunes per legion from equestrian families

senatorial tribune: the single tribune of a legion from a senatorial family

turma: the basic unit of cavalry consisting of 30 to 32 men commanded by a decurion, analog of the basic infantry unit of a century commanded by a centurion

Scripture References

A COMMENT ABOUT CAPITALIZATION OF THE WORDS USED FOR GOD
Some Bible translations capitalize all the pronouns referring to God, with pronouns for God the Father, Jesus as God the Son, and the Holy Spirit all being capitalized. Other Bible translations don't capitalize any of the pronouns referring to God.

I usually capitalize when it's a believer speaking or thinking and don't capitalize when it's someone who doesn't believe in God. I did that in this story. But I also found that some of the conversations between Narina and Rogatus became too confusing about whether their words and thoughts referred to God the Father or Jesus, whom the Britons call Iesu and the Romans Iesus.

So, to avoid that, I decided for this story to capitalize the pronouns for God the Father while making them lower case for Jesus, the Son of God. This does NOT mean that I think Father God is worthy of those special capitals while Jesus isn't. As Jesus told his disciples, "I and the Father are One."—John 10:30 (ESV)

CHAPTER 8:
Narina: "Iesu said, 'Blessed are the peacemakers,' and I want to be one of them."

Blessed are the peacemakers, for they shall be called sons of God. —Matthew 5:9 (NKJV)

CHAPTER 10
Narina: "As far as it depends on me, I do my best to live at peace with everyone."

If possible, so far as it depends on you, live peaceably with all. —Romans 12:18 (ESV)

CHAPTER 16:
Narina: "I think you find it too entertaining to bait the man. But it is amusing to see how he never responds like you want. I've never seen anyone seem so unconcerned when someone tries to insult him."

"You have heard that it was said, 'An eye for an eye and a tooth for a

tooth.' But I tell you not to resist an evil person. But whoever slaps you on your right cheek, turn the other to him also." —Matthew 5:38-39 (NKJV)
Also Luke 6:29-31

CHAPTER 23:
Narina: " I wish everyone around here lived like Apostle Paul told us. 'If it is possible, as far as it depends on me, live at peace with everyone.'" (Rom. 12:18)
Narina (about Rogatus):" He mostly agreed with what Apostle Paul said, even though he didn't know Paul said it. Remember that Jesus said, 'Blessed are the peacemakers, for they will be called children of God.' (Mat 5:9) We should always try to get people to get along better."

CHAPTER 24
Narina: "Apostle Paul told us to show hospitality to strangers, and when we get this taberna running well, we'll keep it a place where strangers can feel welcome."
Do not forget to show hospitality to strangers, for by so doing some people have shown hospitality to angels without knowing it. —Hebrews 13:2 (NIV)

CHAPTER 35
Sulio: Narina's voice played in his head. Love your enemies. Do good to those who hate you.
"But to you who are listening I say: Love your enemies, do good to those who hate you, bless those who curse you, pray for those who mistreat you. —Luke 6:27-28 (NIV)

CHAPTER 42:
Narina paraphrases the story of Mary and the angel in Luke 1:26-38.
And the angel answered and said unto her, The Holy Ghost shall come upon thee, and the power of the Highest shall overshadow thee: therefore also that holy thing which shall be born of thee shall be called the Son of God. —Luke 1: 35 (NKJV)
Narina tells Rogatus that God is the God of everyone.
Indeed He says, 'It is too small a thing that You should be My Servant To raise up the tribes of Jacob,
And to restore the preserved ones of Israel;
I will also give You as a light to the Gentiles,
That You should be My salvation to the ends of the earth.'" —Isaiah 41:6-7 (NKJV)

"Listen to me, my people; hear me, my nation: Instruction will go out from me; my justice will become a light to the nations. —Isaiah 51:4 (NIV)

Narina shares God's greatest commandments

Matthew 22:36–40 , 12:28–34, and Luke 10:25–28:

Narina: "Because Jesus told us that the Holy Spirit would come live with us and even be in us when we believed. Veldicca told me all about God and Iesu. She told me how what Iesu did paid for any sins I confessed so I wouldn't have to pay for them. When I confessed and told God I believed in Iesu, I felt the Holy Spirit come. When we pray for you, the Spirit is here with us as we pray. When I don't know what to pray, I ask Him to pray for me, and I feel him doing it."

"If you love me, keep my commands. And I will ask the Father, and he will give you another advocate to help you and be with you forever—the Spirit of truth. The world cannot accept him, because it neither sees him nor knows him. But you know him, for he lives with you and will be in you. I will not leave you as orphans; I will come to you. —John 14:15-18 (NIV)

Likewise the Spirit also helps in our weaknesses. For we do not know what we should pray for as we ought, but the Spirit Himself makes intercession for us with groanings which cannot be uttered. Now He who searches the hearts knows what the mind of the Spirit is, because He makes intercession for the saints according to the will of God. —Romans 8:26-27 (NKJV)

CHAPTER 48:

Veldicca's chuckle drew Narina's gaze. "Remember, patience is one of the gifts of the Spirit."

"I know, and I am patient...about things that aren't this important to me."

"But the fruit of the Spirit is love, joy, peace, patience, kindness, goodness, faithfulness, gentleness, self-control; against such things there is no law." — Galatians 5:22-23 (ESV)

Acknowledgements

Most of all, I thank God for the opportunity to tell this story of a loner who had dedicated his life to his military career until he learned the importance of friendship, faith, and love.

No one can write the best book possible without the help of many others. Here's a few who helped me more than I can express.

I'm especially thankful for Lisa Garcia, my top alpha beta and dear friend who's helped me with every book in the series. She's the first person I send new scenes to see if they're working well. I'm always amazed by her ability to spot a missing word or typo that I've looked at half a dozen times and never seen. She's as good as a copyeditor. But her prayers are the greatest blessing, both while I'm writing and in life.

I want to thank Carlene Havel for volunteering to alpha-beta read first *River of Life* and now *What Loyalty Demands*. She's a truly gifted author of both contemporary and biblical fiction, and she brings an author's eye to the task that makes her contributions especially valuable. Both her comments and her prayers as I worked on the challenging scenes have been a true blessing.

Christine Dillon is the author of the Light of Nations stand-alone series, biblical fiction about events in the Old Testament through the eyes of non-Israelites. Some, like Trust and Trickery, are perfect for encouraging faith in older teen boys. Her contemporary Grace series deals with faith-challenging events and how God blesses in unexpected ways. With an author's eye and the spiritual insight of a missionary, her help with a manuscript is always a blessing. I'm truly blessed to have her as my author buddy.

Vicki Floyd beta-read the first quarter of the manuscript. I want to thank her for her many useful comments that helped me improve the beginning chapters.

Terry Shoebotham is my local writing buddy and prayer partner for so much of life. She's a joy to talk with about books and life in general, especially over a plate of Indian food at our favorite buffet.

I want to thank Andrew Budek-Schmeisser for being my prayer partner and good friend as I've written all of the books since *The Legacy*. Whenever I needed prayers for something that was giving me problems, an email would get him praying right away. None of the books would have been the same without him.

I also want to thank Katie Powner, for her prayers and wise comments. She is a two-time Christy-Award-winning novelist herself. For wonderful contemporary reads that are light on romance but deep on human relationships, you can't beat Katie's novels.

Thanks also to Mesu Andrews for praying with me for inspiration and for meeting deadlines when they got way too close and especially when they needed to be reset because they flew on by. As a leading writer of Biblical fiction, she shared her author insights as well. Ancient history nerds belong together, and I can count on her to share my excitement about archeological discoveries from Old Testament and Roman times. When I find something new about OT times, my first thought is "Mesu would like this."

Ronda Wells is a fellow writer and medical doctor. I consult her on the medical problems I give my characters and have so much fun sharing with her strange things I learn about ancient medicine. She teaches and writes blogs for authors on medical problems we can give our characters, and she shares my keen interest in the scientifically strange. She's a kindred spirit who prays with and for me as I write, and those are treasures.

Anne Perreault and so many other author friends have all been wonderful when I asked for prayers for inspiration and efficiency. Anne is also my expert consultant on anything related to horses.

My line editor, Wendy Chorot, has once more brought her deep spiritual insight and her editorial skill to bear to make the spiritual scenes feel like real life. These are the most challenging part of the story, and she always helps me make them better. Working with her is a delight, too.

Roseanna White has designed another gorgeous cover for the series. Each one captures the location of the story and the essence of the key characters. I gave her a difficult assignment this time, and she hit it right on the head. Every time I think she can't possibly top the last one, but she always does.

I also thank my family (son Paul, daughter Lydia, her husband Paul, and granddaughters Payton and Kaila) for the balance and joy they bring to my life.

But my greatest thanks to go my amazing husband, Jim, who makes every day a little bit better just by being here. He's also the one who dons my dagger and gladius so I can take pictures with them at exactly the right angle for Roseanna to use. He's the model for the best of my Christian heroes with his never-failing patience, kindness, and humor. I am so blessed to have been his wife for more than forty years.

About the Author

Carol Ashby has been a professional writer for most of her life, but her articles and books were about lasers and compound semiconductors (the electronics that make cell phones, laser pointers, and LED displays work). She still writes about light, but her Light in the Empire series tells stories of difficult friendships and life-changing decisions in dangerous times, where forgiveness and love open hearts to discover their own faith in Christ. Her fascination with the Roman Empire was born during her first middle-school Latin class. A research career in New Mexico inspires her to get every historical detail right so she can spin stories that make her readers feel like they're living under the Caesars themselves.

Read her articles about many facets of life in the Roman Empire at carolashby.com, or join her at her blog, The Beauty of Truth, at carol-ashby.com.

Light *in the* Empire Series

The Light in the Empire Series follows the interconnected lives of several Roman families during the reigns of Trajan and Hadrian. Join them as they travel the Empire, from Germania and Britannia to Thracia, Dacia, North Africa, Egypt, Judaea and, of course, to Rome itself.

Although each can be read stand-alone, here are some groupings based on the appearance of some characters in more than one story.

Drusus family: *The Legacy, True Freedom, Second Chances, Forgiven*
Lentulus family: *Blind Ambition, Faithful*
Crassus family: *Blind Ambition, Faithful, Honor Bound*
Sabinus family: *The Legacy, Honor Bound, More Than Honor, What Matters Most*
Glabrio family: *What Matters Most, Truth and Honor, River of Life*
Martinus family: *Truth and Honor, Crushed Hopes and Hopeful Beginnings, River of Life*
Titianus family: *True Freedom, More Than Honor, What Matters Most, Truth and Honor*
Brutus family: *Faithful, True Freedom, Honor Bound*
The Dacians: *Hope Unchained, Hope's Reward, True Freedom*

For more relationships based on time, location, and the people involved, visit https://carolashby.com/novel-relationships/

Available in paperback and hardcover editions at Amazon, Barnes & Noble, and many other online booksellers. All ebooks are available at Amazon with some in Kindle Unlimited. Some are available at Kobo and for Nook ereaders.

The Drusus Family Stories

Forgiven
Are some wounds too deep to forgive?

With a ruthless father who murdered for the family inheritance, Marcus Drusus plans to do the same. In AD 122, Marcus follows his brother Lucius to Judaea and plots to frame a zealot for his older brother's death. But the plan goes awry, and Lucius is rescued by a Messianic Jewish woman. Her oldest brother is a zealot and a Roman soldier killed her twin, but Rachel still persuades her father Joseph to put his love for Jesus above his anger with Rome and hide Lucius until he heals.

Rachel cares for the enemy, and more than broken bones heal as duty turns to love. Lucius embraces Joseph's faith in Jesus, but sharing a faith doesn't heal all wounds. Even before revealed secrets slice open old scars, Joseph wants no Roman son-in-law. With Rachel's zealot brother suspecting he's a Roman officer and his own brother planning to kill him when he returns, can Lucius survive long enough to change Joseph's mind?

If you're wondering what made the Drusus brothers become what they are, you can find out in *The Legacy*, set eight years earlier, and *True Freedom*, set four years earlier.

The Legacy
When Rome has taken everything, what's left for a man to give?

Betrayed by a ruthless son who'll do anything for power and wealth, Publius Drusus faces death with an unanswered prayer—that his treasured daughter, Claudia, and honorable son, Titus, will someday share his faith. But who will lead them to the truth once he's gone?

Claudia's oldest brother Lucius arranged their father's execution to inherit everything, and now he's forcing her to marry a cruel Roman power broker. If only she could get to Titus—a thousand miles away in Thracia. Then the man who secretly told her father about Jesus arranges for his son Philip to sneak her out of Rome and take her to the brother she can trust.

A childhood accident scarred Philip's face. A woman's rejection scarred his heart.

Claudia's gratitude grows into love, but what can Philip do when the first woman who returns his love hates the God he loves even more?

Titus and Claudia hunger for revenge on their brother and the Christians they blame for their father's deadly conversion. When Titus buys Miriam, a secret Christian, to serve his sister, he starts them all down a path of conflicting loyalties and dangerous decisions. His father's final letter commands the forgiveness Titus refuses to give. What will it take to free him from the hatred poisoning his own heart?

Join the people you met in *Second Chances* eight years earlier in this tale of betrayal, hatred, love, and forgiveness, where even bad things can work together for good.

<u>*Second Chances*</u>
Must the shadows of the past destroy the hope of the future?

In AD 122, Cornelia Scipia, proud daughter of one of Rome's noblest families, learns her adulterous husband plans to betroth their daughter to the vicious son of his best friend. Over her dead body! Cornelia divorces him, reclaims her enormous dowry, and kidnaps her own daughter. She plans to start over with Drusilla a thousand miles away. No more husbands for her. But she didn't count on meeting Hector, the widowed Greek captain of the ship carrying her to her new life.

Devastated by the loss of his wife and daughter, Hector's heart begins to heal as he befriends Drusilla. Cornelia's sacrificial love for Drusilla and her courage and humor in the face of the unknown earn his admiration…as a friend. Is he ready for more?

Marriage to the kind, honest sea captain would give Drusilla the father she deserves…and Cornelia the faithful husband she's always longed for. But while her ex-husband hunts them to drag Drusilla back to Rome, secrets in Hector's past and the chasm between their social classes and different faiths erect complicated barriers to any future together. Will God give two lonely hearts a second chance at happiness?

Join the people you met in *The Legacy* eight years later in this tale of healing and new beginnings. Surprising things happen when God opens the door.

The Crassus, Lentulus, and Brutus Families Stories

<u>*Blind Ambition*</u>
Sometimes you have to almost die to discover how you want to live.

It's AD 114 in the Roman province of Germania Superior, and being a Christian carries a death sentence. Tribune Decimus Lentulus is on the fast track for a stellar political career back in Rome. When he's robbed, blinded, and left for dead, a young German woman who follows the Way finds him. Valeria knows it's his duty to have her and her family killed, but she chooses to obey Jesus's command to love her enemy and takes him home to care for him.

It's not his miraculous recovery that shakes Decimus to his core. It's the way they love him like family and their unconcealed love for Jesus. In spite of himself, he falls in love with the Christian woman Rome wants him to kill. Can Valeria hide her faith to follow him into the circles of Roman power? Or should he abandon his ambition to help rule the Empire and choose to follow a different way?

Discover what happened to the people of *Blind Ambition* eight years later in *Faithful*.

Faithful

Is the price of true friendship ever too high?

In AD 122, Adela, the fiery daughter of a Germanic chieftain, is kidnapped and taken across the Roman frontier to be sold as a slave. When horse-trader Otto wins her while gambling with her kidnappers, he entrusts her to his friend and trading partner, Galen. Then Otto is kidnapped by the same men, and Galen must track them half way across the Empire before his best friend loses a fight to the death in a Roman arena.

Adela joins Galen in the chase, hungry for vengeance. As the perilous journey deepens their friendship, will the kind, faithful man open her eyes to a life she never dreamed she'd want?

A trip to the heart of the Empire poses mortal danger to a man who follows Jesus, especially when he must seek the help of an enemy of the faith for Otto to survive. Tiberius hunted Christians when he governed Germania Superior and banished his own son when he became one.

When Tiberius learns sparing Galen offers a chance at reconciliation, he joins the trio on their journey home. Can his animosity toward the followers of Jesus survive a trip with the Christian man whose courage and faithfulness demand his respect?

Follow the continuing saga of the people you met in *Blind Ambition* from the frontier of Germany to the heart of the Empire in *Faithful*.

Honor Bound

Honor had forced him to protect her. Time would tell if he'd regret it.

Marcus Brutus owns estates, ships, and gladiator schools that increase his fortune daily, but his greatest treasures are his honor and his wife. When she reveals her faith in Jesus before dying after the birth of their son, he's consumed by hatred for the unnamed Christian woman who led his beloved to abandon the Roman gods, making him lose her in this life and the next.

For fifteen years, Licinia's father hid her Christian faith. But now her father is dead, and a ruthless political enemy is hunting for anything to destroy her brother. When she becomes the target, her brother sends her to their estate in Germania. But is that far enough to protect her from an evil man who will stop at nothing?

When a carriage accident leaves Brutus injured and his best friend near death after rescuing Brutus's son, Licinia welcomes and cares for them. But her strange habits and his friend's unexpected recovery make Brutus suspect she's the Christian who corrupted his wife. When her brother's enemies come for her, does honor require him to protect her or turn her over as an enemy of Rome? And when Licinia's heart is drawn toward the pagan man who makes money off death, can she reconcile her growing affection with her love for Christ?

If you read *True Freedom* and wondered what happened to Africanus and Brutus, you can find out in *Honor Bound*.

Find out what happens to Ariana's brother Diegis from *Hope Unchained* twelve years later in this tale of hope and a future never imagined until God opens the door.

The Dacian Stories

Hope Unchained
Can the deepest loss bring the greatest gain?

Rome's conquering army took Ariana's family and freedom, but nothing can take her faith in Jesus. When she rescues a tribune's wife from certain death, her reward is freedom and a chance to free her brother and sister. But first she must catch up with the slave caravan before they vanish forever, and tracking them from Dacia to the coast seems impossible for one woman alone.

Discharged from the legion with a hand crippled by a Dacian knife, Donatus faces a future without hope. When the tribune asks him to escort Ariana on her quest, it's the only work he can find. It means four weeks with a Dacian woman and a gladiator bodyguard, but it takes money to eat. A man without options must take what he can get.

But a lot can happen in four weeks. Even battle-hardened men can be touched by love and forgiveness, and it's easier to face an enemy with a sword than to face the truth. When his moment of truth comes, what will Donatus choose, and what will that mean for both of them?

If you read *True Freedom* and wondered what happened to Leander's beloved sister Ariana, you can find out in *Hope Unchained*. If you wonder what happened to Ursus from *Hope Unchained*, he's the hero in *Hope's Reward*.

<u>Hope's Reward</u>
Must the secrets we hide destroy our hope for a future?

For a gladiator slave, each time you step on the sand, it's kill or die. When Ursus decides to follow Jesus, he must choose to die the next time he's ordered to fight…or run away. He runs, taking again his childhood name, Matti. But he isn't just trying to escape. He's running to Thessalonica, where he hopes to find other Christians like the woman who led him to faith.

When Felicia's new husband, Falco, almost kills her in a fit of rage, her uncle won't help her end the marriage with his business partner. He will send her to her sister in Thessalonica, but only if she tells no one she plans to divorce Falco and demand her dowry back before she gets there. When Matti interrupts a robbery too late to save Felicia's money for traveling by sea, he offers to bodyguard and escort her overland to their mutual destination.

After Matti risks everything to save her from Falco's assassins, Felicia fears taking the danger to her sister's family. When his Christian friends take them in, she discovers the deepest desires of her heart. But will the secrets of Matti's past make a future together impossible?

If you wonder what happened to Ursus in *Hope Unchained*, he's the hero in *Hope's Reward*.

<u>True Freedom</u>
The chains we cannot see can be the hardest ones to break.

When Aulus runs up a gambling debt to his father's political enemy, he's desperate to pay it off before his father returns to Rome. His best friend Marcus suggests they fake the kidnapping of Aulus's sister Julia and use the ransom money. But when the man they hired kidnaps her for real, Aulus is catapulted into a desperate search to find her.

Torn from his childhood home by Rome's conquering armies and sold as a farm slave to labor until he dies, Dacius's faith gives him strength to bear what he must and serve without complaining. After a deadly accident makes him one of Julia's litter bearers, he overhears Marcus advising her brother to kidnap her. When Dacius almost dies thwarting the kidnapping, a Christian couple pretend Julia and Dacius are their children to keep her brother from finding them before her father returns.

But pretending to be free again makes returning to slavery more than Dacius can bear, while acting like a common woman opens Julia's eyes to dreams and destinies she never knew existed. With her brother closing in and her father almost home, can she find a way around Roman law and custom to free them both for the future they long for?

If you wonder what happened to Leander's beloved sister Ariana, you can find out in *Hope Unchained.*

Tribunes of the Urban Cohort: Titianus and Glabrio

<u>More Than Honor</u>

Duty and honor had anchored his life, but only truth could set him free.

Devotion to duty and dogged determination make Tribune Titianus the most feared investigator of the Urban Cohort. Honor drives him to hunt down anyone who breaks Roman law, but it becomes personal when Lenaeus, his old tutor, is murdered in his own classroom. Why kill a respected teacher of the noble sons of Rome, a man who has nothing worth stealing and no known enemies? Had he learned something too dangerous to let him live?

Pompeia was only a girl when Titianus studied with Father before her family became Christians. She and her brother Kaeso can't move their school from the house where their father was killed. But what if the one who killed Father comes to kill again? Kaeso's friend Septimus insists they spend nights at his father's well-guarded home. But danger lurks there as well. As Titianus hunts for the murderer, will he discover their secret faith and arrest them as enemies of the Empire?

When Titianus gets too close to finding the killer, the hunter becomes the hunted. While he recovers at his cousin Septimus's house, Pompeia becomes the first woman to touch his heart. But a tribune's loyalty is sworn to Rome, no matter how he feels. When her faith is revealed, will truth and love mean more to him than honor? Does honor require more than devotion to Rome?

If you're curious about what happens next with Titianus, Pompeia's family, and Septimus, you can find that story in *What Matters Most.*

<u>What Matters Most</u>

When faced with impossible choices, how do you decide what matters most?

For ten years, the incorruptible Tribune Titianus enforced Rome's laws. He's four days from leaving the Urban Cohort to teach at his brother-in-law Kaeso's school when Emperor Hadrian and the Praetorian Prefect draft him to secretly investigate and thwart an assassination plot…one that might involve his own commander. He can't refuse, but if Hadrian's enemies discover his Christian faith, will it mean death for everyone he loves?

Titianus's cousin Sabina returns as a widow to her father's house after six years of misery in a marriage that sealed a political alliance. She's dreading the next marriage Grandfather will arrange with someone seeking his support. When her brother's best friend Kaeso offers the encouragement and friendship she's longed for, can she escape the chains of society's expectations to gain what her heart desires?

The new tribune Glabrio wants two things as Titianus trains him: to discover for their commander who Titianus is investigating and to gain the support of Titianus's powerful relatives. Marrying Sabina would secure the backing of her grandfather, but because of the teacher, she's making choices no noblewoman should. As he gets closer to both his goals, will he realize in time what matters most?

If you're curious about what happened with Manius's family, Kaeso's family, and Titianus a year before *What Matters Most*, you can find that story in *More Than Honor*.

If you're curious about what happens to Glabrio in his next assignment, you can find that story in *Truth and Honor*.

<u>Truth and Honor</u>
Is truth worth the price if it costs you everything?

For Tribune Glabrio, descended from three consuls of Rome and determined to be the fourth, commanding the troops policing Carthago appears ideal for hastening his political rise. Arriving from Rome with the secretly Christian Sartorus as his aide, Glabrio discovers the man he was to replace has vanished without a trace. Was the missing tribune too close to finding the counterfeiters Glabrio is now hunting? But no matter the cost, duty and honor require him to enforce Roman law.

Orphaned as a child and taken to live with her pagan grandfather, Martina met Jesus through her step-grandmother. Their faith was a well-kept secret, even from most of their family. With both grandparents now dead, her uncle helps Martina hide the faith he doesn't share. But after a single dinner at her uncle's, the new tribune is determined to get to know her. No matter what she does to discourage Glabrio, he won't leave her alone. But if he discovers her faith, will it mean her death?

When Martina rescues Glabrio from the counterfeiter's schemes, he learns the people who risked everything to save him share the faith that got his grandfather executed. Embracing that faith could cost him the future he planned on. As an officer of the empire, it's his duty to reject it…but what if it's true?

If you're curious about what happened between Glabrio, Titianus, Kaeso, and their families almost a year before *Truth and Honor*, you can find that story in *What Matters Most.*

The Martinus Family Stories

<u>*Crushed Hopes and Hopeful Beginnings*</u>
Can God work all things for good if you don't even think he's real?

Lusario was content in Cyrene as part of the Philandros household. After he returns from serving the youngest son, Diokles, while he studies in Alexandria, Lusario expects to become a paid tutor for his master, earning the money to buy his freedom. But when Diokles uses him to pay a gambling debt, he must go to Carthago as the slave of a man who hates him. His once-bright future is gone forever. So why does his Christian friend Timon insist things will turn out so much better than he expects?

But Carthago brings new people, like Caelus Martinus, and new possibilities into Lusario's hopeless world. Could Timon be right? When Lusario sees a chance to escape his fate, will going for it give him a future again, or only hasten his death?

Crushed Hopes and Hopeful Beginnings is a short novel about the turbulent lives of Lusario and his friends three years before Carol Ashby's next full-length novel, *River of Life*, when two of them embark on a journey up the Nile that changes everything.

<u>*River of Life*</u>

When the future you dreamed of looks impossible, maybe God has a better one planned.

Driven from home because of her Christian faith, Neferu lands a position tutoring Jason, her childhood friend's young son. Jason's father despises him and banishes both the boy and Neferu to his ancestral estate, where Jason becomes the target of a family member who wants Jason's inheritance for her own boys. How can a mere servant thwart her mistress before her young charge is killed? Knowing what she does, is her life at risk as well?

When Lusario's new master, Caelus Martinus, decided they would train together to work as architects, Lusario's once-bleak future seemed bright. But if they don't get a commission within a month to design a building, both will lose the future they long for.

During their trip up the Nile to compete for a building contract, disaster strikes, forcing Neferu to rescue Lusario and Caelus from certain death. As the threat to Neferu and Jason grows, both men would do anything to protect her and the boy. Might death await them all if they fail?

If you wonder how Lusario and Caelus came to be best friends, you can find out in *Crushed Hopes and Hopeful Beginnings.*

The Light in the Empire novels are available in paperback and hardcover editions at Amazon, Barnes & Noble, and many other online booksellers. All ebooks are available at Amazon with some in Kindle Unlimited. Some are available at Kobo and for Nook ereaders.

I'd Love to Hear from You!

If you enjoyed this book, it would be a real gift to me if you would post a review at the retailer you purchased it from. A good review is like a jewel set in gold for an author. Other great places to share reviews are Goodreads and BookBub. If you've read others in the series, it would be great if you post a review of those, too.

I'd also love to hear from you at carol-ashby.com/newsletter/ or directly at carolashbyauthor@gmail.com.

Want to hear about upcoming releases in the Light in the Empire series and free gifts only for newsletter subscribers?

For free gifts and other special offers, advance notices of upcoming releases, and info about my latest writing adventures, I hope you'll sign up for my newsletter at carol-ashby.com/newsletter/.

Who would you like to see in a future story? Help me pick what to write next!

I grew to love several of the characters in *What Loyalty Demands* while I was writing. That usually happens, and sometimes a future story takes shape in my head even before I finish. But more often the next hero or heroine is chosen because readers tell me who needs to come back as a story lead.

Readers who loved Galen as a teen in *Blind Ambition* wanted to see him as a grown man, so he became the hero in *Faithful*. People who asked for Brutus and Africanus to have their own story found out what happened to them in *Honor Bound*.

Since people kept asking what happened to Leander's beloved but long-lost sister in *True Freedom*, it was clear Ariana would need her own story in *Hope Unchained*. People who met Ursus in *Hope Unchained* asked what happened to him, so he returned with his childhood name of Matti in his quest to know God better in *Hope's Reward*.

In *What Matters Most*, Septimus, who was rather like a Great Dane puppy in *Honor Bound*, comes back four years older, and Tribune Titianus from *More Than Honor* and *True Freedom* faces the most dangerous assignment of his life. I'm SO glad people asked for still more of them after the earlier books.

For those of you who asked for more of Titianus's apprentice Glabrio, I hope you've enjoyed his story in *Truth and Honor*.

But there are many more characters in the books of the series that I would like to spend more time with, and I hope there are some for you, too. Who would you most like to see in a future story? What was it about them that made you want more of them? I'd love to hear what you think. It will guide what I write next.

Some possibilities:
Aulus of *True Freedom?*
Septimus or Manius of *Honor Bound, More Than Honor,* and *What Matters Most?*
Someone from *What Loyalty Demands*: Sulio, Dexter, Lucania?
Someone else I haven't mentioned? (I can't wait to see who shows up here!)

Please tell me who you'd love to see again as a comment at carol-ashby. com/newsletter/. While you're there, I'd love to have you sign up for my newsletter to find out what's going on in my writing life, for background on what's coming next, and for some freebies I'd love to share with you.